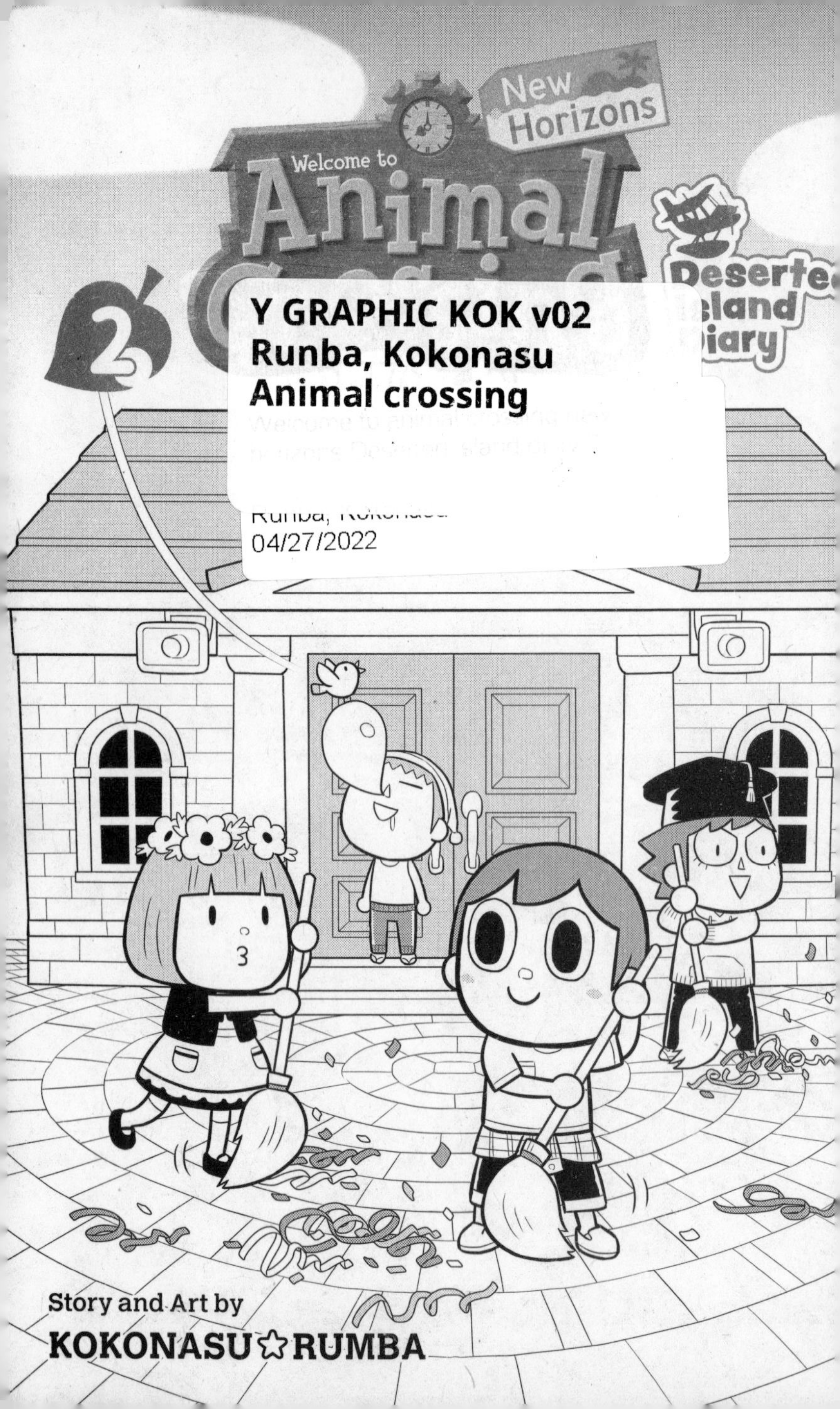
New Horizons
Welcome to
Animal
2
Deserte
sland
iary
Story and Art by
KOKONASU☆RUMBA

DESERTED ISLAND PALS

Himepoyo
One of Coroyuki's friends. This strong-willed princess is richer than rich!

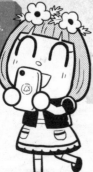

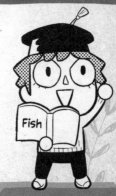

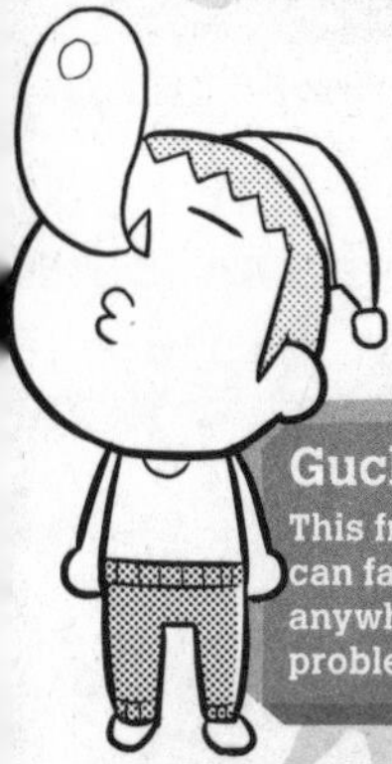

Guchan
This friend of Coroyuki's can fall asleep anytime, anywhere, with no problem!

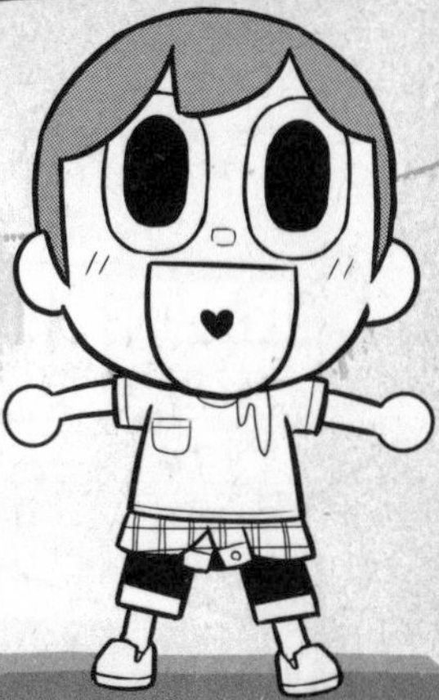

Coroyuki
The leader of this group is a glutton with endless curiosity!

Tom Nook
As the head of Nook Inc., he's here to support everyone's island lifestyle!

Timmy & Tommy
The twins who run Nook's Cranny. Timmy is technically older.

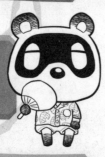

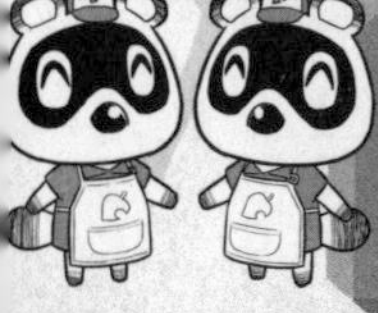

Fish

Benben
The most studious and well-read of Coroyuki's friends!

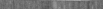

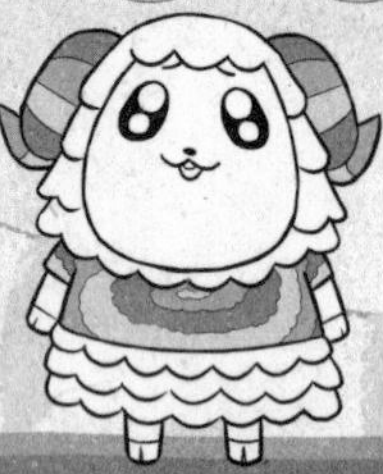

Raymond
This stylish narcissist resides on the island. His catchphrase is “crisp”!

Dom
An excitable sheep villager with adorably round eyes. Fun fact: He’s scared of ghosts.

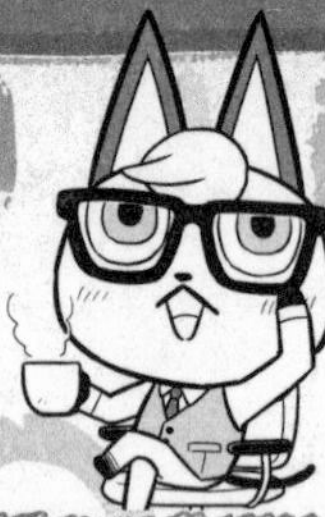

CONTENTS

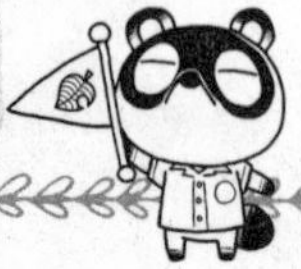

CHALLENGE! CATCH A BLUE MARLIN!

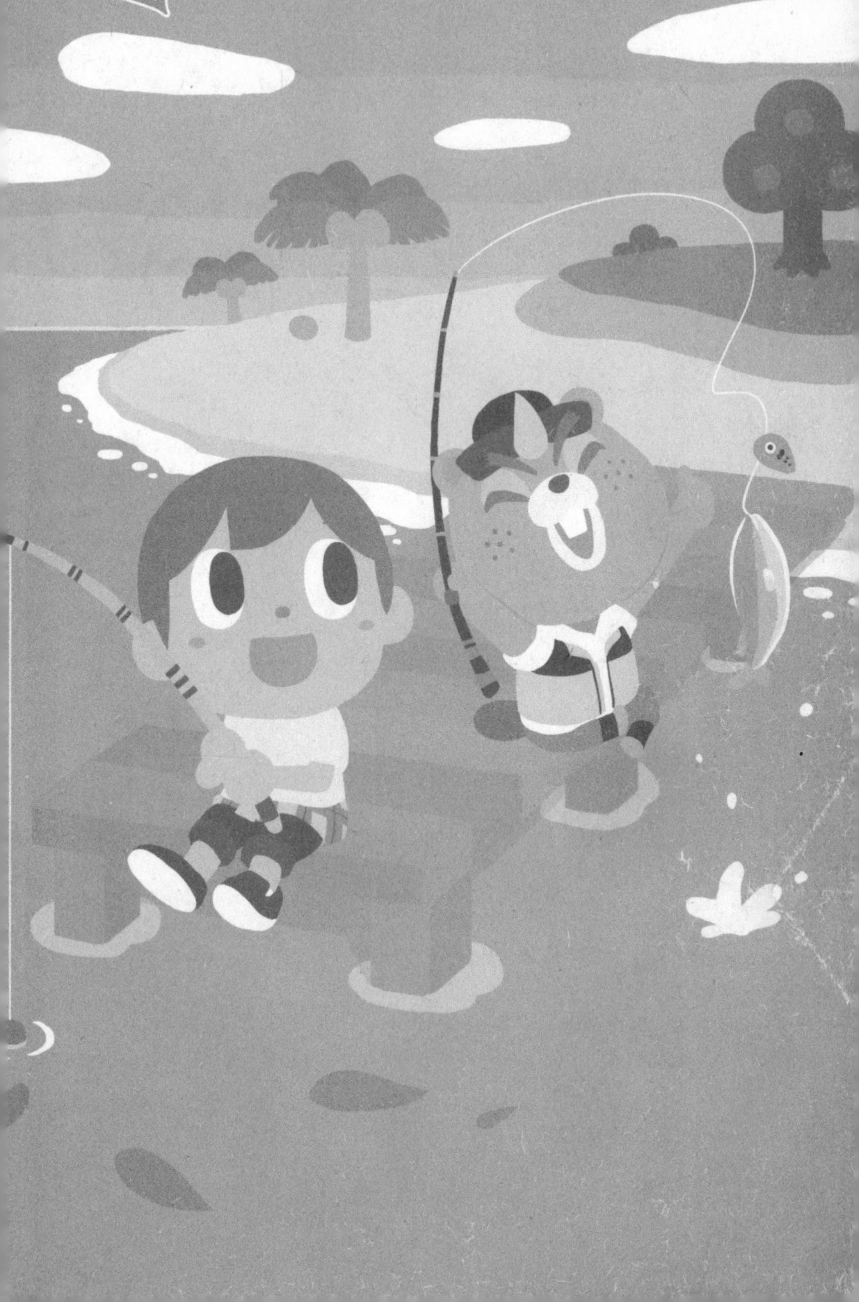

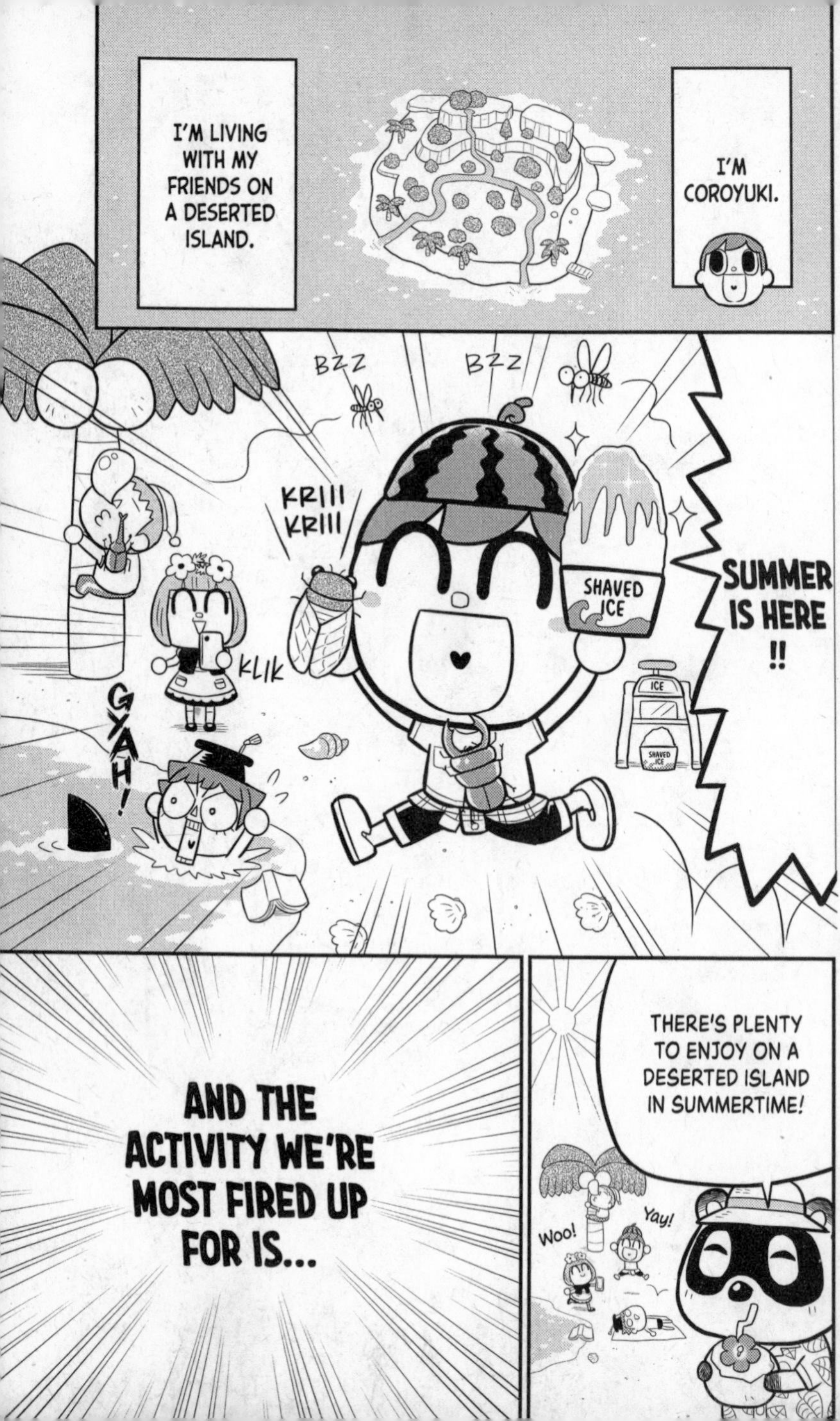
I'M COROYUKI.
I'M LIVING WITH MY FRIENDS ON A DESERTED ISLAND.
SUMMER IS HERE !!
BZZ
BZZ
SHAVED ICE
ICE
SHAVED ICE
KRIII KRIII
KLIK
GYAH!
THERE'S PLENTY TO ENJOY ON A DESERTED ISLAND IN SUMMERTIME!
Yay!
Woo!
AND THE ACTIVITY WE'RE MOST FIRED UP FOR IS...

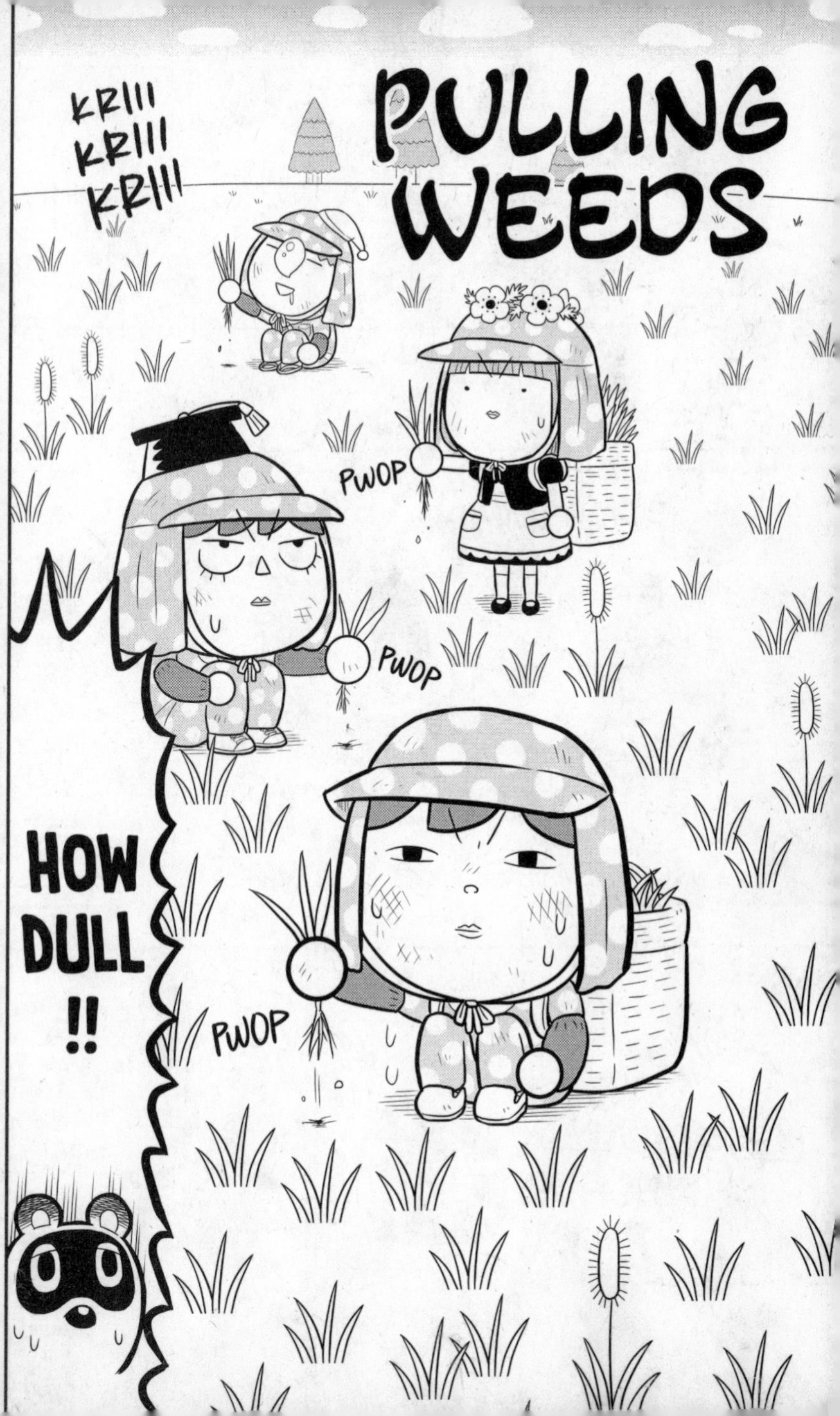
PULLING WEEDS
KRIII KRIII KRIII
PWOP
PWOP
PWOP
HOW DULL !!

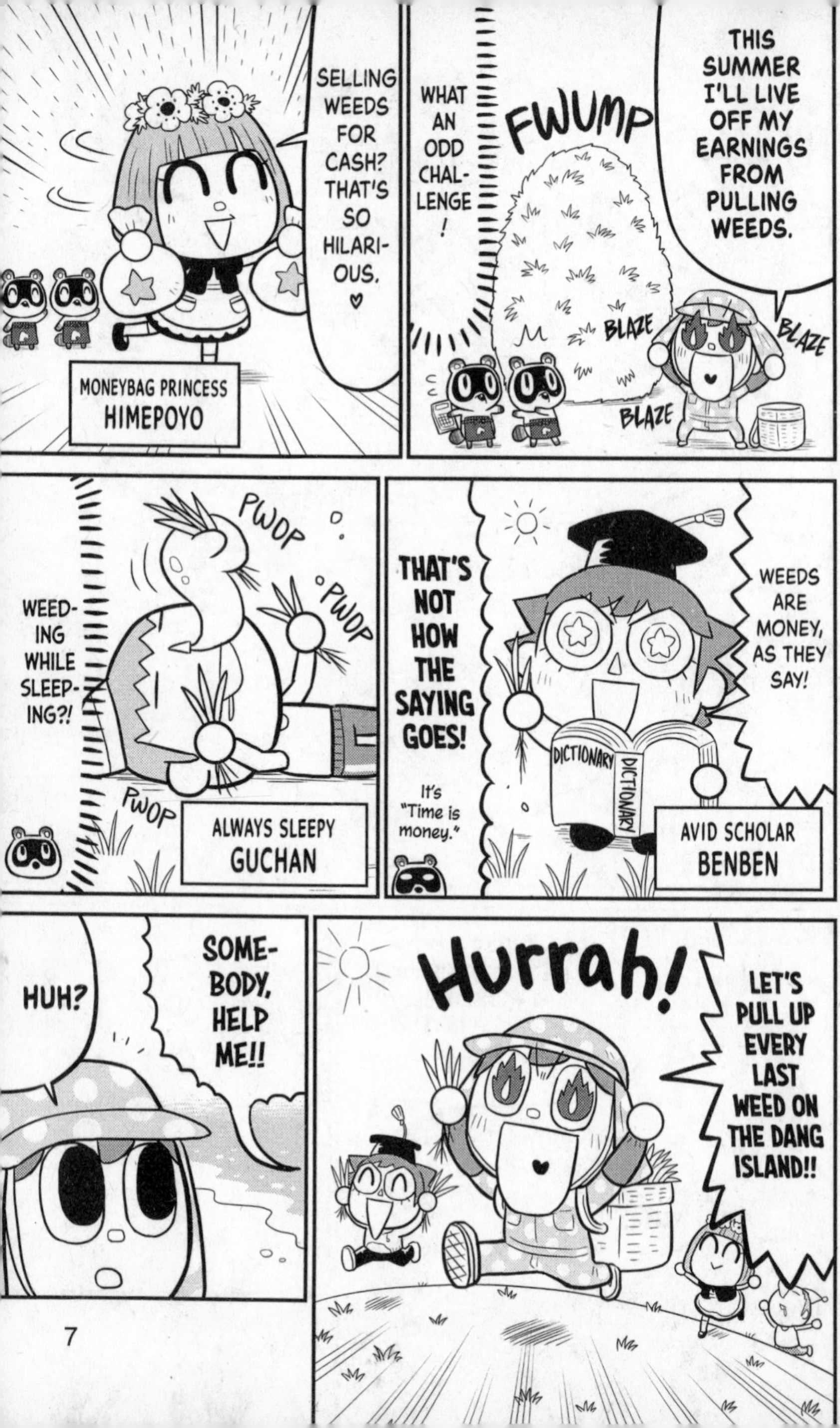
THIS SUMMER I'LL LIVE OFF MY EARNINGS FROM PULLING WEEDS.
FWUMP
BLAZE
BLAZE
BLAZE
WHAT AN ODD CHAL-LENGE!
SELLING WEEDS FOR CASH? THAT'S SO HILARI-OUS. ♡
MONEYBAG PRINCESS HIMEPOYO
WEEDS ARE MONEY, AS THEY SAY!
THAT'S NOT HOW THE SAYING GOES!
It's "Time is money."
DICTIONARY
DICTIONARY
AVID SCHOLAR BENBEN
PWOP
PWOP
WEED-ING WHILE SLEEP-ING?!
PWOP
ALWAYS SLEEPY GUCHAN
Hurrah!
LET'S PULL UP EVERY LAST WEED ON THE DANG ISLAND!!
SOME-BODY, HELP ME!!
HUH?

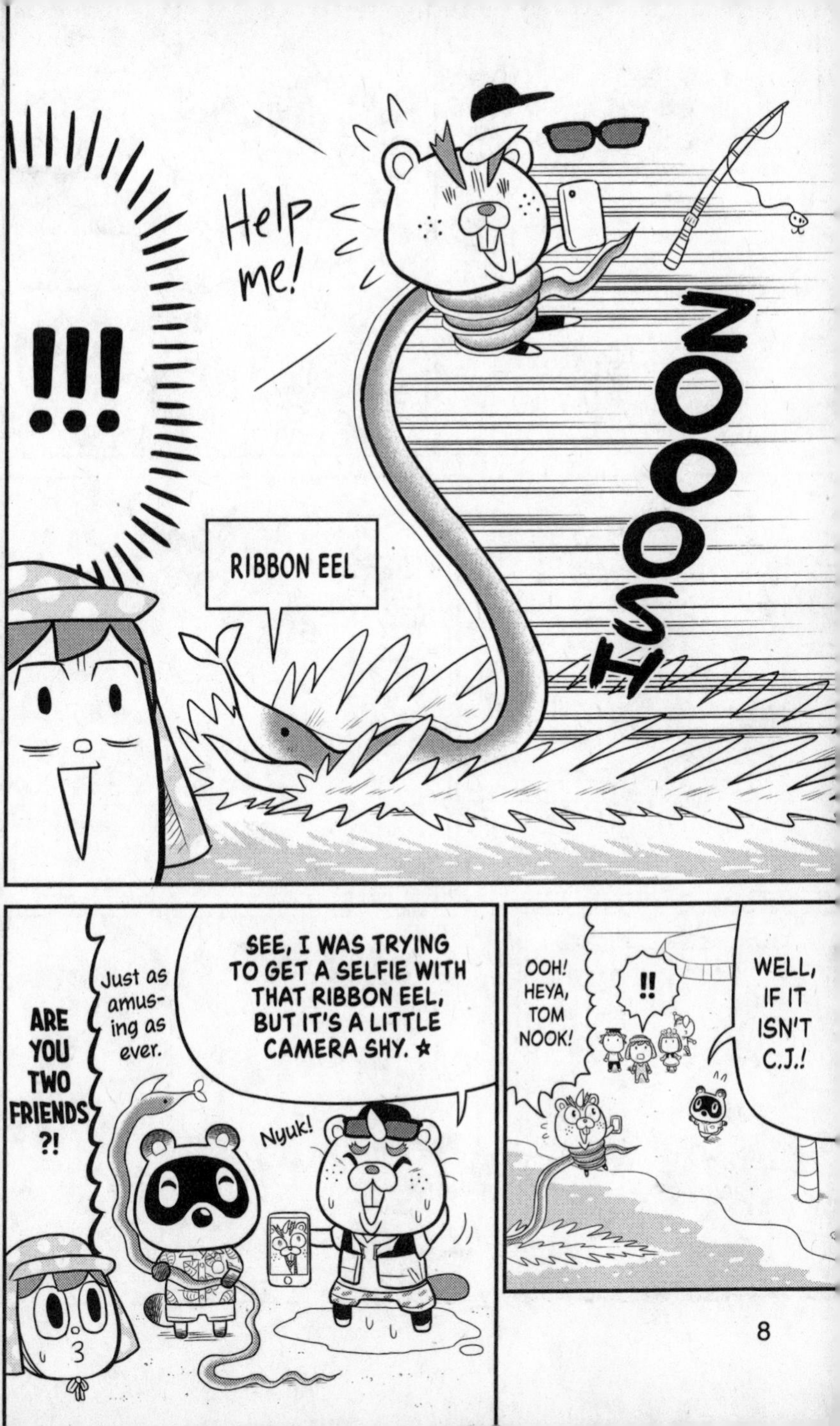
ZOOOSH
Help me!
!!!
RIBBON EEL
WELL, IF IT ISN'T C.J.!
!!
OOH! HEYA, TOM NOOK!
SEE, I WAS TRYING TO GET A SELFIE WITH THAT RIBBON EEL, BUT IT'S A LITTLE CAMERA SHY. ☆
Nyuk!
Just as amus-ing as ever.
ARE YOU TWO FRIENDS?!

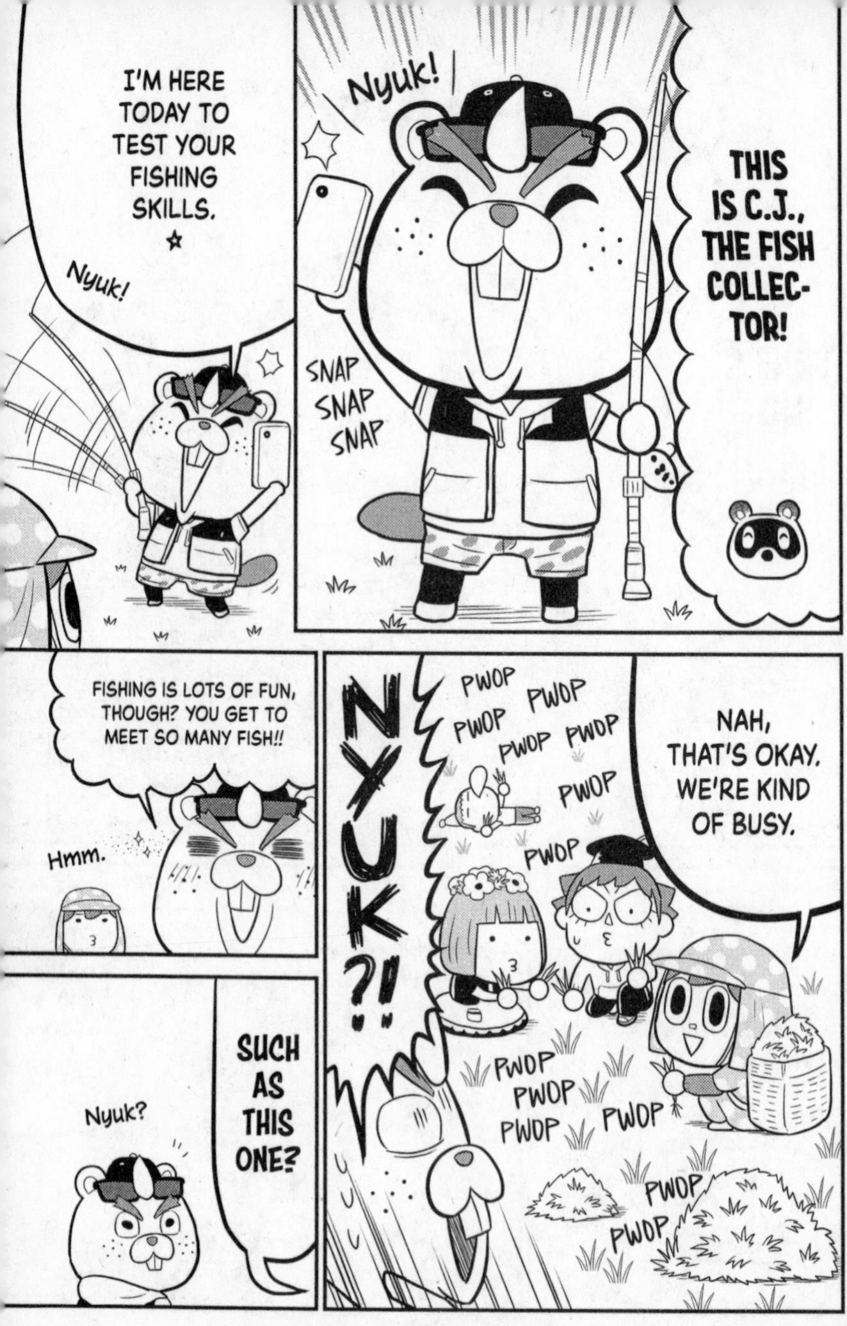
THIS IS C.J., THE FISH COLLECTOR!
Nyuk!
SNAP SNAP SNAP
I'M HERE TODAY TO TEST YOUR FISHING SKILLS. ☆
Nyuk!
NAH, THAT'S OKAY. WE'RE KIND OF BUSY.
PWOP PWOP PWOP PWOP PWOP PWOP PWOP
NYUK?!!
PWOP PWOP PWOP PWOP PWOP PWOP
FISHING IS LOTS OF FUN, THOUGH? YOU GET TO MEET SO MANY FISH!!
Hmm.
SUCH AS THIS ONE?
Nyuk?

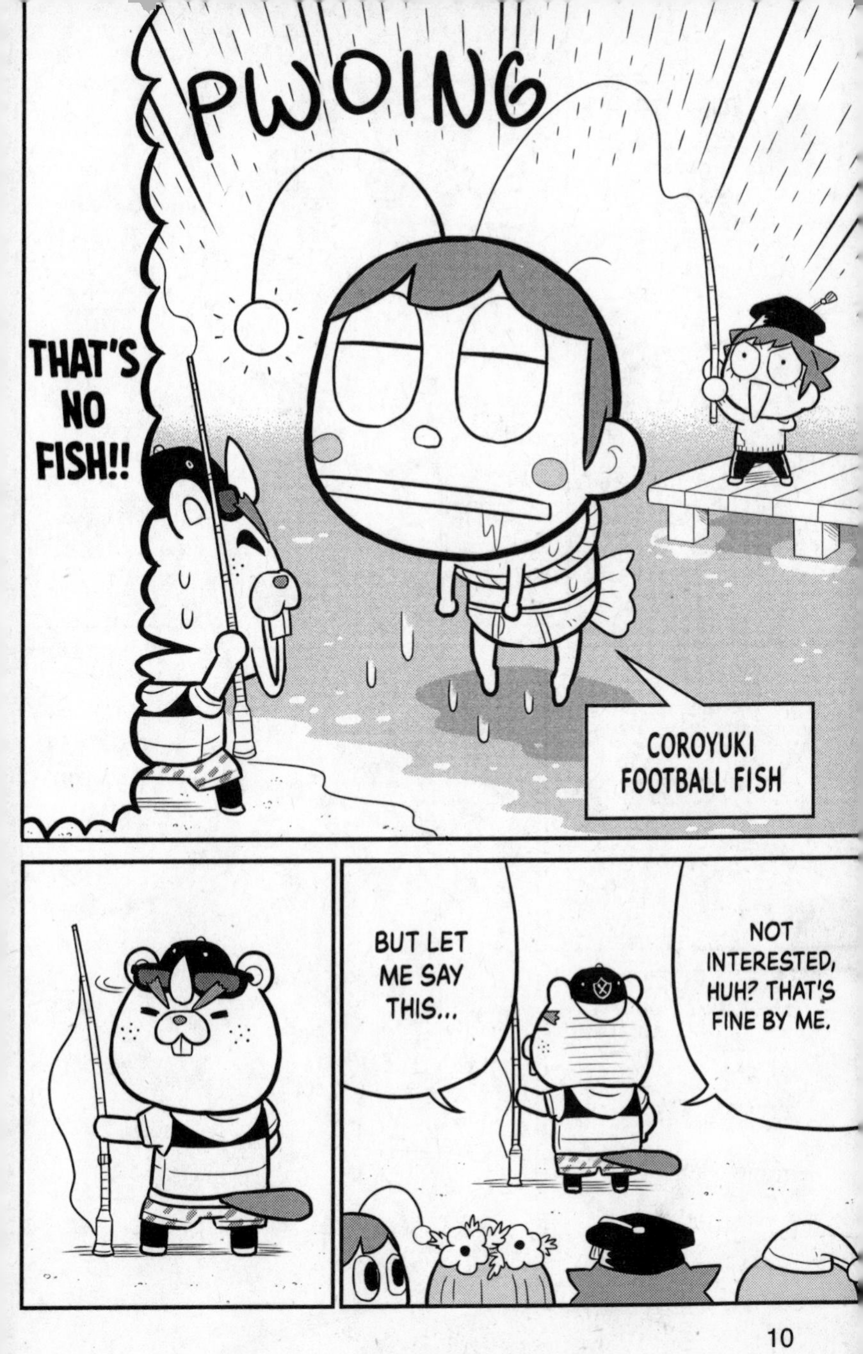
PWOING
THAT'S NO FISH!!
COROYUKI FOOTBALL FISH
NOT INTERESTED, HUH? THAT'S FINE BY ME.
BUT LET ME SAY THIS...

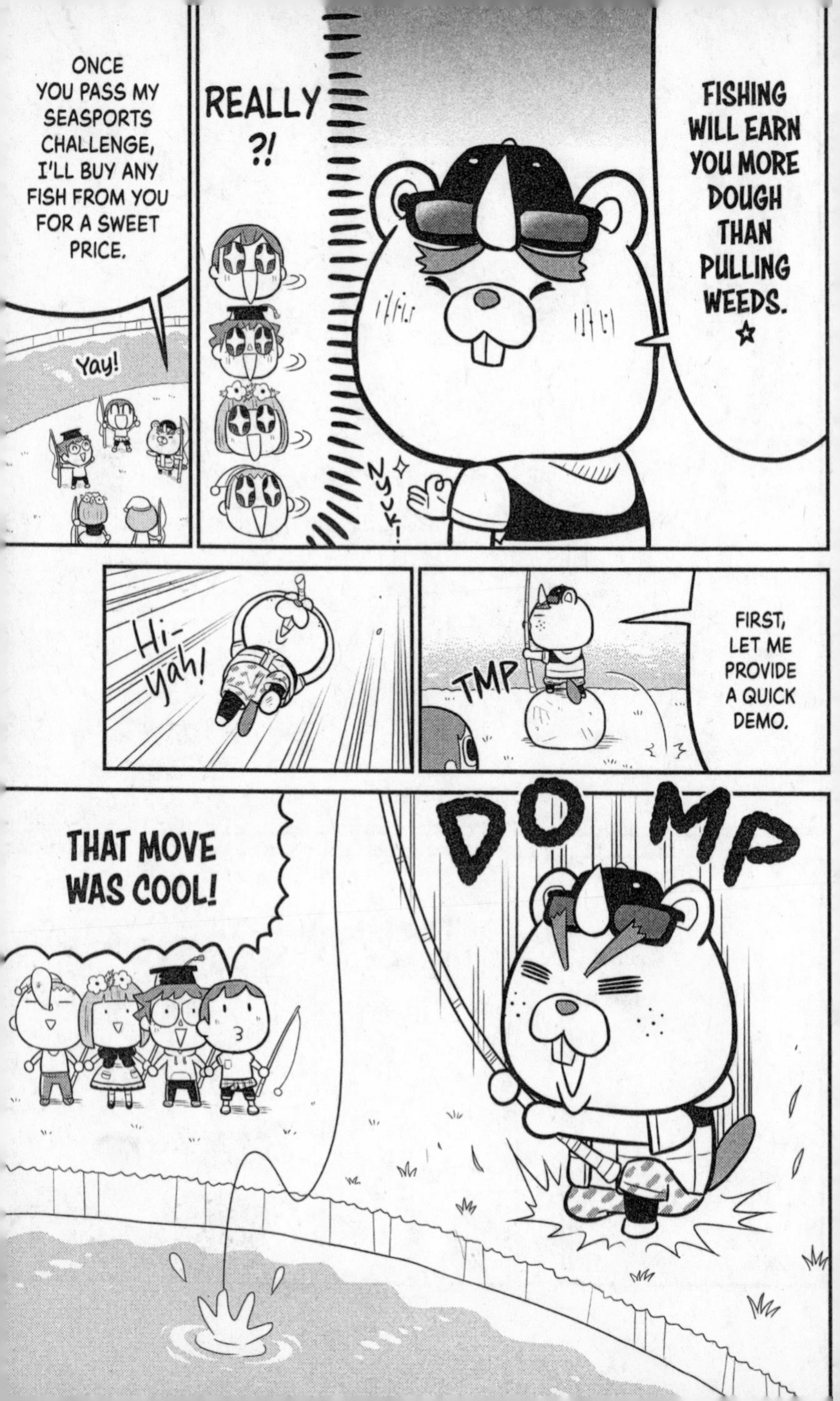
FISHING WILL EARN YOU MORE DOUGH THAN PULLING WEEDS. ☆
NYUK!
REALLY ?!
ONCE YOU PASS MY SEASPORTS CHALLENGE, I'LL BUY ANY FISH FROM YOU FOR A SWEET PRICE.
Yay!
FIRST, LET ME PROVIDE A QUICK DEMO.
TMP
Hi-yah!
DOMP
THAT MOVE WAS COOL!

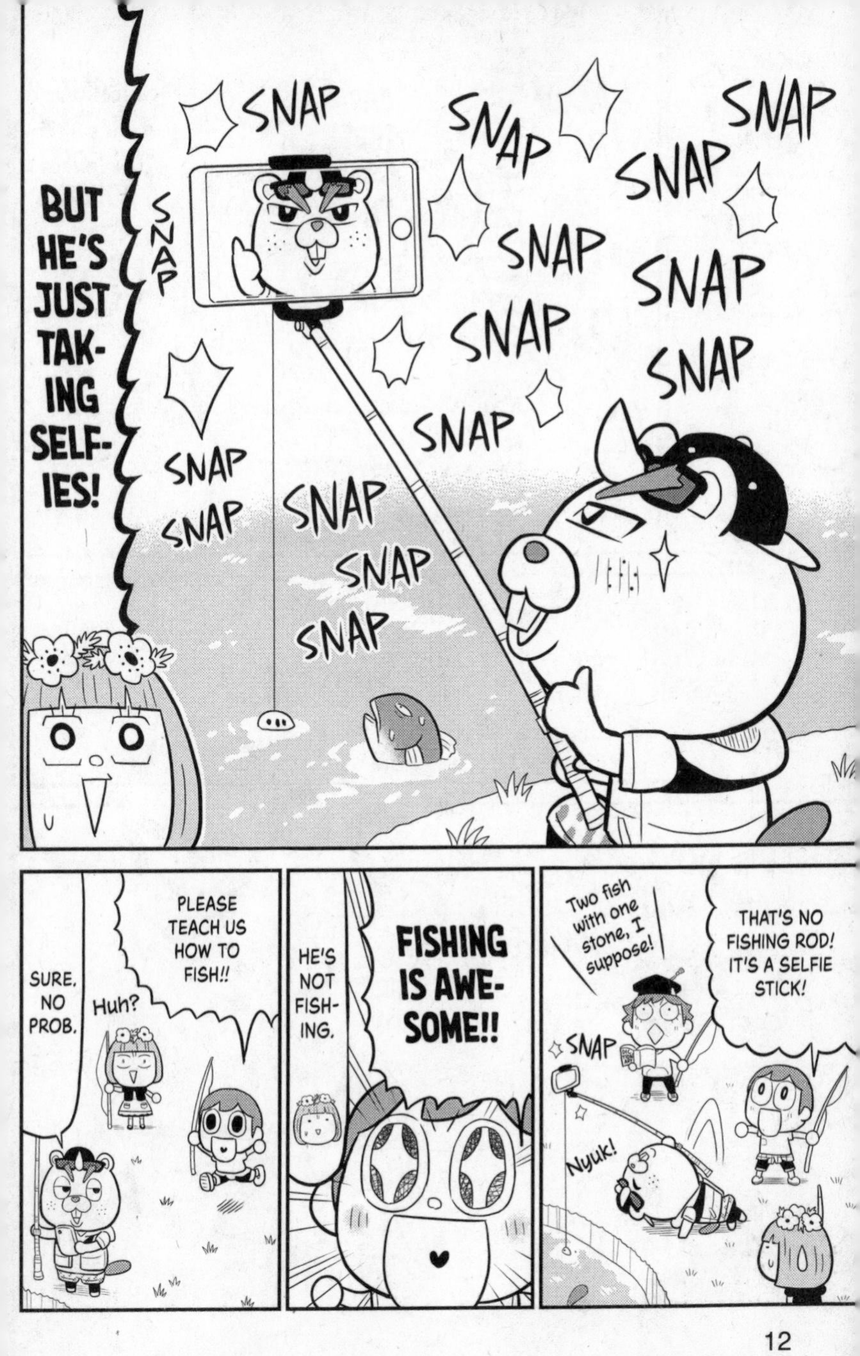
SNAP
SNAP
SNAP
SNAP
SNAP
SNAP
SNAP
SNAP
SNAP
SNAP
SNAP
SNAP
SNAP
SNAP
SNAP
BUT HE'S JUST TAK-ING SELF-IES!
THAT'S NO FISHING ROD! IT'S A SELFIE STICK!
Two fish with one stone, I suppose!
SNAP
Nyuk!
FISHING IS AWE-SOME!!
HE'S NOT FISH-ING.
PLEASE TEACH US HOW TO FISH!!
Huh?
SURE, NO PROB.

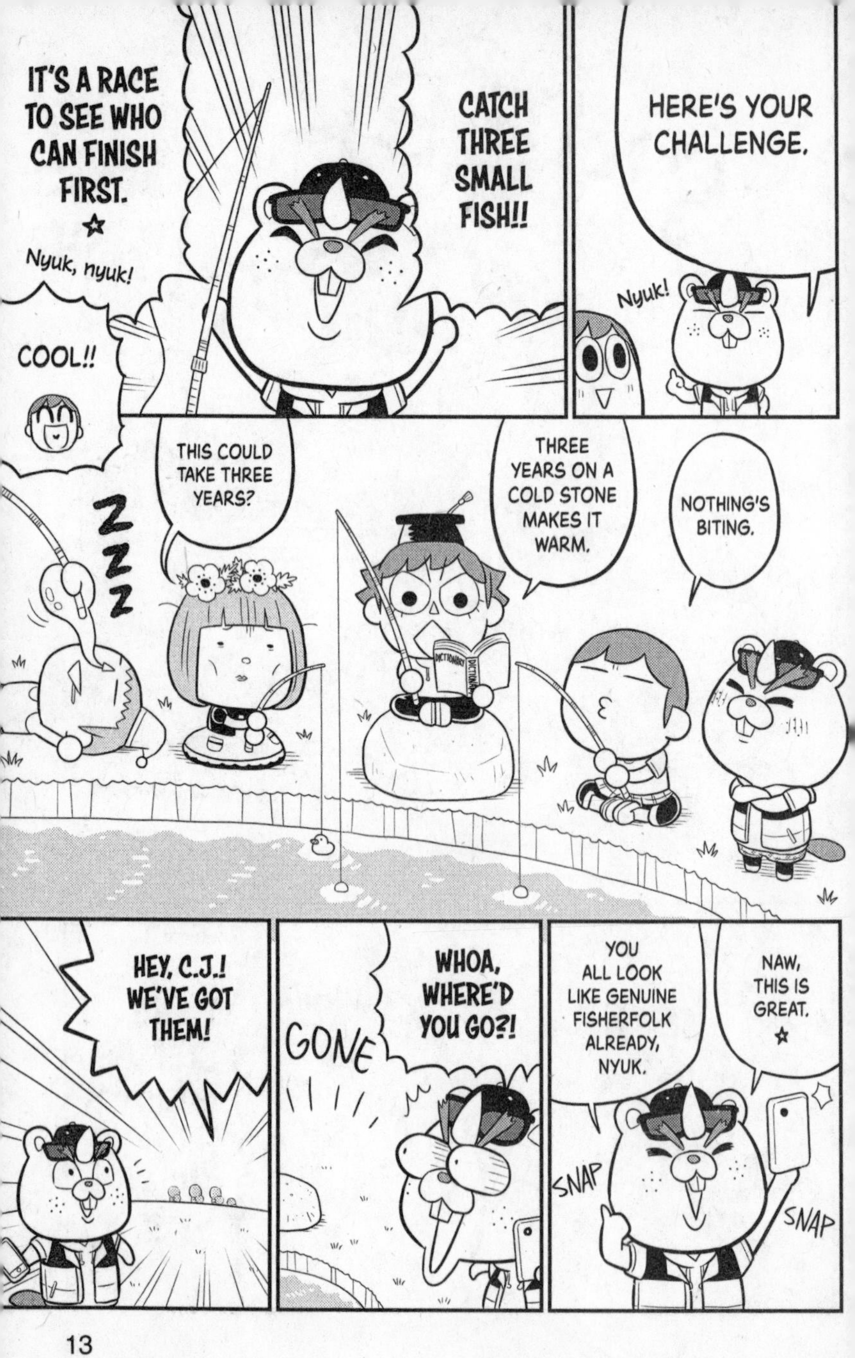
HERE'S YOUR CHALLENGE.
Nyuk!
CATCH THREE SMALL FISH!!
IT'S A RACE TO SEE WHO CAN FINISH FIRST. ☆
Nyuk, nyuk!
COOL!!
NOTHING'S BITING.
THREE YEARS ON A COLD STONE MAKES IT WARM.
THIS COULD TAKE THREE YEARS?
ZZZ
NAW, THIS IS GREAT. ☆
YOU ALL LOOK LIKE GENUINE FISHERFOLK ALREADY, NYUK.
SNAP
SNAP
WHOA, WHERE'D YOU GO?!
GONE
HEY, C.J.! WE'VE GOT THEM!

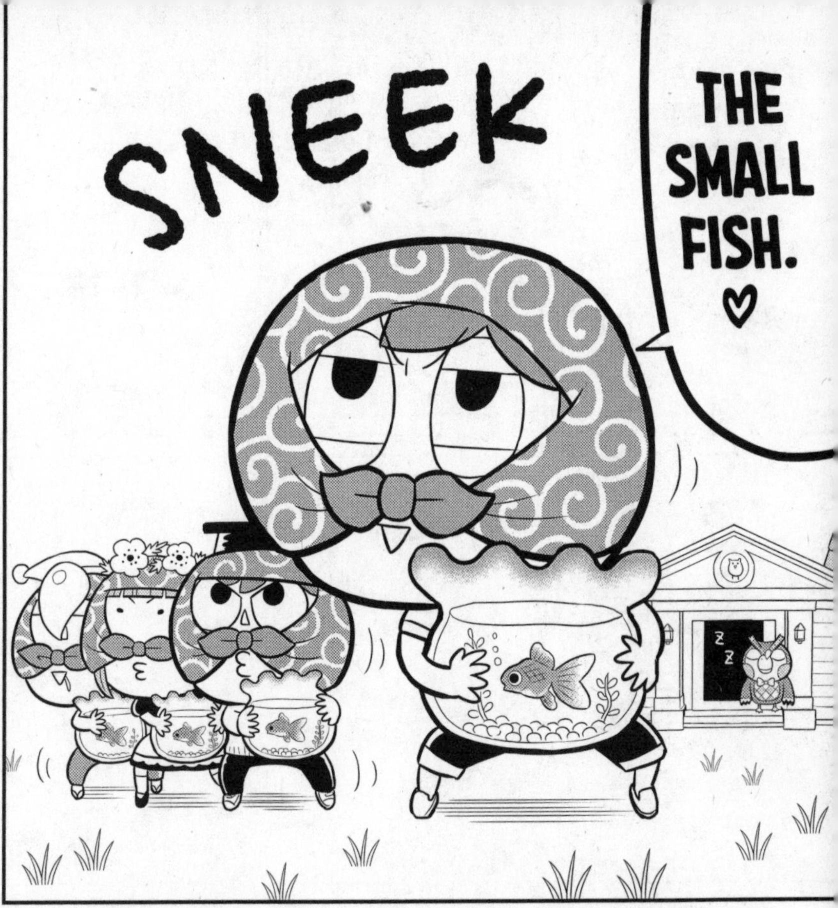
THE SMALL FISH. ♡
SNEEK

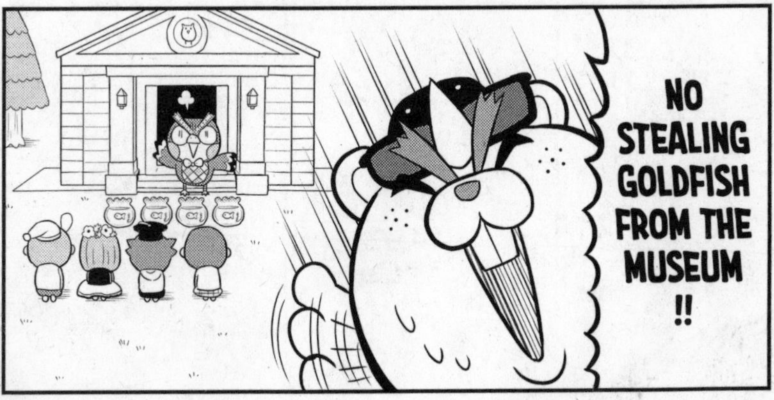
NO STEALING GOLDFISH FROM THE MUSEUM !!

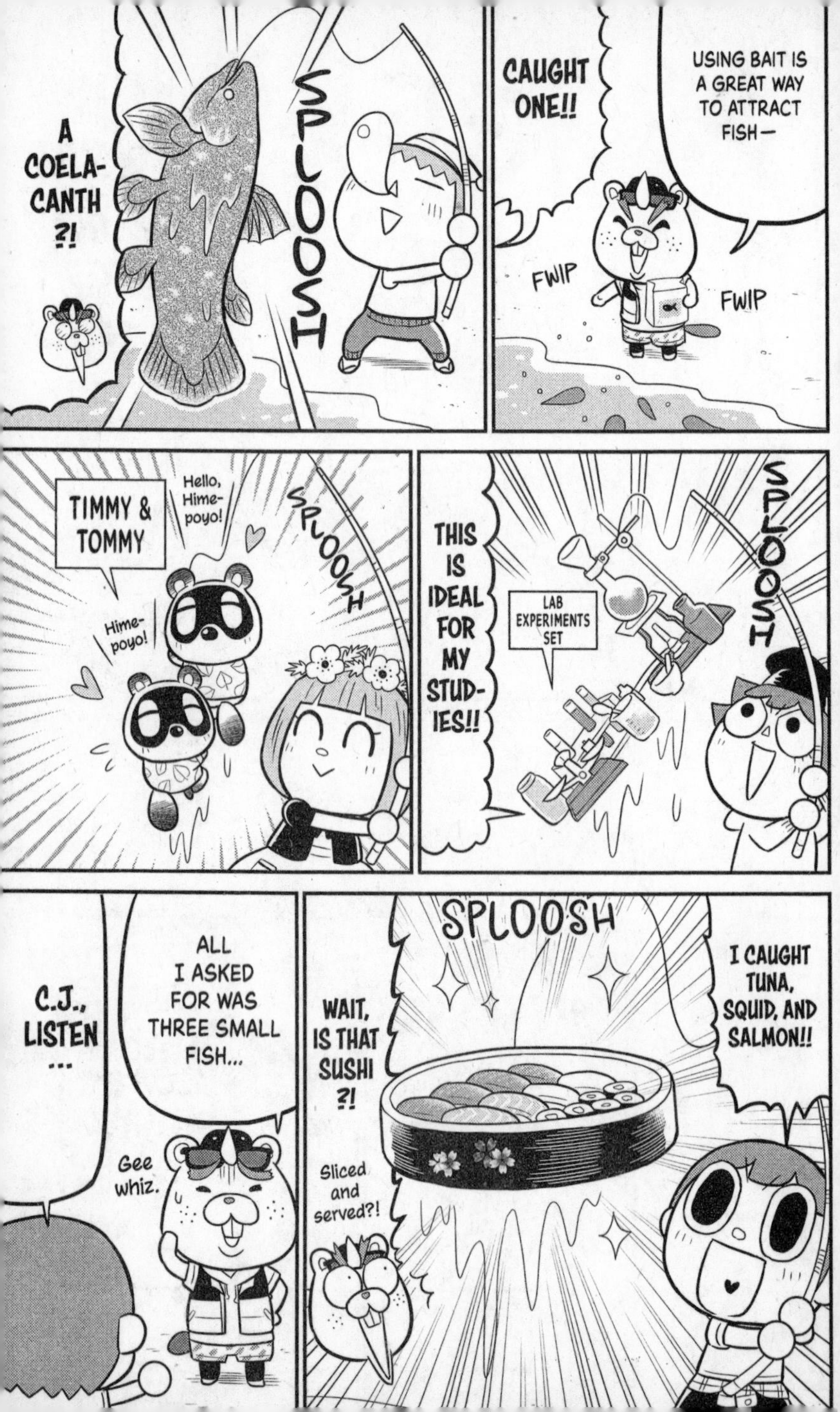
USING BAIT IS A GREAT WAY TO ATTRACT FISH—
CAUGHT ONE!!
FWIP
FWIP
SPLOOSH
A COELACANTH?!
SPLOOSH
THIS IS IDEAL FOR MY STUDIES!!
LAB EXPERIMENTS SET
SPLOOSH
Hello, Hime-poyo!
TIMMY & TOMMY
Hime-poyo!
SPLOOSH
I CAUGHT TUNA, SQUID, AND SALMON!!
WAIT, IS THAT SUSHI?!
Sliced and served?!
ALL I ASKED FOR WAS THREE SMALL FISH...
C.J., LISTEN...
Gee whiz.

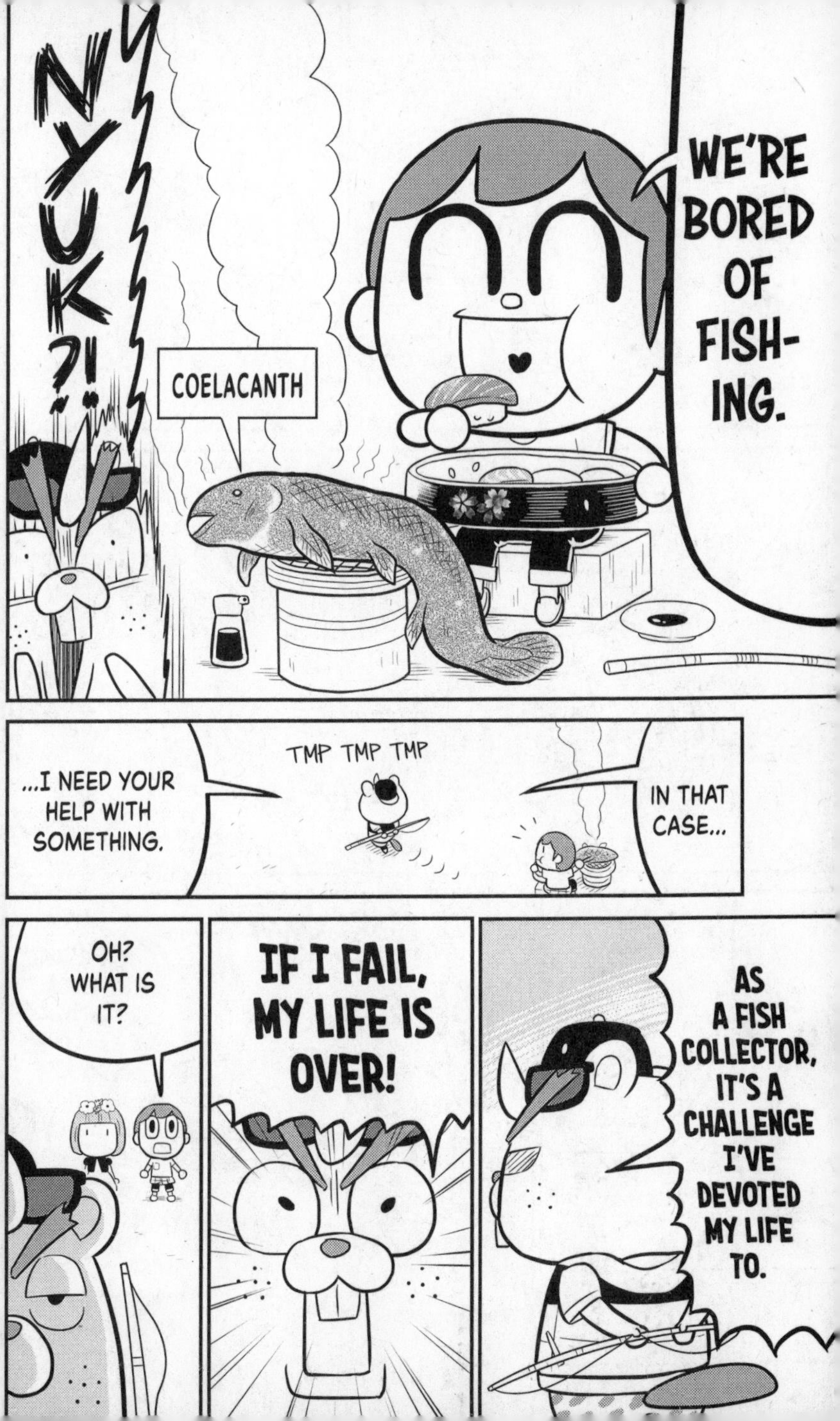
WE'RE BORED OF FISHING.
COELACANTH
NYUK?!
IN THAT CASE...
TMP TMP TMP
...I NEED YOUR HELP WITH SOMETHING.
AS A FISH COLLECTOR, IT'S A CHALLENGE I'VE DEVOTED MY LIFE TO.
IF I FAIL, MY LIFE IS OVER!
OH? WHAT IS IT?

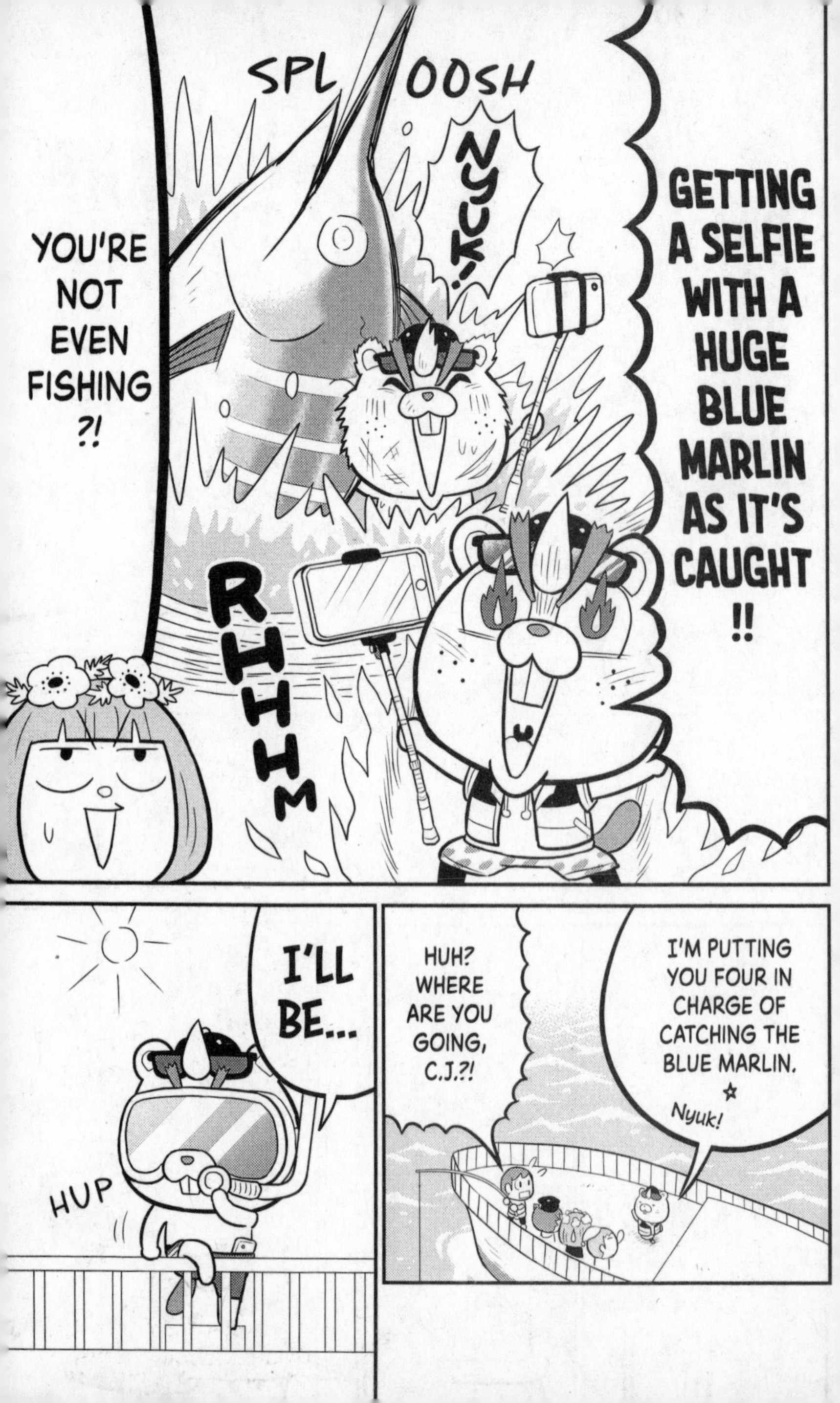
GETTING A SELFIE WITH A HUGE BLUE MARLIN AS IT'S CAUGHT !!
NYUK!
SPLOOSH
YOU'RE NOT EVEN FISHING ?!
RHHHHM
I'M PUTTING YOU FOUR IN CHARGE OF CATCHING THE BLUE MARLIN. ☆ Nyuk!
HUH? WHERE ARE YOU GOING, C.J.?!
I'LL BE...
HUP

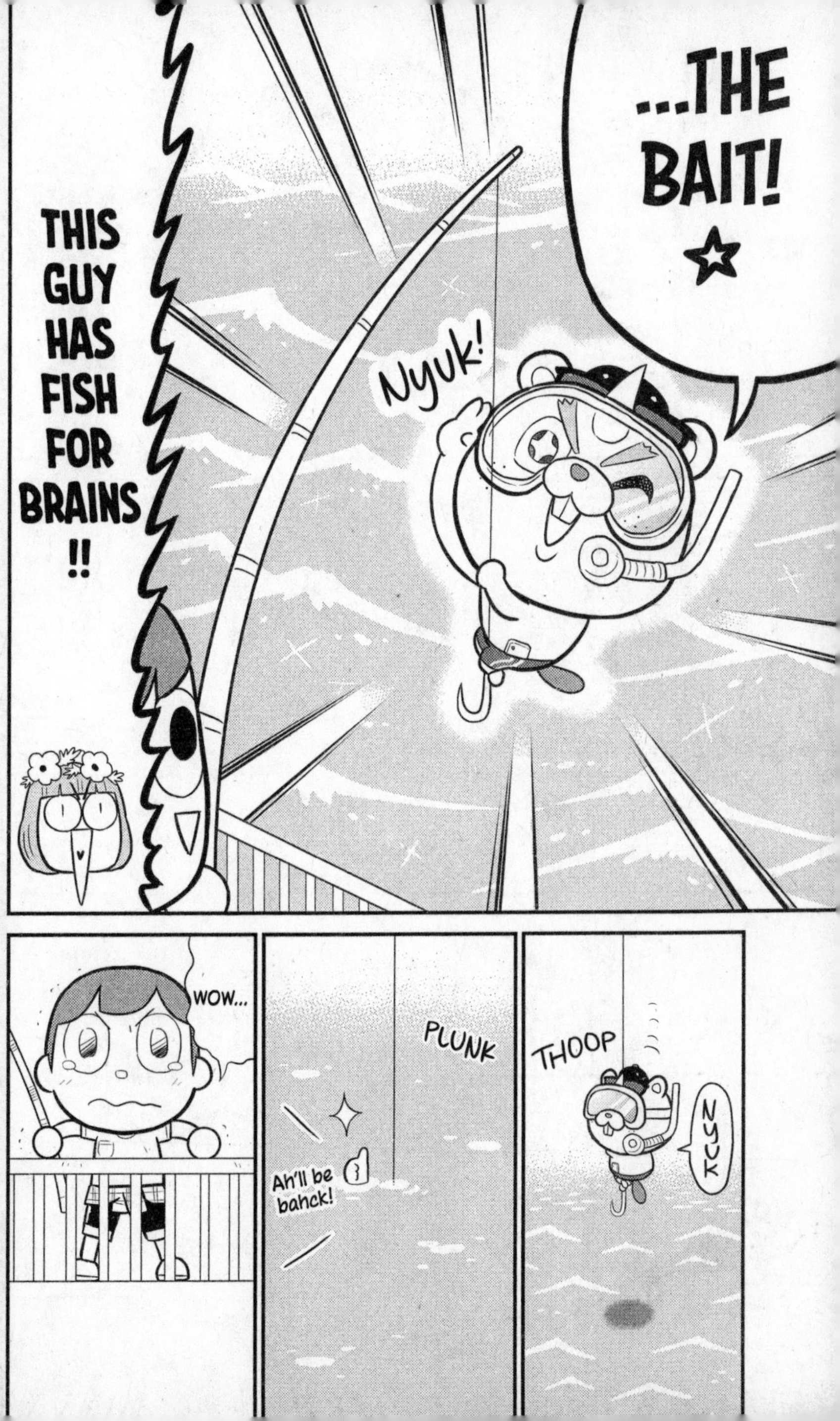
...THE BAIT! ☆
Nyuk!
THIS GUY HAS FISH FOR BRAINS !!
THOOP
NYUK
PLUNK
Ah'll be bahck!
WOW...

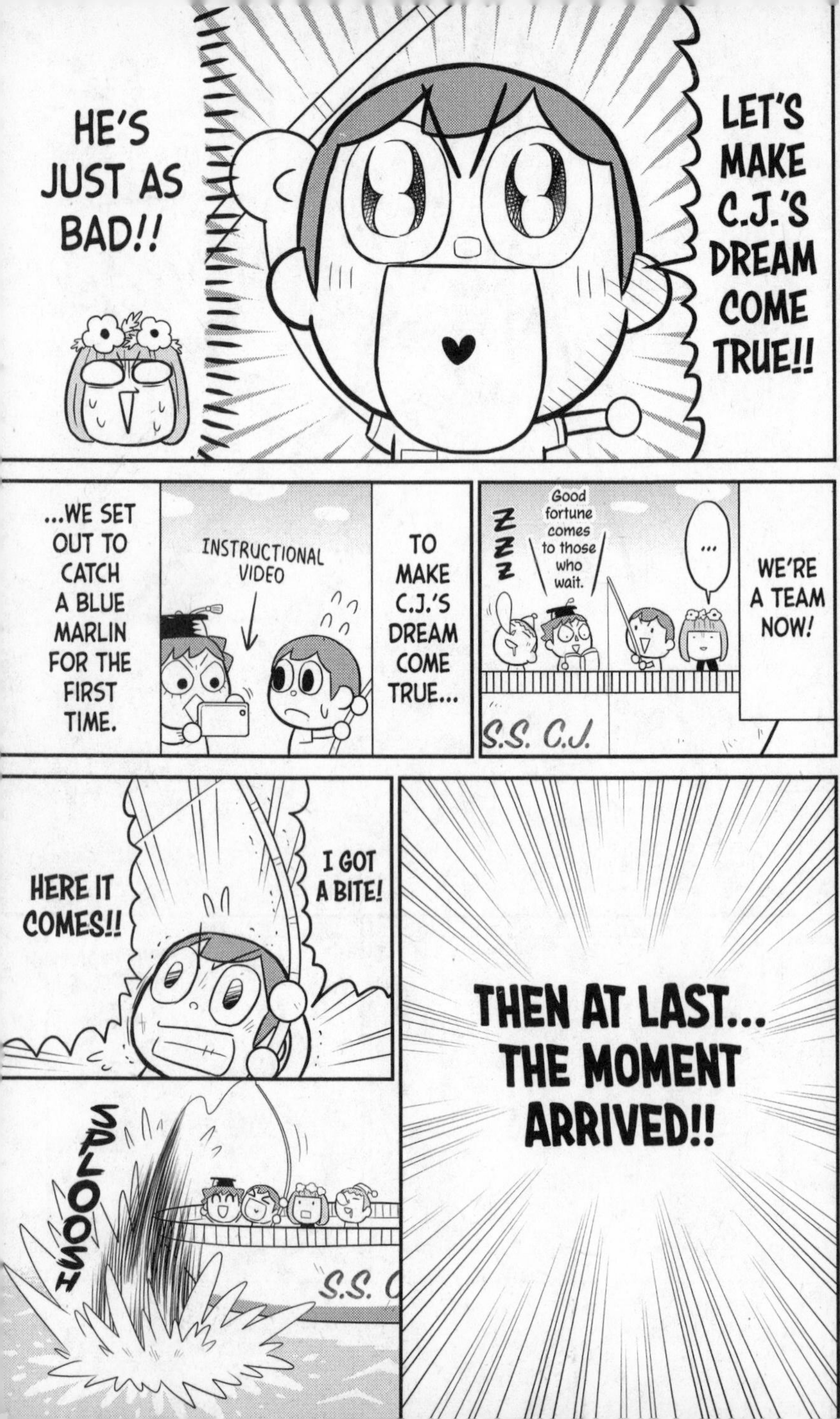
LET'S MAKE C.J.'S DREAM COME TRUE!!
HE'S JUST AS BAD!!
WE'RE A TEAM NOW!
...
Good fortune comes to those who wait.
ZZZ
S.S. C.J.
TO MAKE C.J.'S DREAM COME TRUE...
INSTRUCTIONAL VIDEO
...WE SET OUT TO CATCH A BLUE MARLIN FOR THE FIRST TIME.
THEN AT LAST... THE MOMENT ARRIVED!!
I GOT A BITE!
HERE IT COMES!!
SPLOOSH
S.S. C

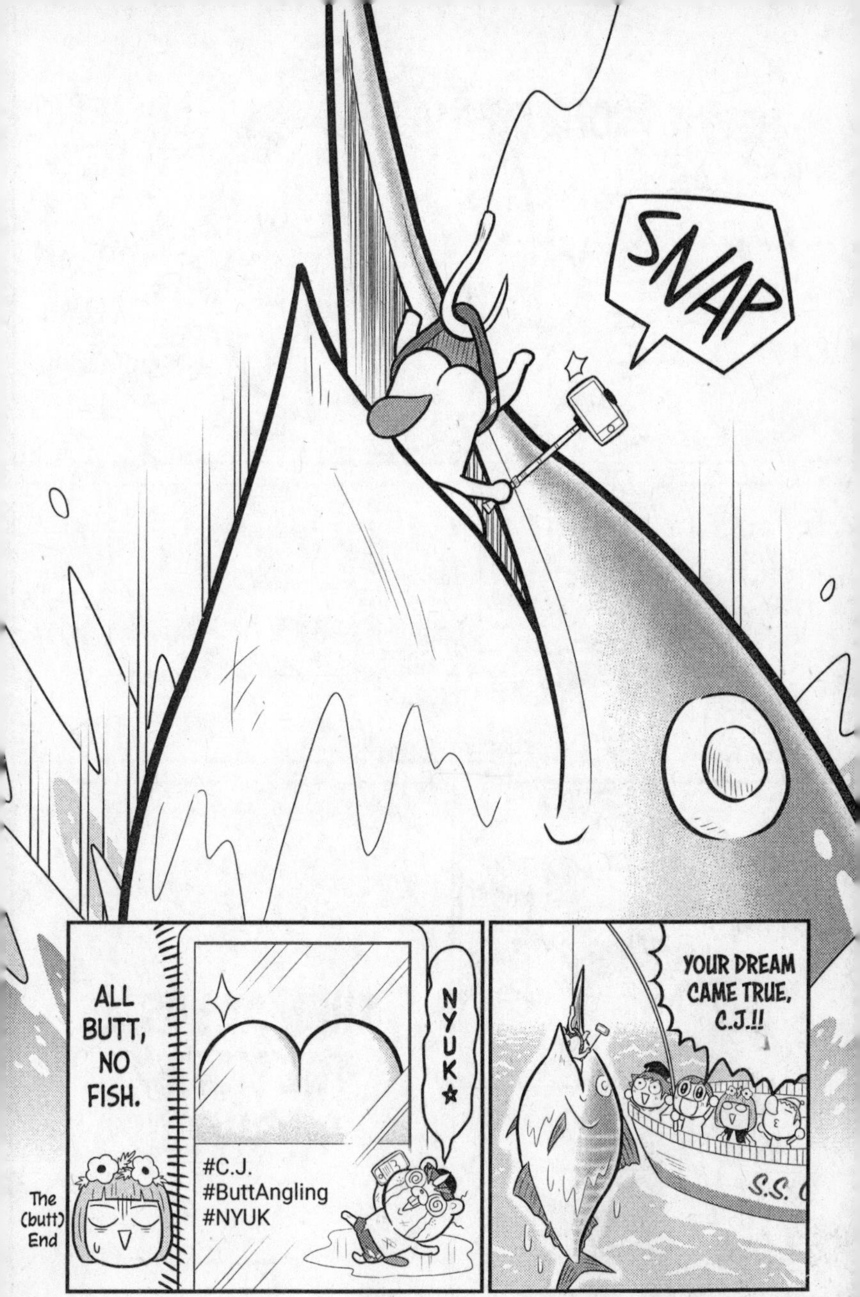
SNAP
YOUR DREAM CAME TRUE, C.J.!!
NYUK☆
#C.J.
#ButtAngling
#NYUK
ALL BUTT, NO FISH.
The (butt) End

THE PROFOUND WORLD OF SCALLOPS

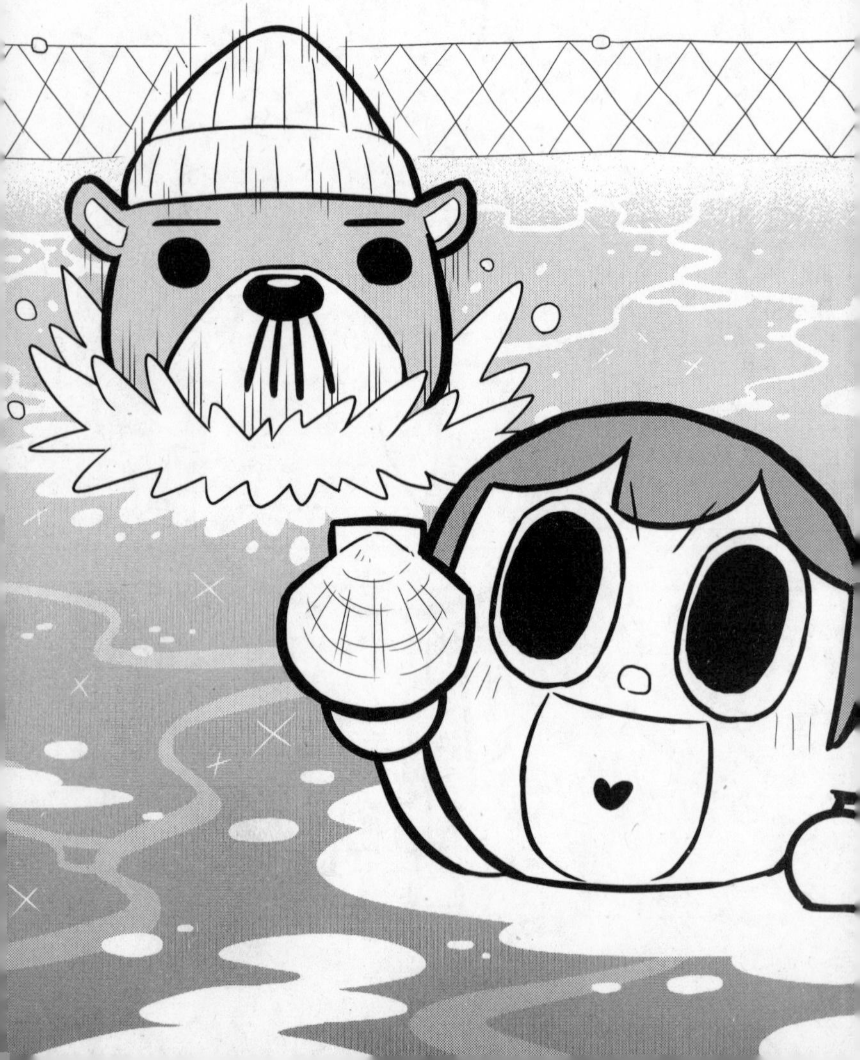

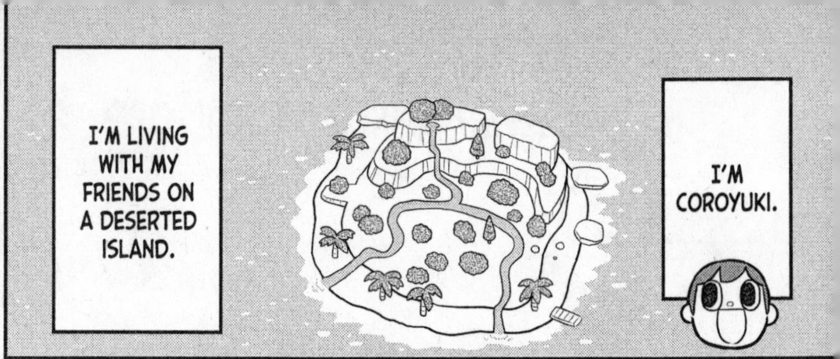
I'M COROYUKI.
I'M LIVING WITH MY FRIENDS ON A DESERTED ISLAND.
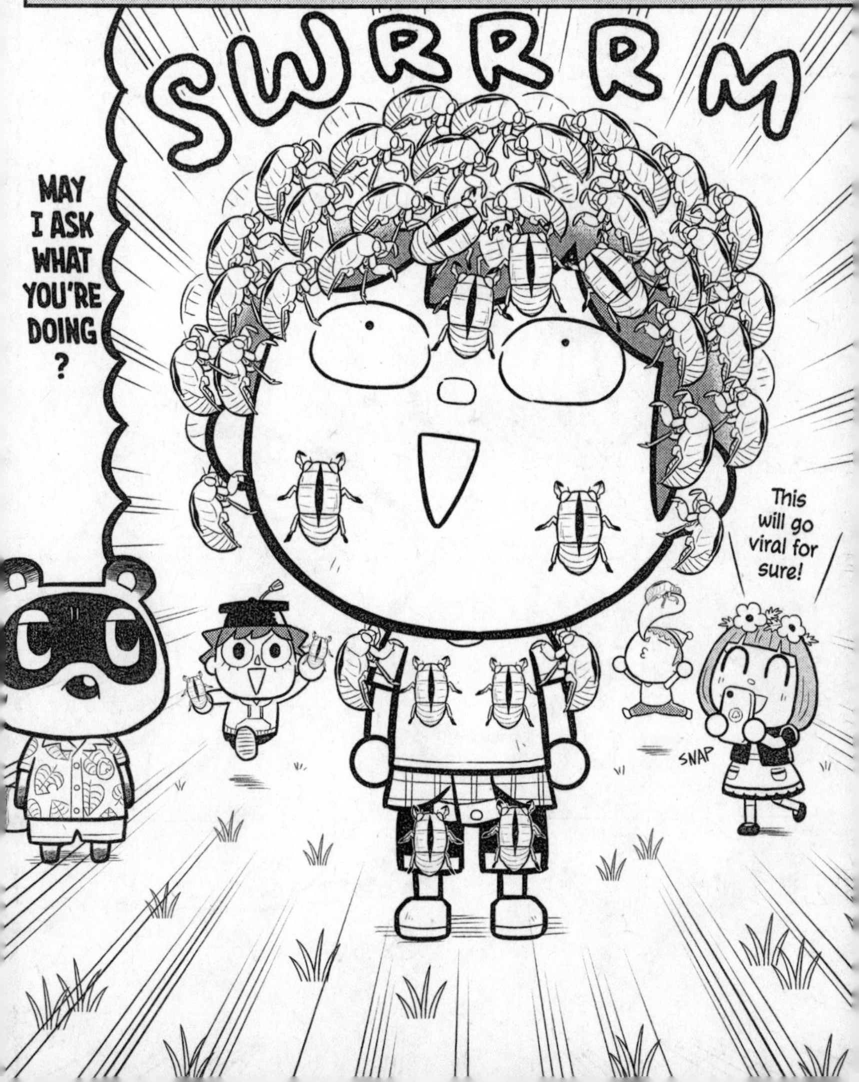
SWRRRM
MAY I ASK WHAT YOU'RE DOING?
This will go viral for sure!
SNAP

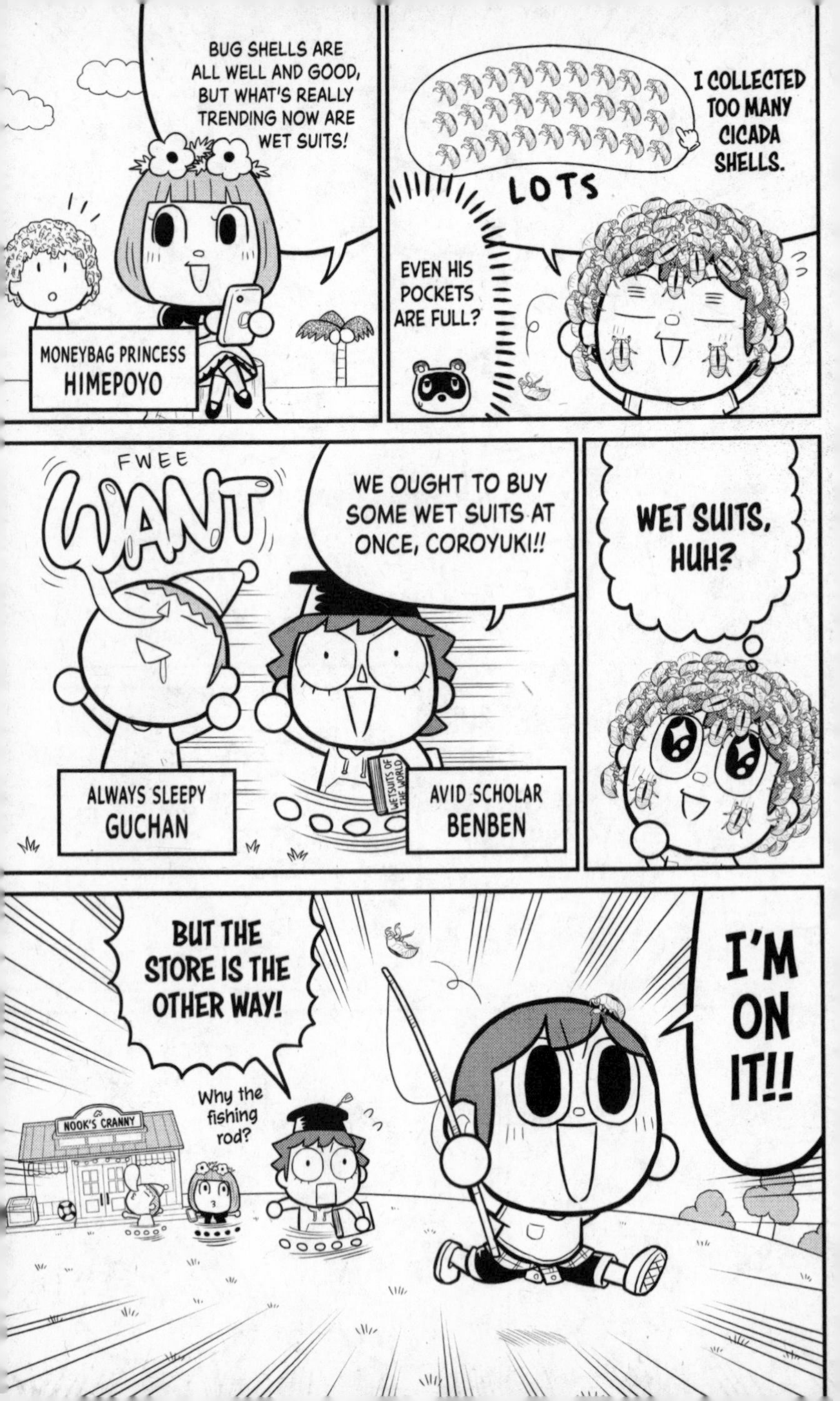

I COLLECTED TOO MANY CICADA SHELLS.
LOTS
EVEN HIS POCKETS ARE FULL?
BUG SHELLS ARE ALL WELL AND GOOD, BUT WHAT'S REALLY TRENDING NOW ARE WET SUITS!
MONEYBAG PRINCESS HIMEPOYO
WET SUITS, HUH?
WE OUGHT TO BUY SOME WET SUITS AT ONCE, COROYUKI!!
AVID SCHOLAR BENBEN
WETSUITS OF THE WORLD
FWEE
WANT
ALWAYS SLEEPY GUCHAN
I'M ON IT!!
BUT THE STORE IS THE OTHER WAY!
Why the fishing rod?
NOOK'S CRANNY

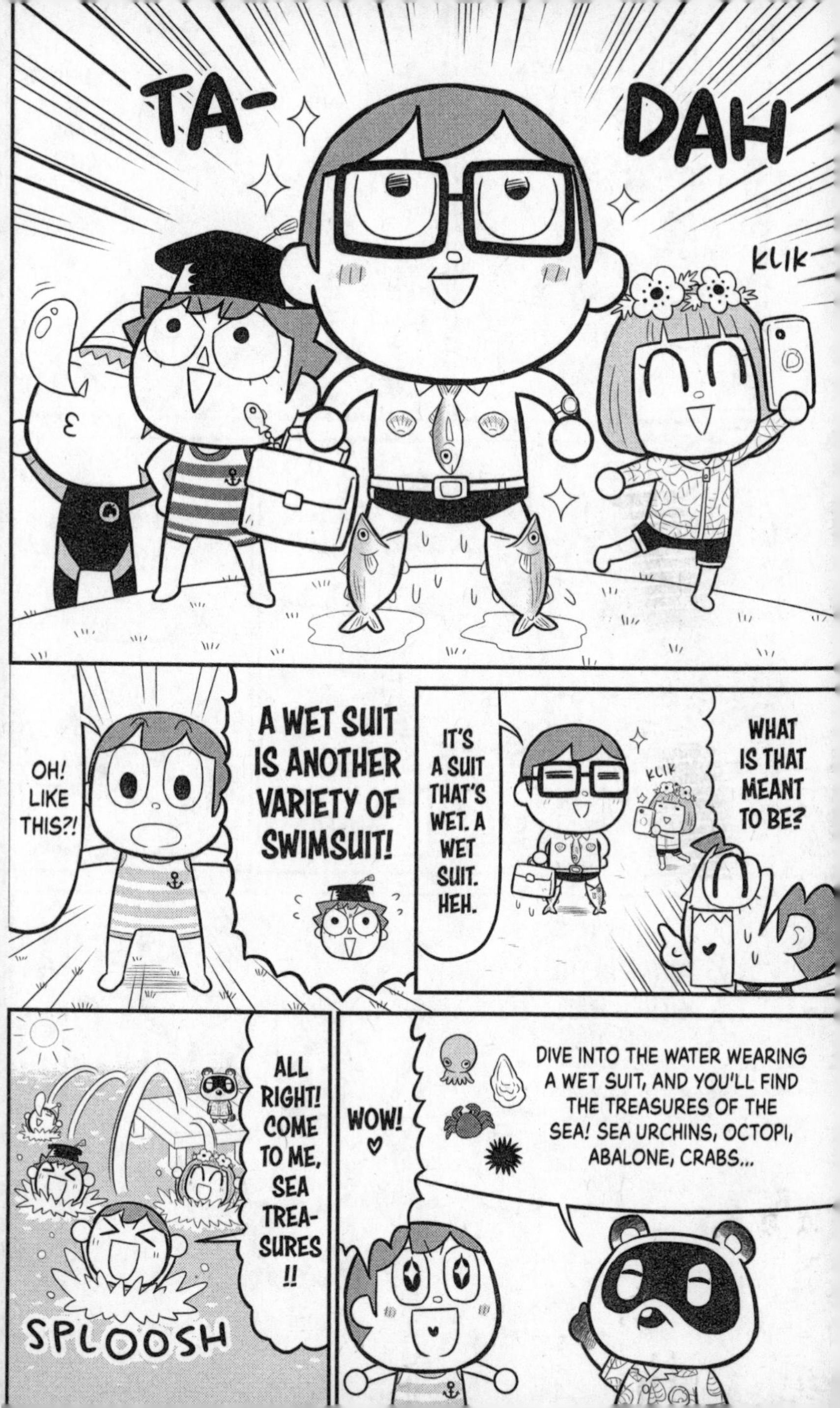
TA- DAH
KLIK
WHAT IS THAT MEANT TO BE?
KLIK
IT'S A SUIT THAT'S WET. A WET SUIT. HEH.
A WET SUIT IS ANOTHER VARIETY OF SWIMSUIT!
OH! LIKE THIS?!
DIVE INTO THE WATER WEARING A WET SUIT, AND YOU'LL FIND THE TREASURES OF THE SEA! SEA URCHINS, OCTOPI, ABALONE, CRABS...
WOW! ♥
ALL RIGHT! COME TO ME, SEA TREA-SURES!!
SPLOOSH

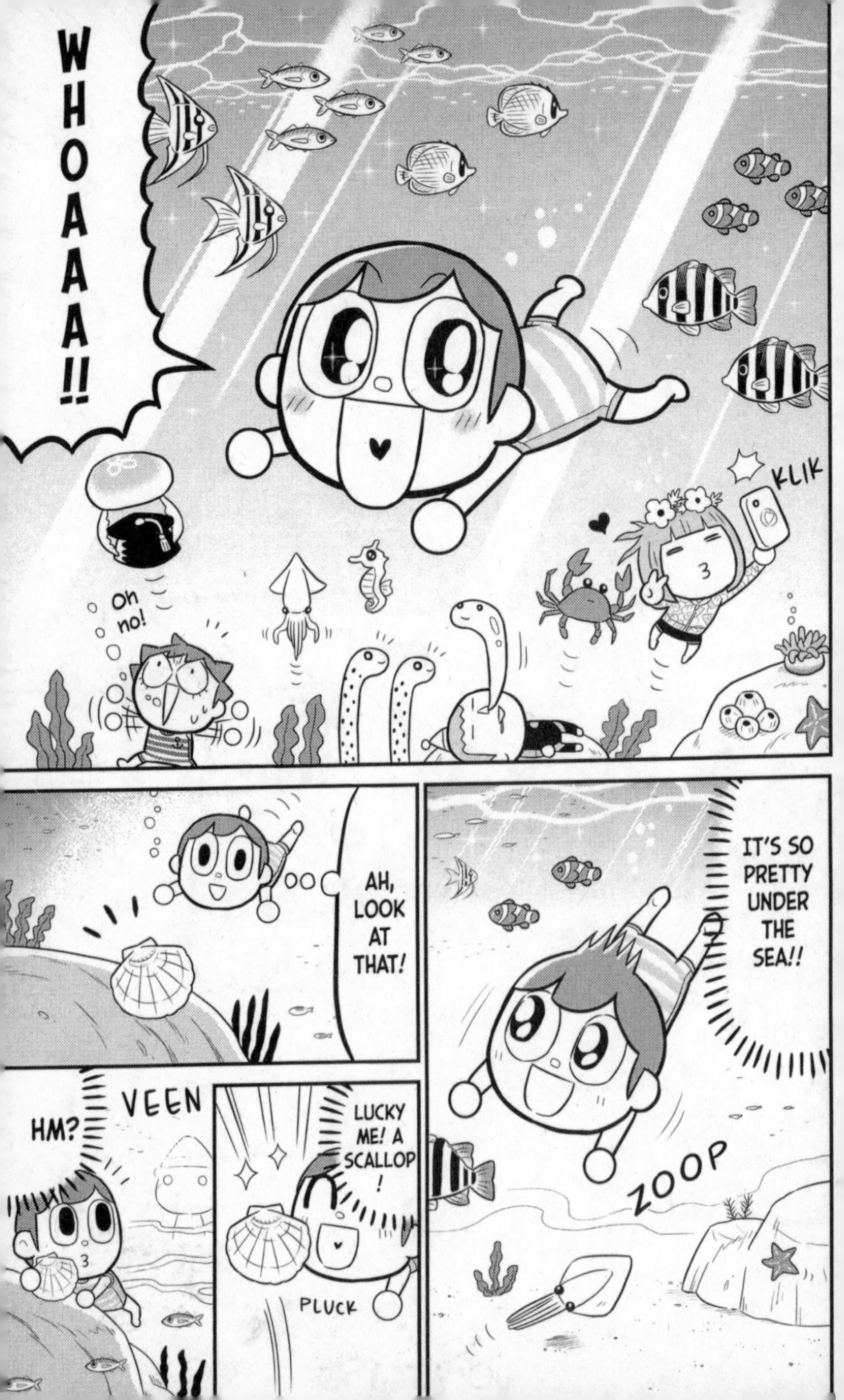
WHOAAA!!
KLIK
Oh no!
IT'S SO PRETTY UNDER THE SEA!!
ZOOP
AH, LOOK AT THAT!
LUCKY ME! A SCALLOP!
PLUCK
HM?
VEEN

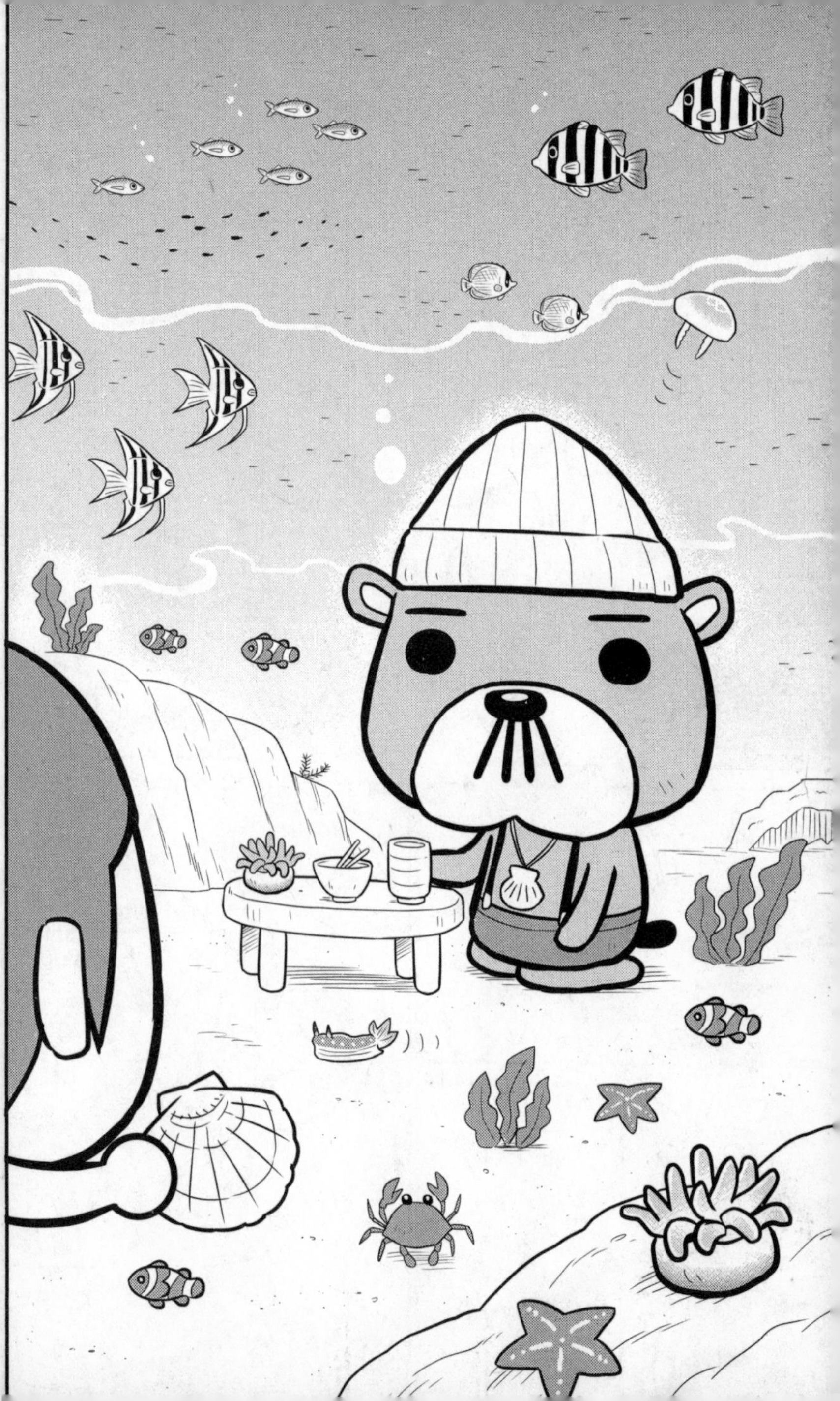

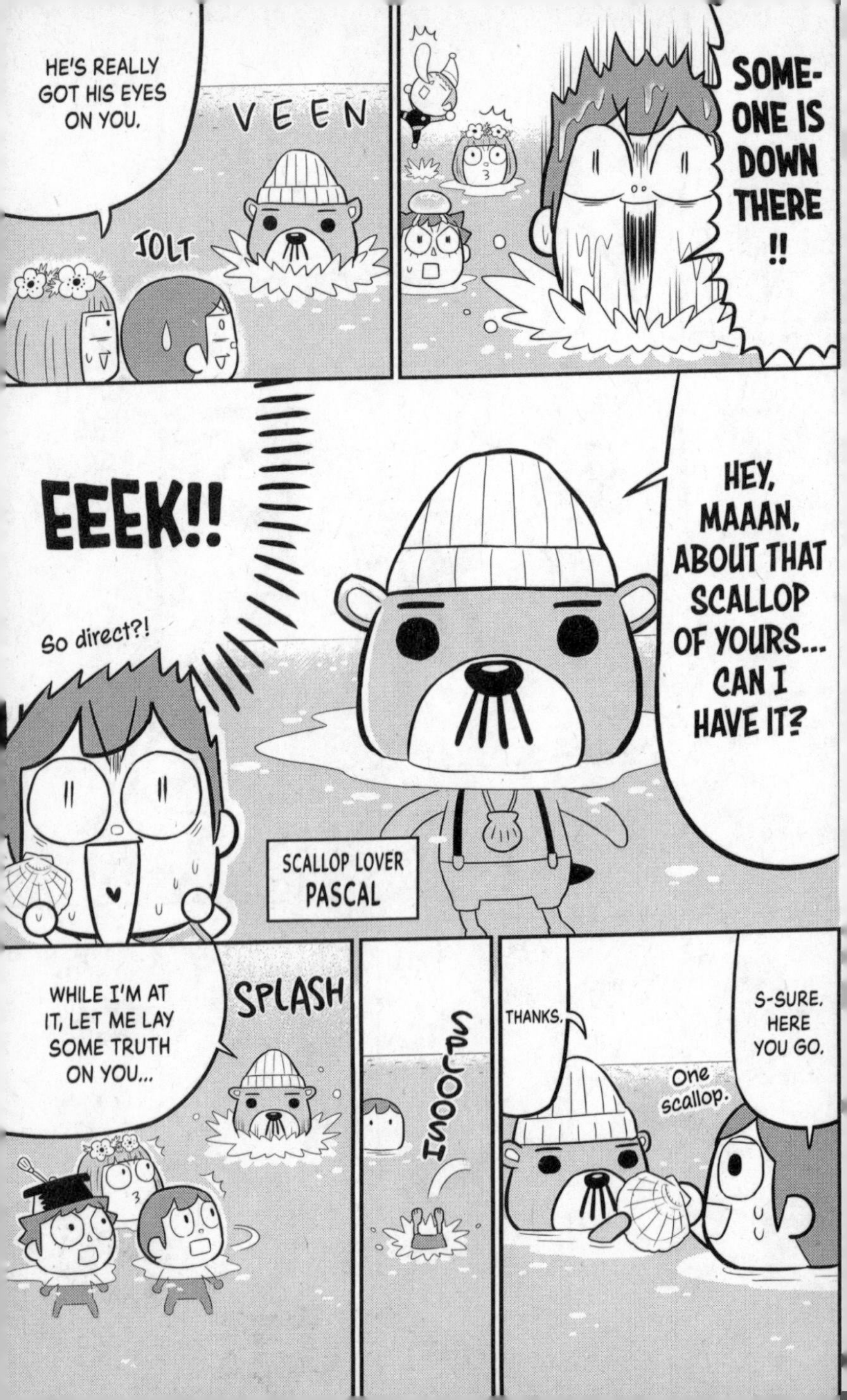
SOME-ONE IS DOWN THERE!!
VEEN
HE'S REALLY GOT HIS EYES ON YOU.
JOLT
HEY, MAAAN, ABOUT THAT SCALLOP OF YOURS... CAN I HAVE IT?
EEEK!!
SCALLOP LOVER PASCAL
So direct?!
S-SURE. HERE YOU GO.
One scallop.
THANKS.
SPLOOSH
SPLASH
WHILE I'M AT IT, LET ME LAY SOME TRUTH ON YOU...

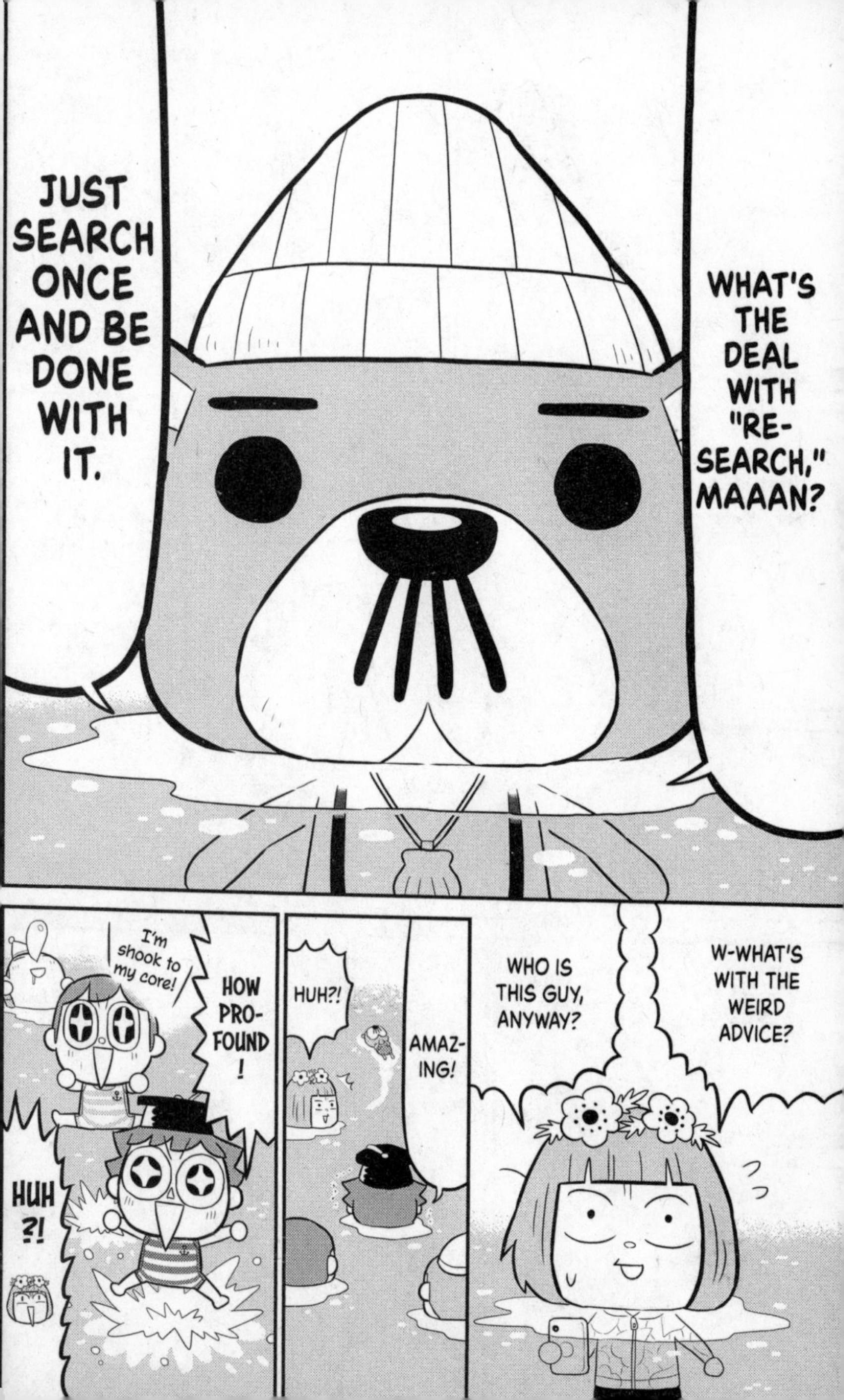
WHAT'S THE DEAL WITH "RE-SEARCH," MAAAN?
JUST SEARCH ONCE AND BE DONE WITH IT.
W-WHAT'S WITH THE WEIRD ADVICE?
WHO IS THIS GUY, ANYWAY?
AMAZ-ING!
HUH?!
HOW PRO-FOUND!
I'm shook to my core!
HUH ?!

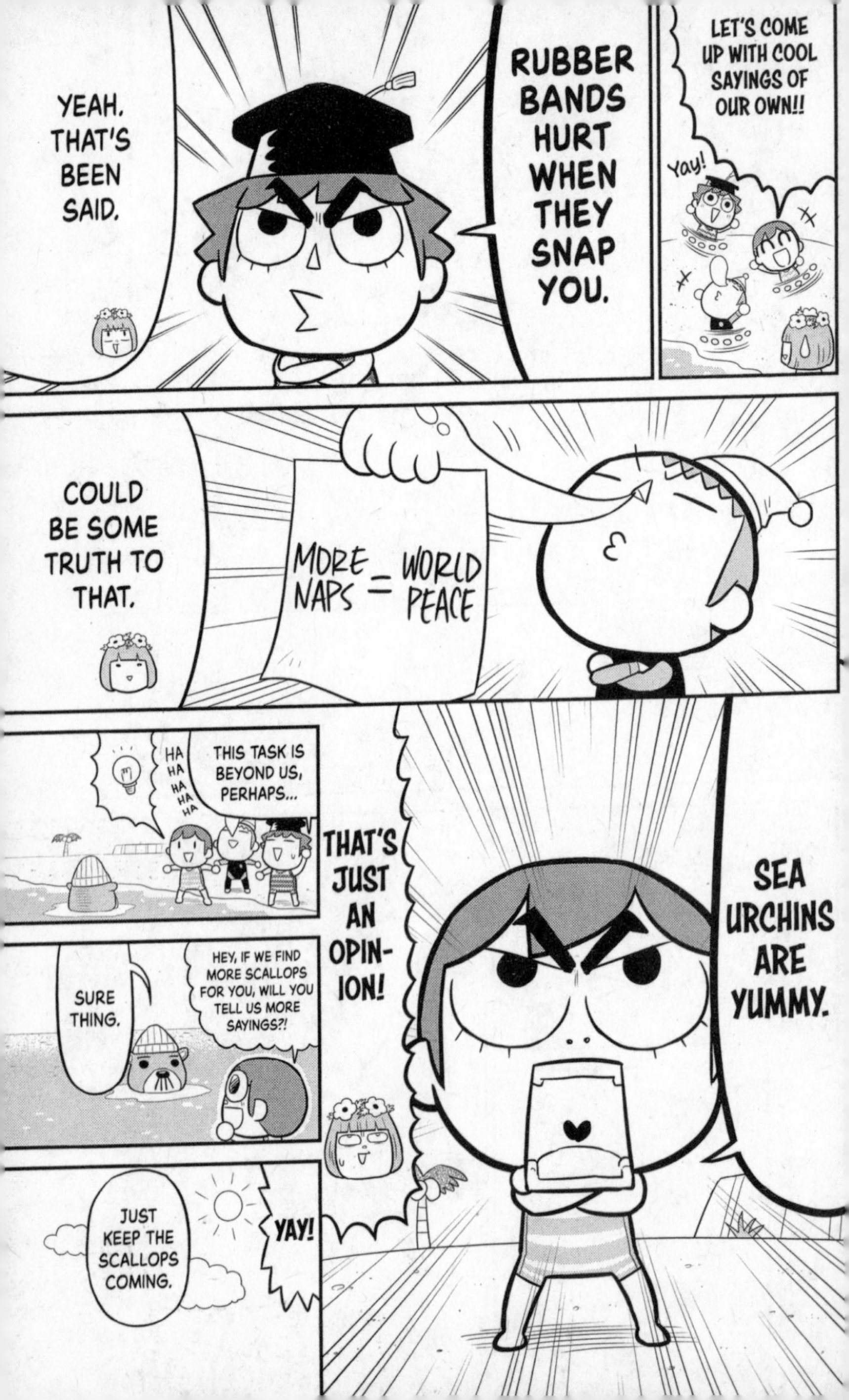
LET'S COME UP WITH COOL SAYINGS OF OUR OWN!!
Yay!
RUBBER BANDS HURT WHEN THEY SNAP YOU.
YEAH. THAT'S BEEN SAID.
MORE NAPS = WORLD PEACE
COULD BE SOME TRUTH TO THAT.
SEA URCHINS ARE YUMMY.
THAT'S JUST AN OPIN-ION!
THIS TASK IS BEYOND US, PERHAPS...
HA HA HA HA HA
HEY, IF WE FIND MORE SCALLOPS FOR YOU, WILL YOU TELL US MORE SAYINGS?!
SURE THING.
YAY!
JUST KEEP THE SCALLOPS COMING.

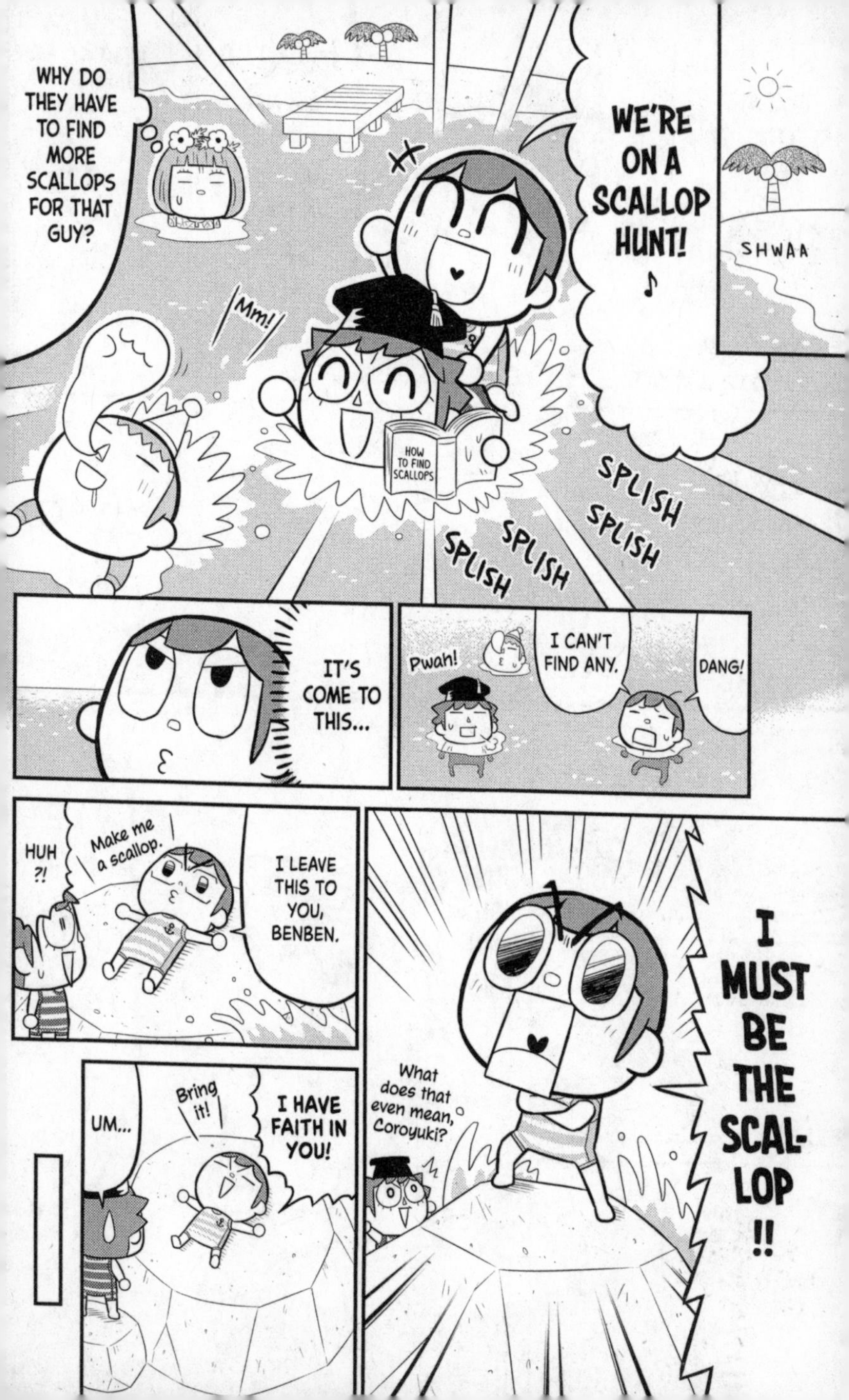
SHWAA
WE'RE ON A SCALLOP HUNT! ♪
Mm!
WHY DO THEY HAVE TO FIND MORE SCALLOPS FOR THAT GUY?
HOW TO FIND SCALLOPS
SPLISH
SPLISH
SPLISH
SPLISH
DANG!
I CAN'T FIND ANY.
Pwah!
IT'S COME TO THIS...
I MUST BE THE SCAL-LOP!!
What does that even mean, Coroyuki?
I LEAVE THIS TO YOU, BENBEN.
Make me a scallop.
HUH?!
I HAVE FAITH IN YOU!
Bring it!
UM...

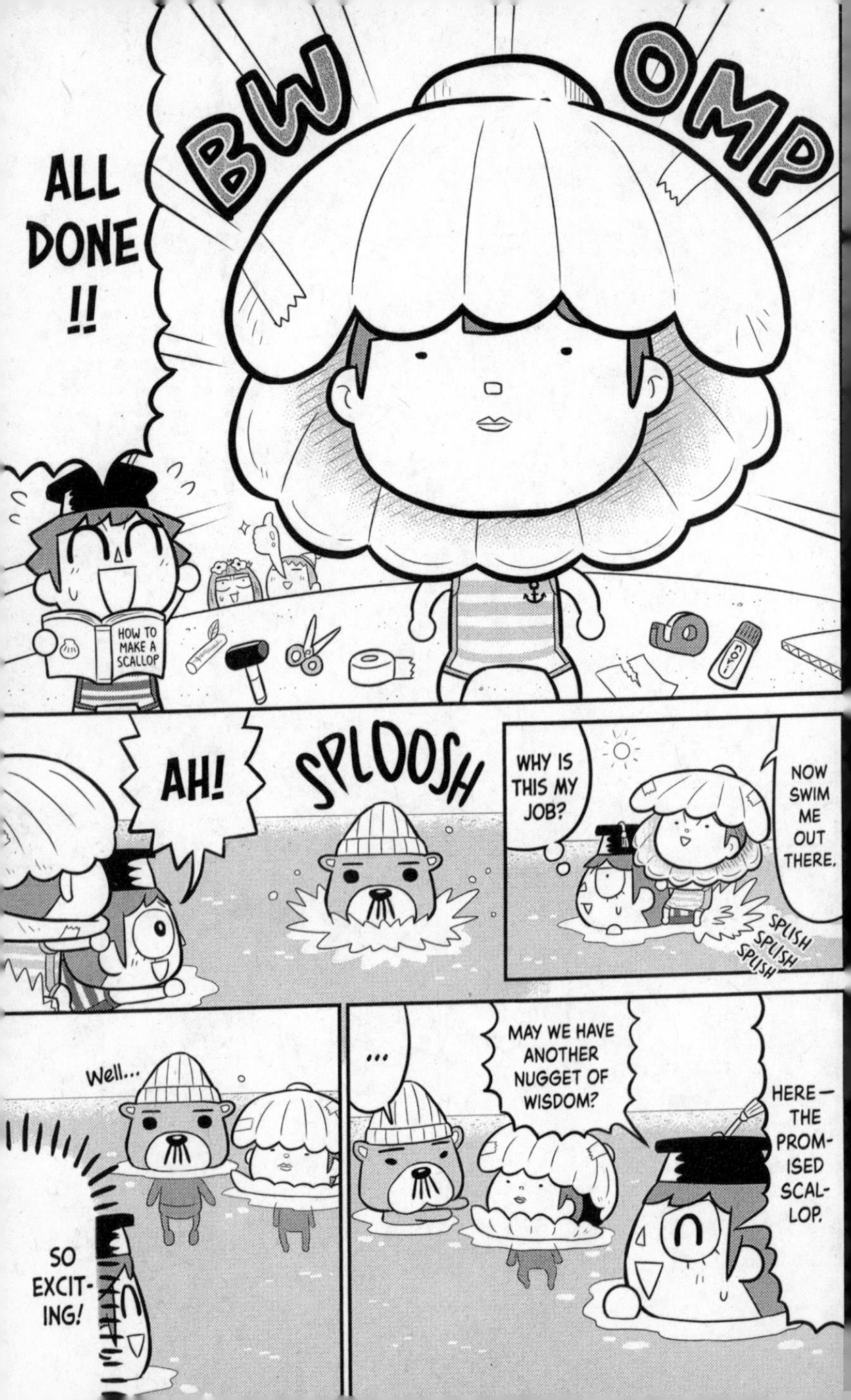
BWOMP
ALL DONE!!
HOW TO MAKE A SCALLOP
NOW SWIM ME OUT THERE.
WHY IS THIS MY JOB?
SPLISH SPLISH SPLISH
SPLOOSH
AH!
HERE—THE PROMISED SCALLOP.
MAY WE HAVE ANOTHER NUGGET OF WISDOM?
...
Well...
SO EXCITING!

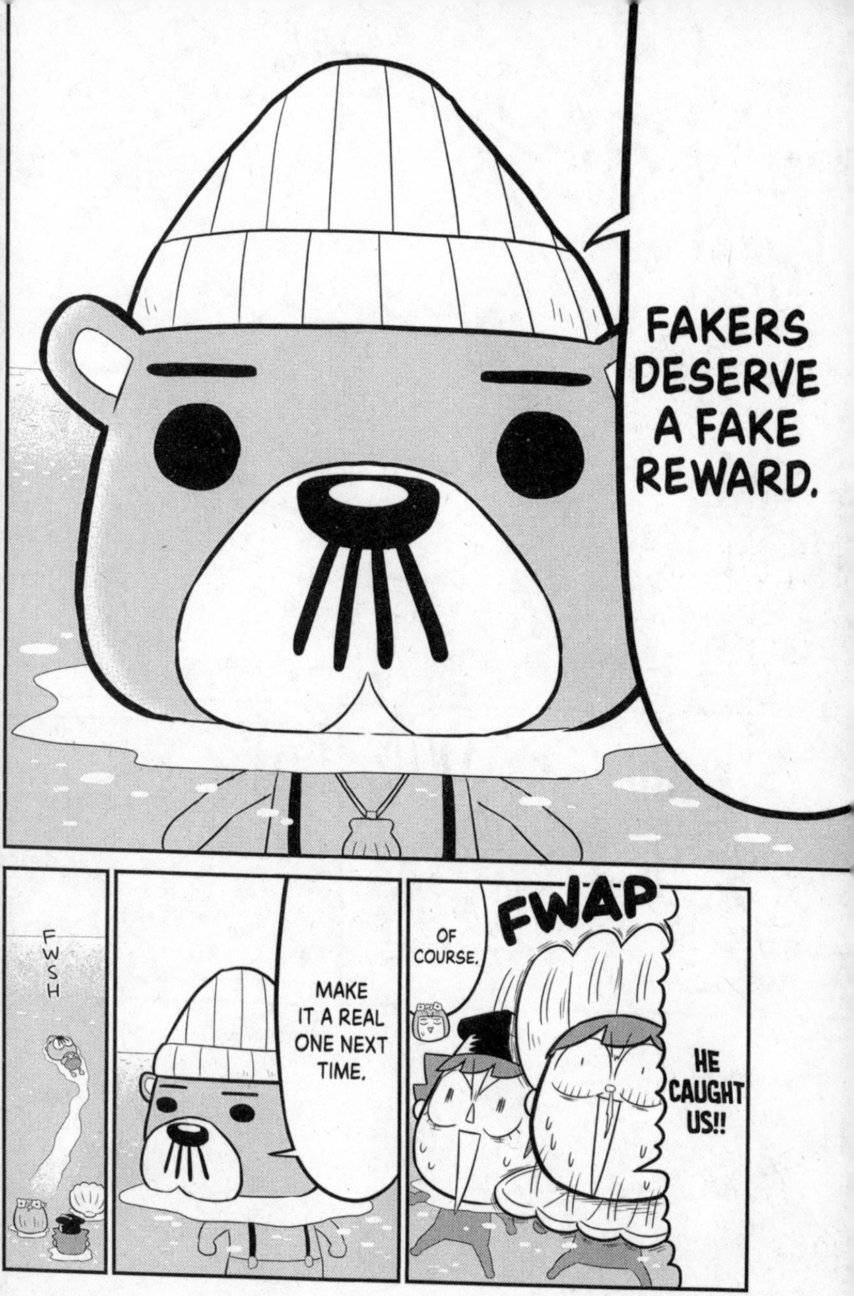
FAKERS DESERVE A FAKE REWARD.
FWAP
OF COURSE.
HE CAUGHT US!!
MAKE IT A REAL ONE NEXT TIME.
FWSH

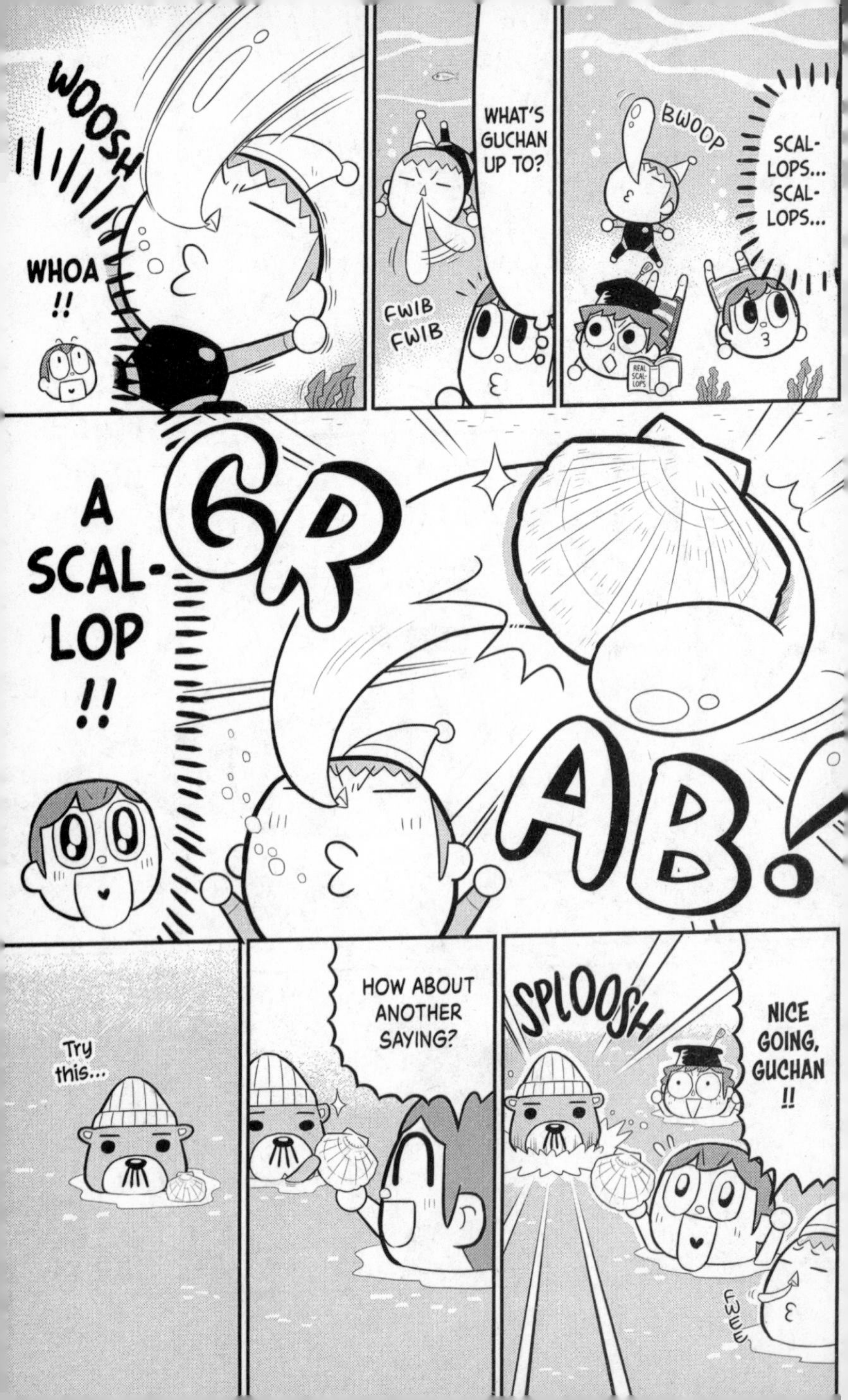
SCAL-LOPS... SCAL-LOPS...
BWOOP
REAL SCALLOPS
WHAT'S GUCHAN UP TO?
FWIB FWIB
WOOSH
WHOA!!
GRAB!
A SCAL-LOP!!
NICE GOING, GUCHAN!!
SPLOOSH
FWEE
HOW ABOUT ANOTHER SAYING?
Try this...

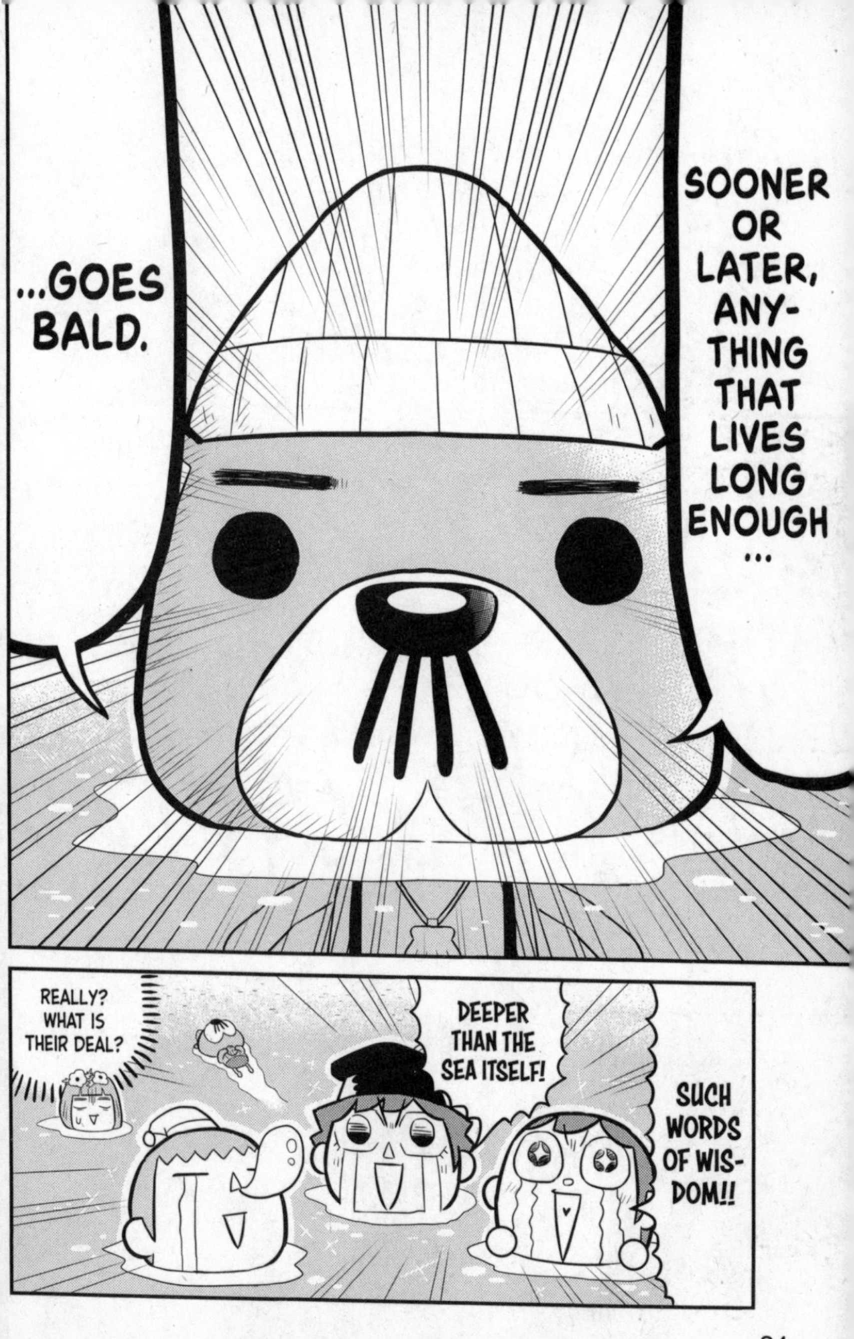
SOONER OR LATER, ANY-THING THAT LIVES LONG ENOUGH...
...GOES BALD.
SUCH WORDS OF WIS-DOM!!
DEEPER THAN THE SEA ITSELF!
REALLY? WHAT IS THEIR DEAL?

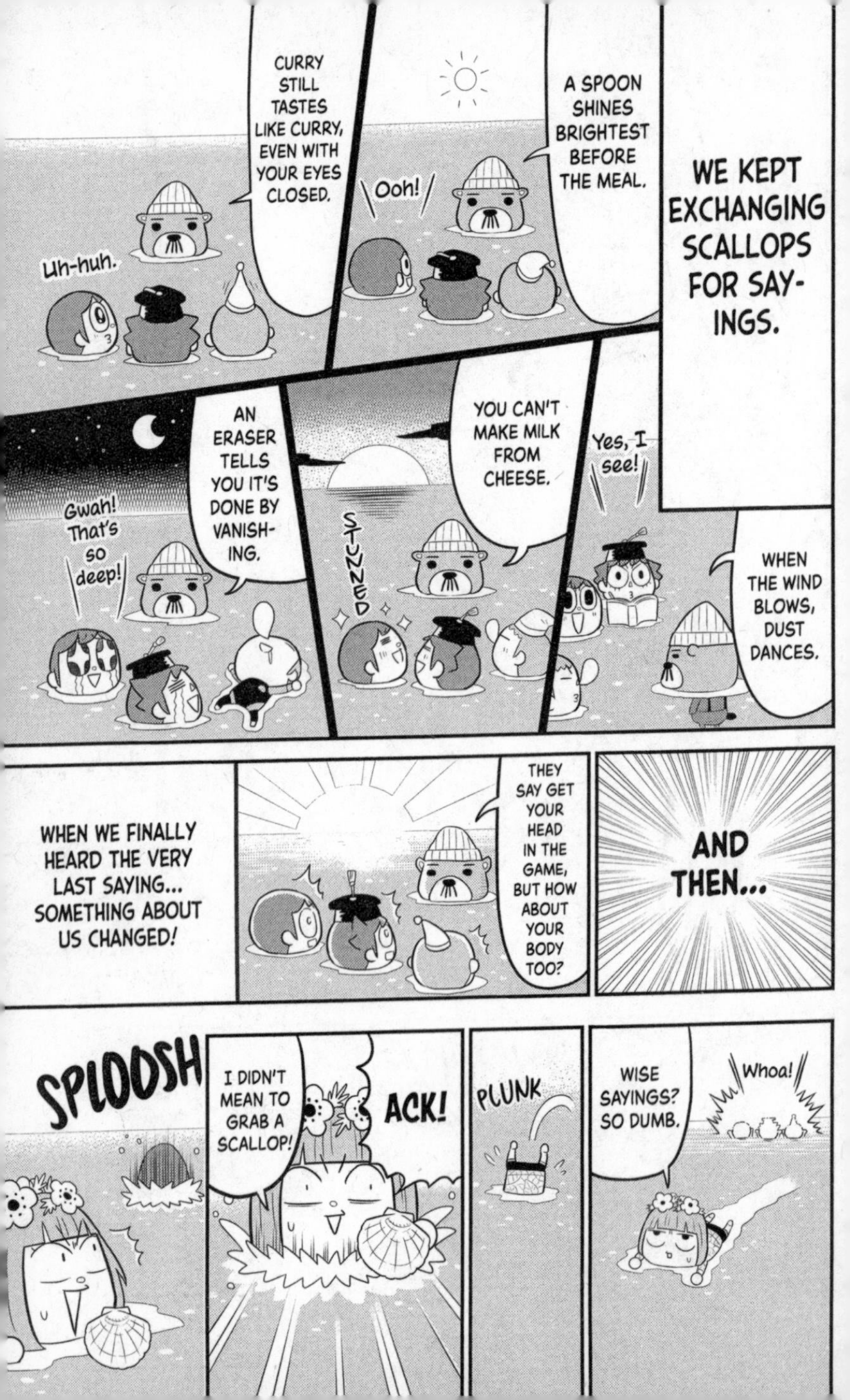
WE KEPT EXCHANGING SCALLOPS FOR SAYINGS.
A SPOON SHINES BRIGHTEST BEFORE THE MEAL.
Ooh!
CURRY STILL TASTES LIKE CURRY, EVEN WITH YOUR EYES CLOSED.
Uh-huh.
Yes, I see!
WHEN THE WIND BLOWS, DUST DANCES.
YOU CAN'T MAKE MILK FROM CHEESE.
STUNNED
AN ERASER TELLS YOU IT'S DONE BY VANISHING.
Gwah! That's so deep!
AND THEN...
THEY SAY GET YOUR HEAD IN THE GAME, BUT HOW ABOUT YOUR BODY TOO?
WHEN WE FINALLY HEARD THE VERY LAST SAYING... SOMETHING ABOUT US CHANGED!
Whoa!
WISE SAYINGS? SO DUMB.
PLUNK
ACK!
I DIDN'T MEAN TO GRAB A SCALLOP!
SPLOOSH

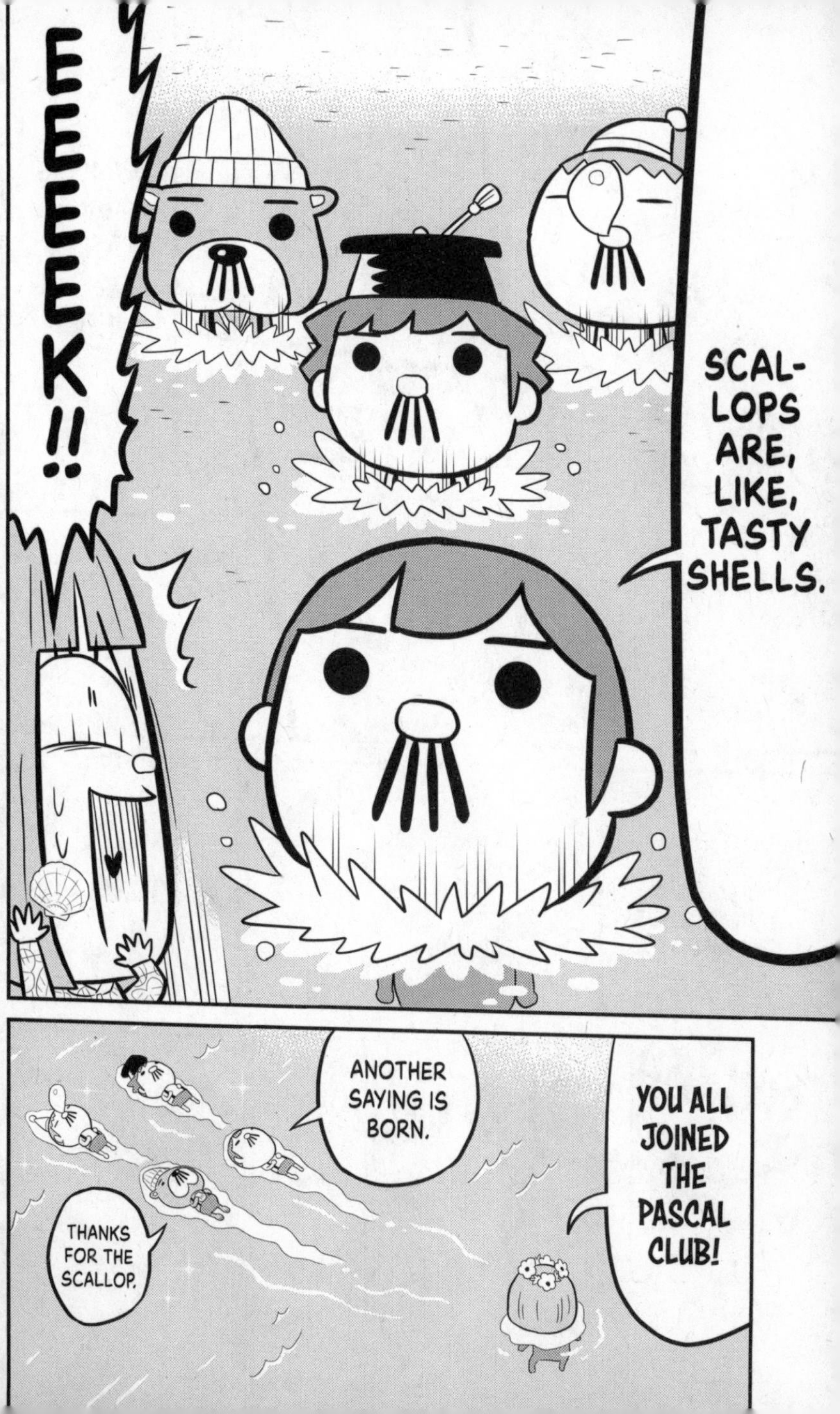
SCAL-LOPS ARE, LIKE, TASTY SHELLS.
EEEEEK!!
YOU ALL JOINED THE PASCAL CLUB!
ANOTHER SAYING IS BORN.
THANKS FOR THE SCALLOP.

New Horizons
Welcome to Animal Crossing
Deserted Island Diary

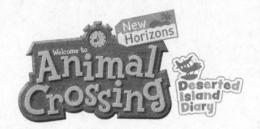

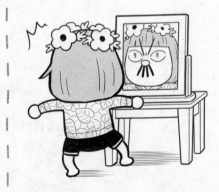

LET'S RAISE THE ISLAND'S RATING!

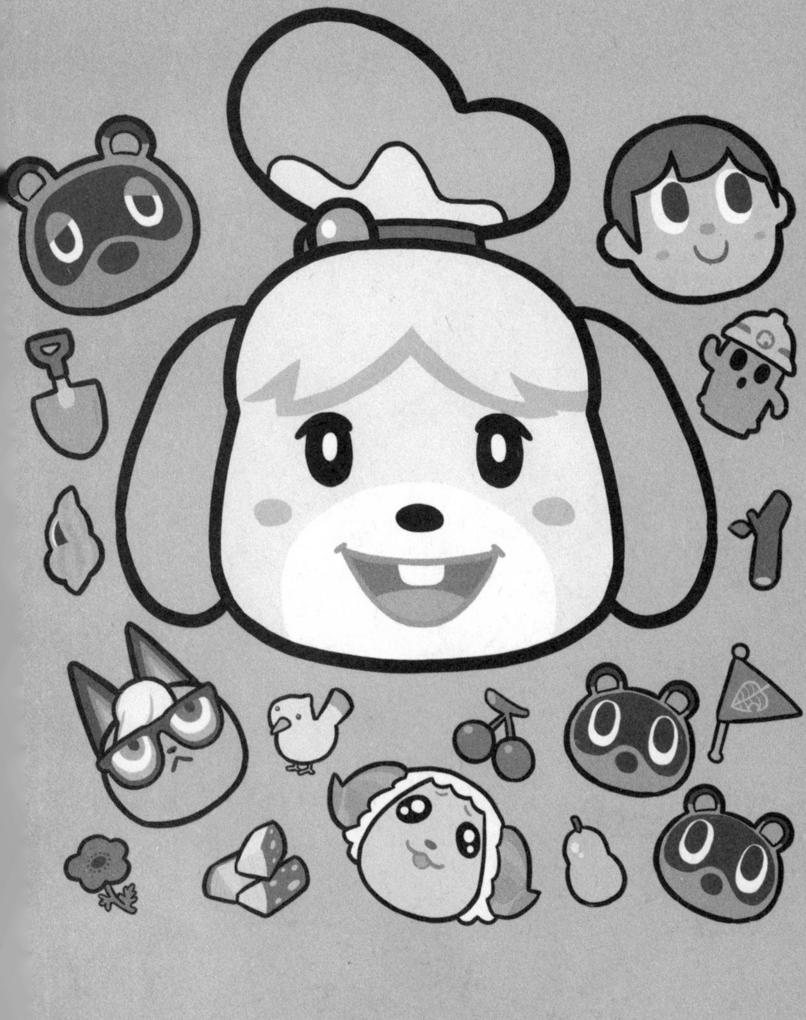

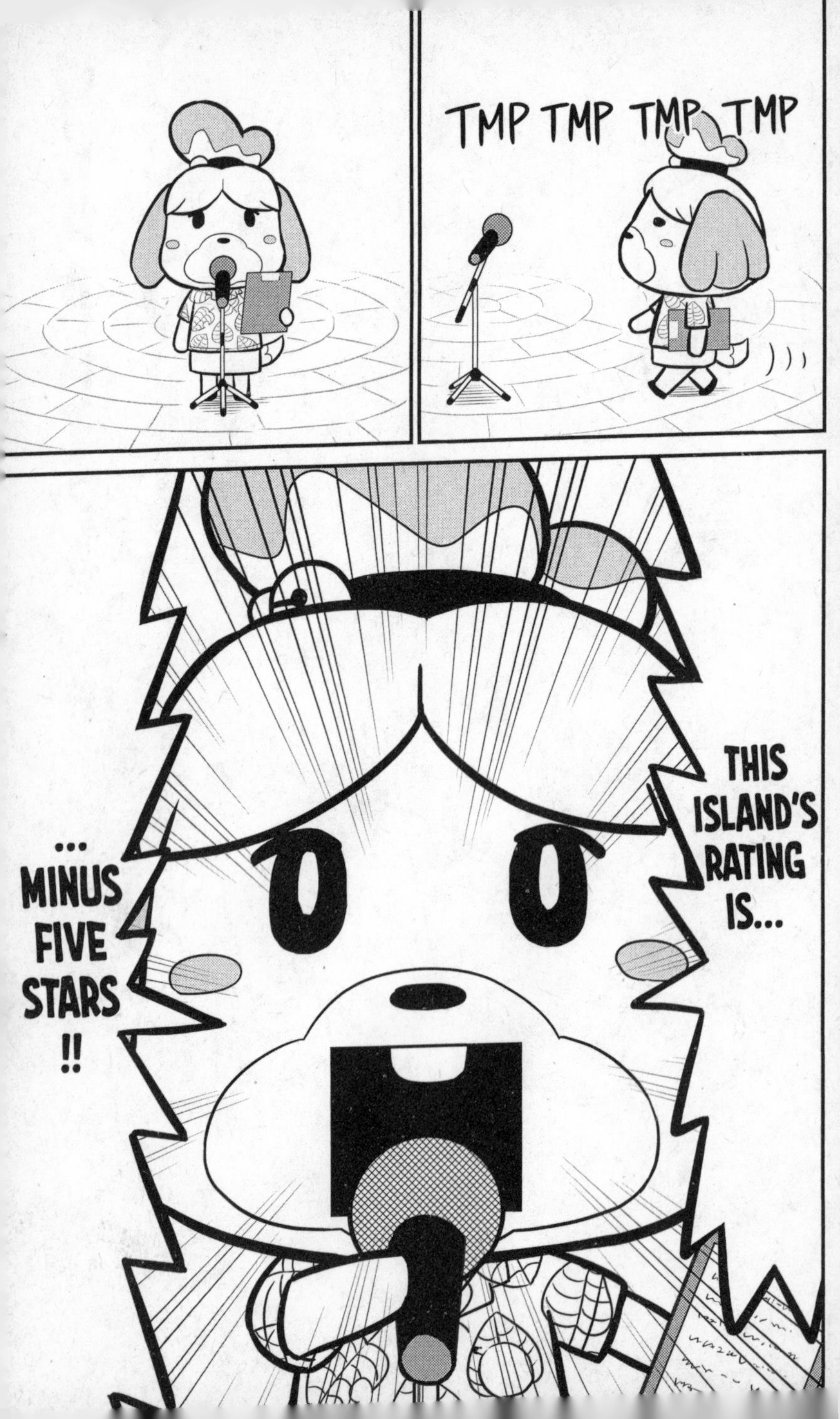
TMP TMP TMP TMP
THIS ISLAND'S RATING IS...
...MINUS FIVE STARS!!

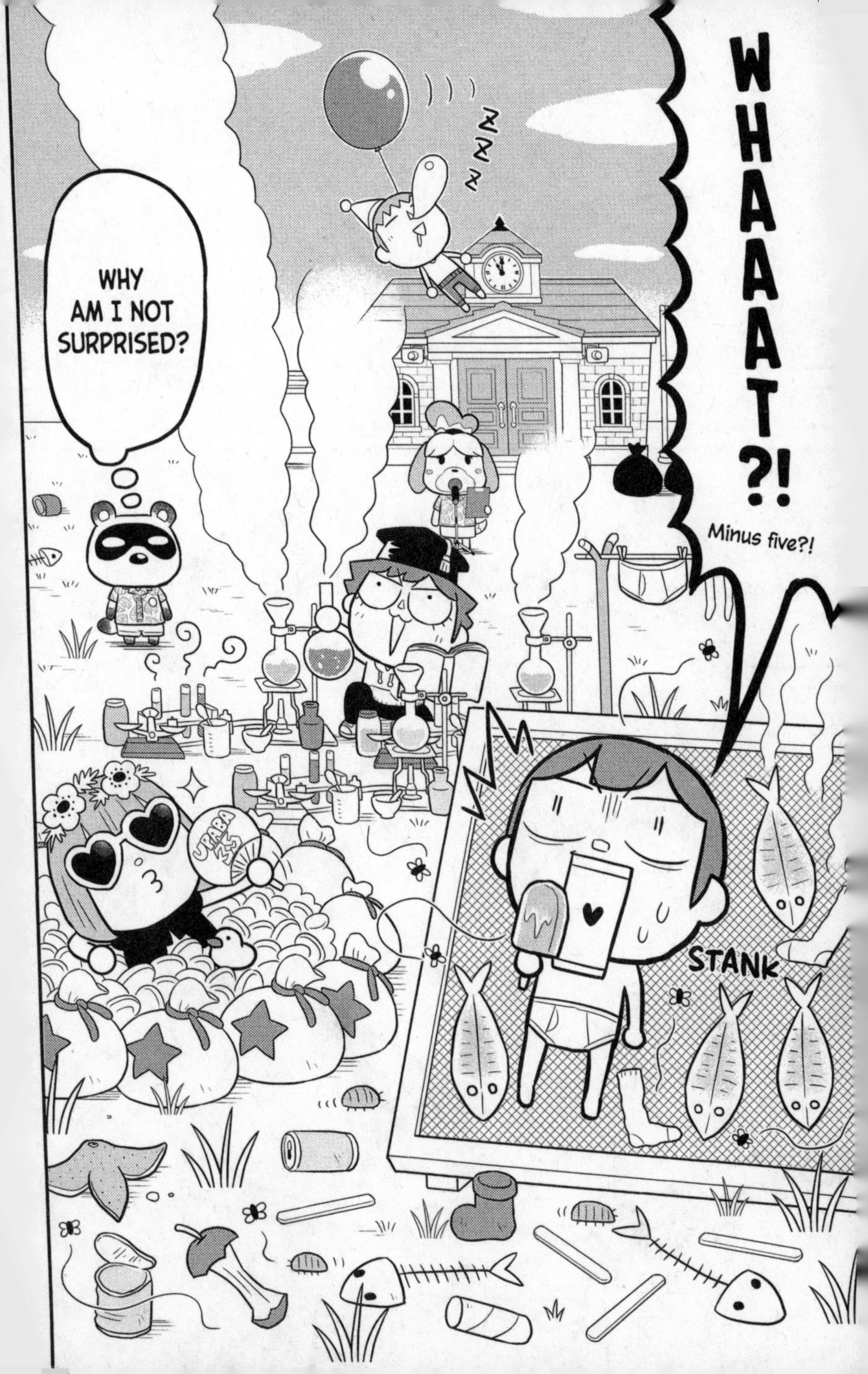
WHAAAT?!
Minus five?!
WHY AM I NOT SURPRISED?
STANK

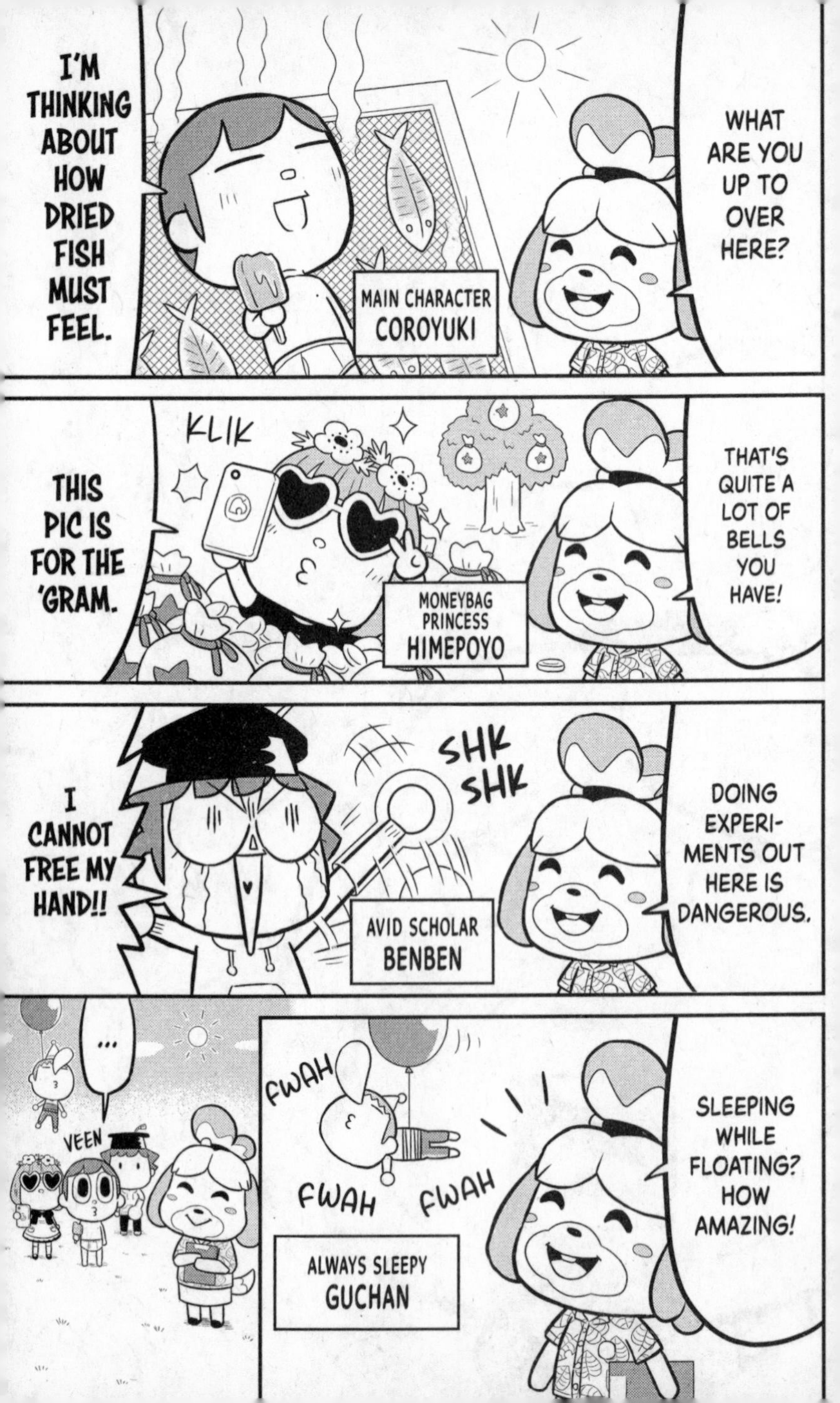
WHAT ARE YOU UP TO OVER HERE?
MAIN CHARACTER COROYUKI
I'M THINKING ABOUT HOW DRIED FISH MUST FEEL.
THAT'S QUITE A LOT OF BELLS YOU HAVE!
KLIK
MONEYBAG PRINCESS HIMEPOYO
THIS PIC IS FOR THE 'GRAM.
DOING EXPERI-MENTS OUT HERE IS DANGEROUS.
SHK SHK
AVID SCHOLAR BENBEN
I CANNOT FREE MY HAND!!
SLEEPING WHILE FLOATING? HOW AMAZING!
FWAH
FWAH FWAH
ALWAYS SLEEPY GUCHAN
...
VEEN

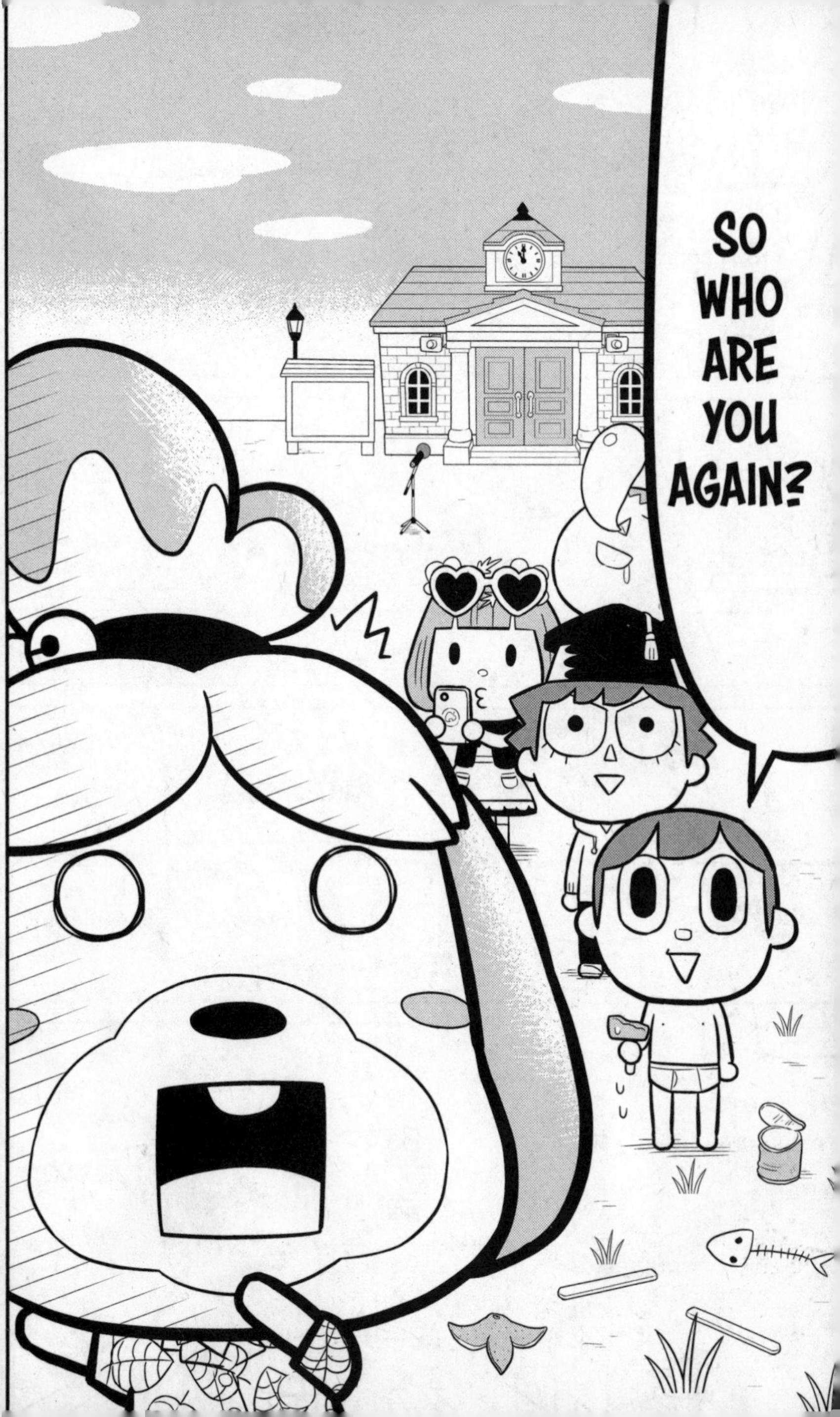
SO WHO ARE YOU AGAIN?

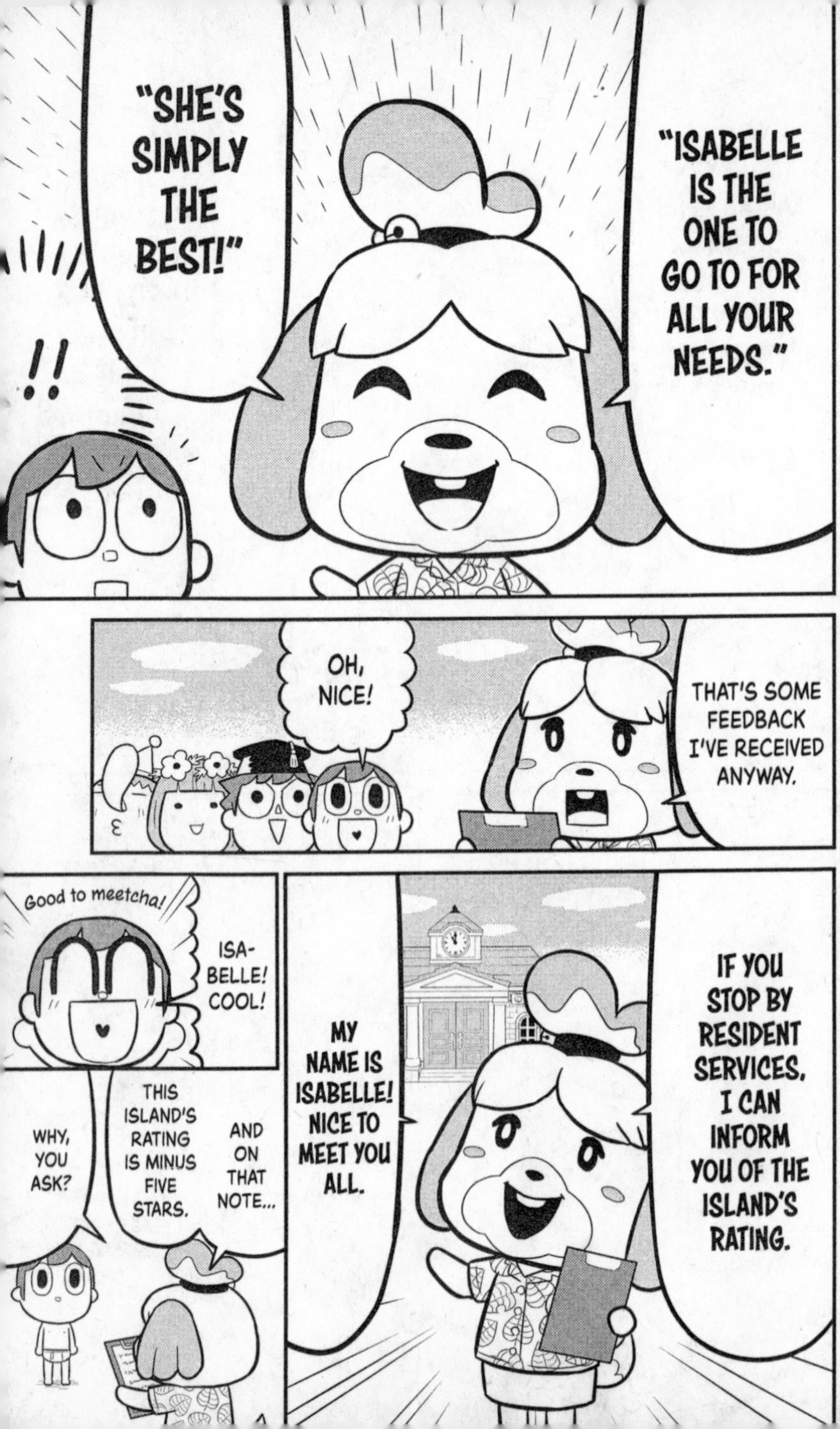

"ISABELLE IS THE ONE TO GO TO FOR ALL YOUR NEEDS."
"SHE'S SIMPLY THE BEST!"
!!
THAT'S SOME FEEDBACK I'VE RECEIVED ANYWAY.
OH, NICE!
IF YOU STOP BY RESIDENT SERVICES, I CAN INFORM YOU OF THE ISLAND'S RATING.
MY NAME IS ISABELLE! NICE TO MEET YOU ALL.
ISA-BELLE! COOL!
Good to meetcha!
AND ON THAT NOTE...
THIS ISLAND'S RATING IS MINUS FIVE STARS.
WHY, YOU ASK?

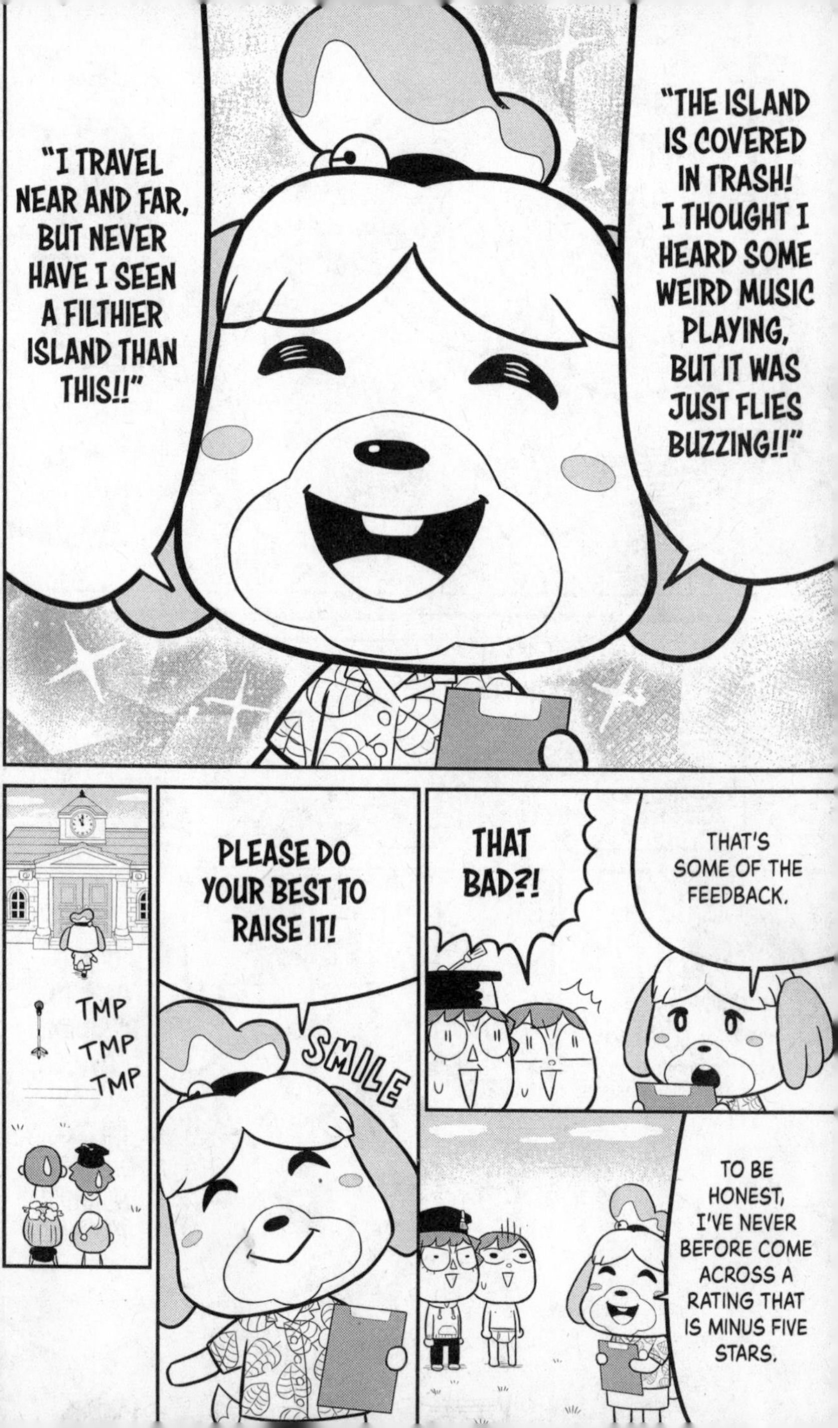
"THE ISLAND IS COVERED IN TRASH! I THOUGHT I HEARD SOME WEIRD MUSIC PLAYING, BUT IT WAS JUST FLIES BUZZING!!"
"I TRAVEL NEAR AND FAR, BUT NEVER HAVE I SEEN A FILTHIER ISLAND THAN THIS!!"
THAT'S SOME OF THE FEEDBACK.
THAT BAD?!
TO BE HONEST, I'VE NEVER BEFORE COME ACROSS A RATING THAT IS MINUS FIVE STARS.
PLEASE DO YOUR BEST TO RAISE IT!
SMILE
TMP
TMP
TMP

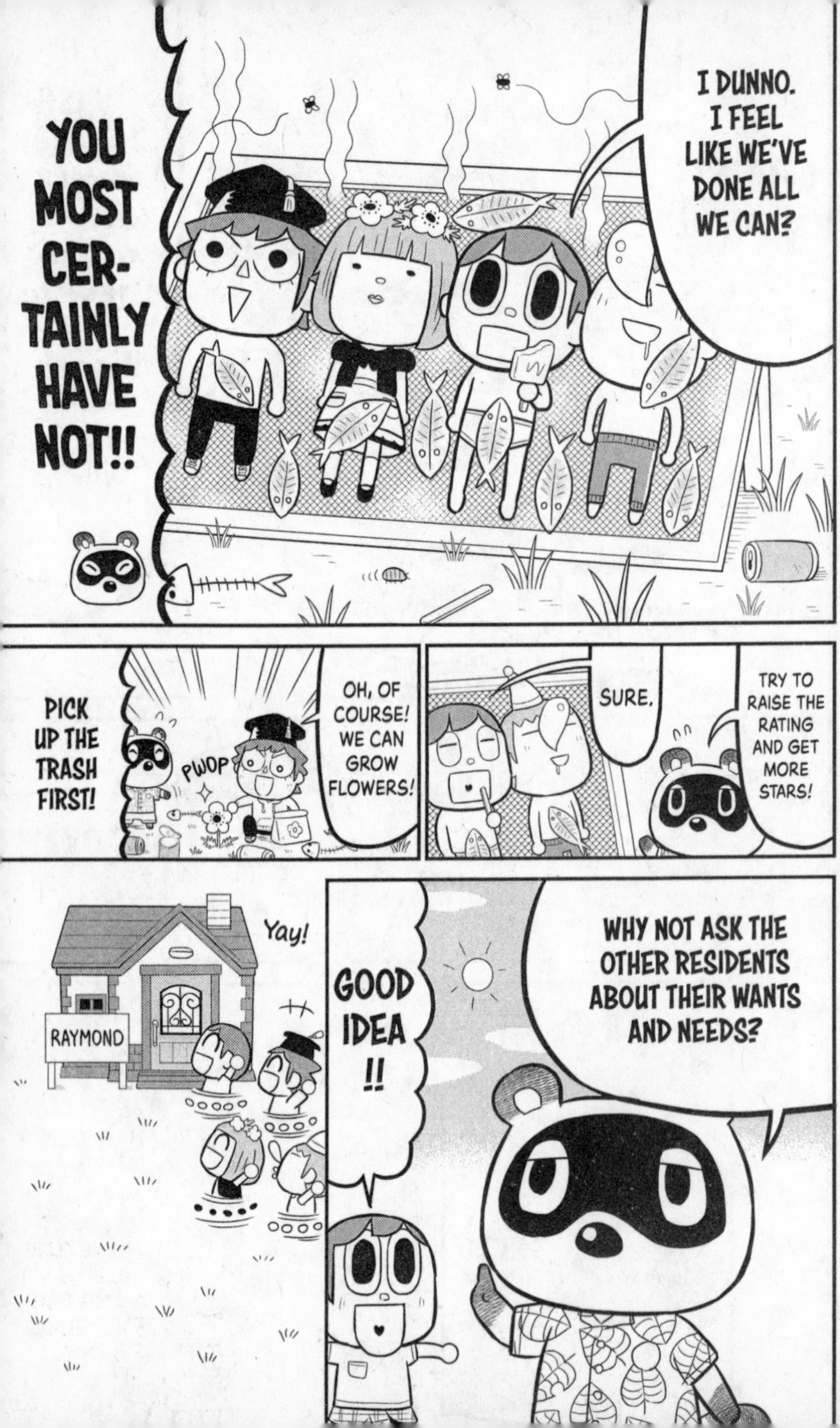
I DUNNO. I FEEL LIKE WE'VE DONE ALL WE CAN?
YOU MOST CER-TAINLY HAVE NOT!!
TRY TO RAISE THE RATING AND GET MORE STARS!
SURE.
OH, OF COURSE! WE CAN GROW FLOWERS!
PWOP
PICK UP THE TRASH FIRST!
WHY NOT ASK THE OTHER RESIDENTS ABOUT THEIR WANTS AND NEEDS?
GOOD IDEA!!
Yay!
RAYMOND

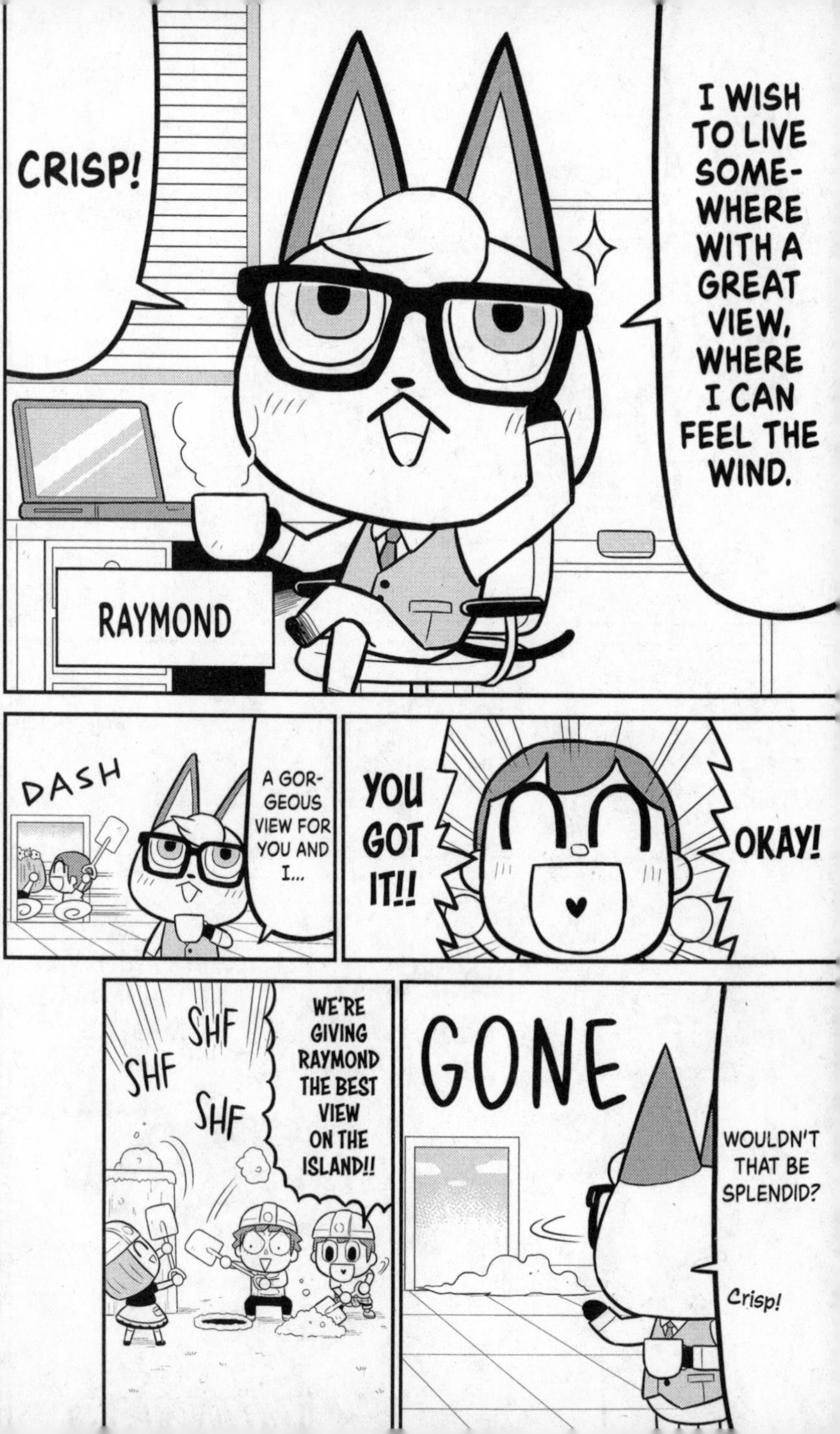
I WISH TO LIVE SOMEWHERE WITH A GREAT VIEW, WHERE I CAN FEEL THE WIND.
CRISP!
RAYMOND
OKAY!
YOU GOT IT!!
A GORGEOUS VIEW FOR YOU AND I...
DASH
GONE
WOULDN'T THAT BE SPLENDID?
Crisp!
WE'RE GIVING RAYMOND THE BEST VIEW ON THE ISLAND!!
SHF
SHF
SHF

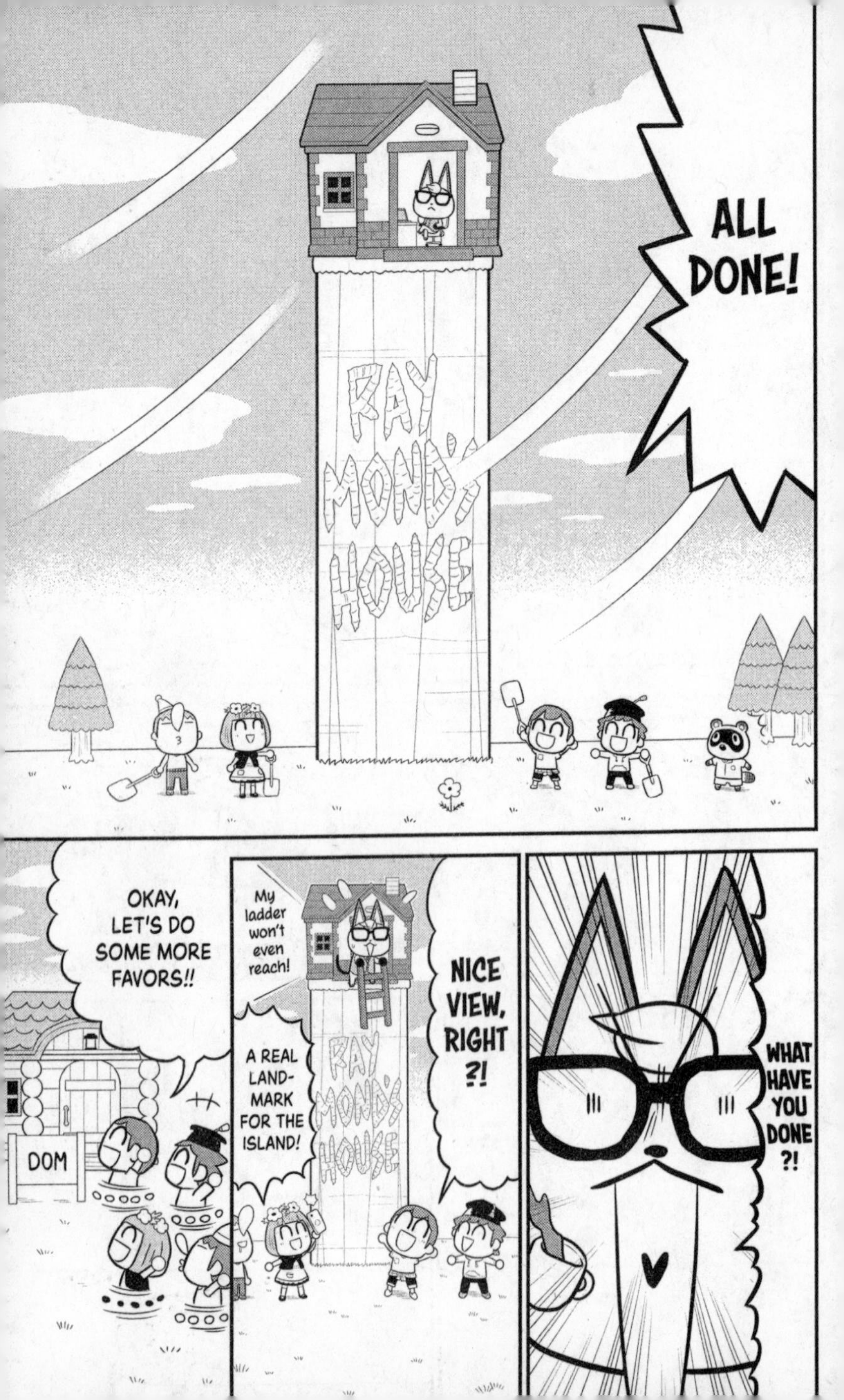
ALL DONE!
RAYMOND'S HOUSE
WHAT HAVE YOU DONE?!
NICE VIEW, RIGHT?!
My ladder won't even reach!
A REAL LANDMARK FOR THE ISLAND!
OKAY, LET'S DO SOME MORE FAVORS!!
DOM

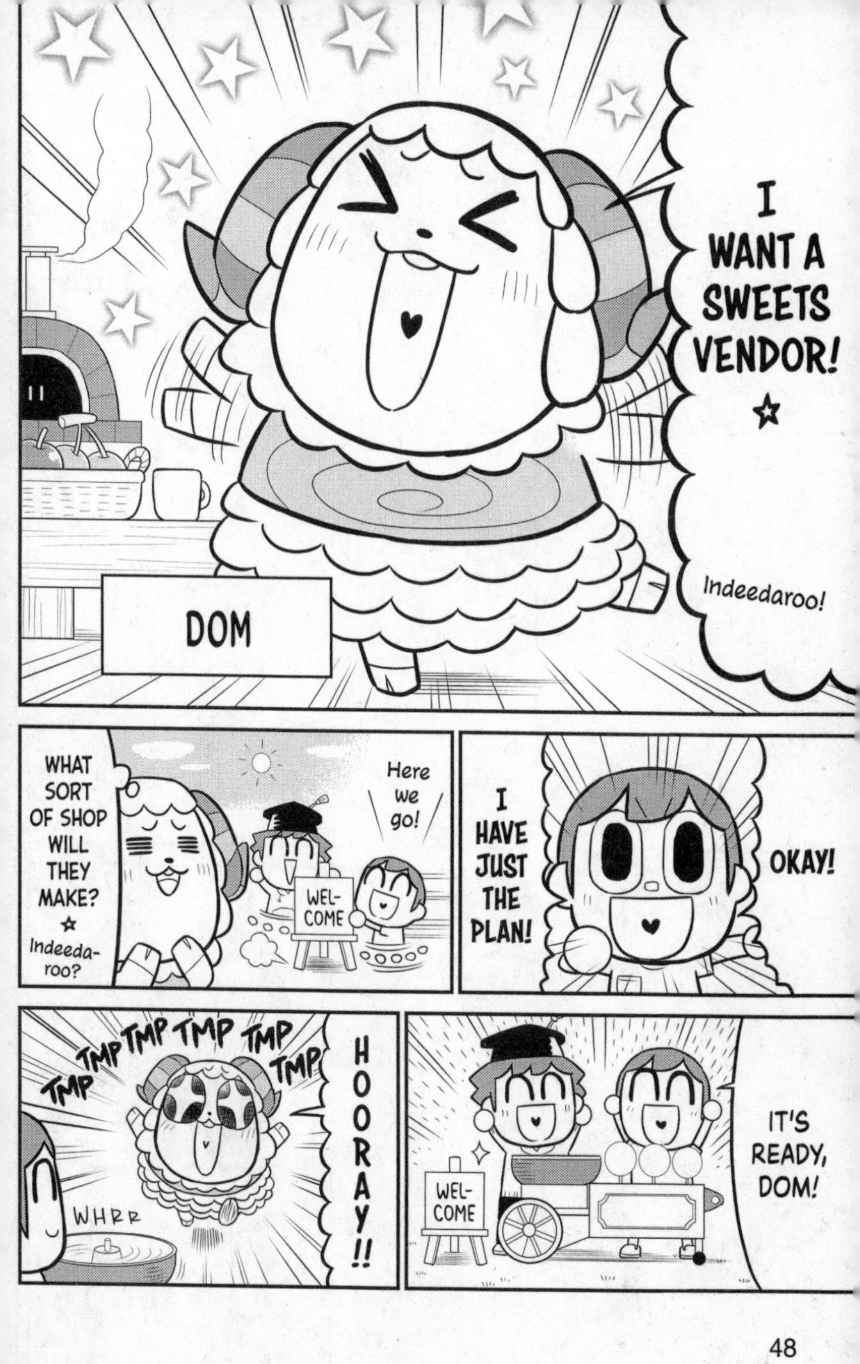
I WANT A SWEETS VENDOR! ☆
Indeedaroo!
DOM
OKAY!
I HAVE JUST THE PLAN!
Here we go!
WEL-COME
WHAT SORT OF SHOP WILL THEY MAKE? ☆ Indeeda-roo?
IT'S READY, DOM!
WEL-COME
HOORAY!!
TMP TMP TMP TMP TMP TMP
WHRR

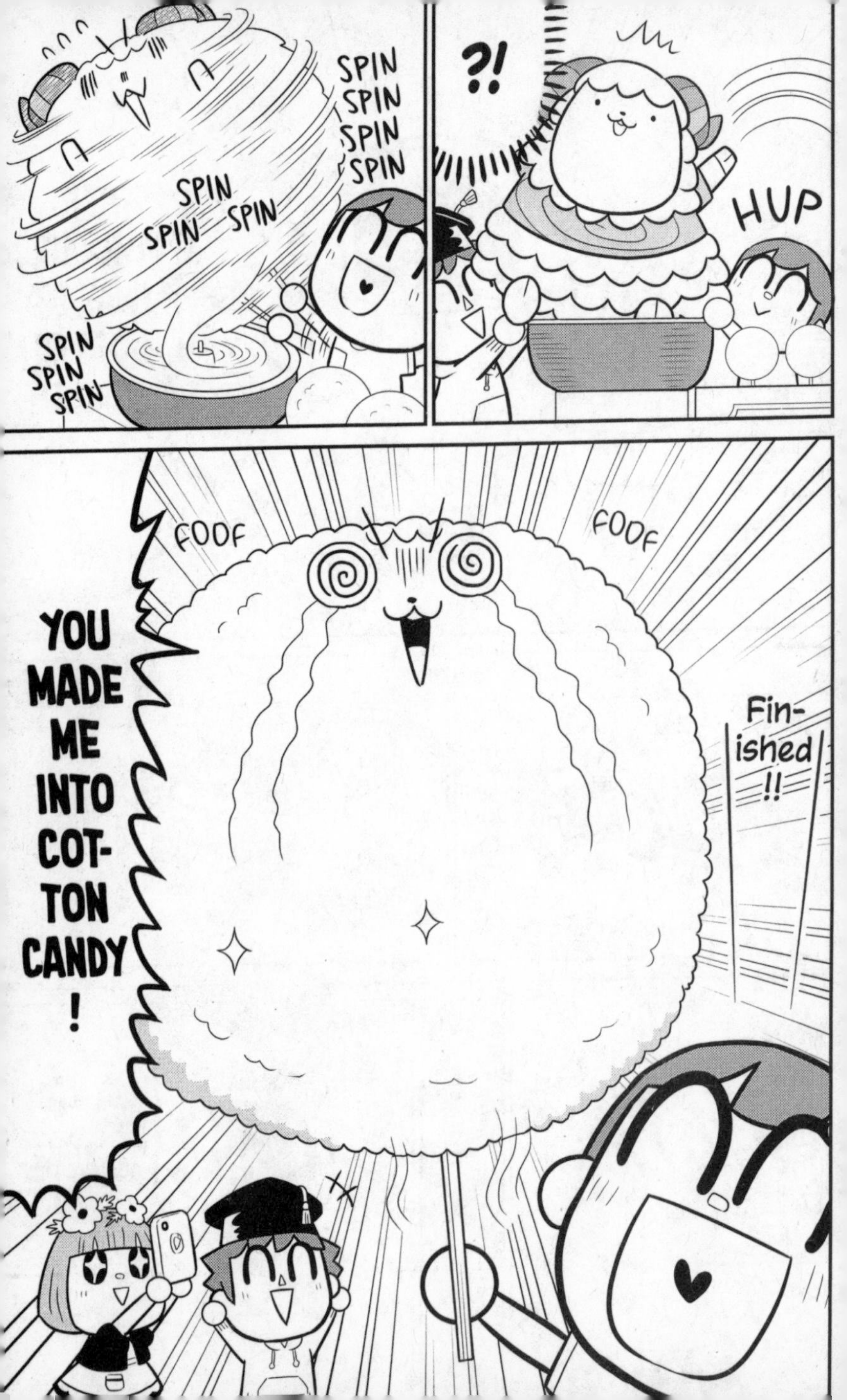
?!
HUP
SPIN SPIN SPIN SPIN
SPIN SPIN SPIN
SPIN SPIN SPIN
FOOF
Fin-ished!!
FOOF
YOU MADE ME INTO COT-TON CANDY!

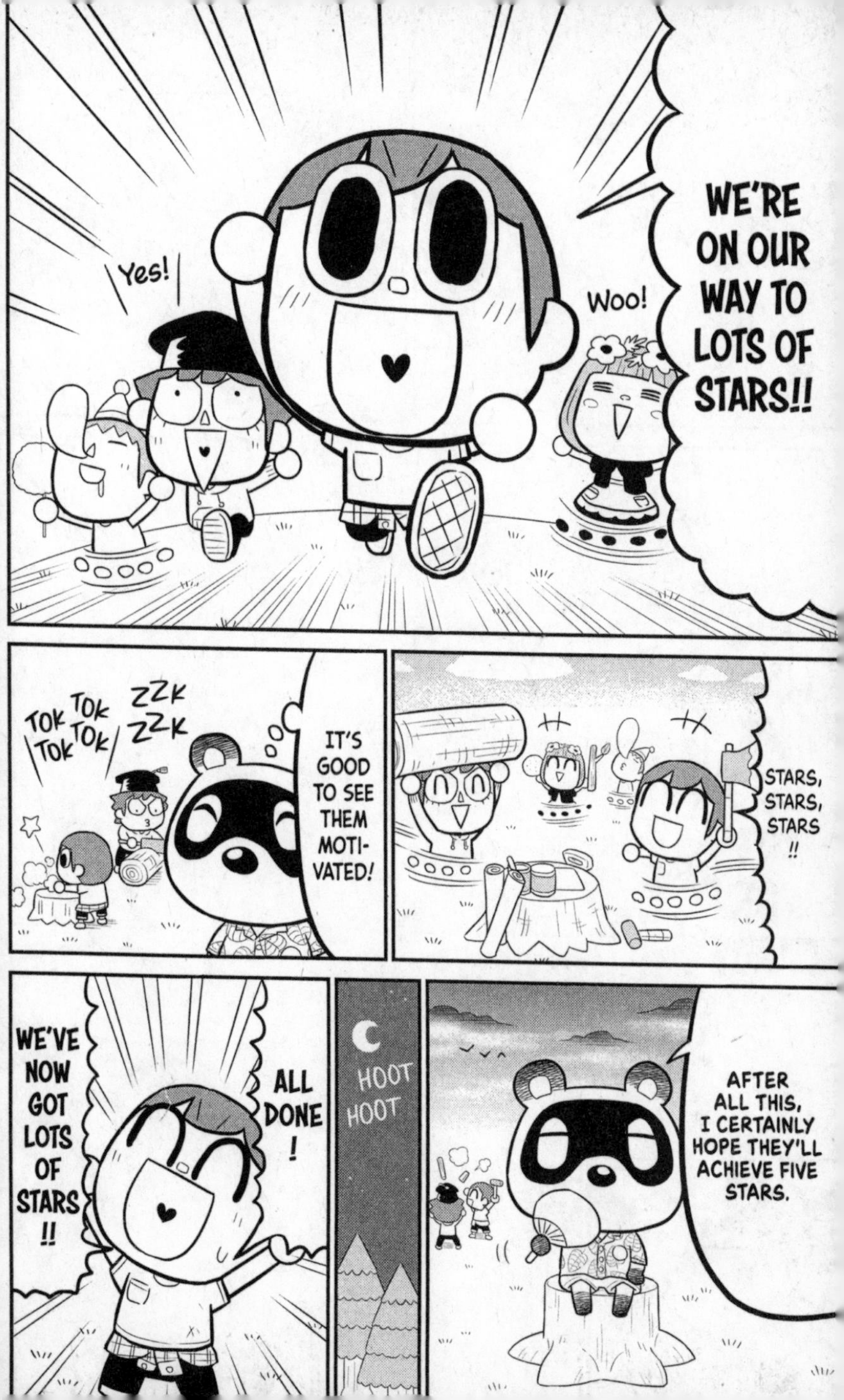
WE'RE ON OUR WAY TO LOTS OF STARS!!
Woo!
Yes!
STARS, STARS, STARS!!
IT'S GOOD TO SEE THEM MOTI-VATED!
ZZK ZZK
TOK TOK TOK TOK
AFTER ALL THIS, I CERTAINLY HOPE THEY'LL ACHIEVE FIVE STARS.
HOOT HOOT
ALL DONE!
WE'VE NOW GOT LOTS OF STARS!!

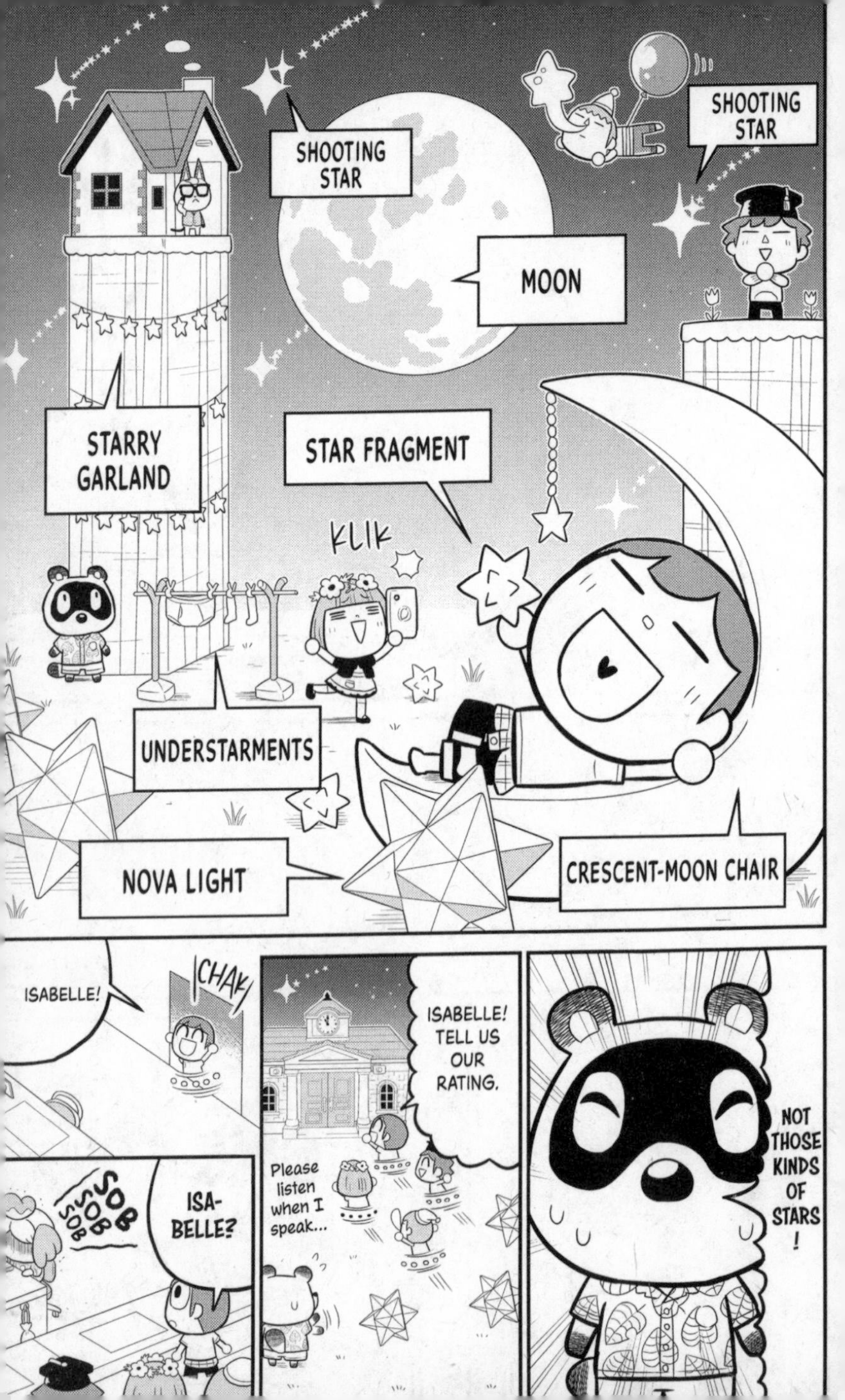
SHOOTING STAR
SHOOTING STAR
MOON
STAR FRAGMENT
STARRY GARLAND
KLIK
CRESCENT-MOON CHAIR
UNDERSTARMENTS
NOVA LIGHT
NOT THOSE KINDS OF STARS!
ISABELLE! TELL US OUR RATING.
Please listen when I speak...
CHAK
ISABELLE!
ISA-BELLE?
SOB SOB SOB

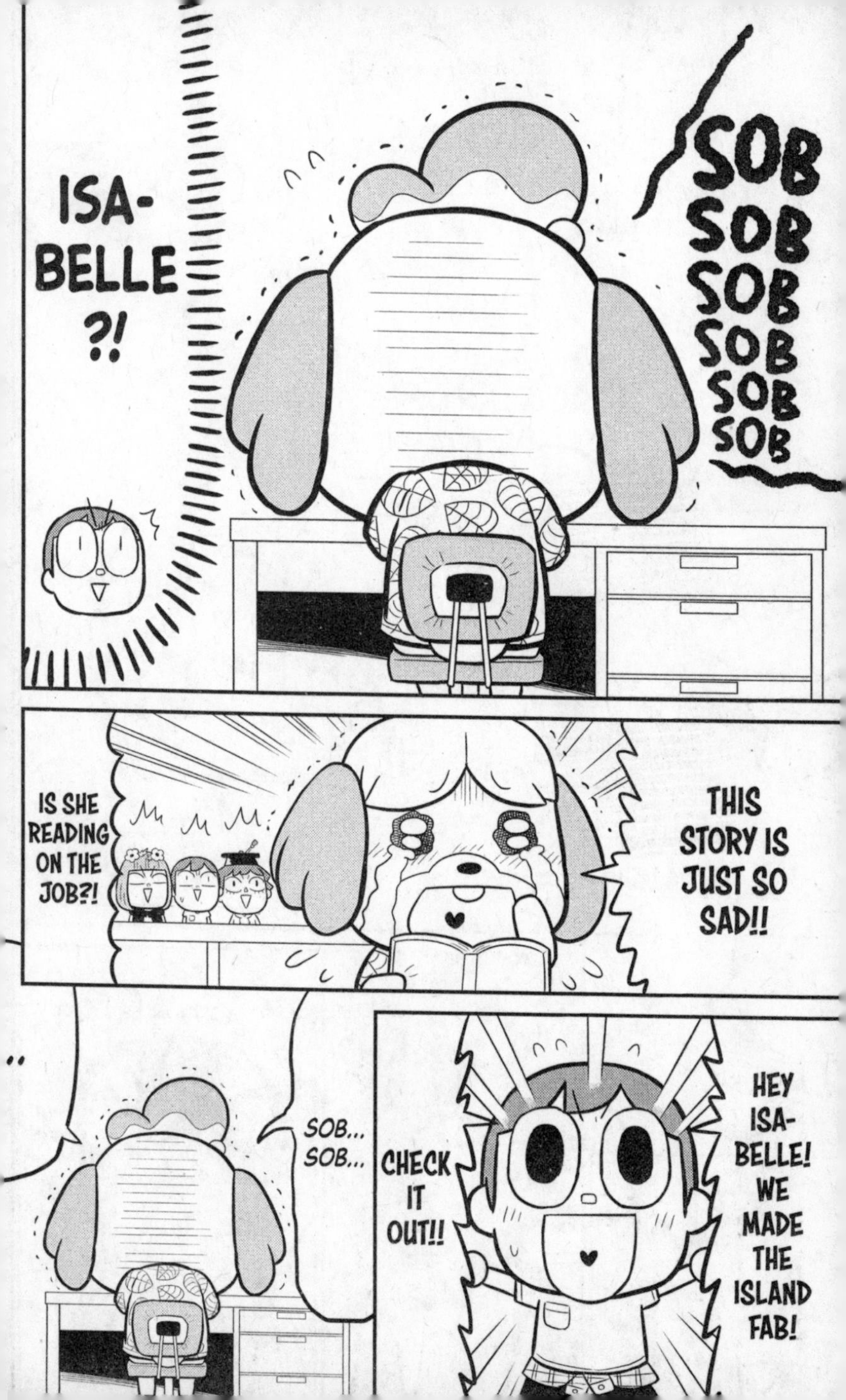
SOB SOB SOB SOB SOB SOB
ISA-BELLE?!
THIS STORY IS JUST SO SAD!!
IS SHE READING ON THE JOB?!
HEY ISA-BELLE! WE MADE THE ISLAND FAB!
CHECK IT OUT!!
SOB... SOB...
..

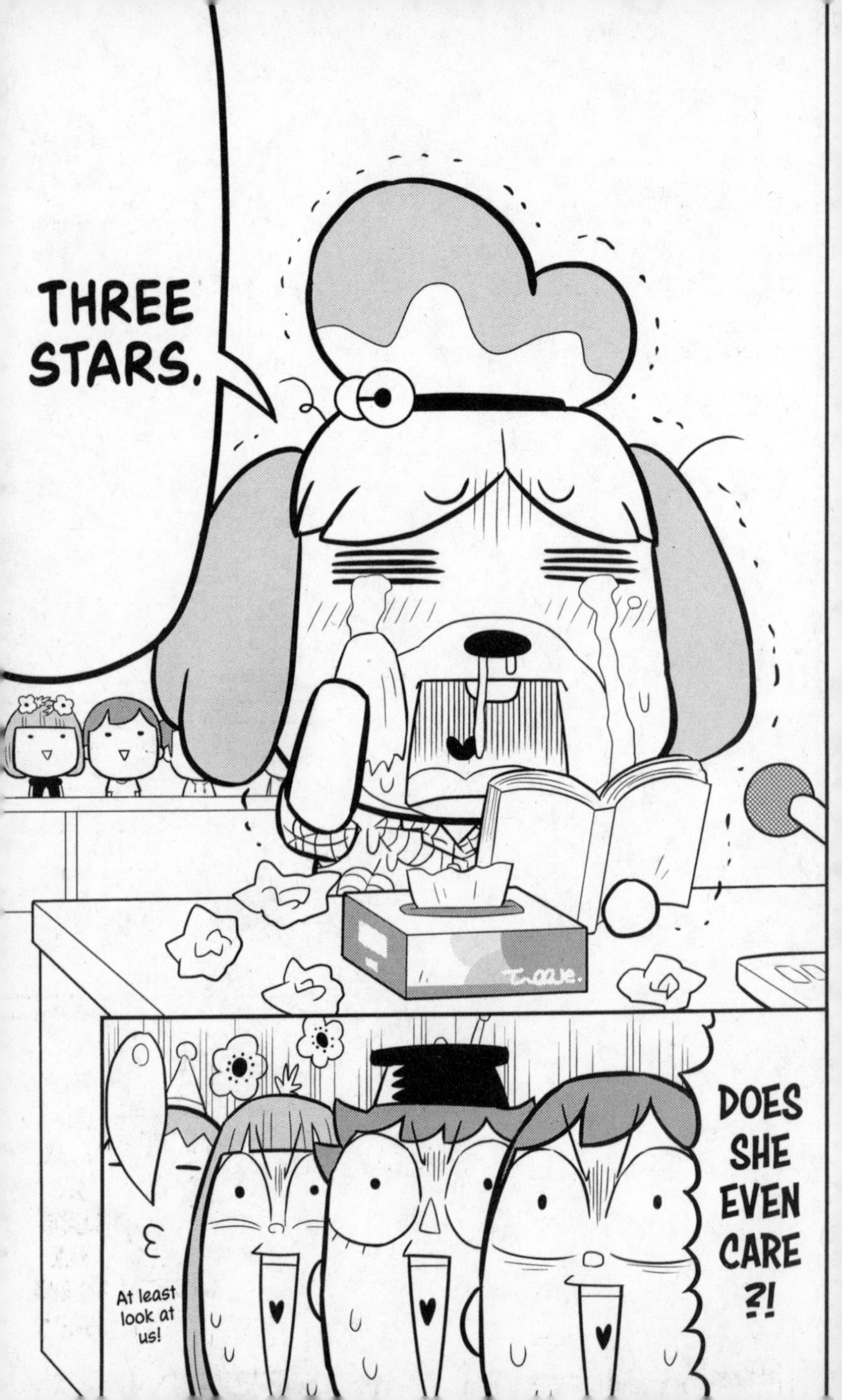
THREE STARS.
DOES SHE EVEN CARE ?!
At least look at us!

Welcome to Animal Crossing New Horizons

Deserted Island Diary

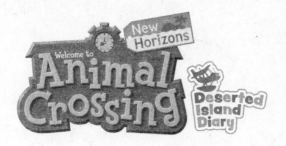

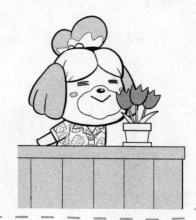

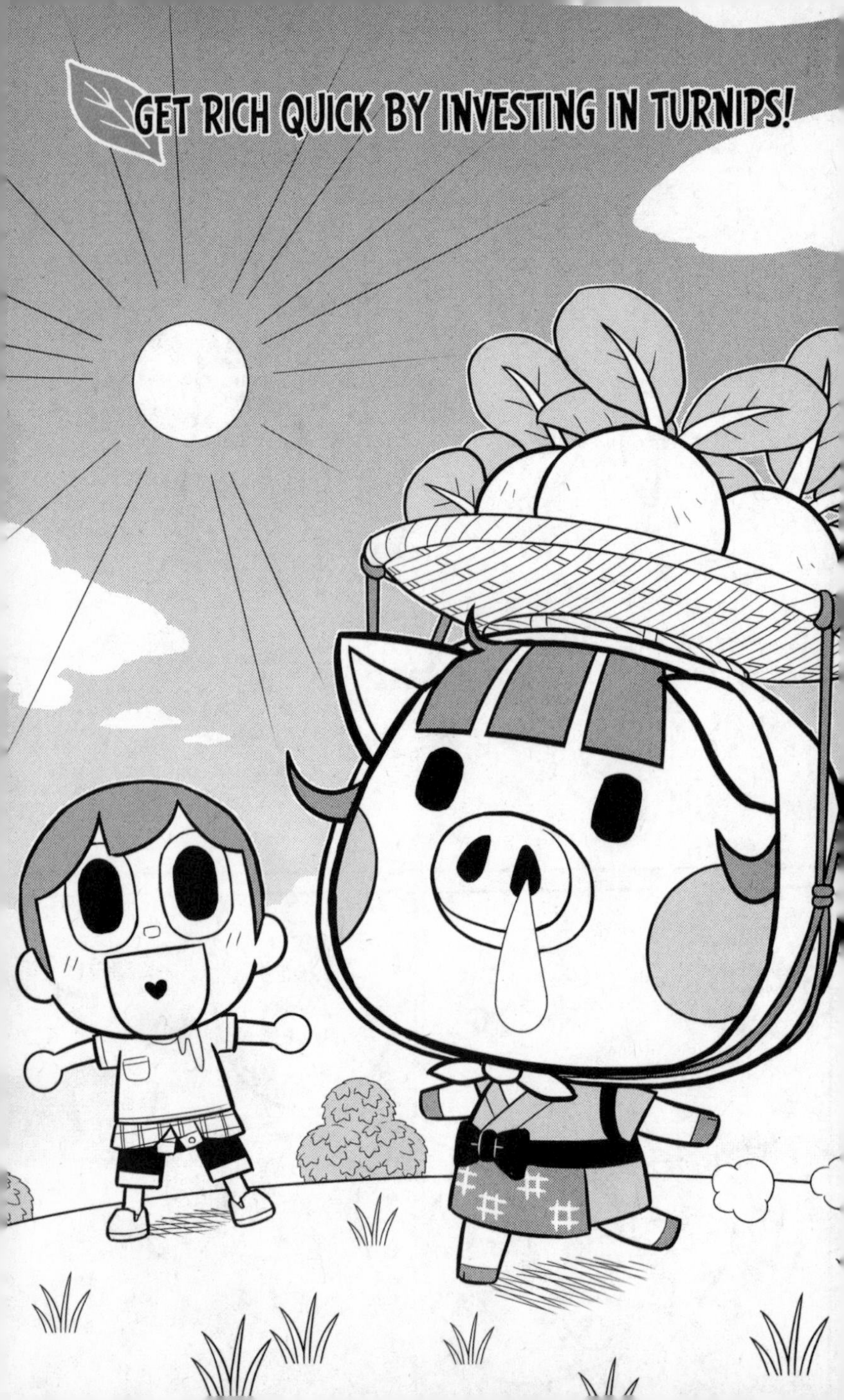
GET RICH QUICK BY INVESTING IN TURNIPS!

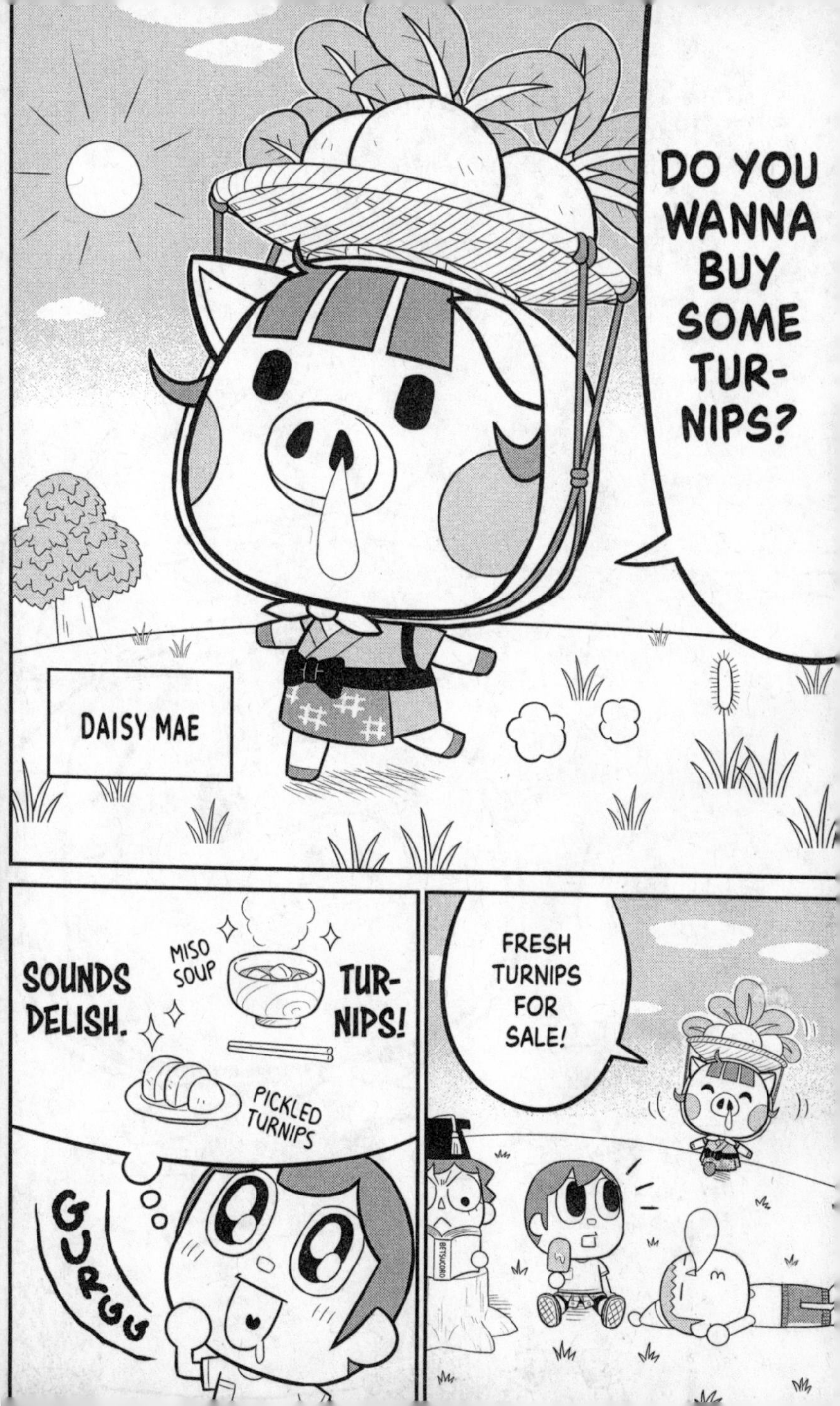
DO YOU WANNA BUY SOME TUR-NIPS?
DAISY MAE
FRESH TURNIPS FOR SALE!
TUR-NIPS!
MISO SOUP
SOUNDS DELISH.
PICKLED TURNIPS
GURGU

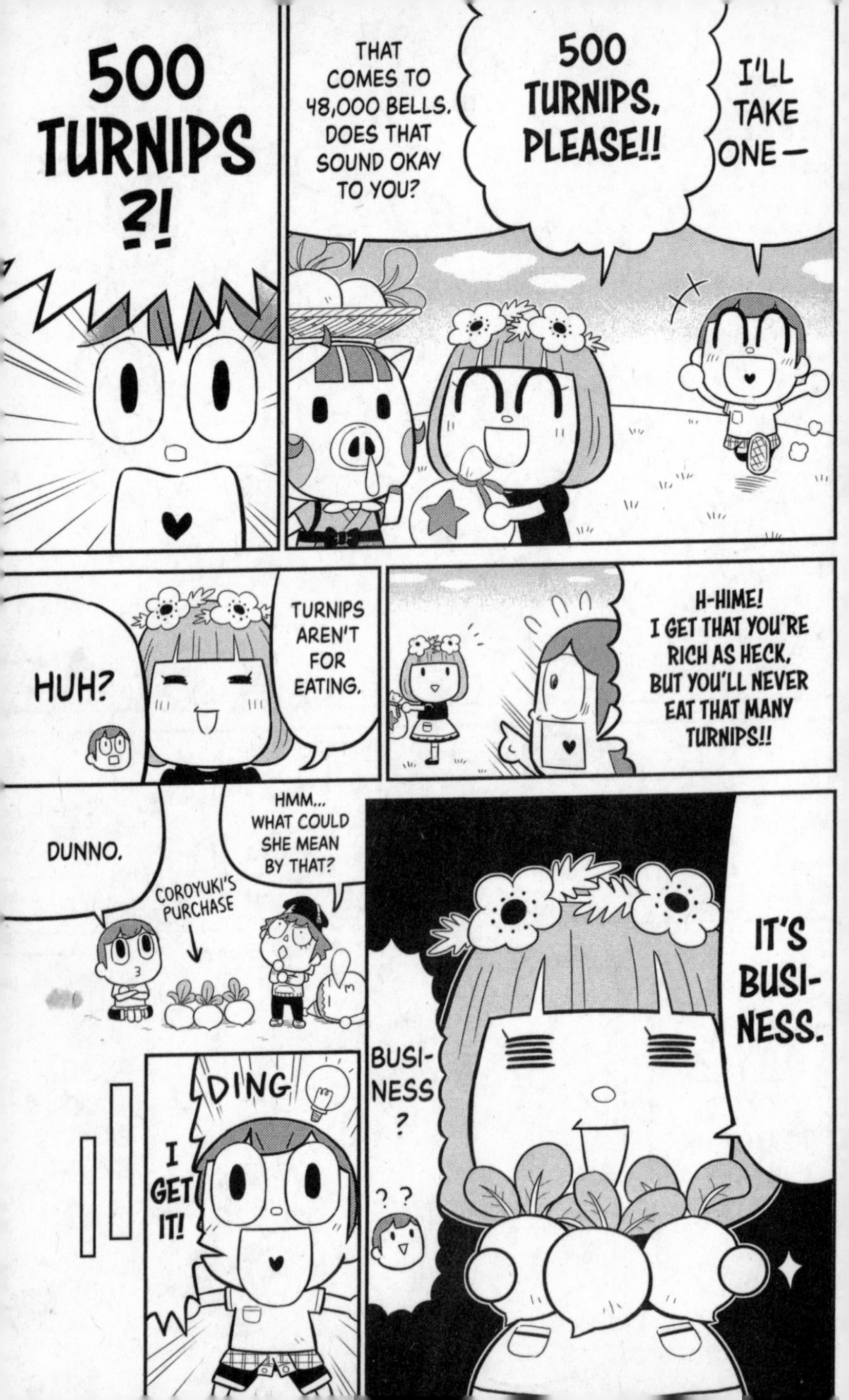
I'LL TAKE ONE—
500 TURNIPS, PLEASE!!
THAT COMES TO 48,000 BELLS. DOES THAT SOUND OKAY TO YOU?
500 TURNIPS ?!
H-HIME! I GET THAT YOU'RE RICH AS HECK, BUT YOU'LL NEVER EAT THAT MANY TURNIPS!!
TURNIPS AREN'T FOR EATING.
HUH?
IT'S BUSI-NESS.
BUSI-NESS?
HMM... WHAT COULD SHE MEAN BY THAT?
DUNNO.
COROYUKI'S PURCHASE
DING
I GET IT!

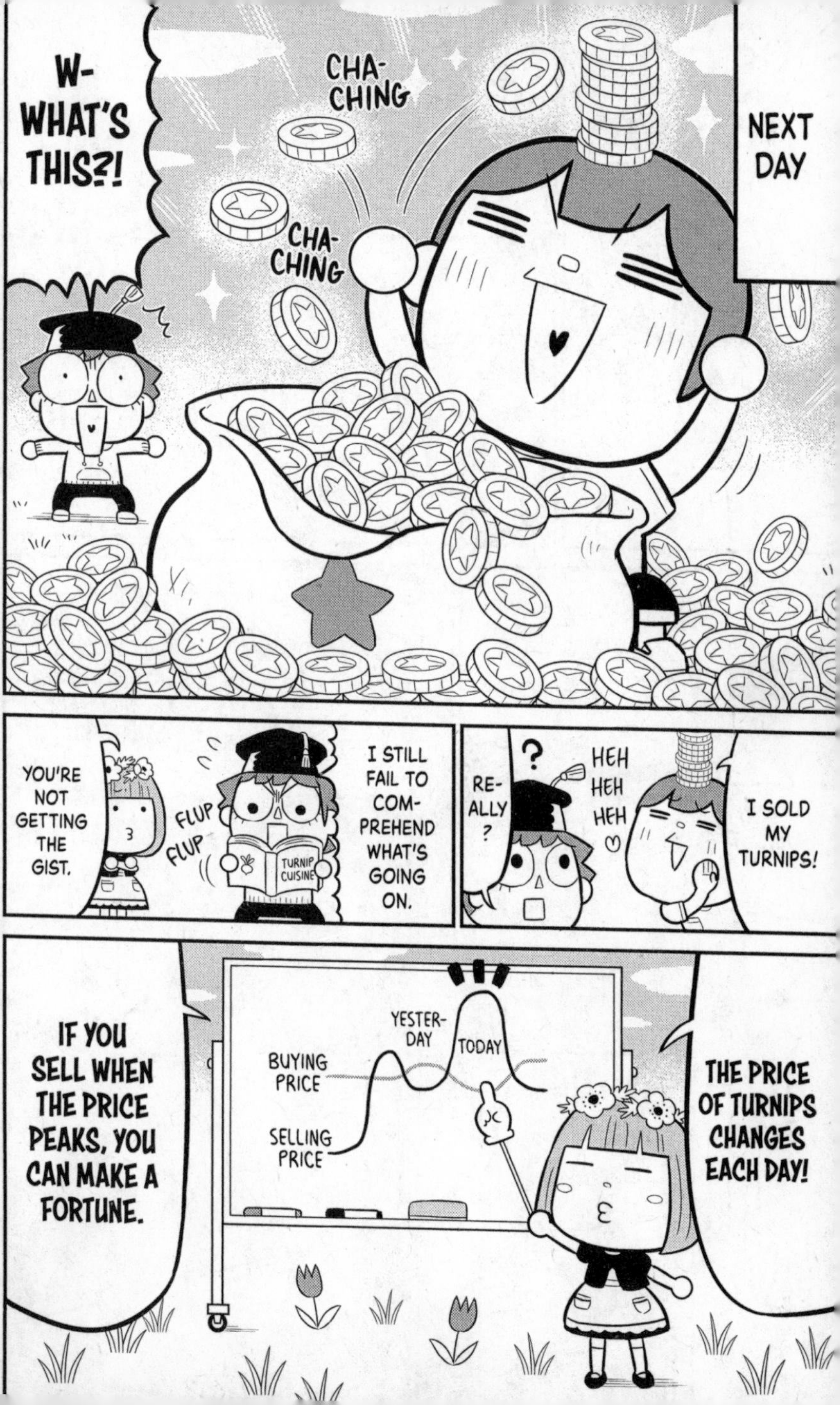
NEXT DAY
CHA-CHING
CHA-CHING
W-WHAT'S THIS?!
I SOLD MY TURNIPS!
HEH HEH HEH
RE-ALLY?
I STILL FAIL TO COM-PREHEND WHAT'S GOING ON.
FLUP FLUP
TURNIP CUISINE
YOU'RE NOT GETTING THE GIST.
THE PRICE OF TURNIPS CHANGES EACH DAY!
TODAY
YESTER-DAY
BUYING PRICE
SELLING PRICE
IF YOU SELL WHEN THE PRICE PEAKS, YOU CAN MAKE A FORTUNE.

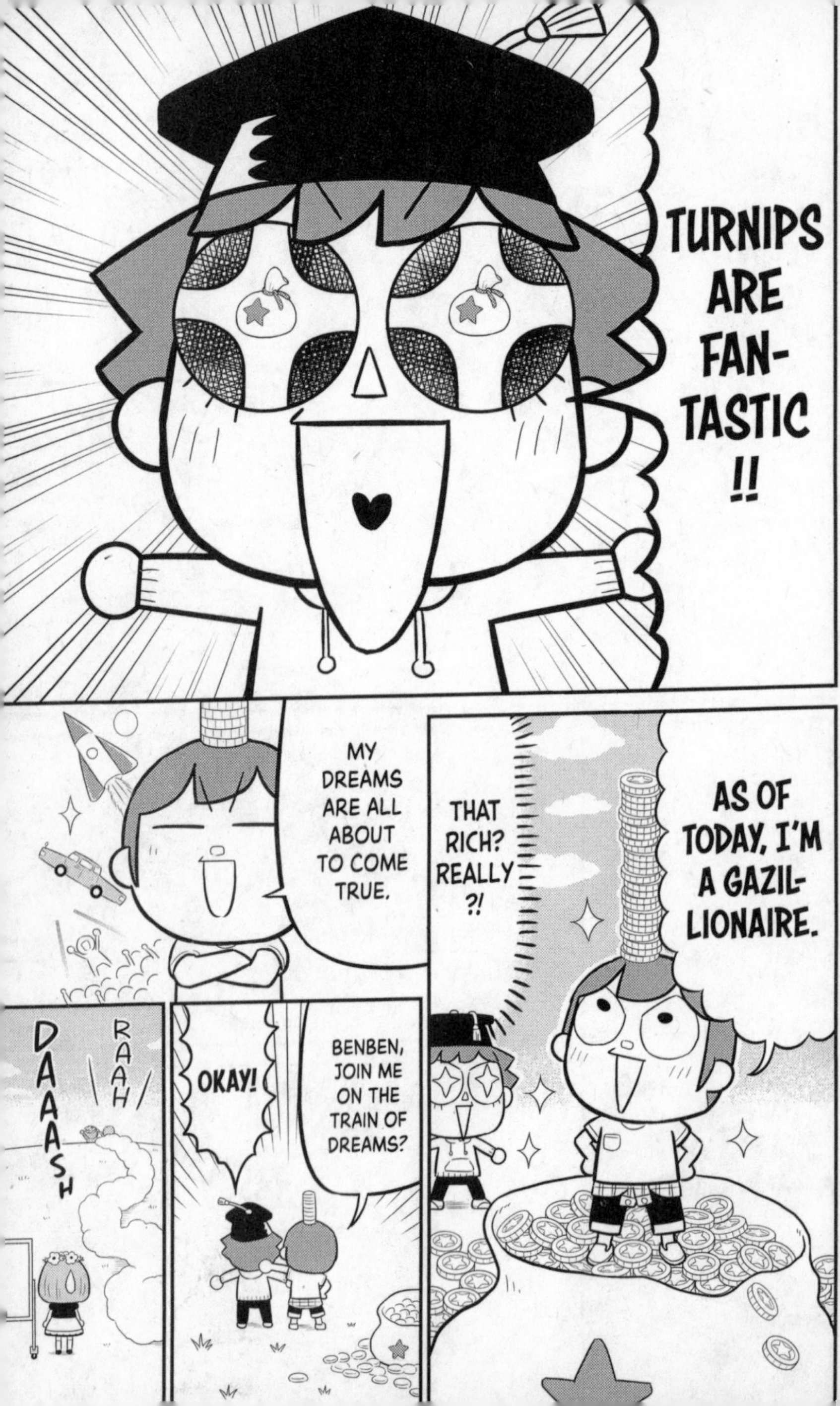
TURNIPS ARE FAN-TASTIC !!
AS OF TODAY, I'M A GAZIL-LIONAIRE.
THAT RICH? REALLY ?!
MY DREAMS ARE ALL ABOUT TO COME TRUE.
BENBEN, JOIN ME ON THE TRAIN OF DREAMS?
OKAY!
RAAH
DAAAASH

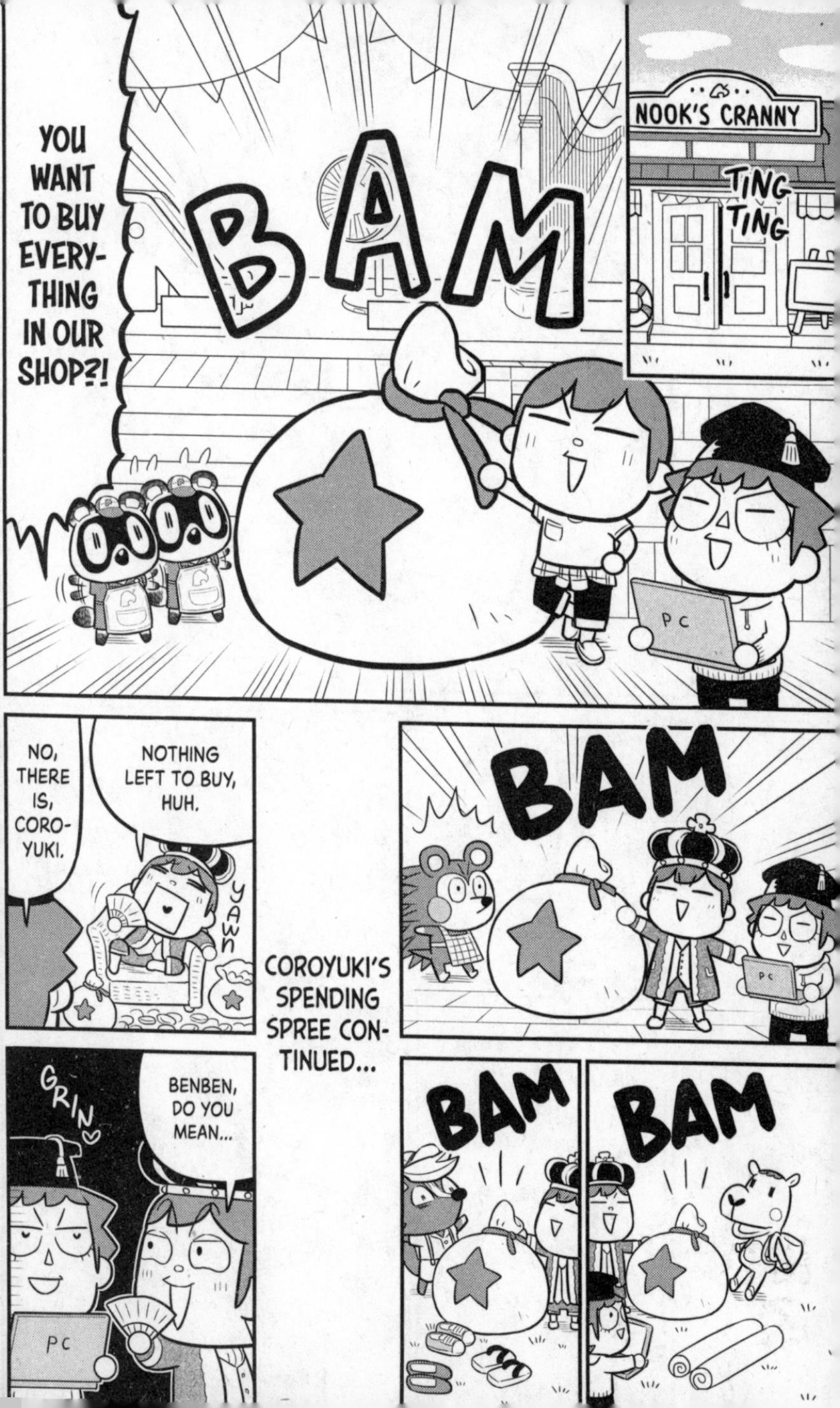

NOOK'S CRANNY
TING TING
BAM
YOU WANT TO BUY EVERYTHING IN OUR SHOP?!
BAM
COROYUKI'S SPENDING SPREE CONTINUED...
BAM
BAM
NOTHING LEFT TO BUY, HUH.
NO, THERE IS, COROYUKI.
YAWN
BENBEN, DO YOU MEAN...
GRIN

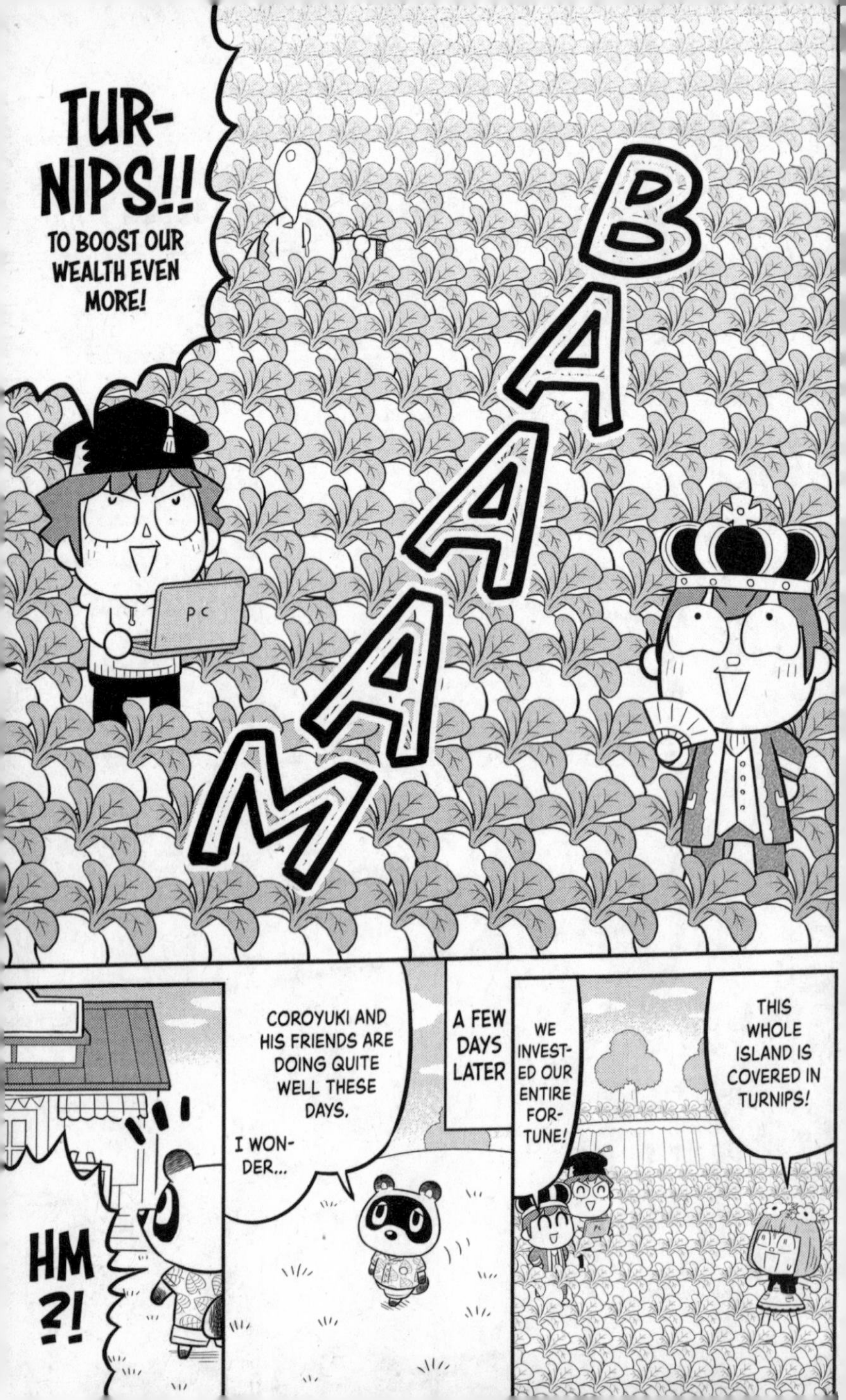
TUR-NIPS!!
TO BOOST OUR WEALTH EVEN MORE!
BAAAAM
THIS WHOLE ISLAND IS COVERED IN TURNIPS!
WE INVEST-ED OUR ENTIRE FOR-TUNE!
A FEW DAYS LATER
COROYUKI AND HIS FRIENDS ARE DOING QUITE WELL THESE DAYS.
I WON-DER...
HM ?!

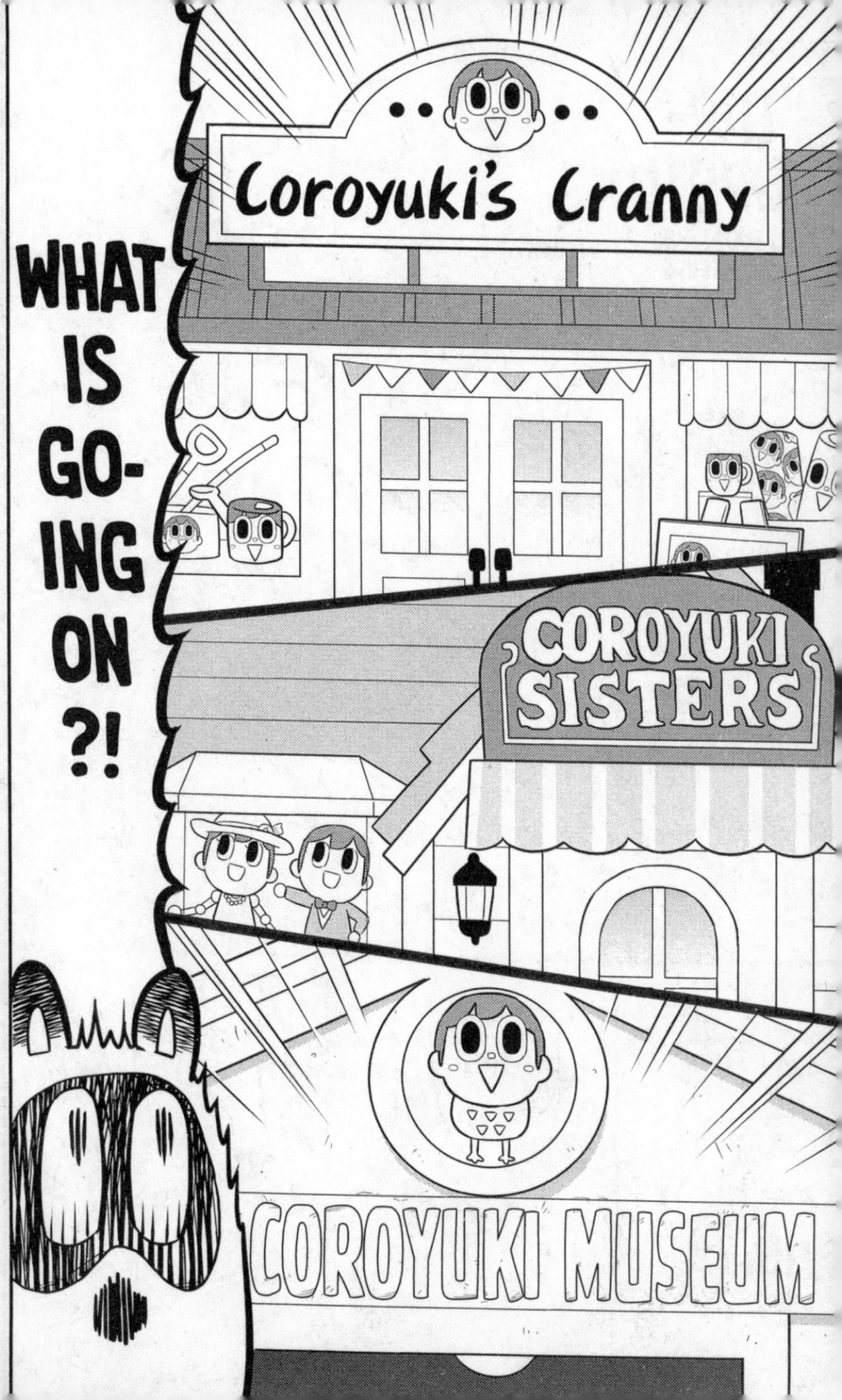
Coroyuki's Cranny
COROYUKI SISTERS
COROYUKI MUSEUM
WHAT IS GO-ING ON ?!

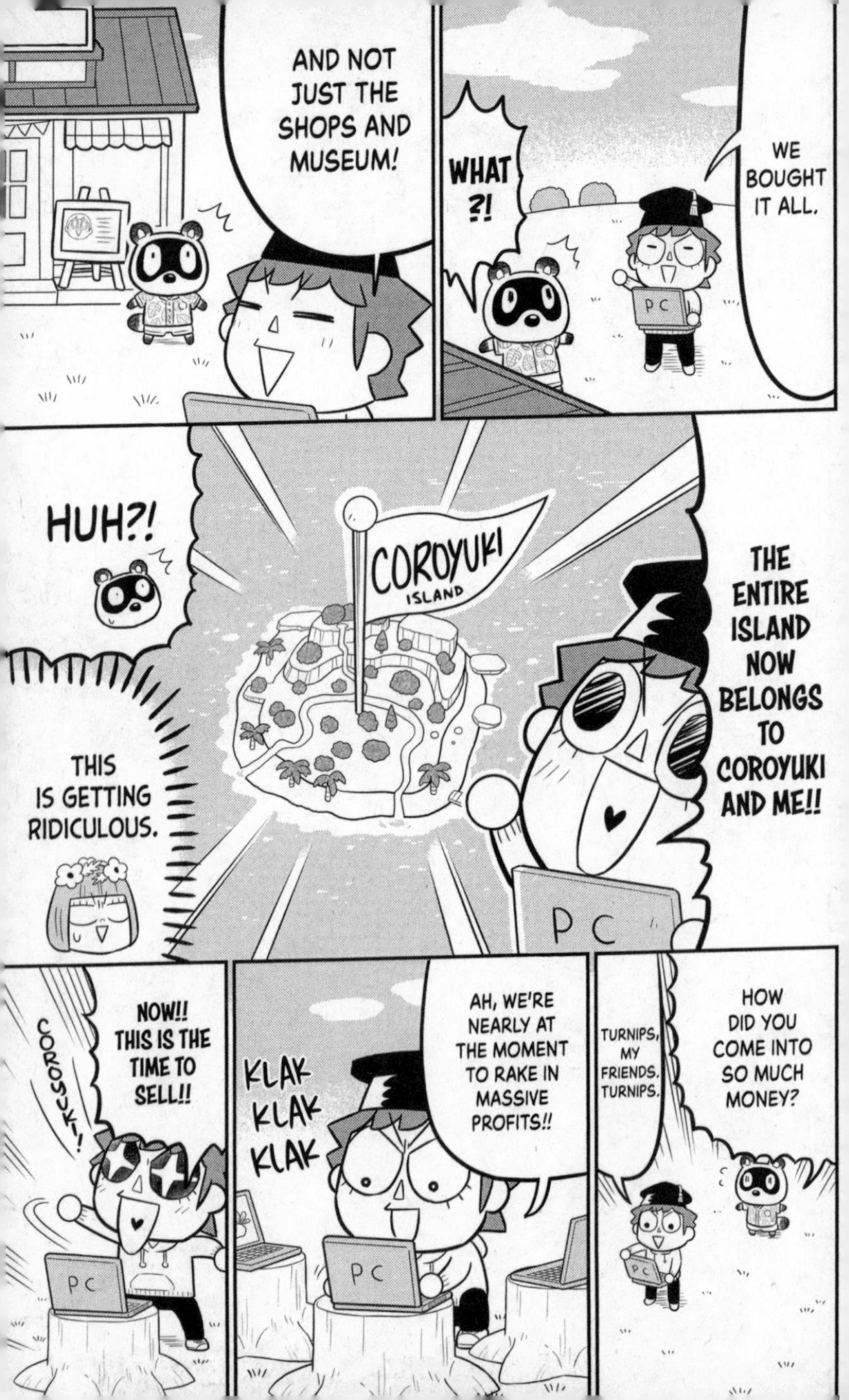
WE BOUGHT IT ALL.
WHAT?!
AND NOT JUST THE SHOPS AND MUSEUM!
THE ENTIRE ISLAND NOW BELONGS TO COROYUKI AND ME!!
COROYUKI ISLAND
HUH?!
THIS IS GETTING RIDICULOUS.
HOW DID YOU COME INTO SO MUCH MONEY?
TURNIPS, MY FRIENDS. TURNIPS.
AH, WE'RE NEARLY AT THE MOMENT TO RAKE IN MASSIVE PROFITS!!
KLAK KLAK KLAK
NOW!! THIS IS THE TIME TO SELL!!
COROSUKI!

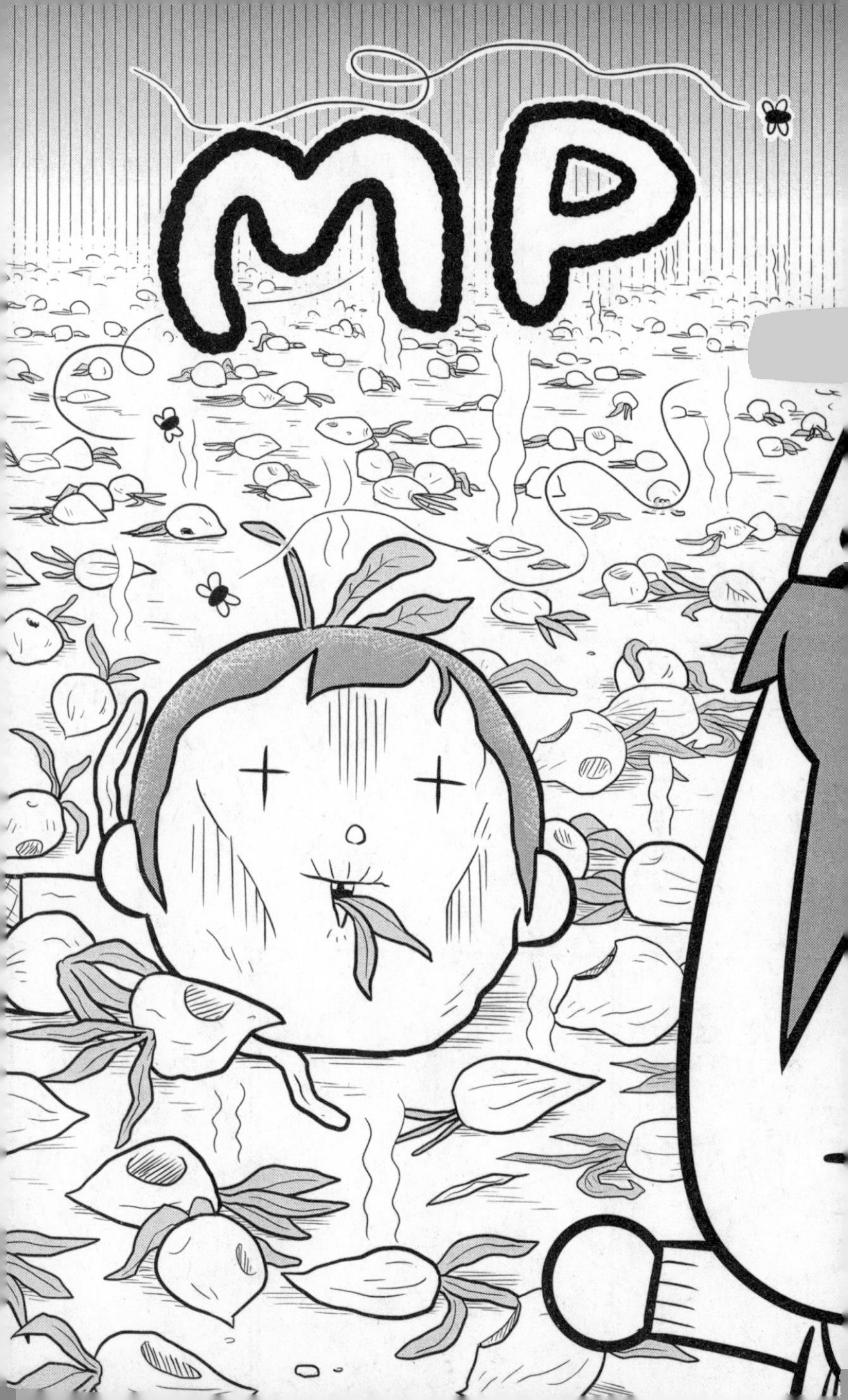
MP

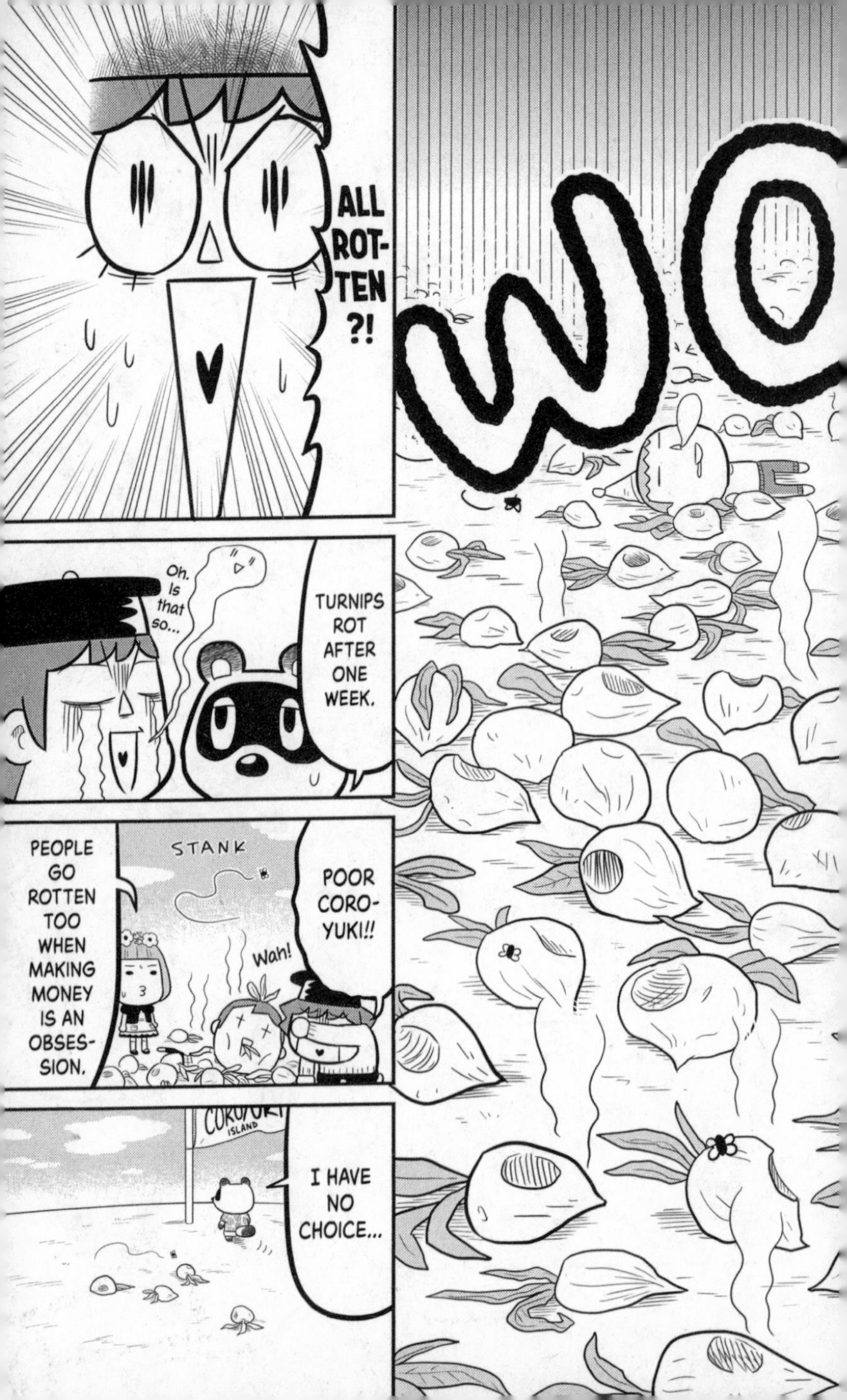
WO
ALL ROT-TEN?!
TURNIPS ROT AFTER ONE WEEK.
Oh. Is that so...
POOR CORO-YUKI!!
Wah!
STANK
PEOPLE GO ROTTEN TOO WHEN MAKING MONEY IS AN OBSES-SION.
ISLAND
I HAVE NO CHOICE...

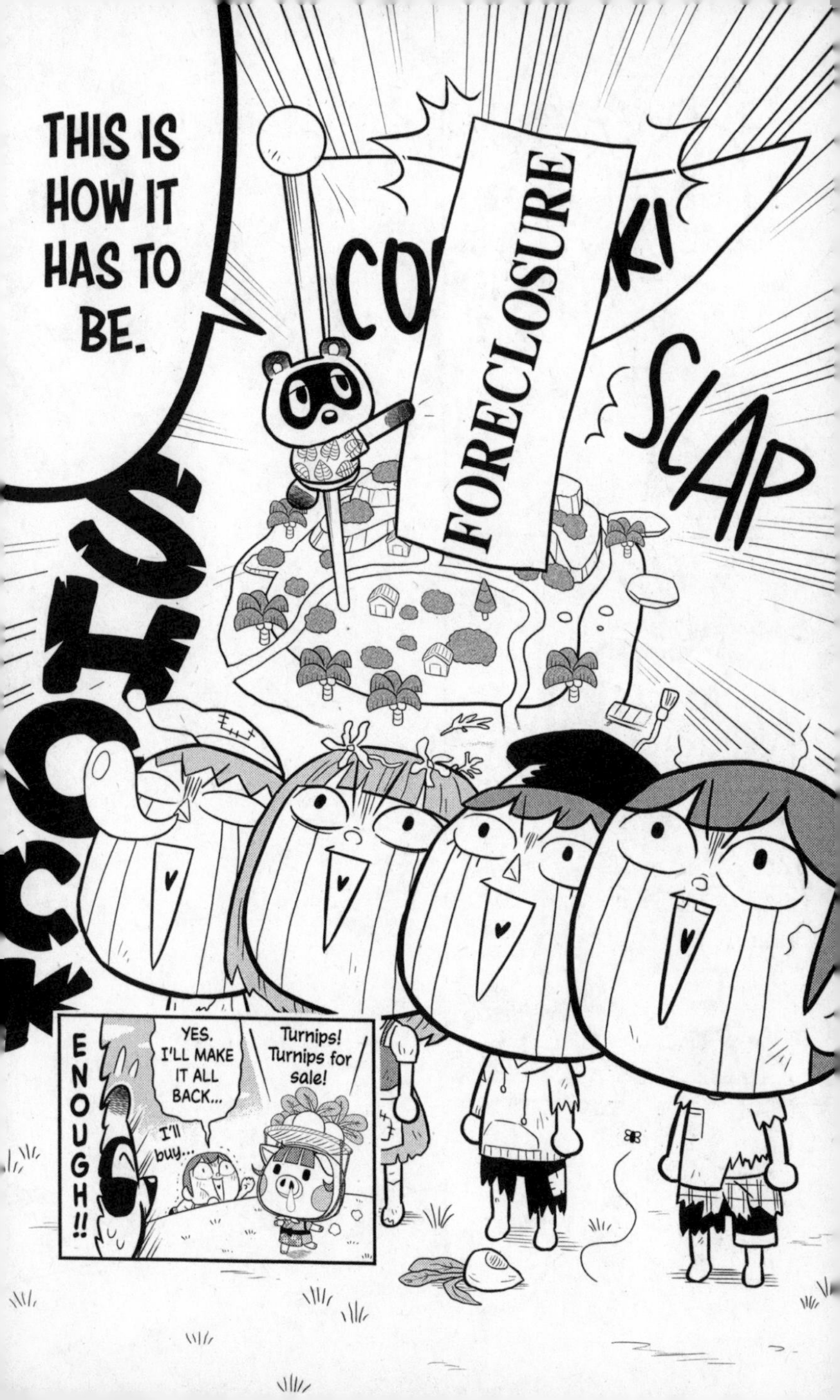

THIS IS HOW IT HAS TO BE.
CO K!
FORECLOSURE
SLAP
SHOCK
Turnips! Turnips for sale!
YES. I'LL MAKE IT ALL BACK...
I'll buy...
ENOUGH!!

BEWARE OF DUBIOUS ARTWORK?!

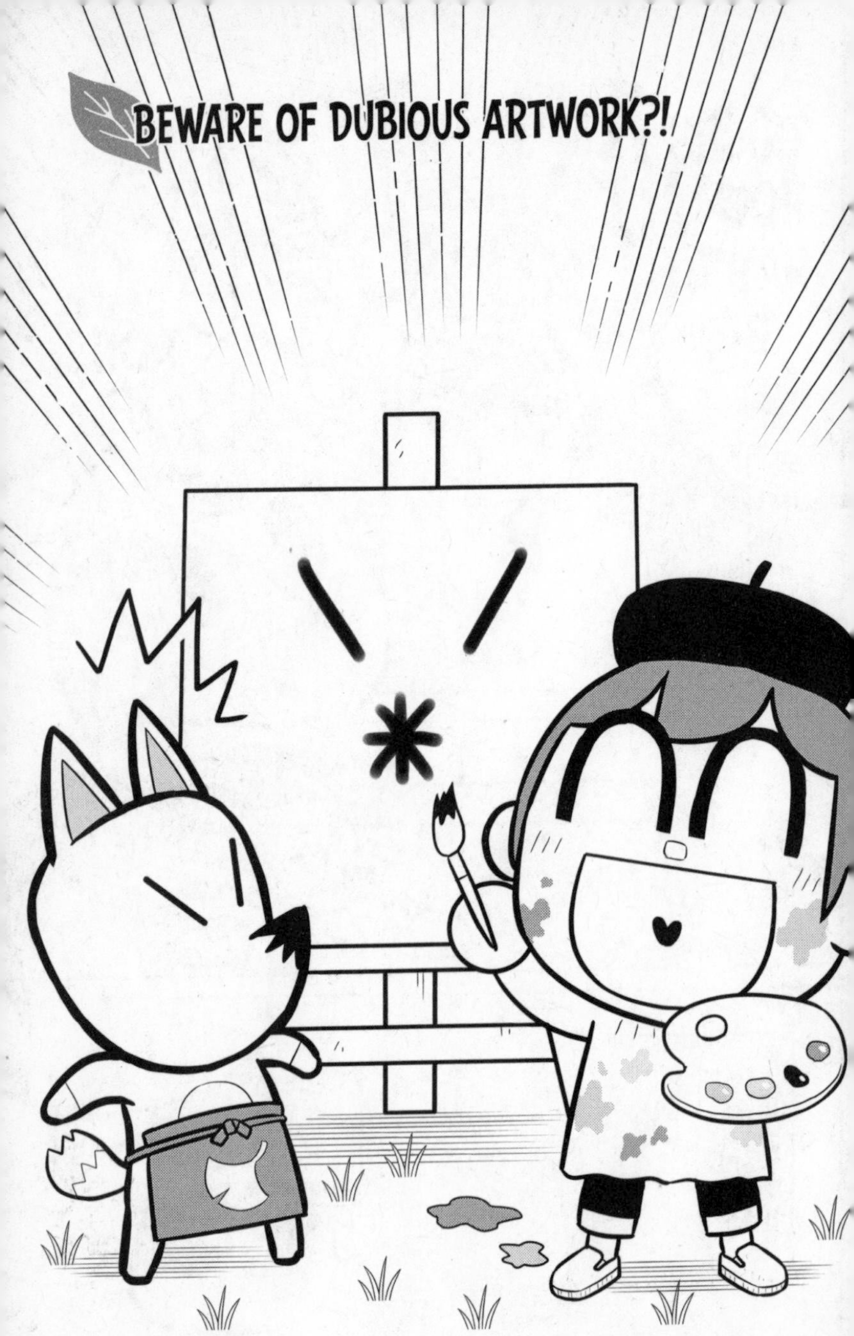

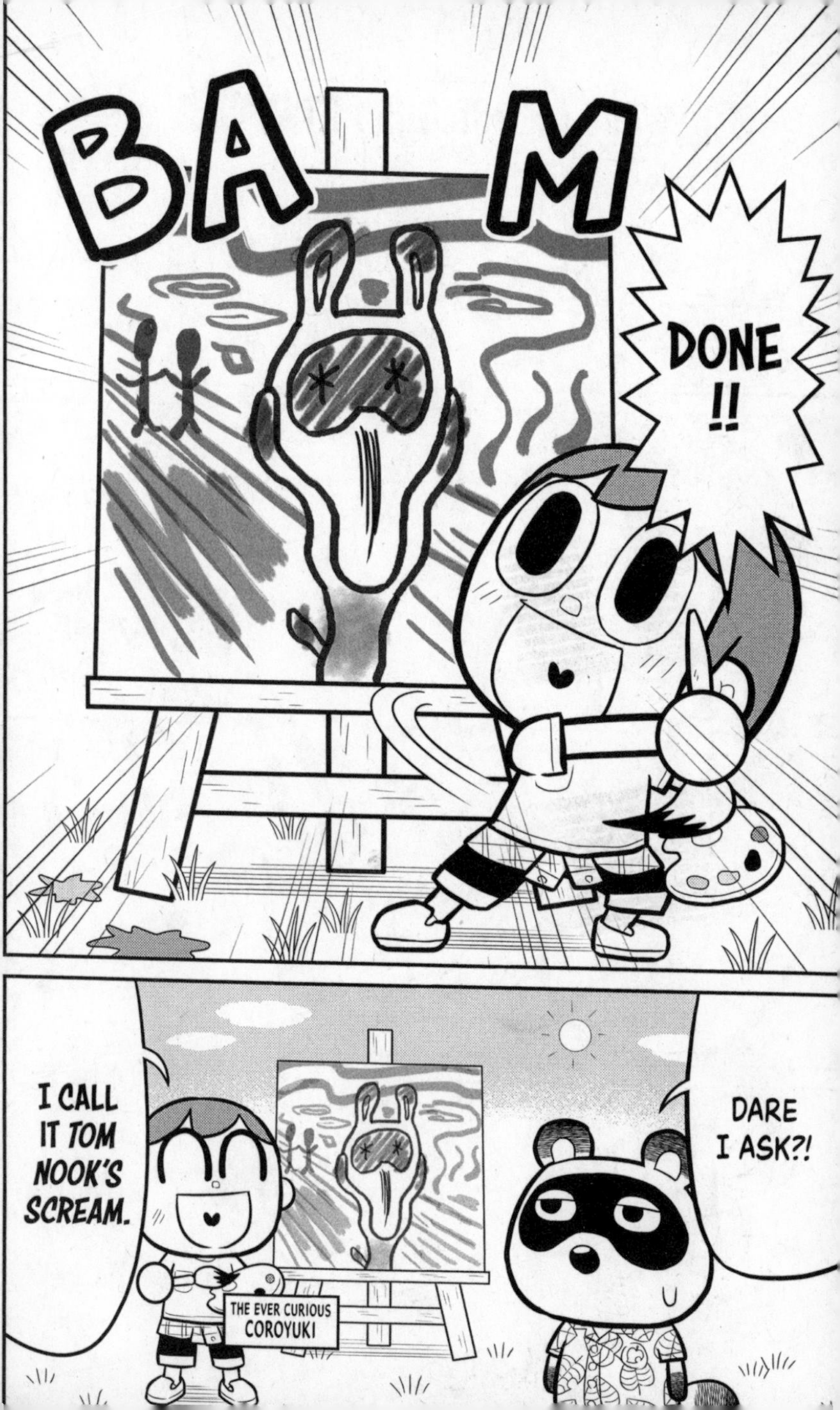
BAM
DONE!!
DARE I ASK?!
I CALL IT TOM NOOK'S SCREAM.
THE EVER CURIOUS COROYUKI

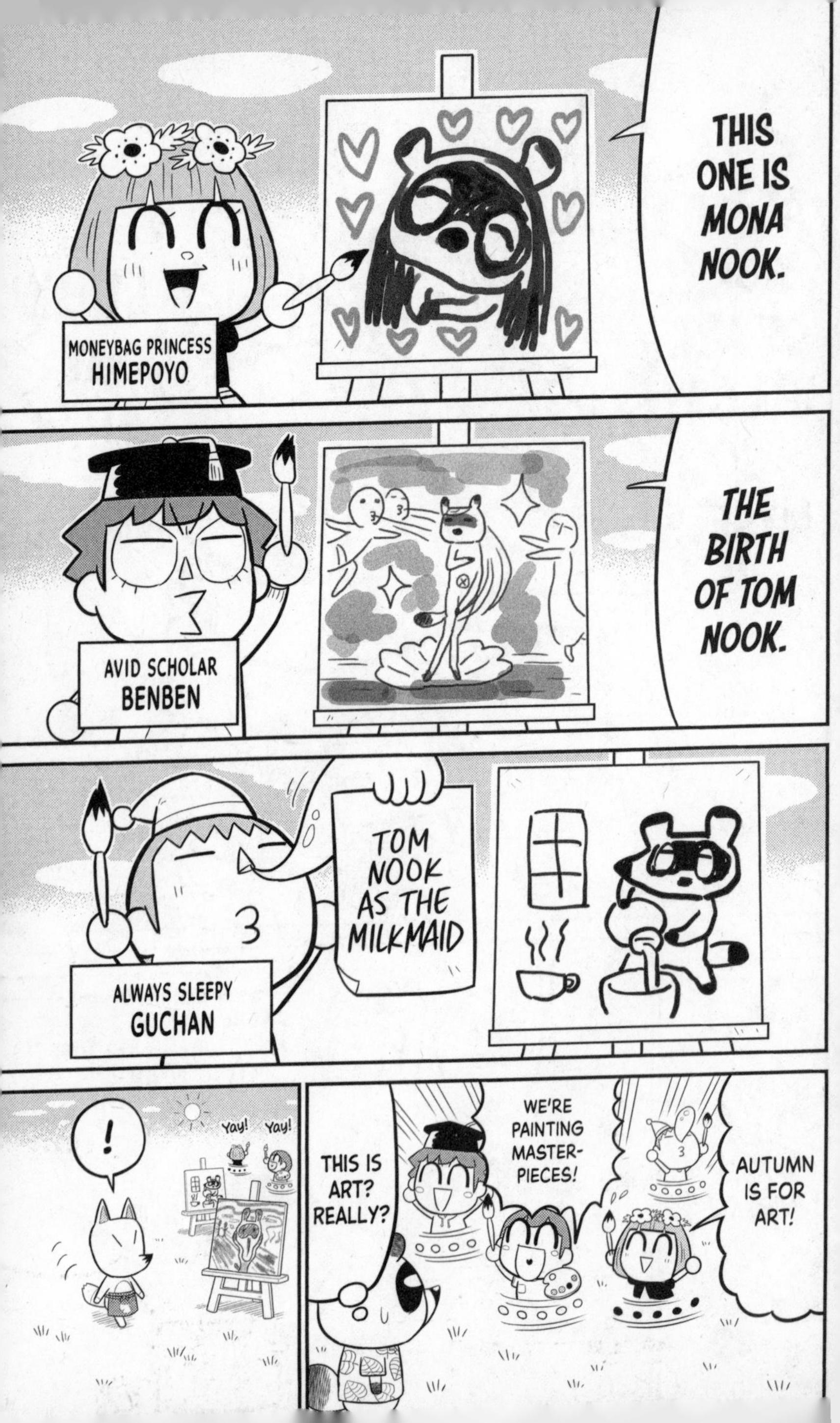
THIS ONE IS MONA NOOK.
MONEYBAG PRINCESS HIMEPOYO
THE BIRTH OF TOM NOOK.
AVID SCHOLAR BENBEN
TOM NOOK AS THE MILKMAID
ALWAYS SLEEPY GUCHAN
AUTUMN IS FOR ART!
WE'RE PAINTING MASTER-PIECES!
THIS IS ART? REALLY?
Yay! Yay!
!

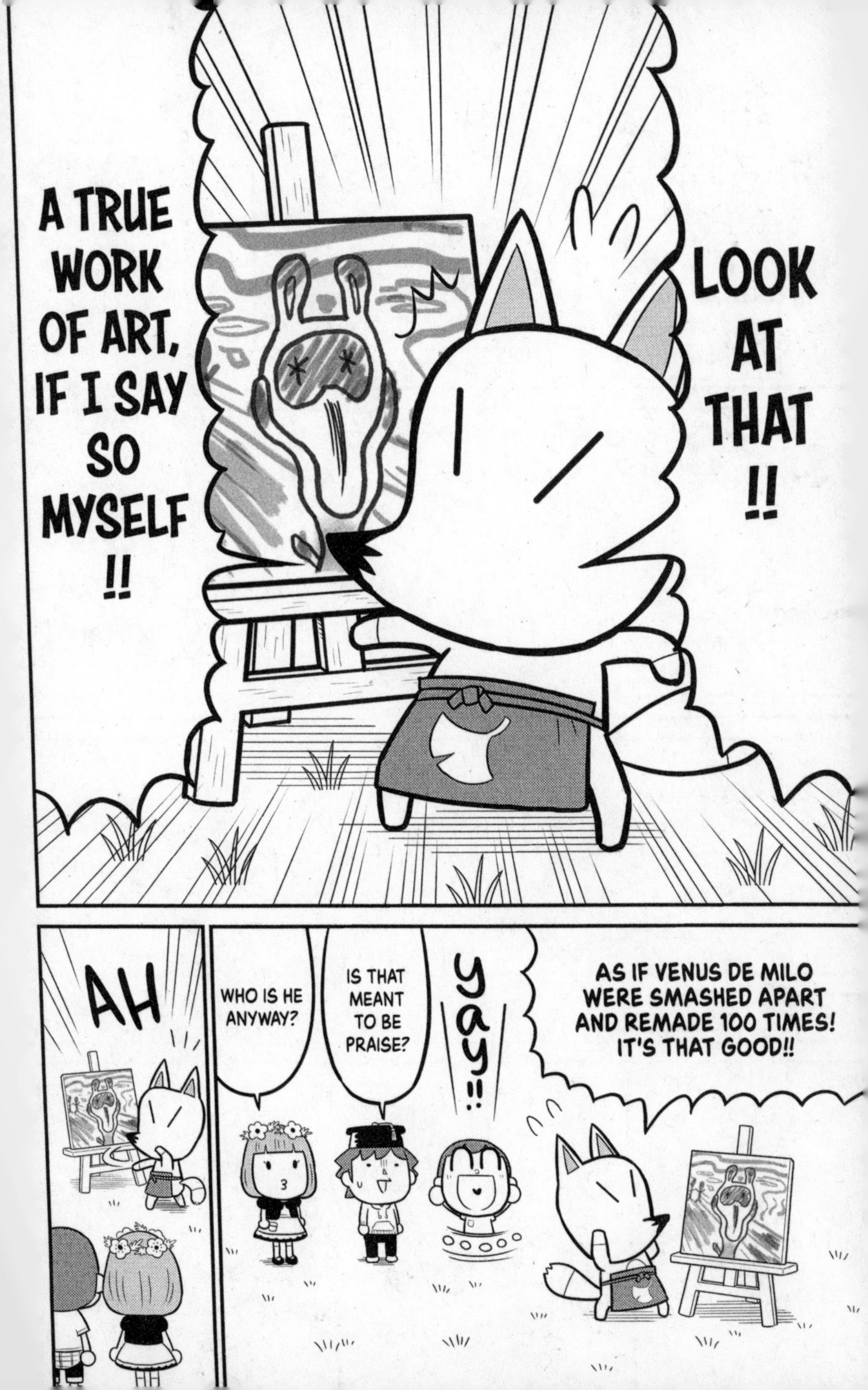

LOOK AT THAT!!
A TRUE WORK OF ART, IF I SAY SO MYSELF!!
AS IF VENUS DE MILO WERE SMASHED APART AND REMADE 100 TIMES! IT'S THAT GOOD!!
yay!!
IS THAT MEANT TO BE PRAISE?
WHO IS HE ANYWAY?
AH

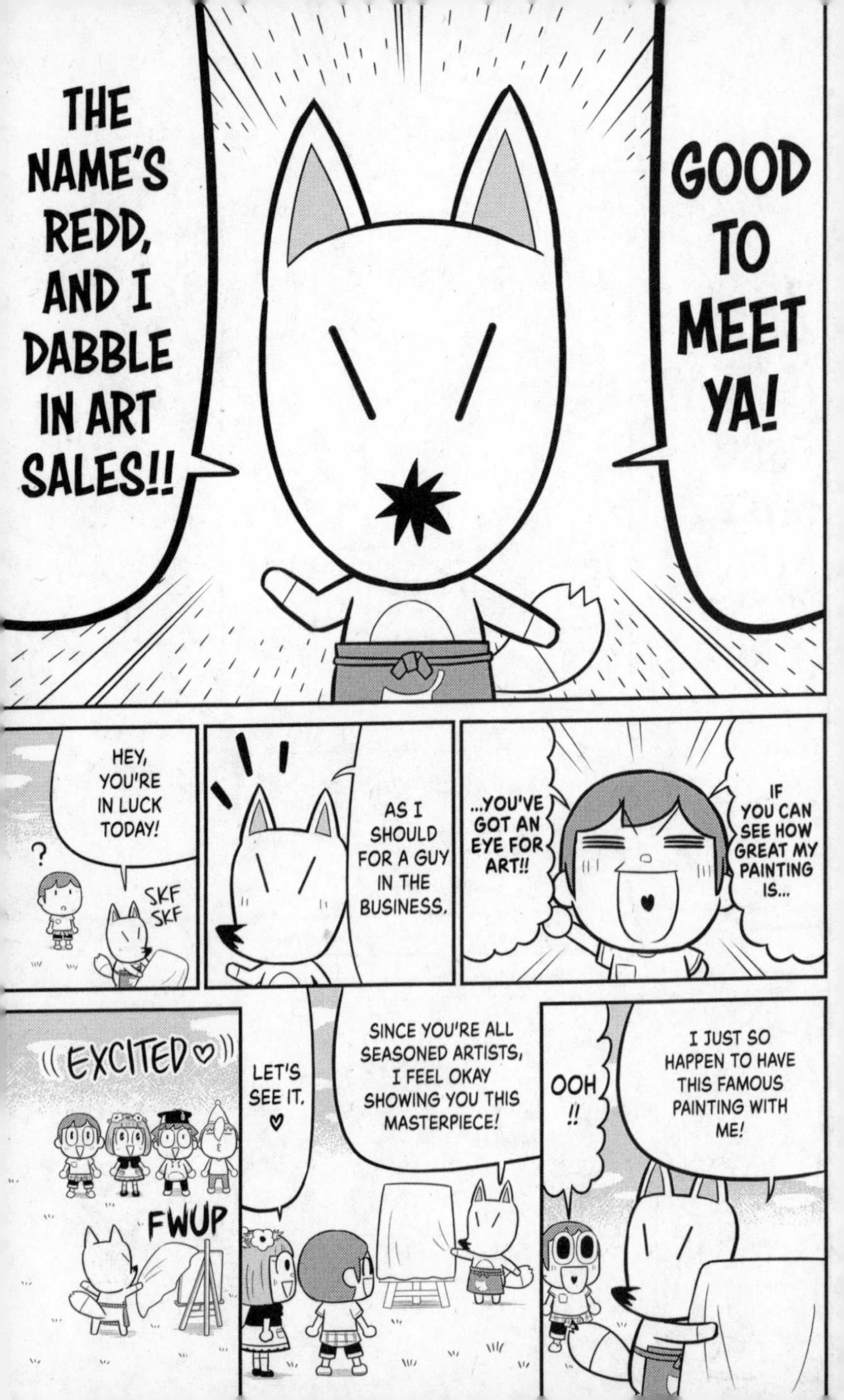
THE NAME'S REDD, AND I DABBLE IN ART SALES!!
GOOD TO MEET YA!
IF YOU CAN SEE HOW GREAT MY PAINTING IS...
...YOU'VE GOT AN EYE FOR ART!!
AS I SHOULD FOR A GUY IN THE BUSINESS.
HEY, YOU'RE IN LUCK TODAY!
?
SKF SKF
I JUST SO HAPPEN TO HAVE THIS FAMOUS PAINTING WITH ME!
OOH !!
SINCE YOU'RE ALL SEASONED ARTISTS, I FEEL OKAY SHOWING YOU THIS MASTERPIECE!
LET'S SEE IT. ♡
EXCITED ♡
FWUP

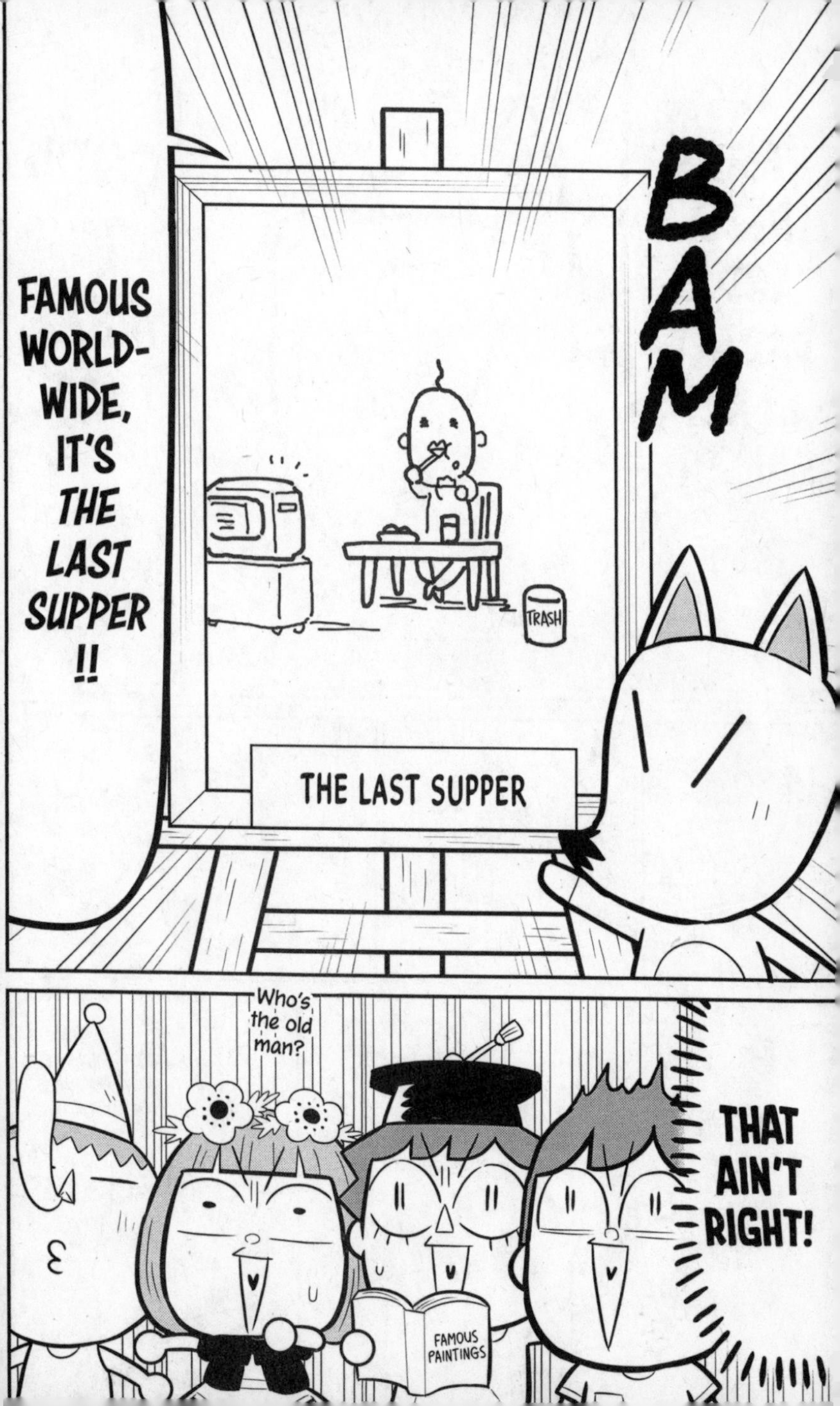
BAM
FAMOUS WORLD-WIDE, IT'S THE LAST SUPPER!!
TRASH
THE LAST SUPPER
THAT AIN'T RIGHT!
Who's the old man?
FAMOUS PAINTINGS

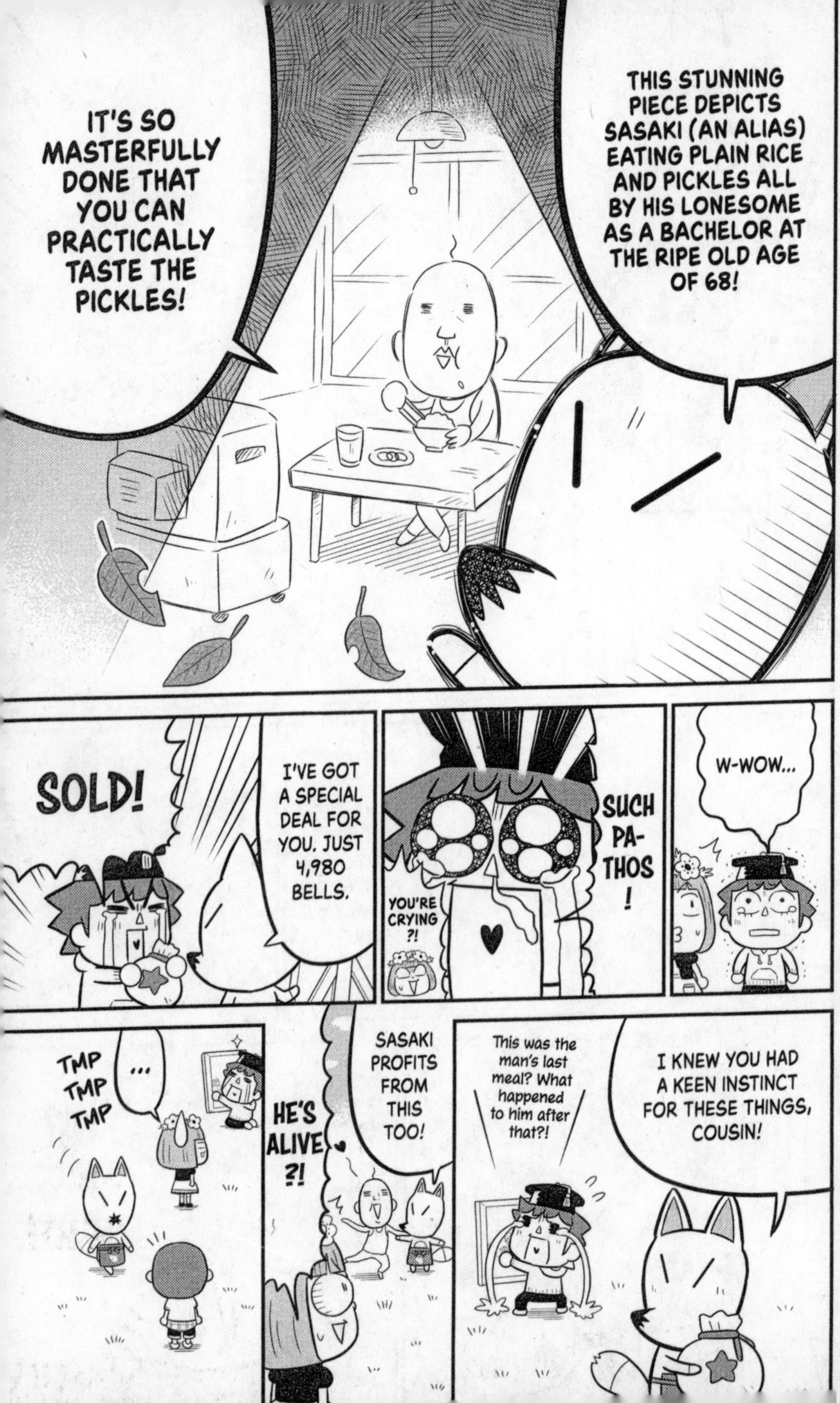
THIS STUNNING PIECE DEPICTS SASAKI (AN ALIAS) EATING PLAIN RICE AND PICKLES ALL BY HIS LONESOME AS A BACHELOR AT THE RIPE OLD AGE OF 68!
IT'S SO MASTERFULLY DONE THAT YOU CAN PRACTICALLY TASTE THE PICKLES!
W-WOW...
SUCH PA-THOS!
YOU'RE CRYING?!
I'VE GOT A SPECIAL DEAL FOR YOU. JUST 4,980 BELLS.
SOLD!
I KNEW YOU HAD A KEEN INSTINCT FOR THESE THINGS, COUSIN!
This was the man's last meal? What happened to him after that?!
SASAKI PROFITS FROM THIS TOO!
HE'S ALIVE?!
...
TMP TMP TMP

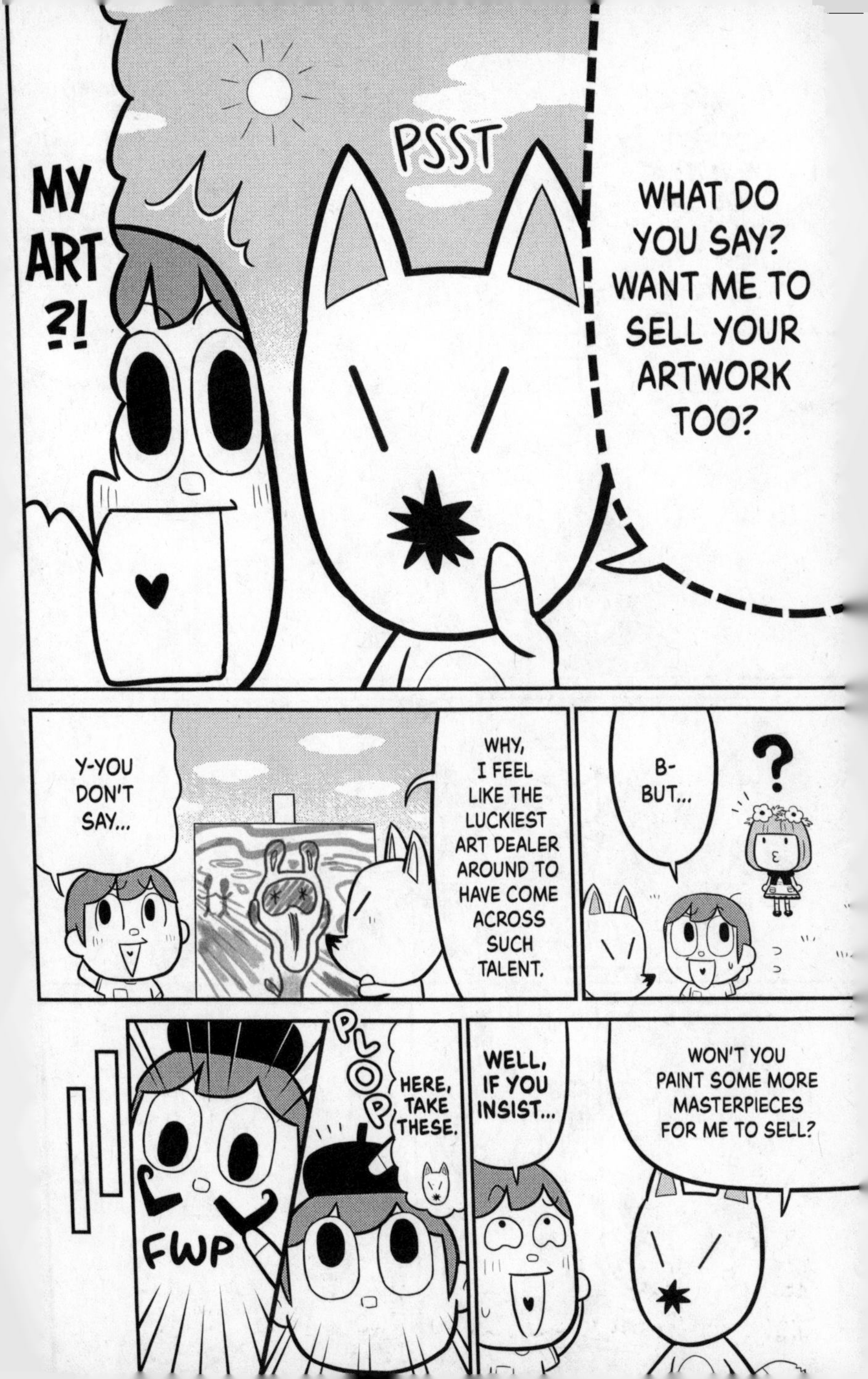
WHAT DO YOU SAY? WANT ME TO SELL YOUR ARTWORK TOO?
PSST
MY ART ?!
?
B-BUT...
WHY, I FEEL LIKE THE LUCKIEST ART DEALER AROUND TO HAVE COME ACROSS SUCH TALENT.
Y-YOU DON'T SAY...
WON'T YOU PAINT SOME MORE MASTERPIECES FOR ME TO SELL?
WELL, IF YOU INSIST...
HERE, TAKE THESE.
PLOP
FWP

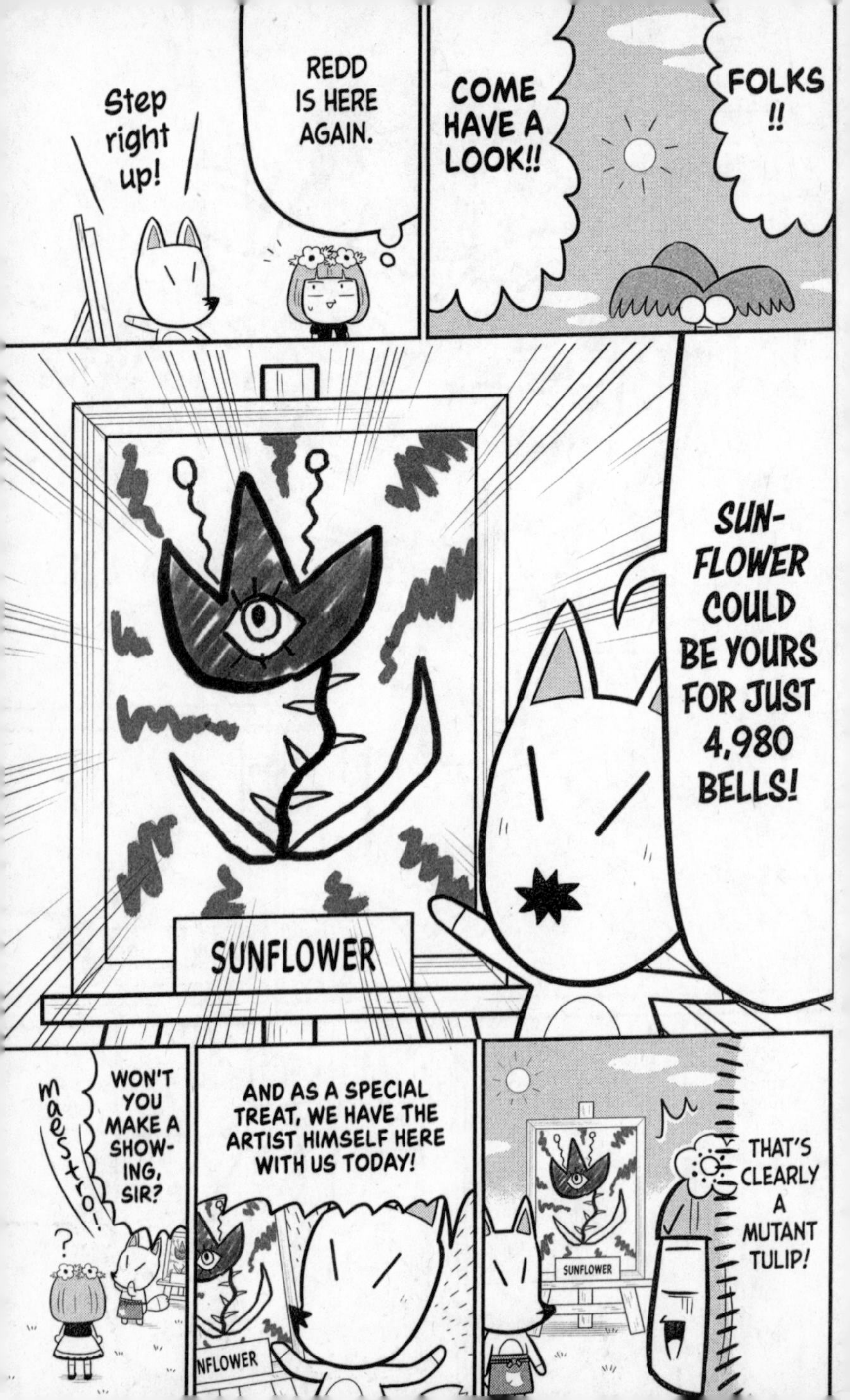
FOLKS !!
COME HAVE A LOOK!!
REDD IS HERE AGAIN.
Step right up!
SUN-FLOWER COULD BE YOURS FOR JUST 4,980 BELLS!
SUNFLOWER
THAT'S CLEARLY A MUTANT TULIP!
SUNFLOWER
AND AS A SPECIAL TREAT, WE HAVE THE ARTIST HIMSELF HERE WITH US TODAY!
NFLOWER
WON'T YOU MAKE A SHOW-ING, SIR?
maestro!
?

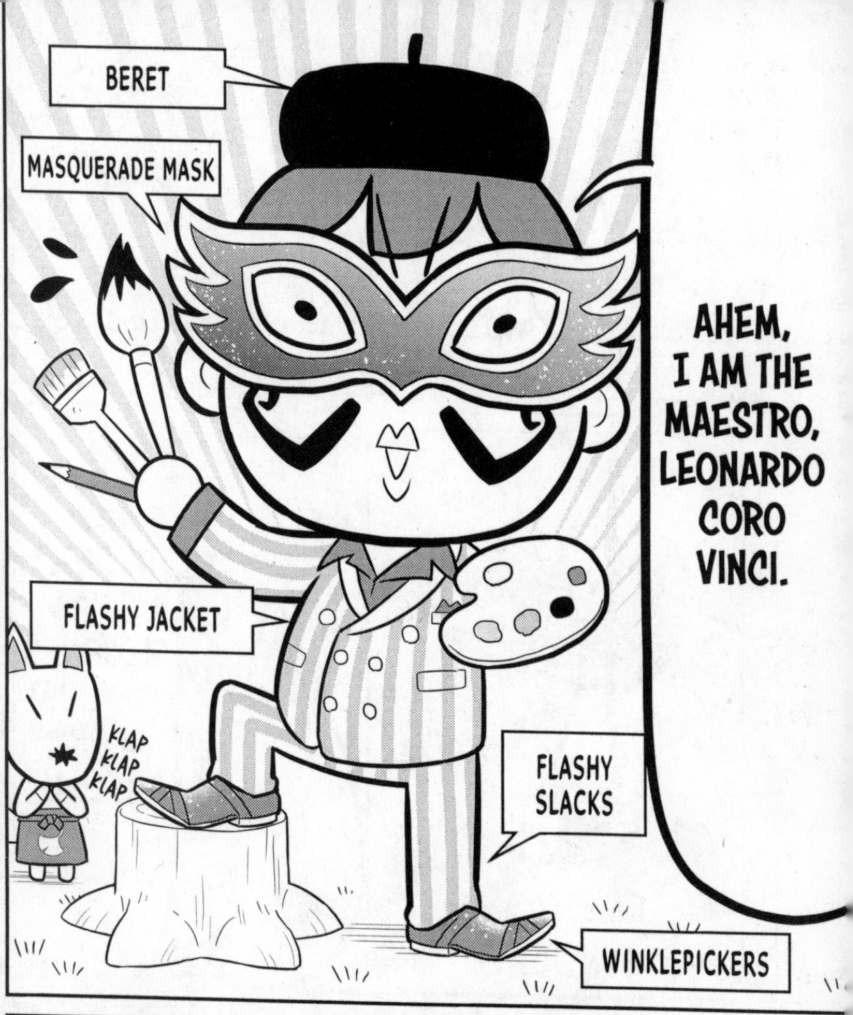
AHEM, I AM THE MAESTRO, LEONARDO CORO VINCI.
BERET
MASQUERADE MASK
FLASHY JACKET
FLASHY SLACKS
KLAP KLAP KLAP
WINKLEPICKERS
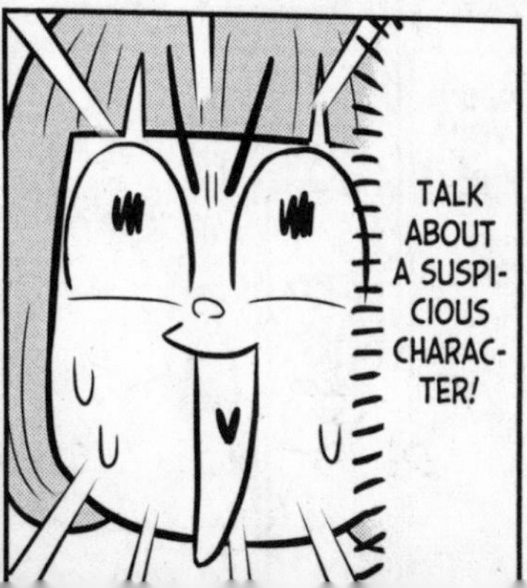
TALK ABOUT A SUSPI-CIOUS CHARAC-TER!
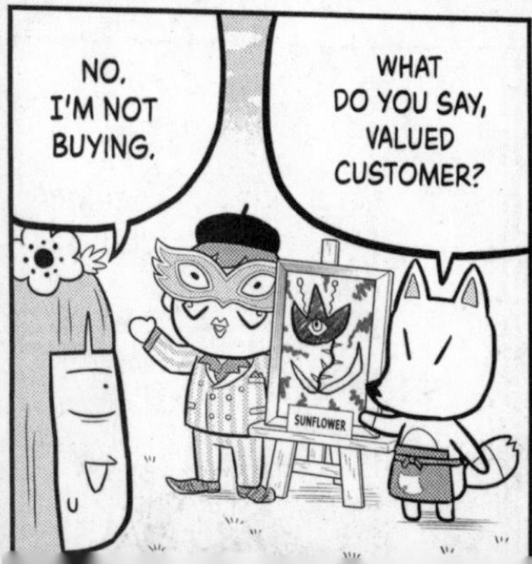
WHAT DO YOU SAY, VALUED CUSTOMER?
SUNFLOWER
NO. I'M NOT BUYING.

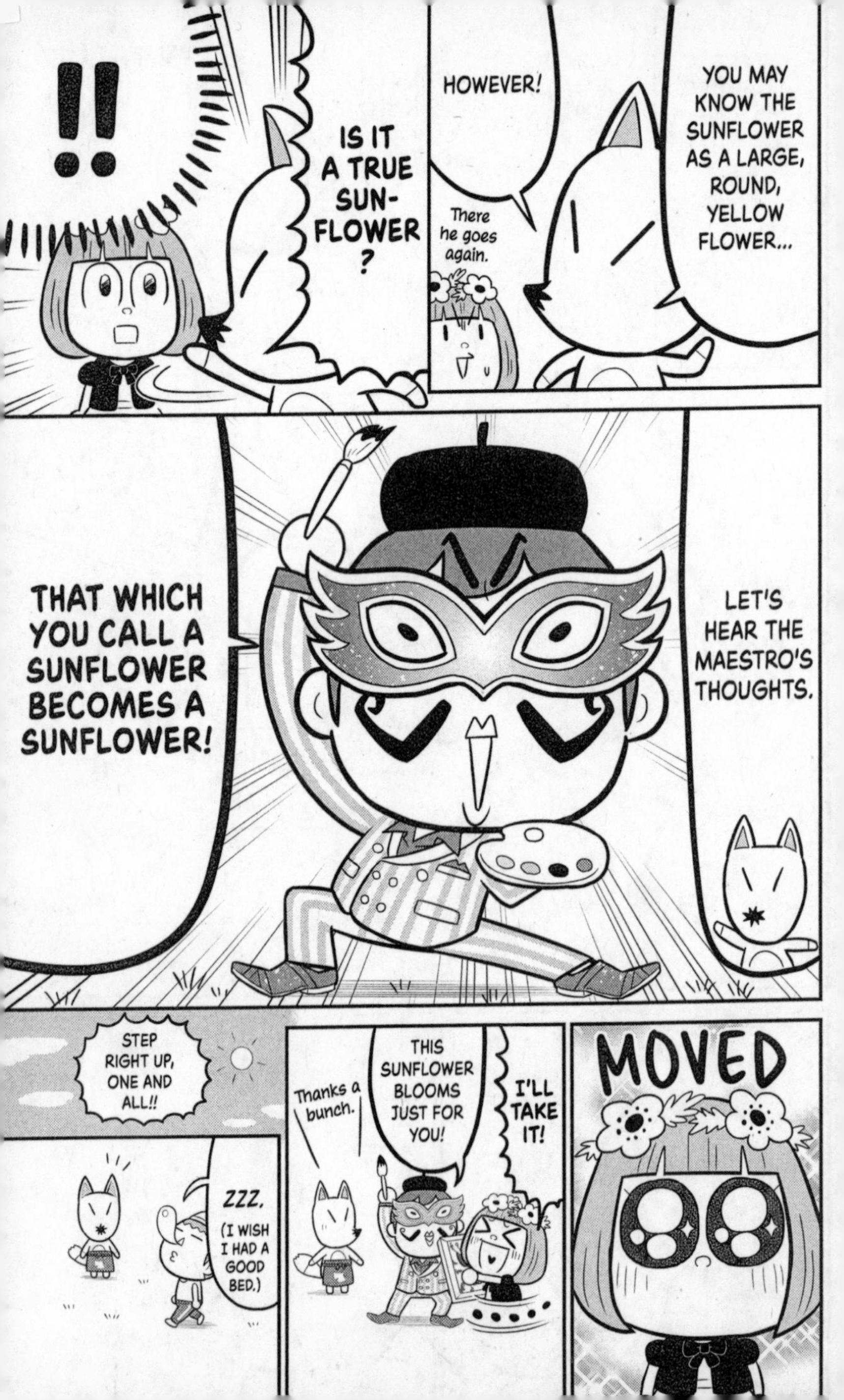
YOU MAY KNOW THE SUNFLOWER AS A LARGE, ROUND, YELLOW FLOWER...
HOWEVER!
There he goes again.
IS IT A TRUE SUN-FLOWER?
!!
LET'S HEAR THE MAESTRO'S THOUGHTS.
THAT WHICH YOU CALL A SUNFLOWER BECOMES A SUNFLOWER!
MOVED
THIS SUNFLOWER BLOOMS JUST FOR YOU!
I'LL TAKE IT!
Thanks a bunch.
STEP RIGHT UP, ONE AND ALL!!
ZZZ.
(I WISH I HAD A GOOD BED.)

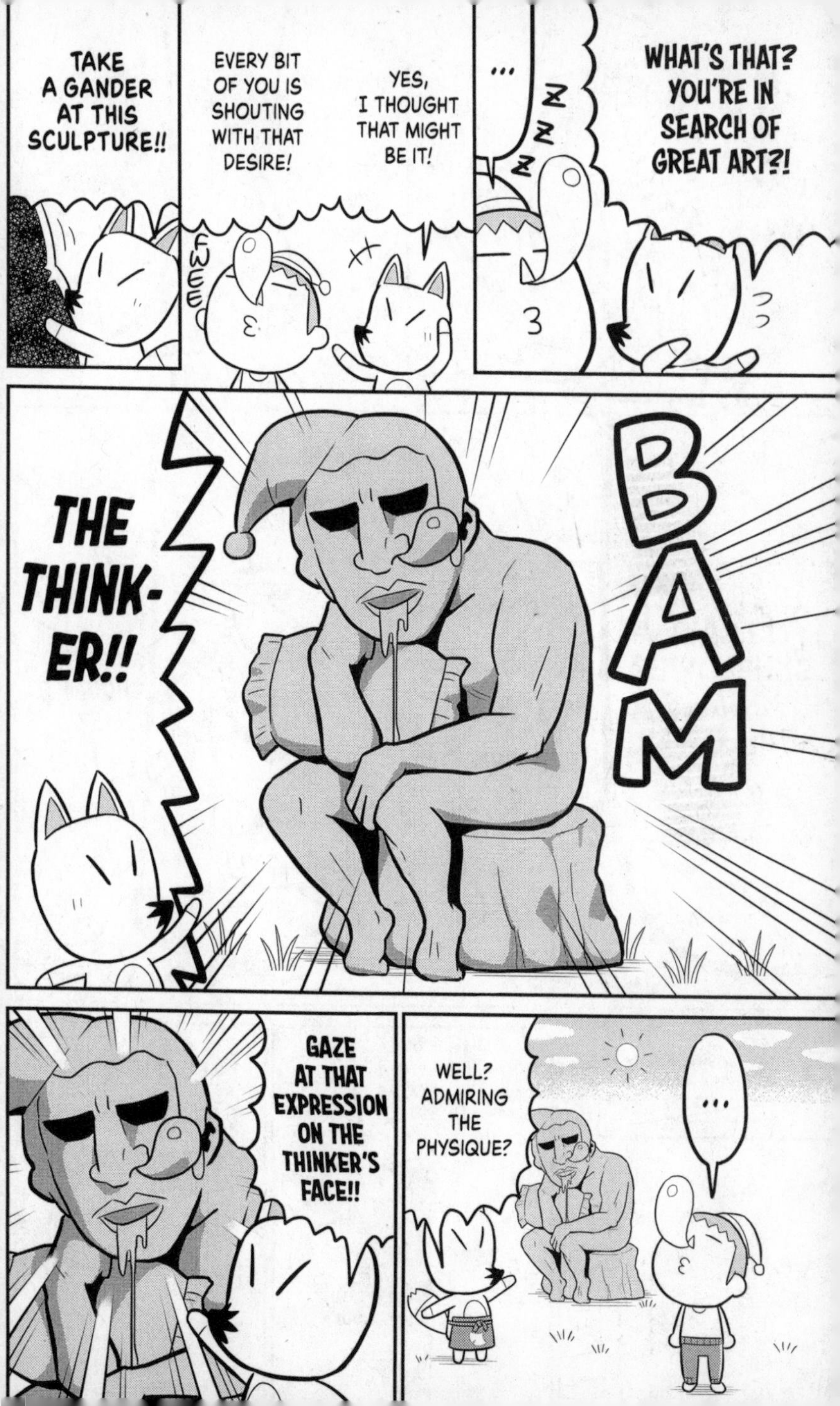
WHAT'S THAT? YOU'RE IN SEARCH OF GREAT ART?!
...
ZZZ
YES, I THOUGHT THAT MIGHT BE IT!
EVERY BIT OF YOU IS SHOUTING WITH THAT DESIRE!
FWEE
TAKE A GANDER AT THIS SCULPTURE!!
BAM
THE THINK-ER!!
...
WELL? ADMIRING THE PHYSIQUE?
GAZE AT THAT EXPRESSION ON THE THINKER'S FACE!!

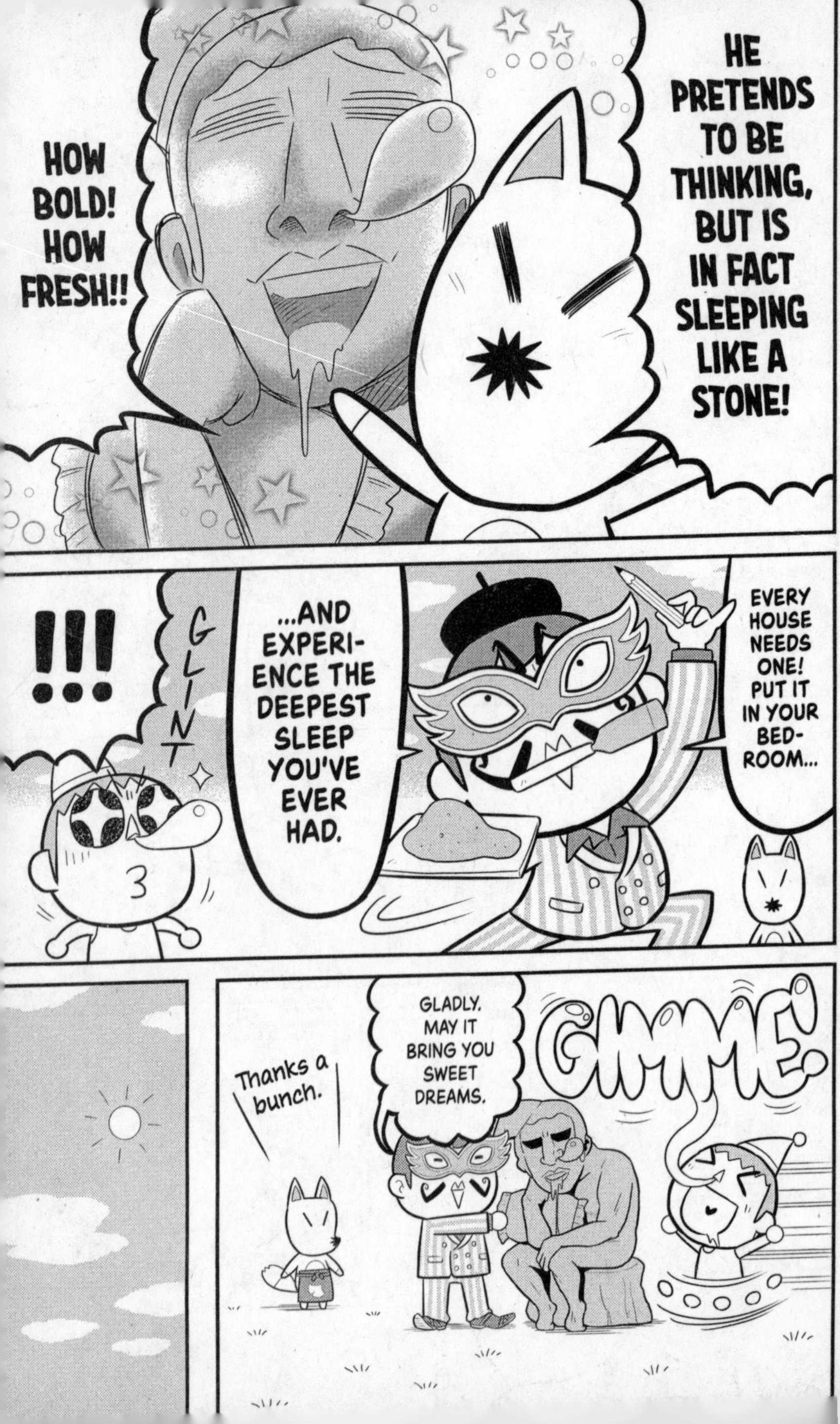

HE PRETENDS TO BE THINKING, BUT IS IN FACT SLEEPING LIKE A STONE!
HOW BOLD! HOW FRESH!!
EVERY HOUSE NEEDS ONE! PUT IT IN YOUR BED-ROOM...
...AND EXPERI-ENCE THE DEEPEST SLEEP YOU'VE EVER HAD.
GLINT
!!!
GIMME!
GLADLY. MAY IT BRING YOU SWEET DREAMS.
Thanks a bunch.

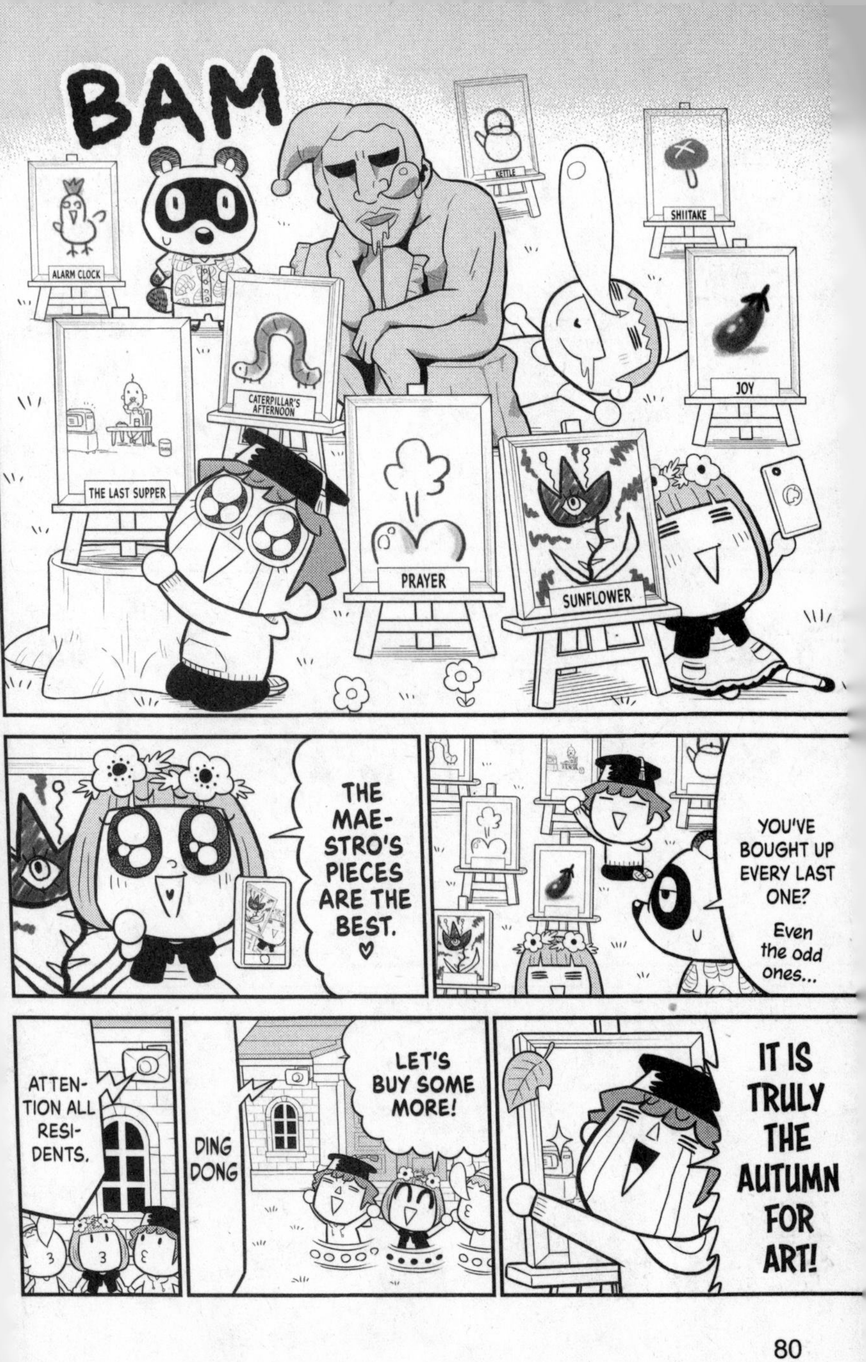
SHIITAKE
KETTLE
BAM
ALARM CLOCK
JOY
CATERPILLAR'S AFTERNOON
THE LAST SUPPER
SUNFLOWER
PRAYER
YOU'VE BOUGHT UP EVERY LAST ONE?
Even the odd ones...
THE MAESTRO'S PIECES ARE THE BEST. ♥
IT IS TRULY THE AUTUMN FOR ART!
LET'S BUY SOME MORE!
DING DONG
ATTENTION ALL RESIDENTS.

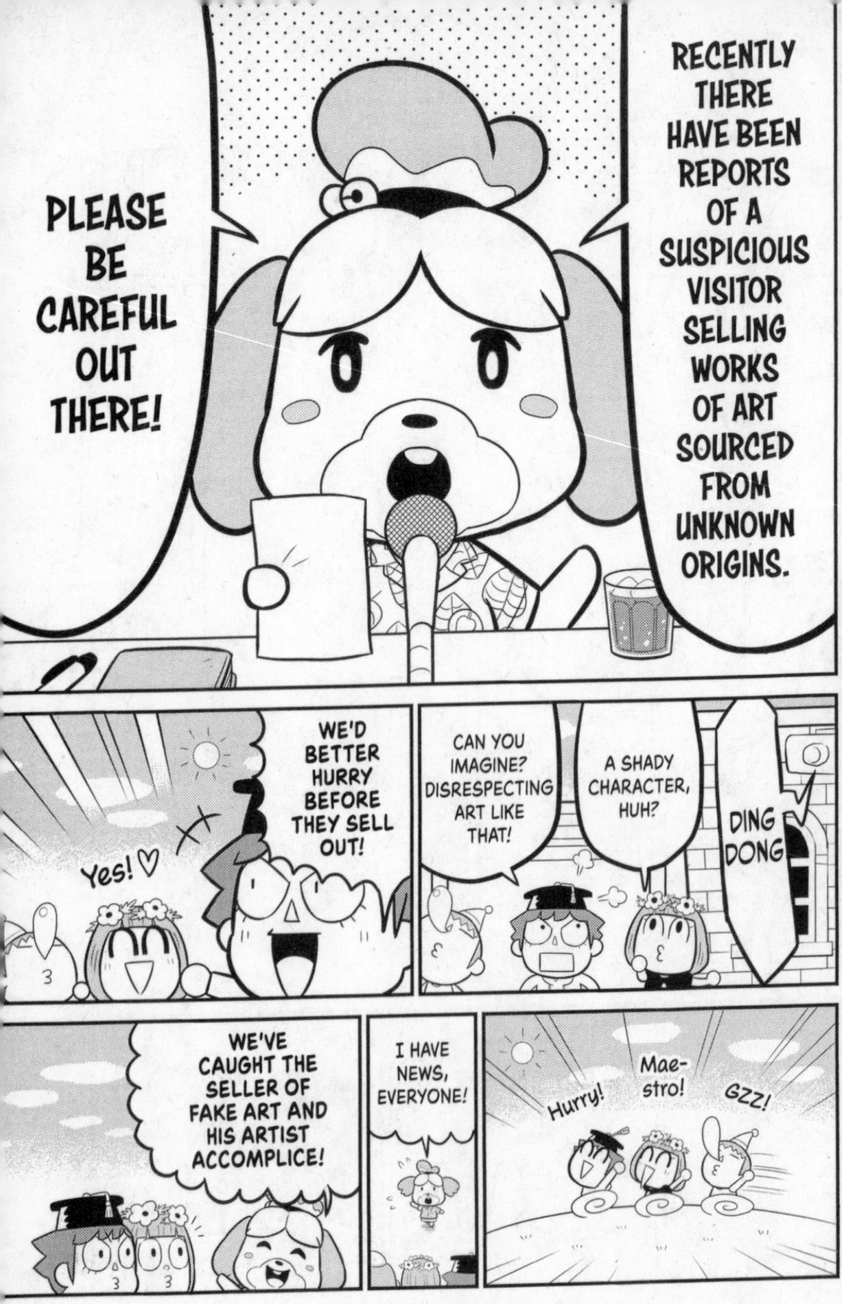
RECENTLY THERE HAVE BEEN REPORTS OF A SUSPICIOUS VISITOR SELLING WORKS OF ART SOURCED FROM UNKNOWN ORIGINS.
PLEASE BE CAREFUL OUT THERE!
DING DONG
A SHADY CHARACTER, HUH?
CAN YOU IMAGINE? DISRESPECTING ART LIKE THAT!
WE'D BETTER HURRY BEFORE THEY SELL OUT!
Yes! ♡
GZZ!
Mae-stro!
Hurry!
I HAVE NEWS, EVERYONE!
WE'VE CAUGHT THE SELLER OF FAKE ART AND HIS ARTIST ACCOMPLICE!

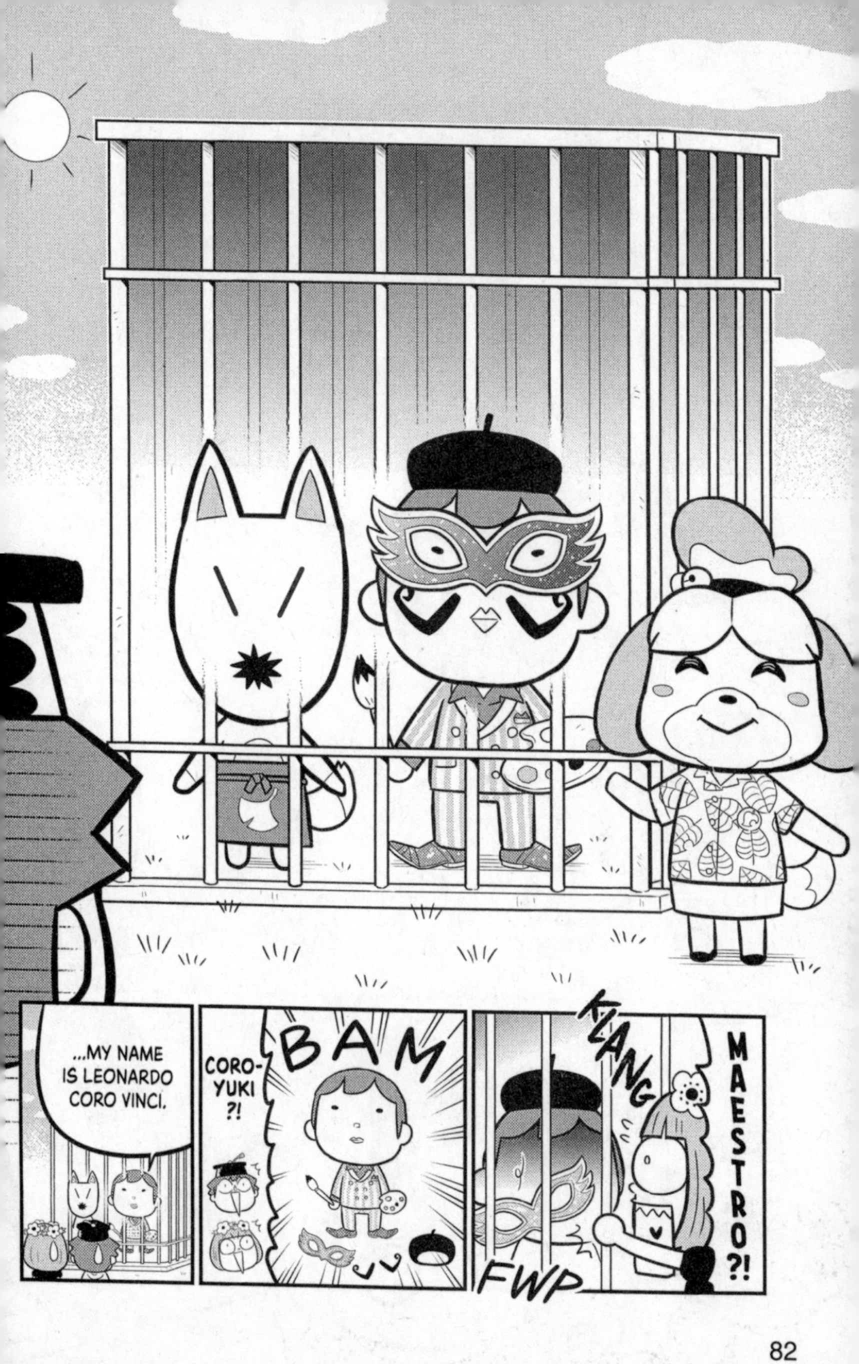
KLANG
MAESTRO?!
FWP
BAM
CORO-YUKI ?!
...MY NAME IS LEONARDO CORO VINCI.

THE PRINCE FROM PARADISE

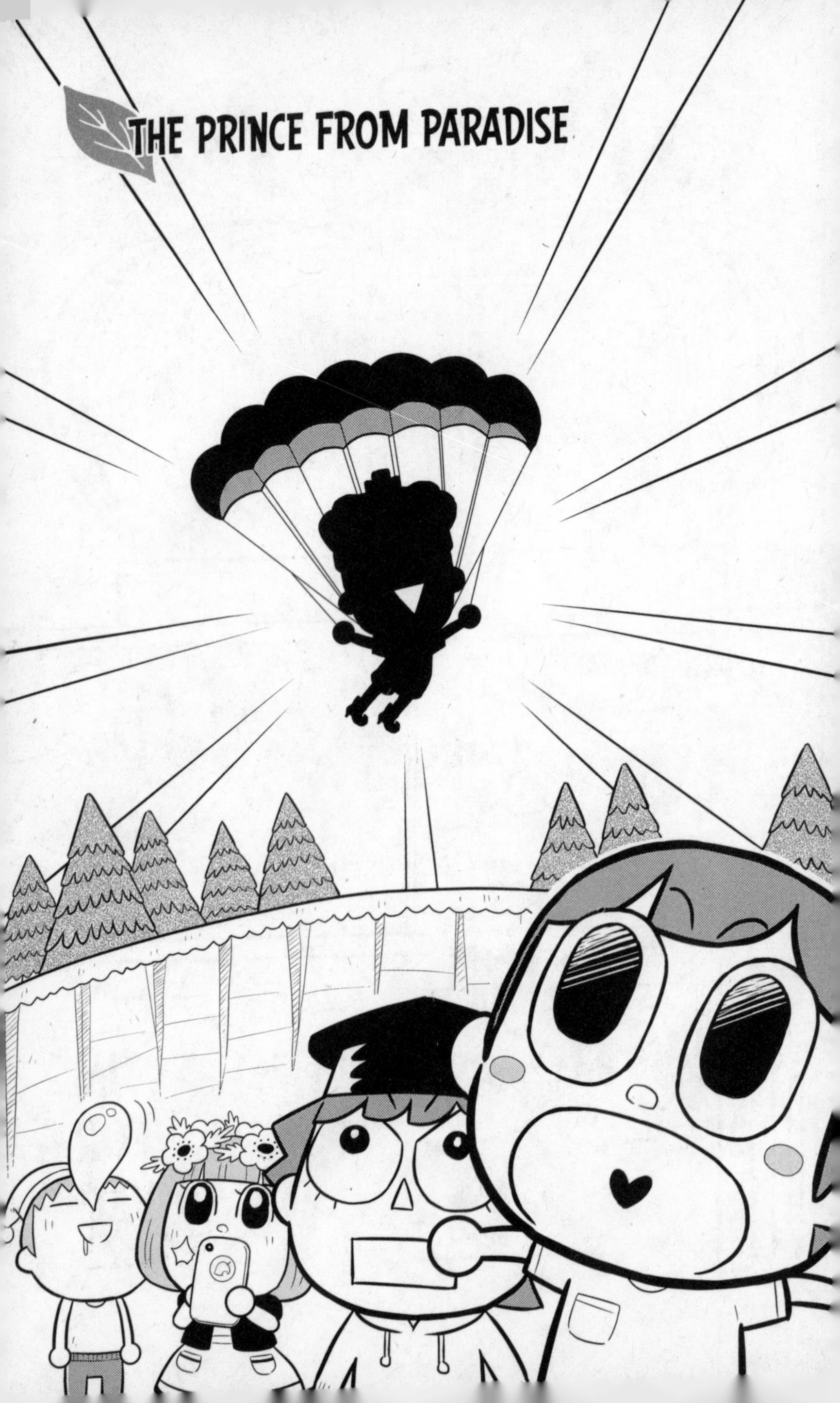

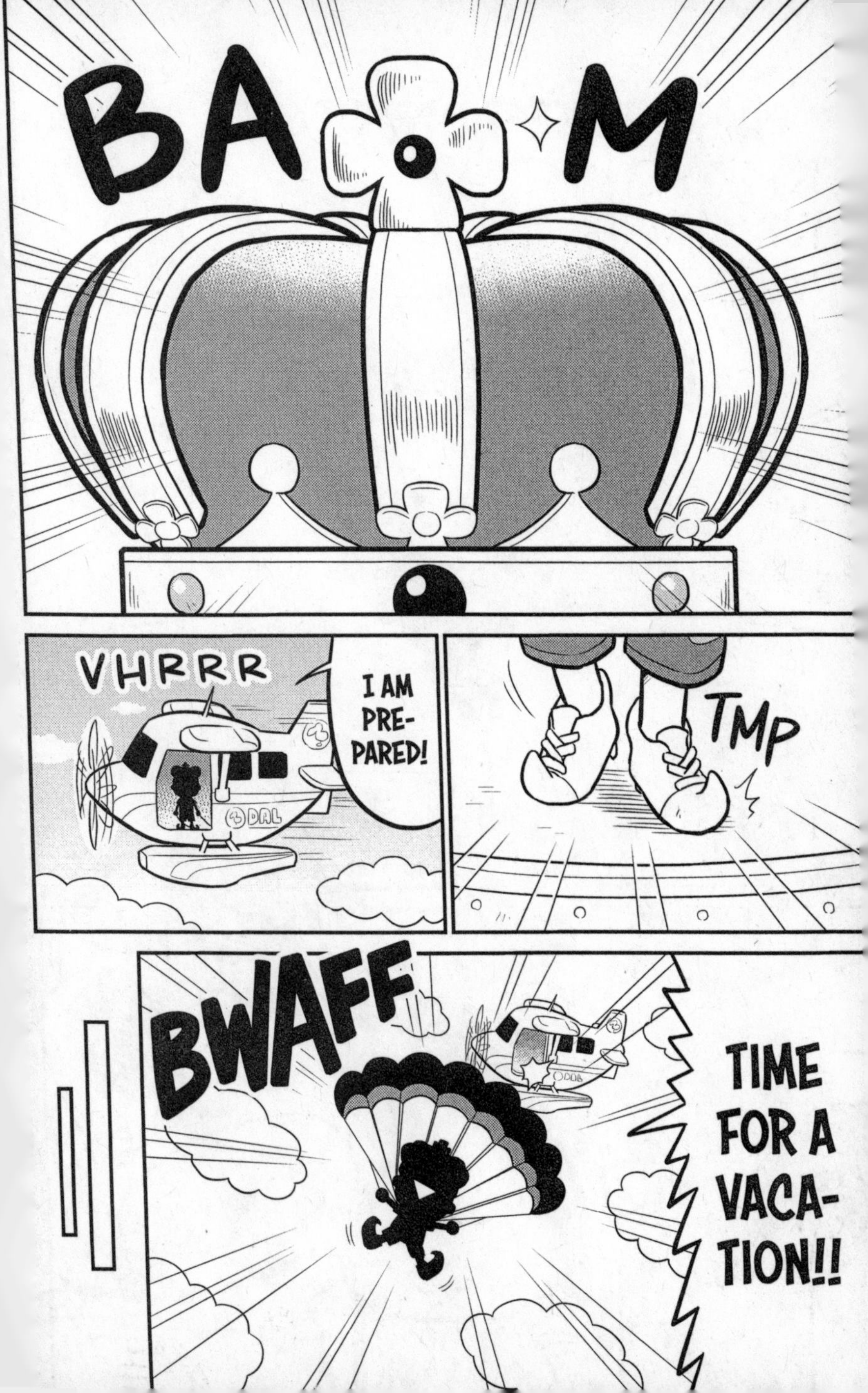
BA M
TMP
I AM PRE-PARED!
VHRRR
TIME FOR A VACA-TION!!
BWAFF

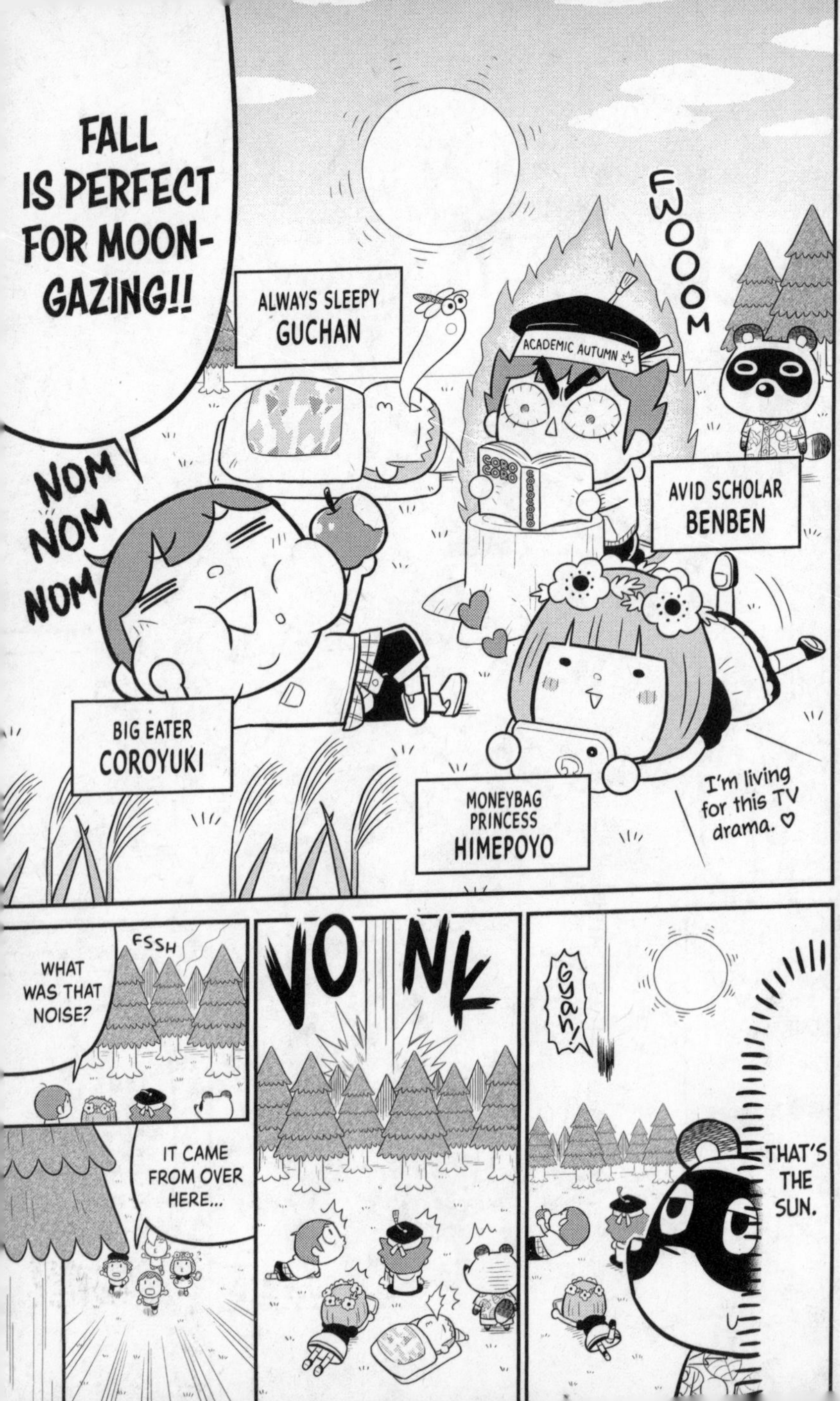

FALL IS PERFECT FOR MOON-GAZING!!
ALWAYS SLEEPY GUCHAN
ACADEMIC AUTUMN
FWOOOM
COROCORO
AVID SCHOLAR BENBEN
NOM NOM NOM
BIG EATER COROYUKI
MONEYBAG PRINCESS HIMEPOYO
I'm living for this TV drama. ♡
FSSH
WHAT WAS THAT NOISE?
IT CAME FROM OVER HERE...
VONK
Gyan!
THAT'S THE SUN.

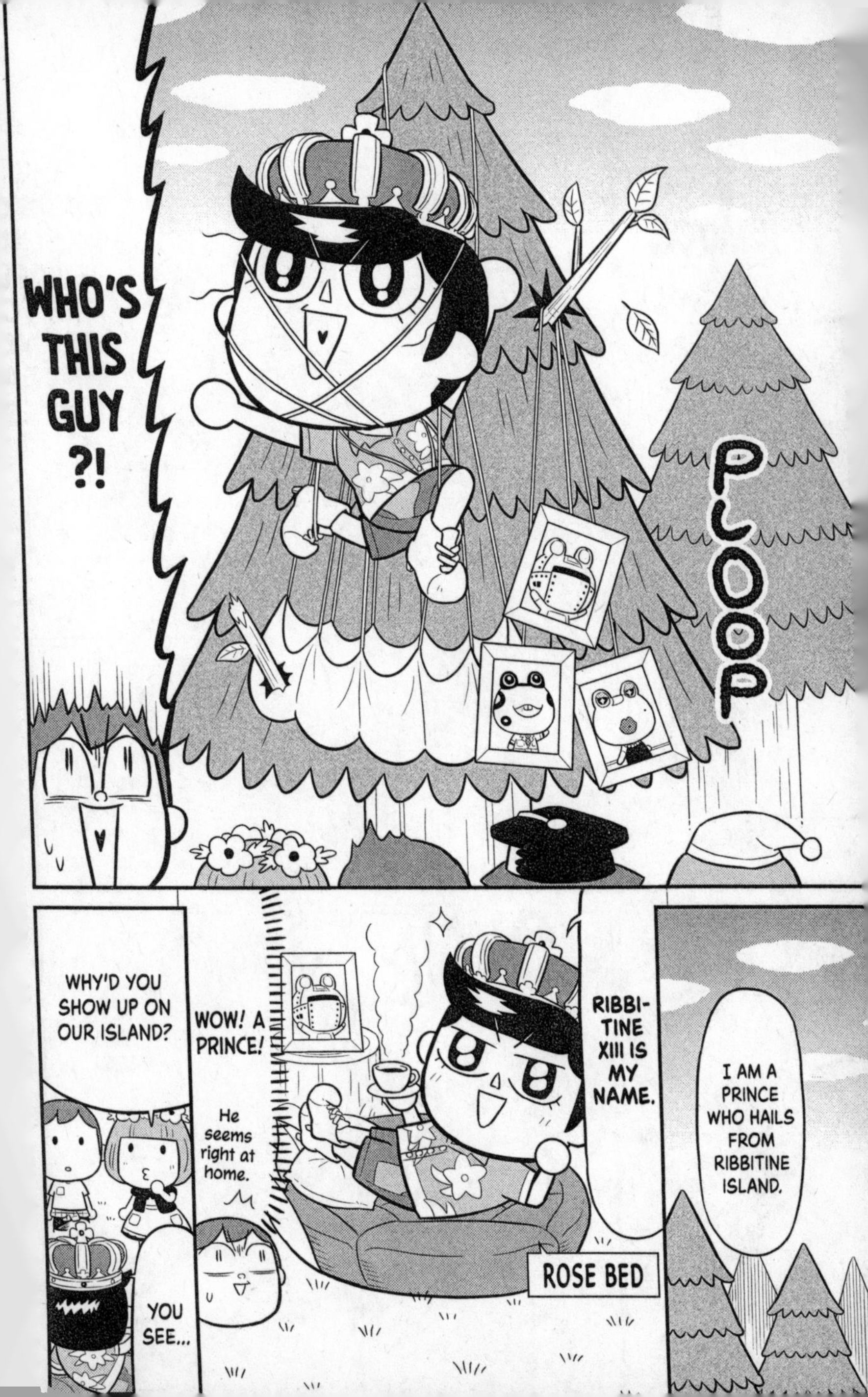
PLOOP
WHO'S THIS GUY ?!
I AM A PRINCE WHO HAILS FROM RIBBITINE ISLAND.
RIBBITINE XIII IS MY NAME.
ROSE BED
WOW! A PRINCE!
He seems right at home.
WHY'D YOU SHOW UP ON OUR ISLAND?
YOU SEE...

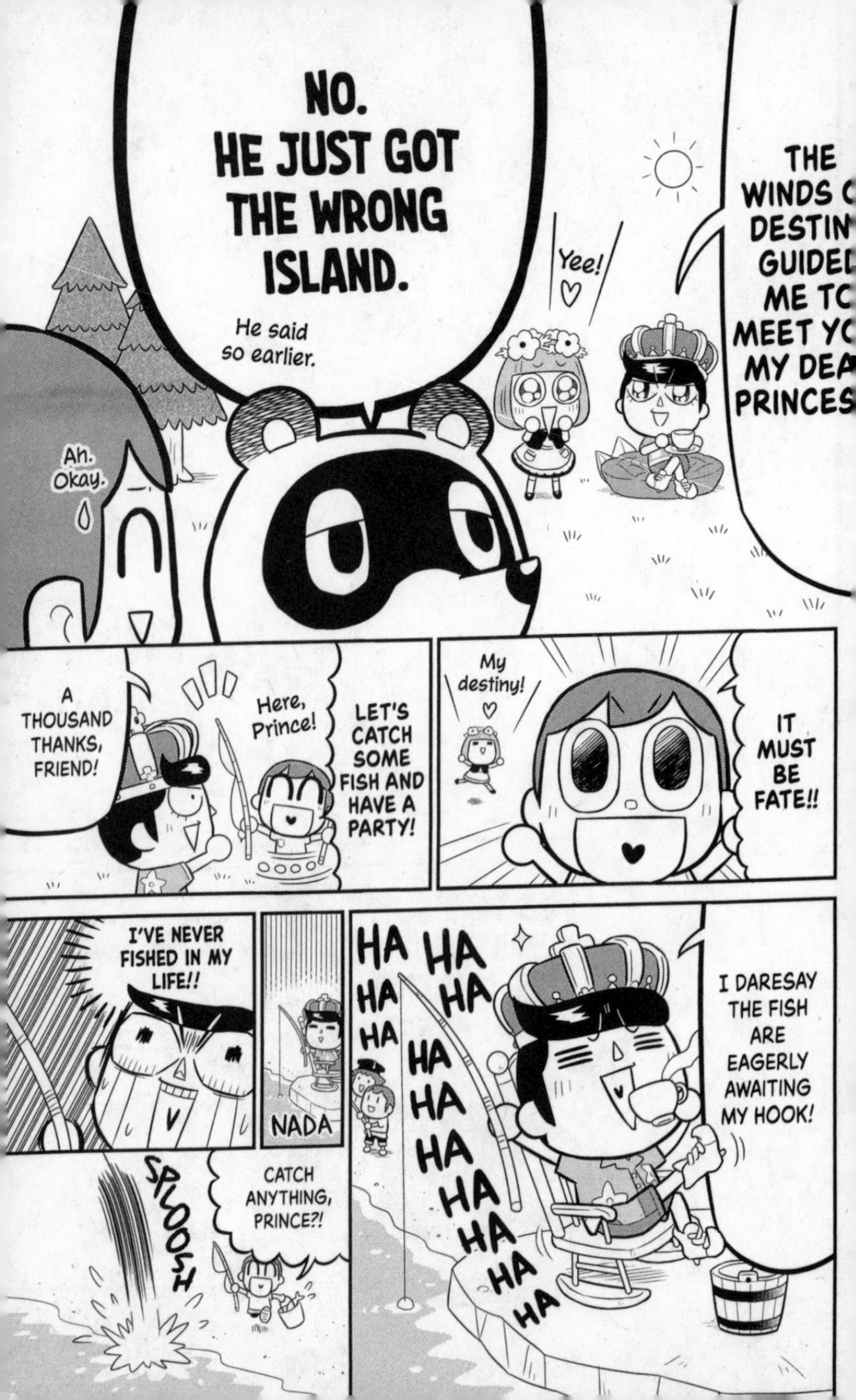
THE WINDS C DESTIN GUIDED ME TC MEET YC MY DEA PRINCES
Yee! ♡
NO. HE JUST GOT THE WRONG ISLAND.
He said so earlier.
Ah. Okay.
IT MUST BE FATE!!
My destiny! ♡
LET'S CATCH SOME FISH AND HAVE A PARTY!
Here, Prince!
A THOUSAND THANKS, FRIEND!
I DARESAY THE FISH ARE EAGERLY AWAITING MY HOOK!
HA HA HA HA HA HA HA HA HA HA HA HA HA HA
NADA
I'VE NEVER FISHED IN MY LIFE!!
CATCH ANYTHING, PRINCE?!
SPLOOSH

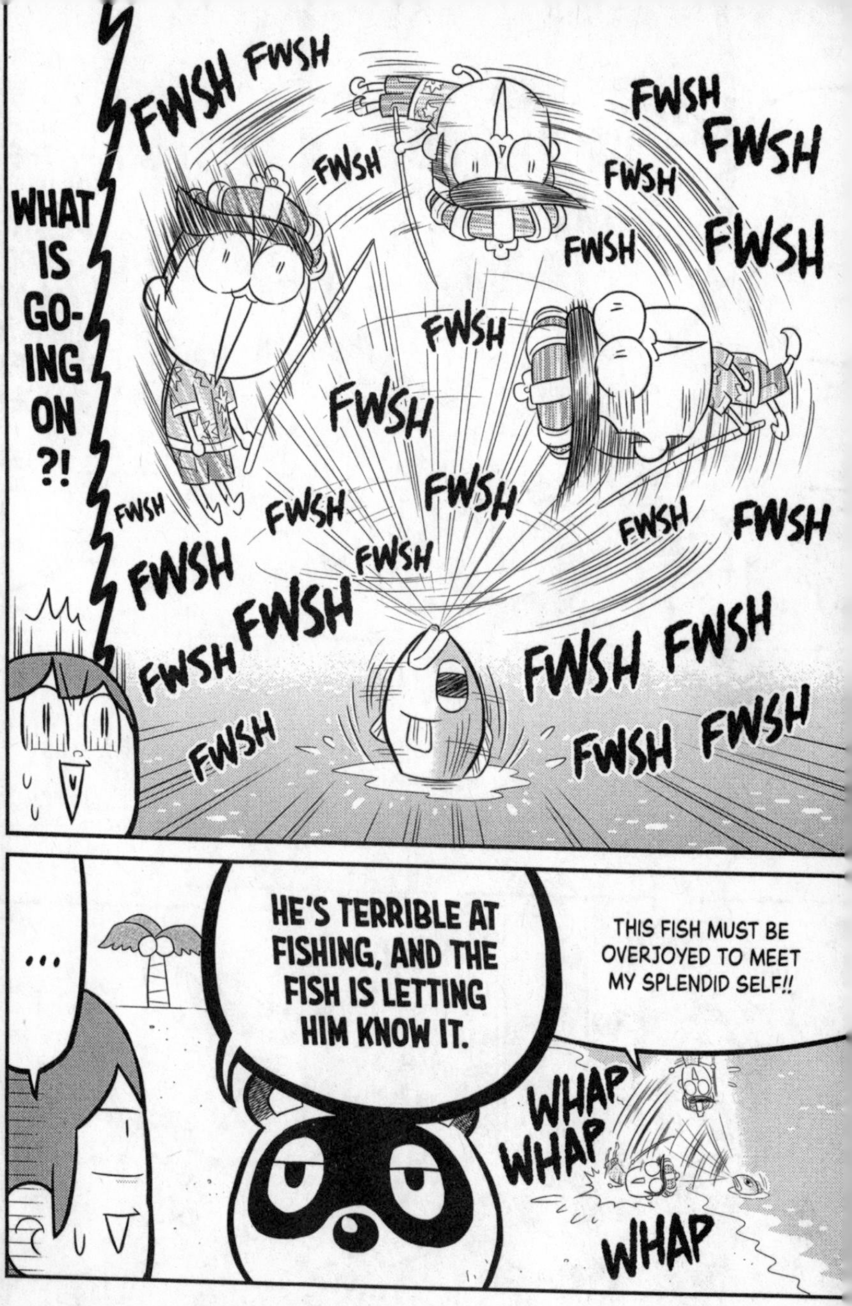
FWSH FWSH
FWSH
FWSH
FWSH
FWSH
FWSH
FWSH
WHAT IS GO-ING ON ?!
FWSH
FWSH
FWSH
FWSH
FWSH
FWSH
FWSH
FWSH
FWSH FWSH
FWSH
FWSH FWSH
FWSH
THIS FISH MUST BE OVERJOYED TO MEET MY SPLENDID SELF!!
WHAP WHAP
WHAP
HE'S TERRIBLE AT FISHING, AND THE FISH IS LETTING HIM KNOW IT.
...

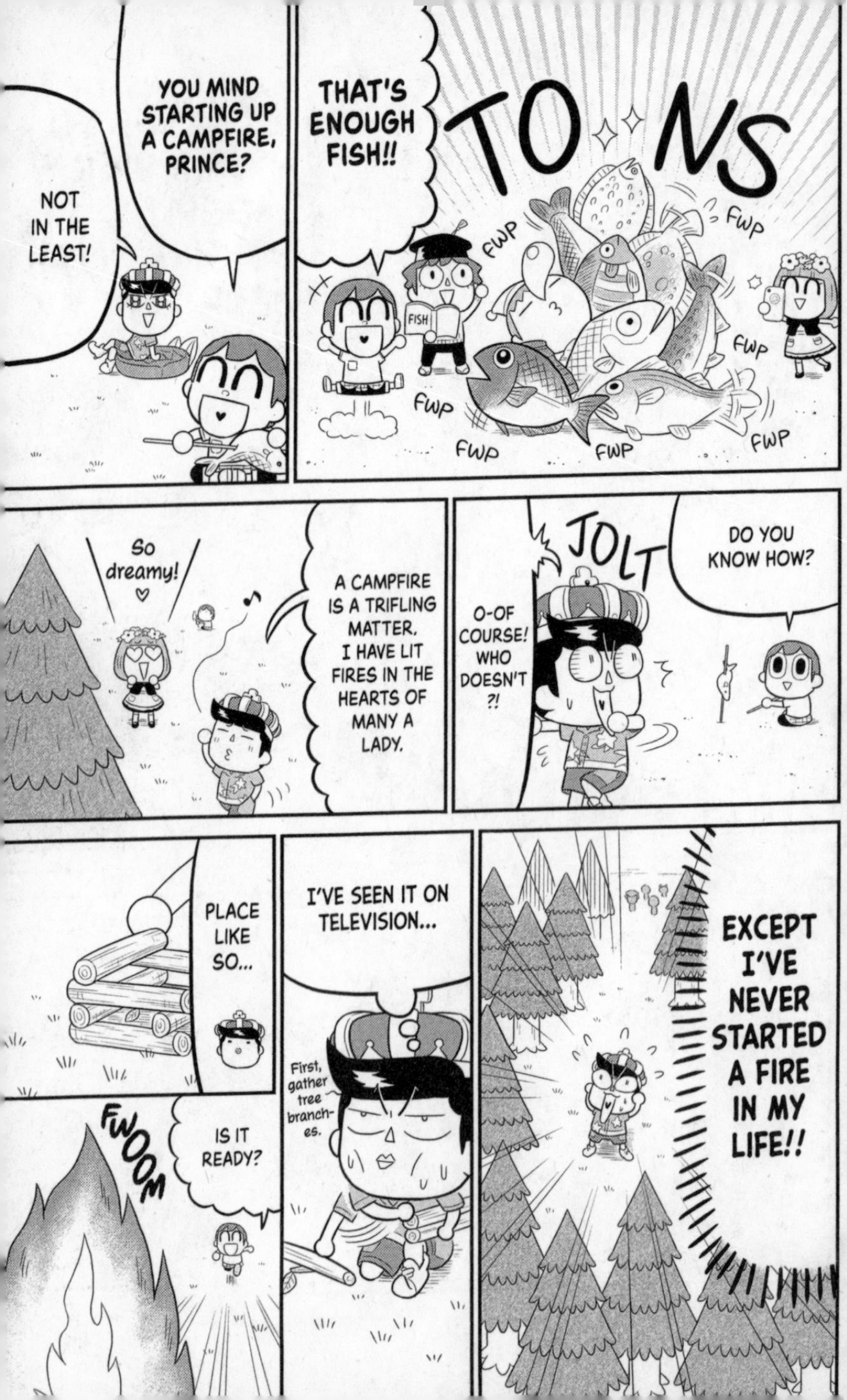
THAT'S ENOUGH FISH!!
TONS
FISH
FWP
FWP
FWP
FWP
FWP
FWP
FWP
YOU MIND STARTING UP A CAMPFIRE, PRINCE?
NOT IN THE LEAST!
DO YOU KNOW HOW?
JOLT
O-OF COURSE! WHO DOESN'T ?!
A CAMPFIRE IS A TRIFLING MATTER. I HAVE LIT FIRES IN THE HEARTS OF MANY A LADY.
So dreamy! ♡
EXCEPT I'VE NEVER STARTED A FIRE IN MY LIFE!!
I'VE SEEN IT ON TELEVISION...
First, gather tree branches.
PLACE LIKE SO...
IS IT READY?
FWOOM

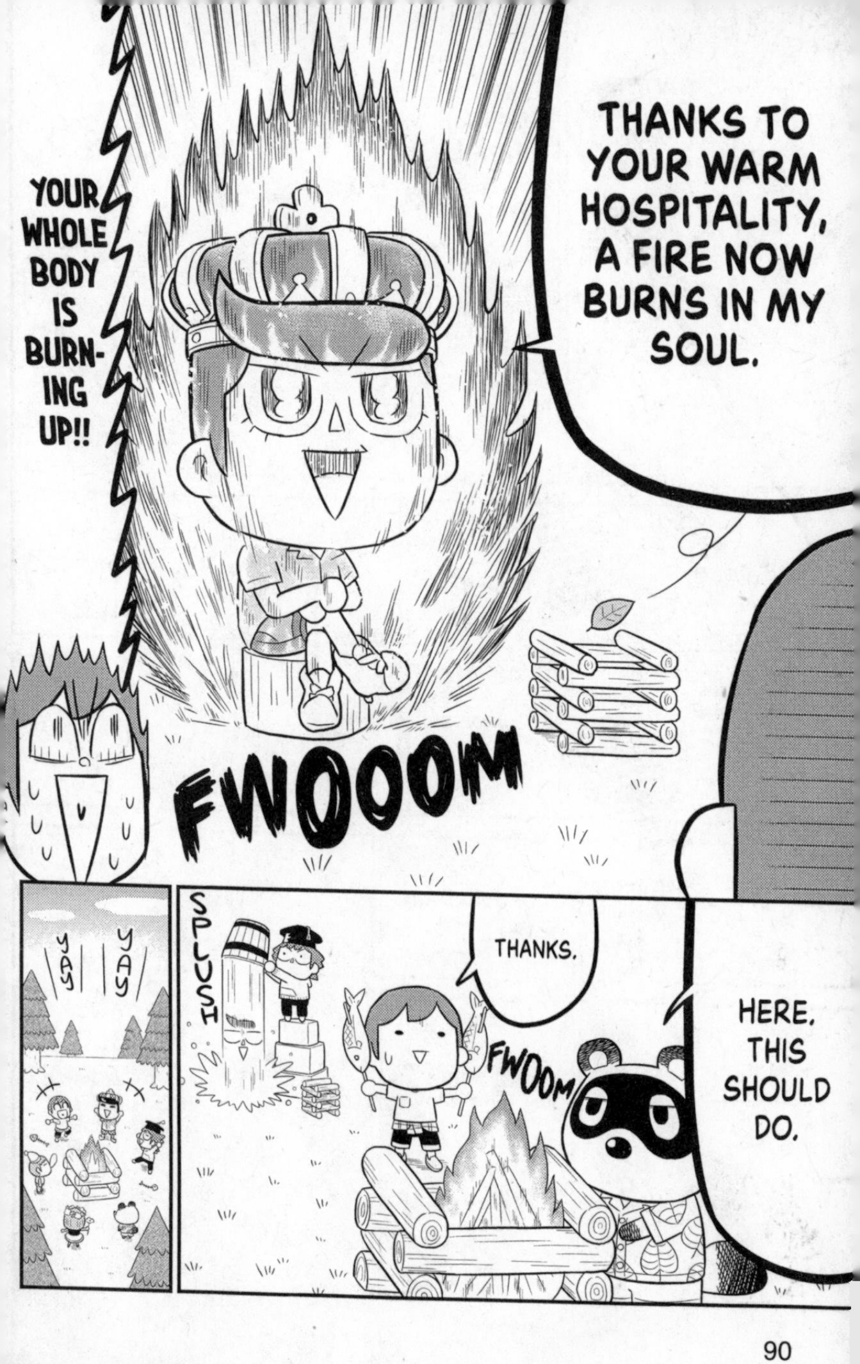
THANKS TO YOUR WARM HOSPITALITY, A FIRE NOW BURNS IN MY SOUL.
YOUR WHOLE BODY IS BURNING UP!!
FWOOOM
HERE, THIS SHOULD DO.
THANKS.
FWOOM
SPLUSH
YAY
YAY

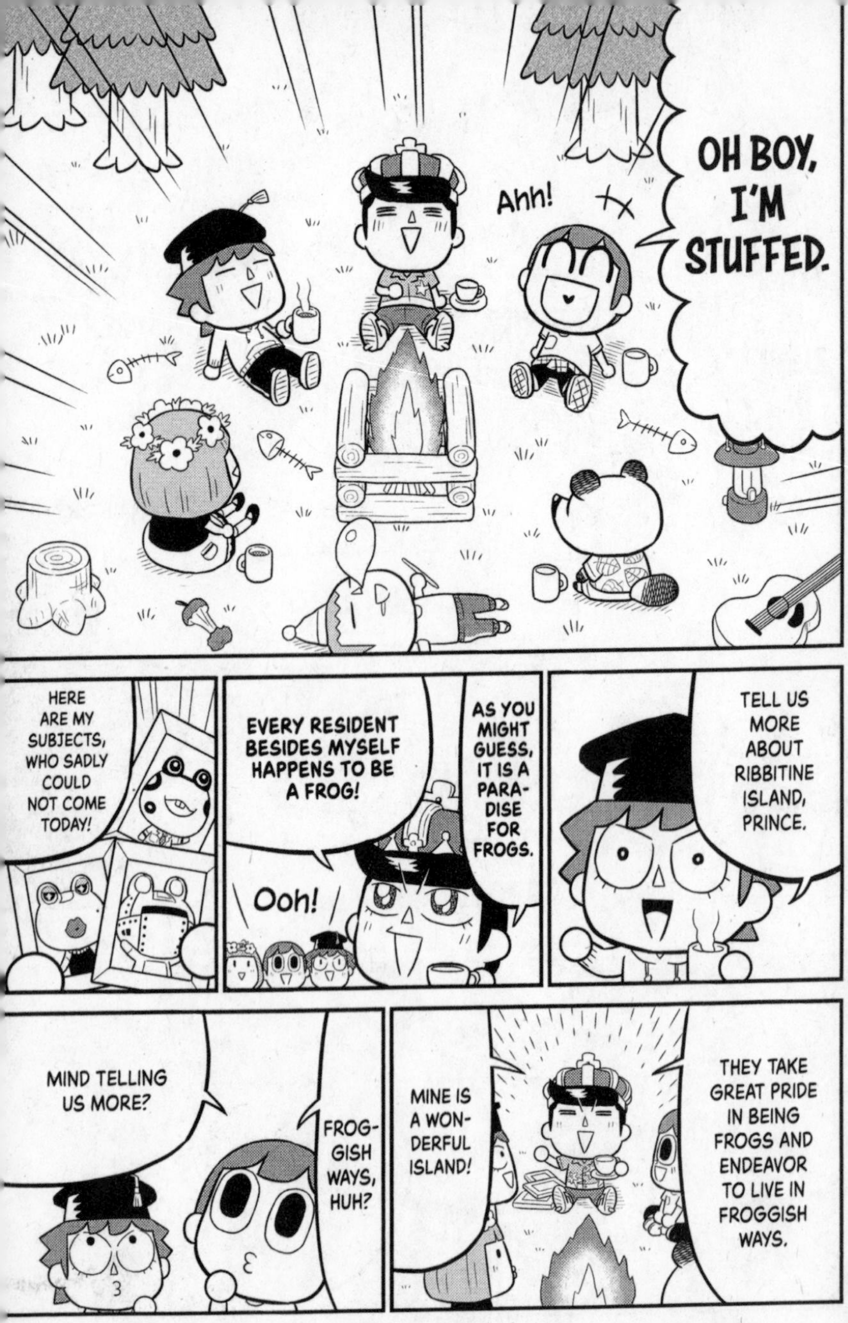
OH BOY, I'M STUFFED.
Ahh!
TELL US MORE ABOUT RIBBITINE ISLAND, PRINCE.
AS YOU MIGHT GUESS, IT IS A PARA-DISE FOR FROGS.
EVERY RESIDENT BESIDES MYSELF HAPPENS TO BE A FROG!
Ooh!
HERE ARE MY SUBJECTS, WHO SADLY COULD NOT COME TODAY!
THEY TAKE GREAT PRIDE IN BEING FROGS AND ENDEAVOR TO LIVE IN FROGGISH WAYS.
MINE IS A WON-DERFUL ISLAND!
FROG-GISH WAYS, HUH?
MIND TELLING US MORE?

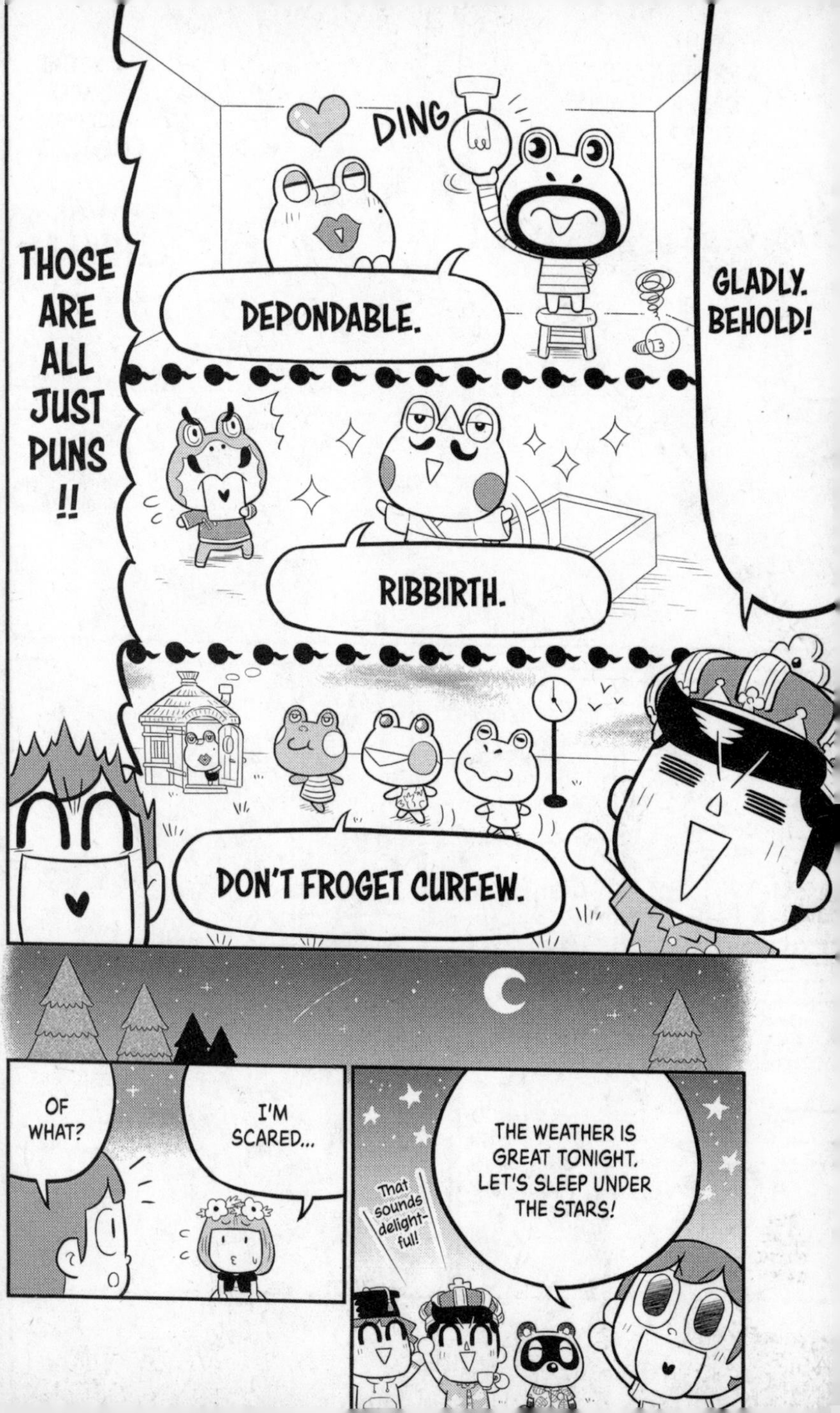
GLADLY. BEHOLD!
DING
DEPONDABLE.
RIBBIRTH.
DON'T FROGET CURFEW.
THOSE ARE ALL JUST PUNS!!
THE WEATHER IS GREAT TONIGHT. LET'S SLEEP UNDER THE STARS!
That sounds delight-ful!
I'M SCARED...
OF WHAT?

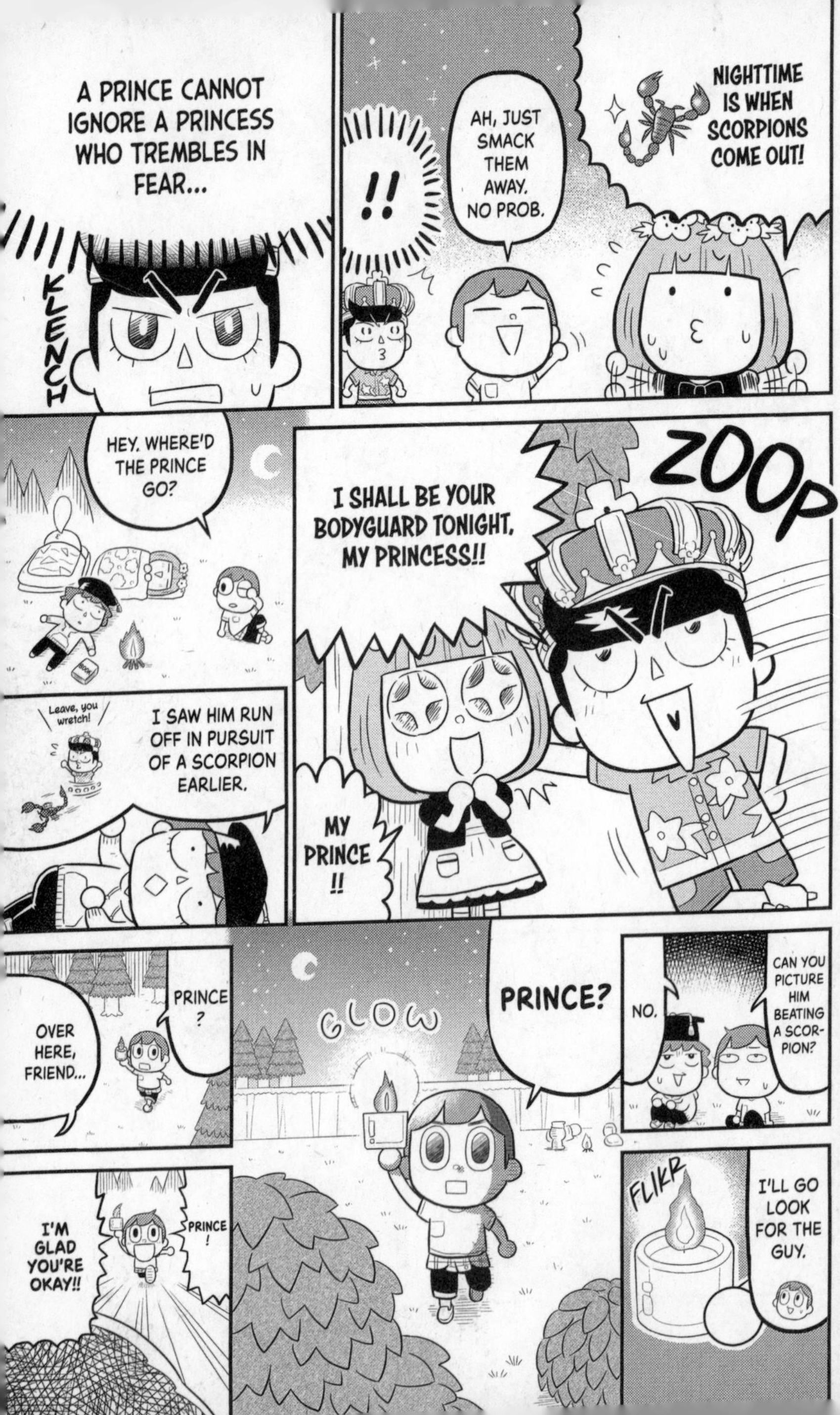

NIGHTTIME IS WHEN SCORPIONS COME OUT!
!!
AH, JUST SMACK THEM AWAY. NO PROB.
A PRINCE CANNOT IGNORE A PRINCESS WHO TREMBLES IN FEAR...
KLENCH
ZOOP
I SHALL BE YOUR BODYGUARD TONIGHT, MY PRINCESS!!
MY PRINCE!!
HEY. WHERE'D THE PRINCE GO?
BOOK
I SAW HIM RUN OFF IN PURSUIT OF A SCORPION EARLIER.
Leave, you wretch!
CAN YOU PICTURE HIM BEATING A SCORPION?
NO.
I'LL GO LOOK FOR THE GUY.
FLIKR
PRINCE?
GLOW
PRINCE?
OVER HERE, FRIEND...
PRINCE!
I'M GLAD YOU'RE OKAY!!

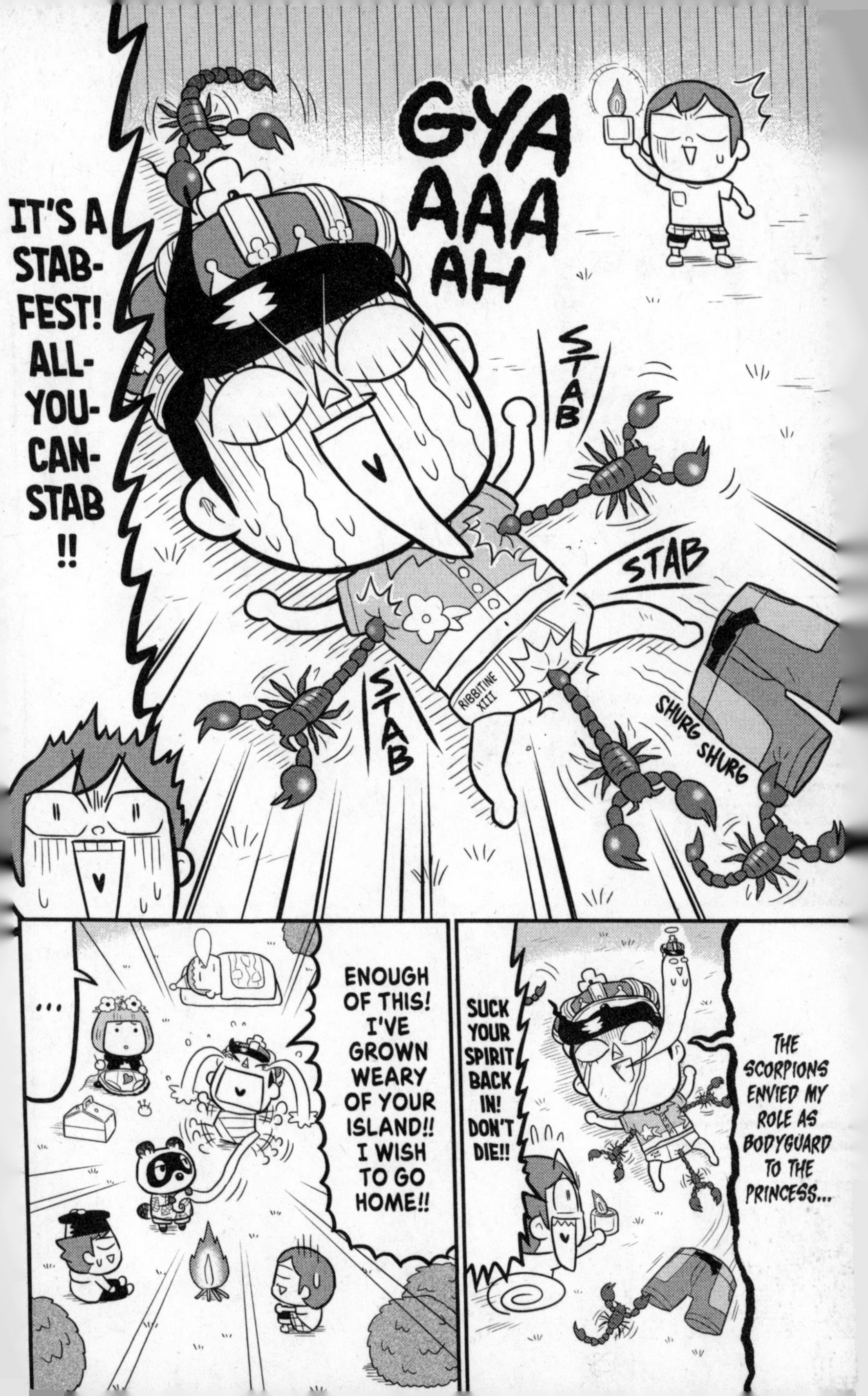
GYA AAA AH
STAB
STAB
RIBBITINE XIII
STAB
SHURG SHURG
IT'S A STAB-FEST! ALL-YOU-CAN-STAB!!
THE SCORPIONS ENVIED MY ROLE AS BODYGUARD TO THE PRINCESS...
SUCK YOUR SPIRIT BACK IN! DON'T DIE!!
ENOUGH OF THIS! I'VE GROWN WEARY OF YOUR ISLAND!! I WISH TO GO HOME!!
...

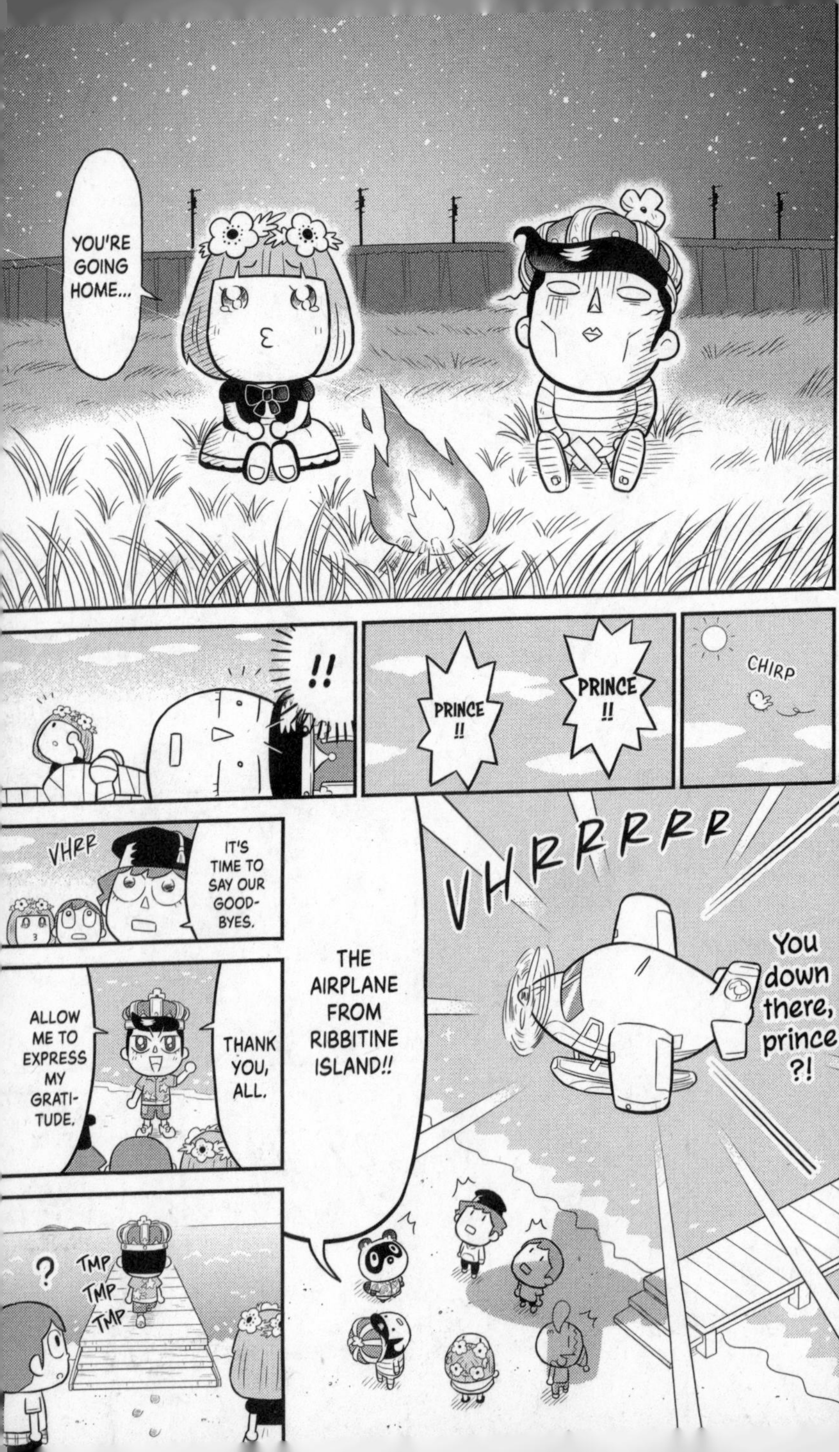

YOU'RE GOING HOME...
CHIRP
PRINCE!!
PRINCE!!
!!
VHRRRRRR
You down there, prince?!
THE AIRPLANE FROM RIBBITINE ISLAND!!
VHRR
IT'S TIME TO SAY OUR GOOD-BYES.
THANK YOU, ALL.
ALLOW ME TO EXPRESS MY GRATI-TUDE.
TMP
TMP
TMP
?

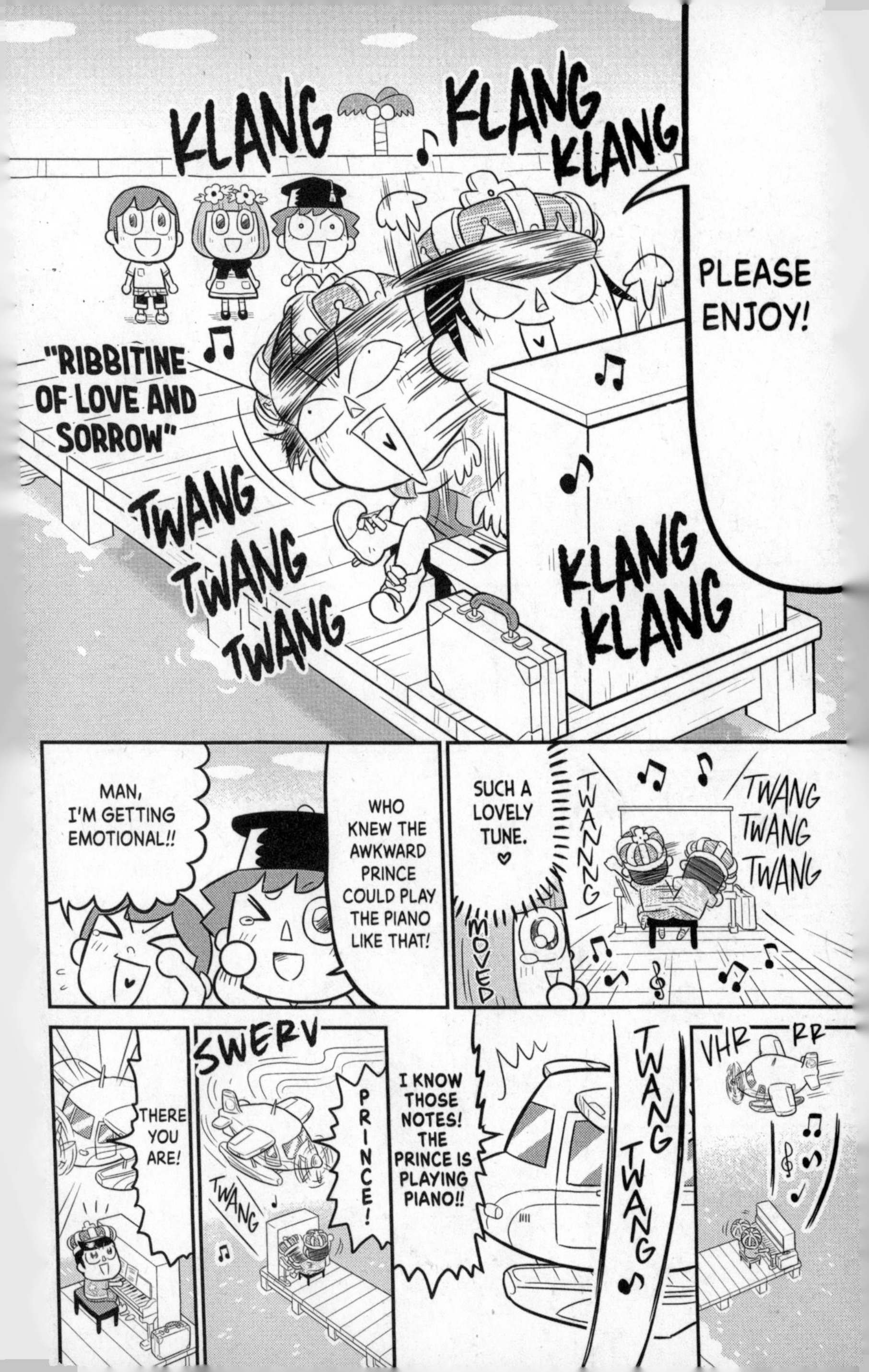
PLEASE ENJOY!
KLANG KLANG KLANG
"RIBBITINE OF LOVE AND SORROW"
TWANG TWANG TWANG
KLANG KLANG
TWANG TWANG TWANG
TWANNNG
SUCH A LOVELY TUNE.
MOVED
WHO KNEW THE AWKWARD PRINCE COULD PLAY THE PIANO LIKE THAT!
MAN, I'M GETTING EMOTIONAL!!
VHR RR
TWANG TWANG
I KNOW THOSE NOTES! THE PRINCE IS PLAYING PIANO!!
SWERV
PRINCE!
TWANG
THERE YOU ARE!

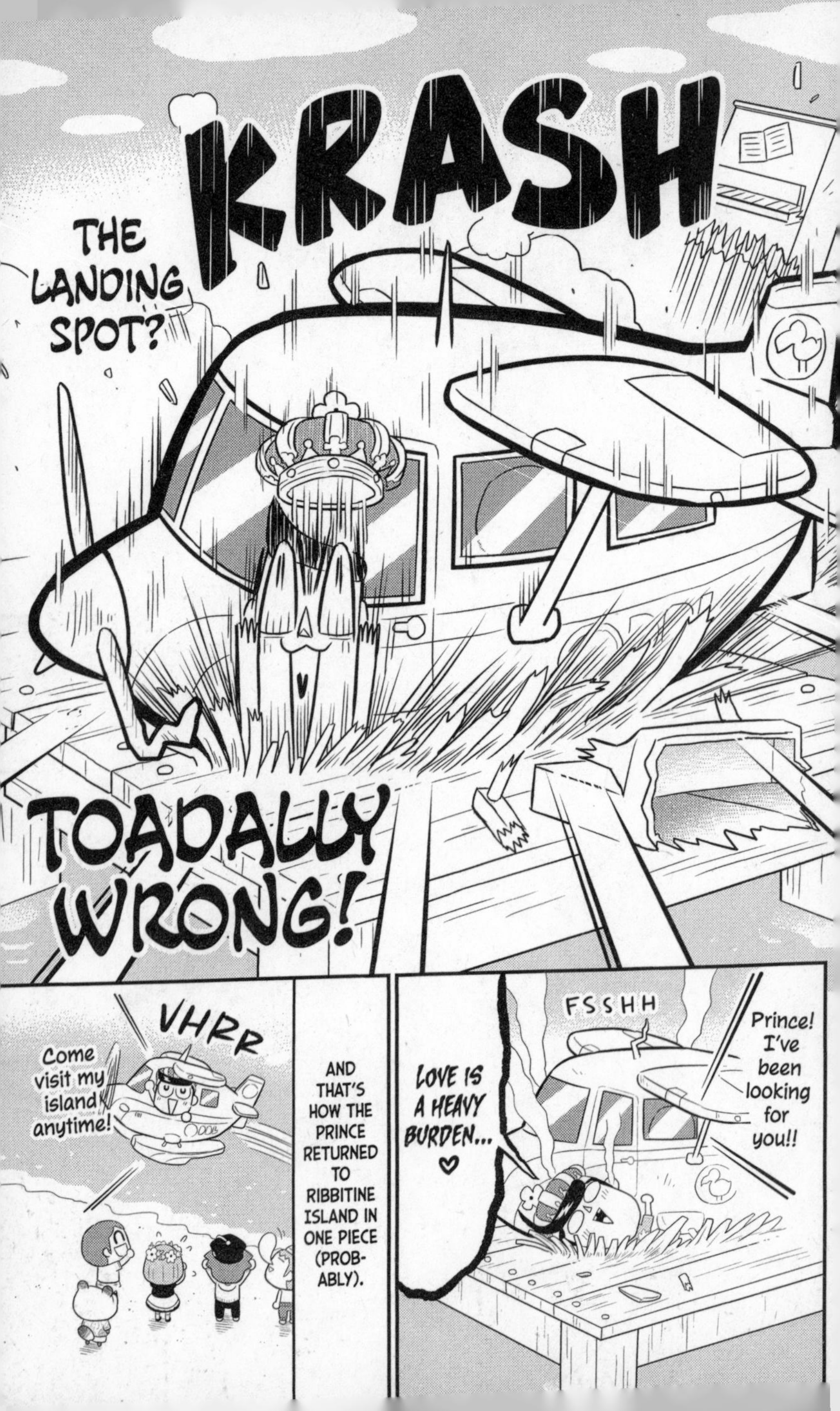
KRASH
THE LANDING SPOT?
TOADALLY WRONG!
FSSHH
Prince! I've been looking for you!!
LOVE IS A HEAVY BURDEN... ♡
AND THAT'S HOW THE PRINCE RETURNED TO RIBBITINE ISLAND IN ONE PIECE (PROB-ABLY).
VHRR
Come visit my island anytime!

Welcome to Animal Crossing New Horizons

Deserted Island Diary

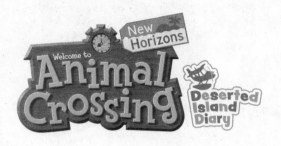

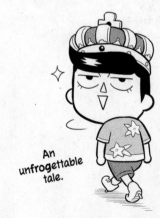

An unfrogettable tale.

HOW TO HAVE A PROPER HALLOWEEN

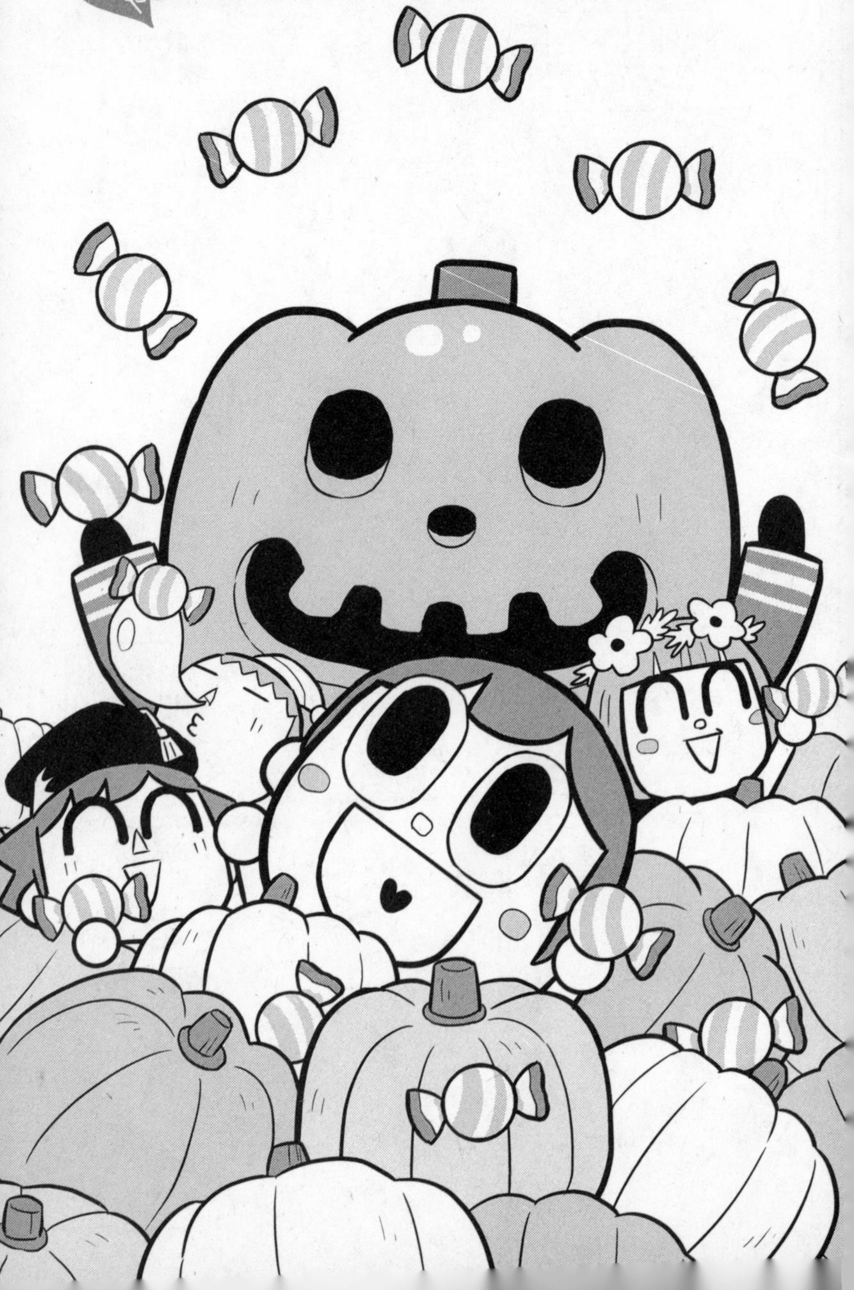

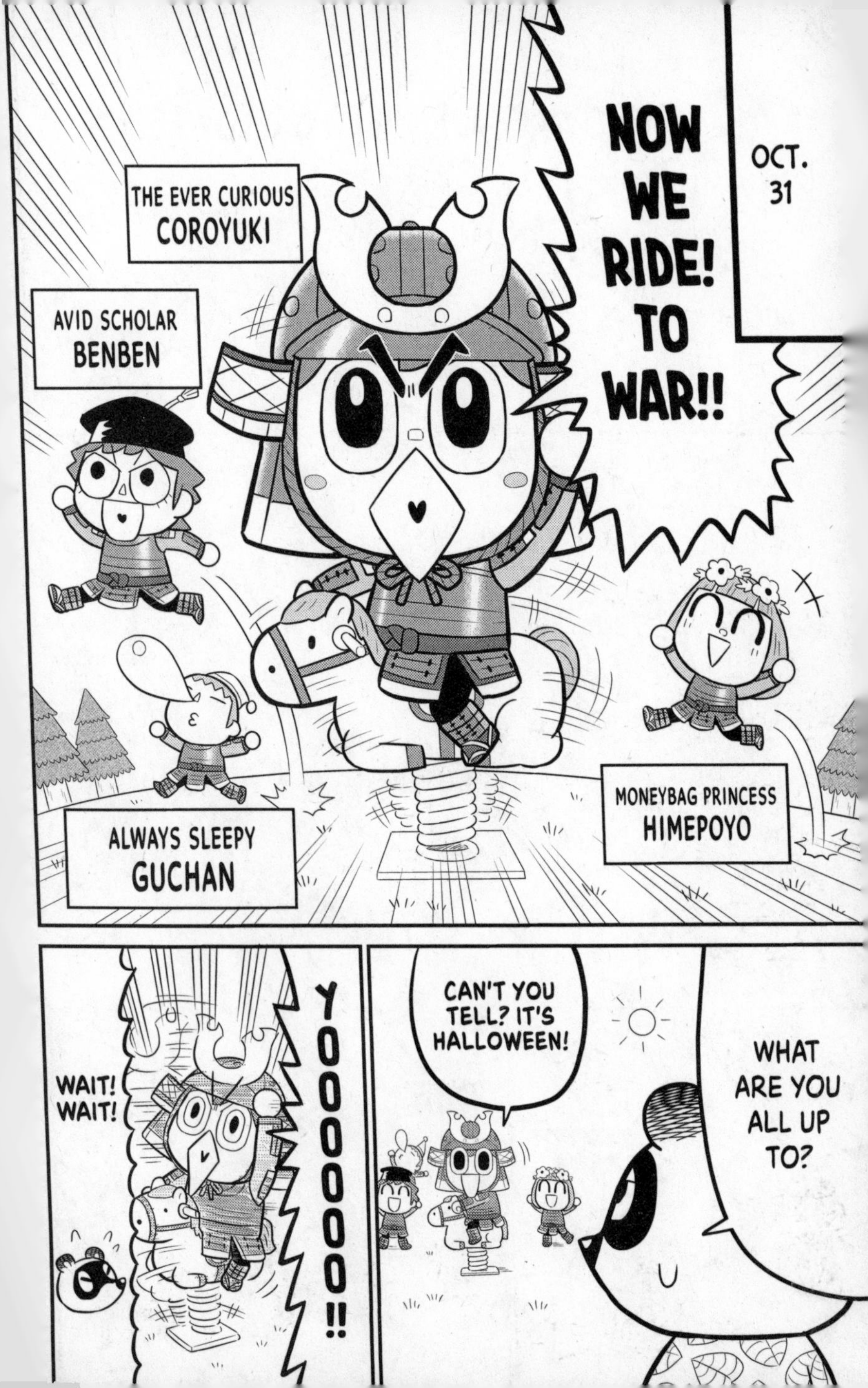
OCT. 31
NOW WE RIDE! TO WAR!!
THE EVER CURIOUS COROYUKI
AVID SCHOLAR BENBEN
MONEYBAG PRINCESS HIMEPOYO
ALWAYS SLEEPY GUCHAN
WHAT ARE YOU ALL UP TO?
CAN'T YOU TELL? IT'S HALLOWEEN!
YOOOOOOO!!
WAIT! WAIT!

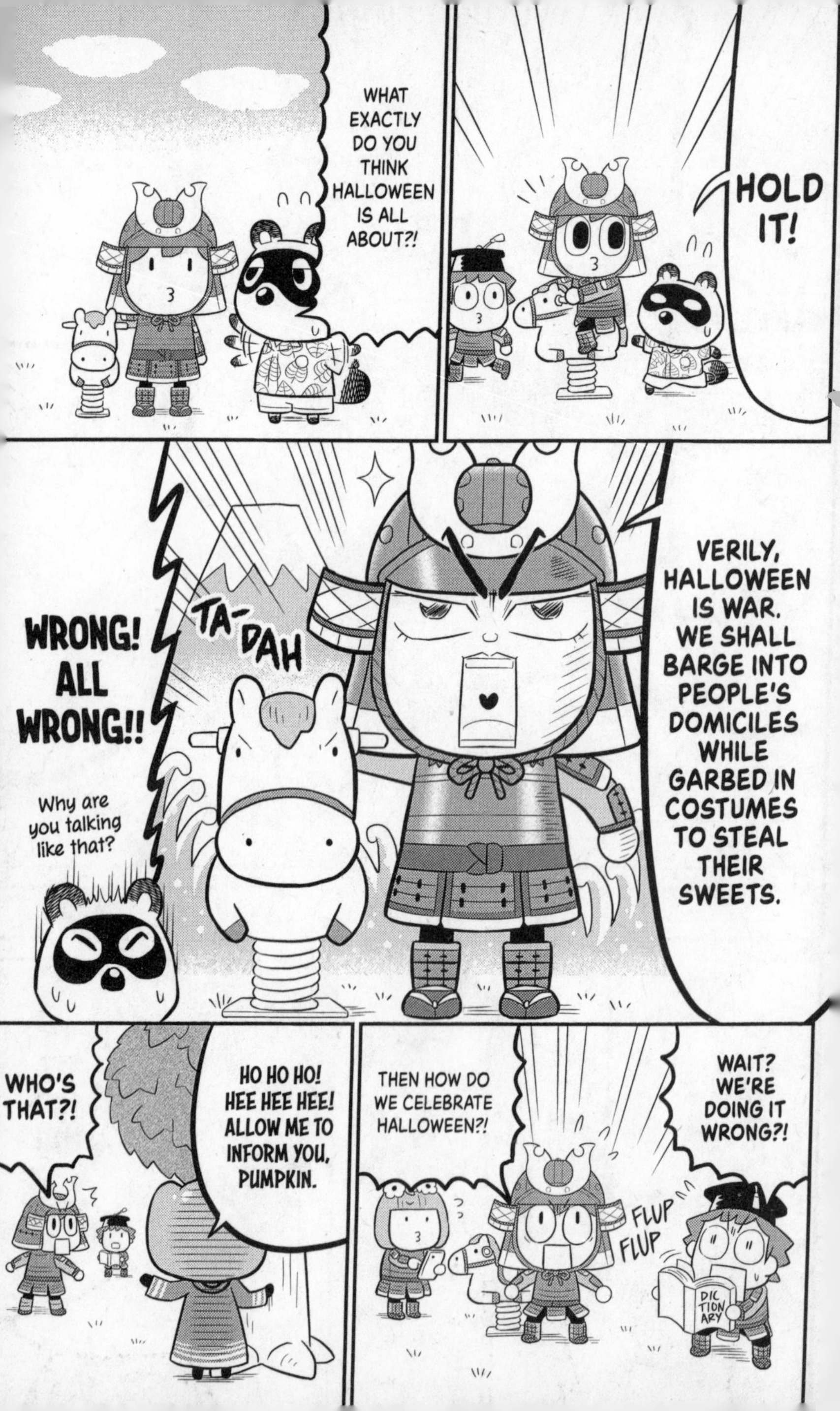
HOLD IT!
WHAT EXACTLY DO YOU THINK HALLOWEEN IS ALL ABOUT?!
VERILY, HALLOWEEN IS WAR. WE SHALL BARGE INTO PEOPLE'S DOMICILES WHILE GARBED IN COSTUMES TO STEAL THEIR SWEETS.
TA-DAH
WRONG! ALL WRONG!!
Why are you talking like that?
WAIT? WE'RE DOING IT WRONG?!
THEN HOW DO WE CELEBRATE HALLOWEEN?!
FLUP FLUP
DICTIONARY
HO HO HO! HEE HEE HEE! ALLOW ME TO INFORM YOU, PUMPKIN.
WHO'S THAT?!

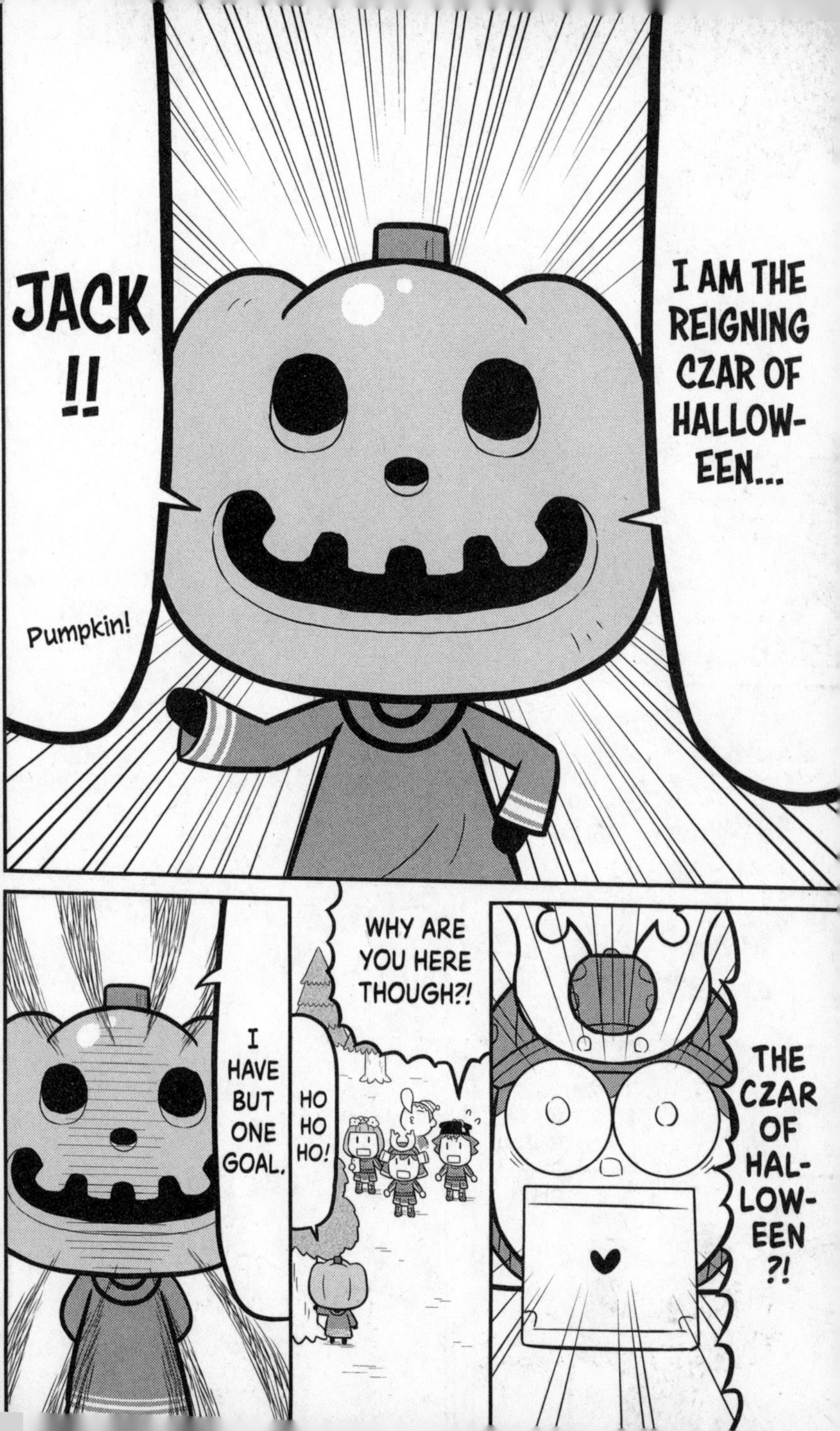
I AM THE REIGNING CZAR OF HALLOW-EEN...
JACK !!
Pumpkin!
THE CZAR OF HAL-LOW-EEN ?!
WHY ARE YOU HERE THOUGH?!
HO HO HO!
I HAVE BUT ONE GOAL.

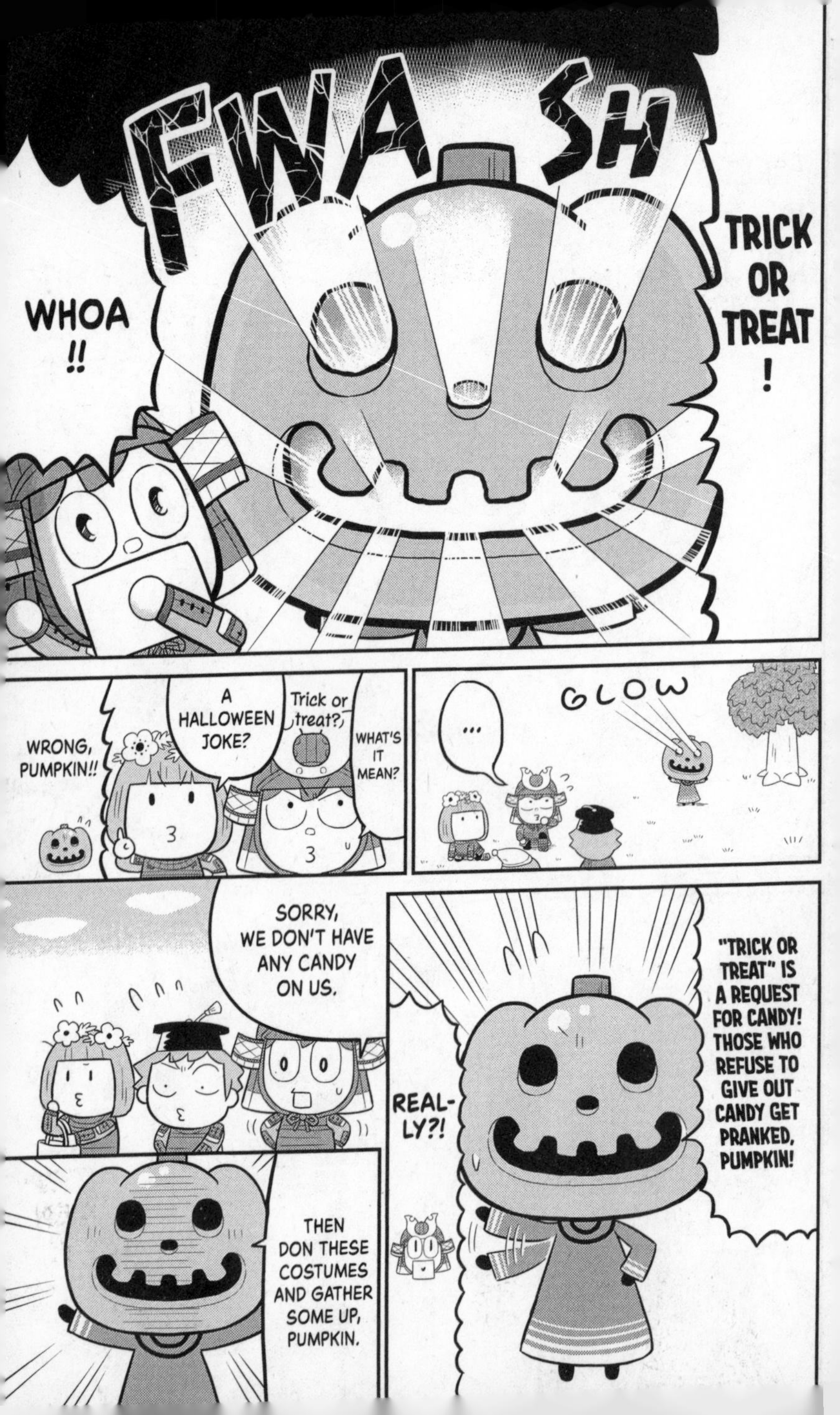
TRICK OR TREAT!
FWA SH
WHOA!!
GLOW
...
WHAT'S IT MEAN?
Trick or treat?
A HALLOWEEN JOKE?
WRONG, PUMPKIN!!
"TRICK OR TREAT" IS A REQUEST FOR CANDY! THOSE WHO REFUSE TO GIVE OUT CANDY GET PRANKED, PUMPKIN!
REAL-LY?!
SORRY, WE DON'T HAVE ANY CANDY ON US.
THEN DON THESE COSTUMES AND GATHER SOME UP, PUMPKIN.

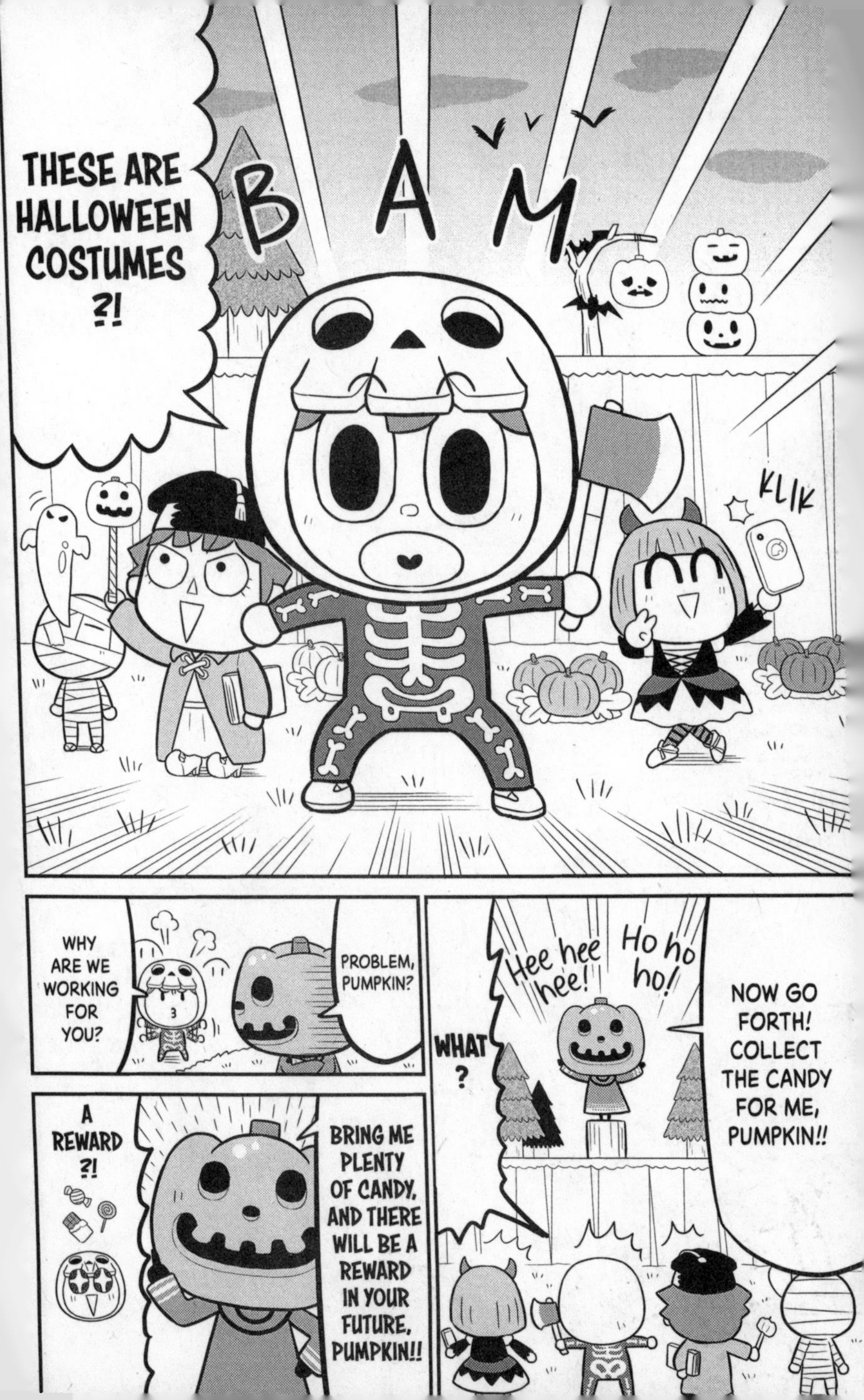
BAM
THESE ARE HALLOWEEN COSTUMES ?!
KLIK
Ho ho ho!
Hee hee hee!
NOW GO FORTH! COLLECT THE CANDY FOR ME, PUMPKIN!!
WHAT ?
PROBLEM, PUMPKIN?
WHY ARE WE WORKING FOR YOU?
BRING ME PLENTY OF CANDY, AND THERE WILL BE A REWARD IN YOUR FUTURE, PUMPKIN!!
A REWARD ?!

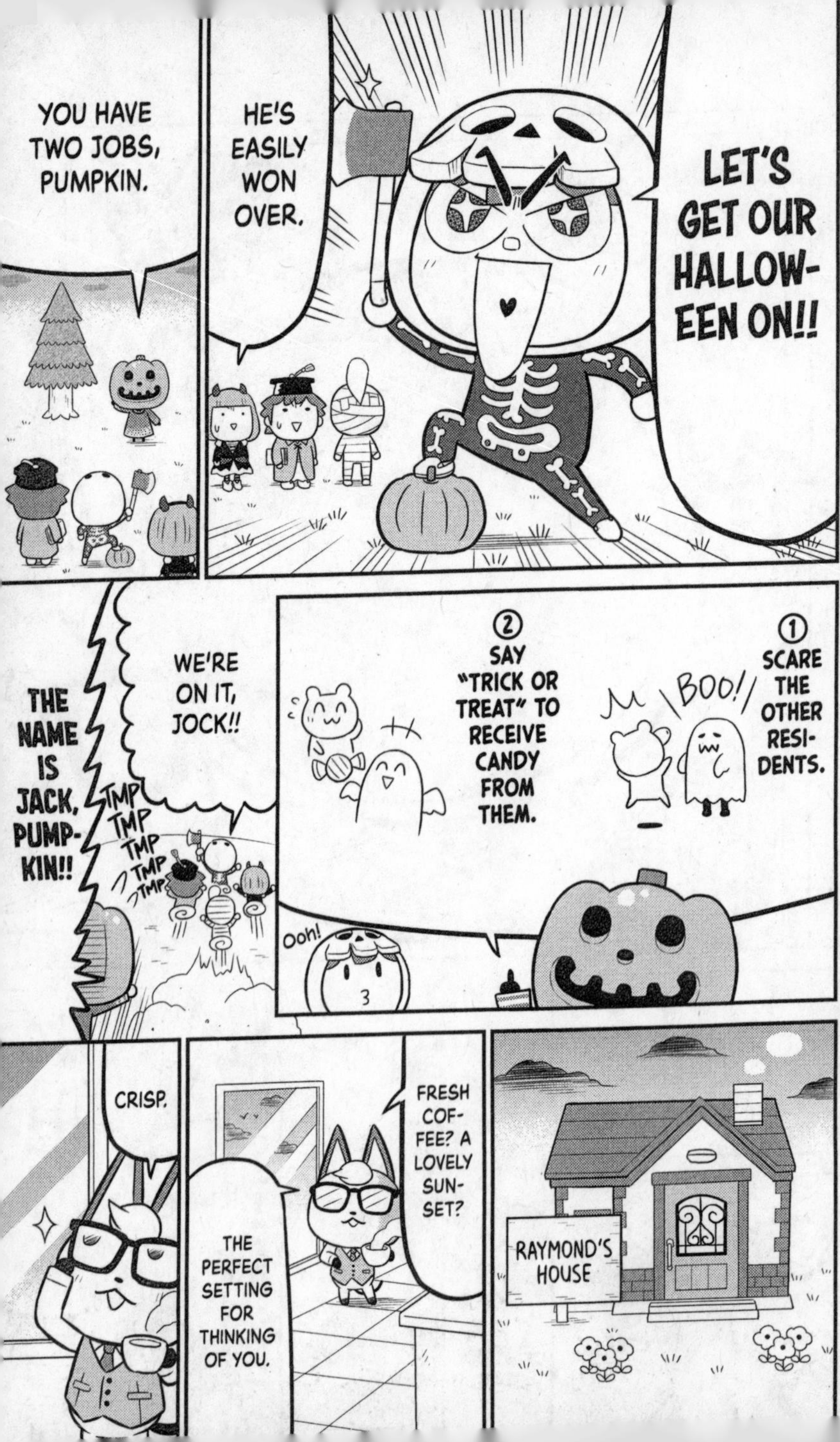

LET'S GET OUR HALLOW-EEN ON!!
HE'S EASILY WON OVER.
YOU HAVE TWO JOBS, PUMPKIN.
① SCARE THE OTHER RESI-DENTS.
BOO!!
② SAY "TRICK OR TREAT" TO RECEIVE CANDY FROM THEM.
Ooh!
WE'RE ON IT, JOCK!!
THE NAME IS JACK, PUMP-KIN!!
TMP TMP TMP TMP TMP
RAYMOND'S HOUSE
FRESH COF-FEE? A LOVELY SUN-SET?
THE PERFECT SETTING FOR THINKING OF YOU.
CRISP.

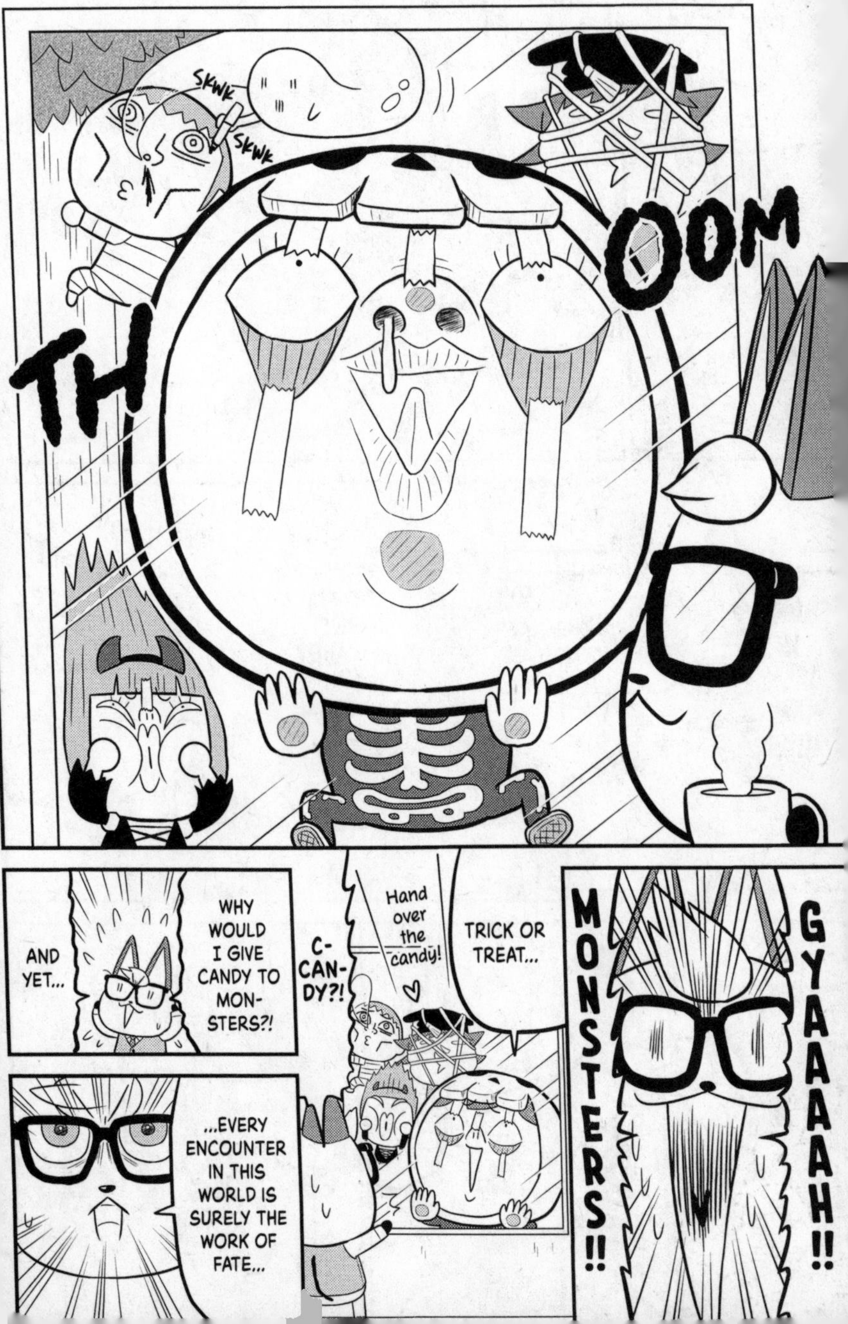
SKWK
SKWK
THOOM
GYAAAAH!!
MONSTERS!!
TRICK OR TREAT...
Hand over the candy! ♥
C-CANDY?!
WHY WOULD I GIVE CANDY TO MONSTERS?!
AND YET...
...EVERY ENCOUNTER IN THIS WORLD IS SURELY THE WORK OF FATE...

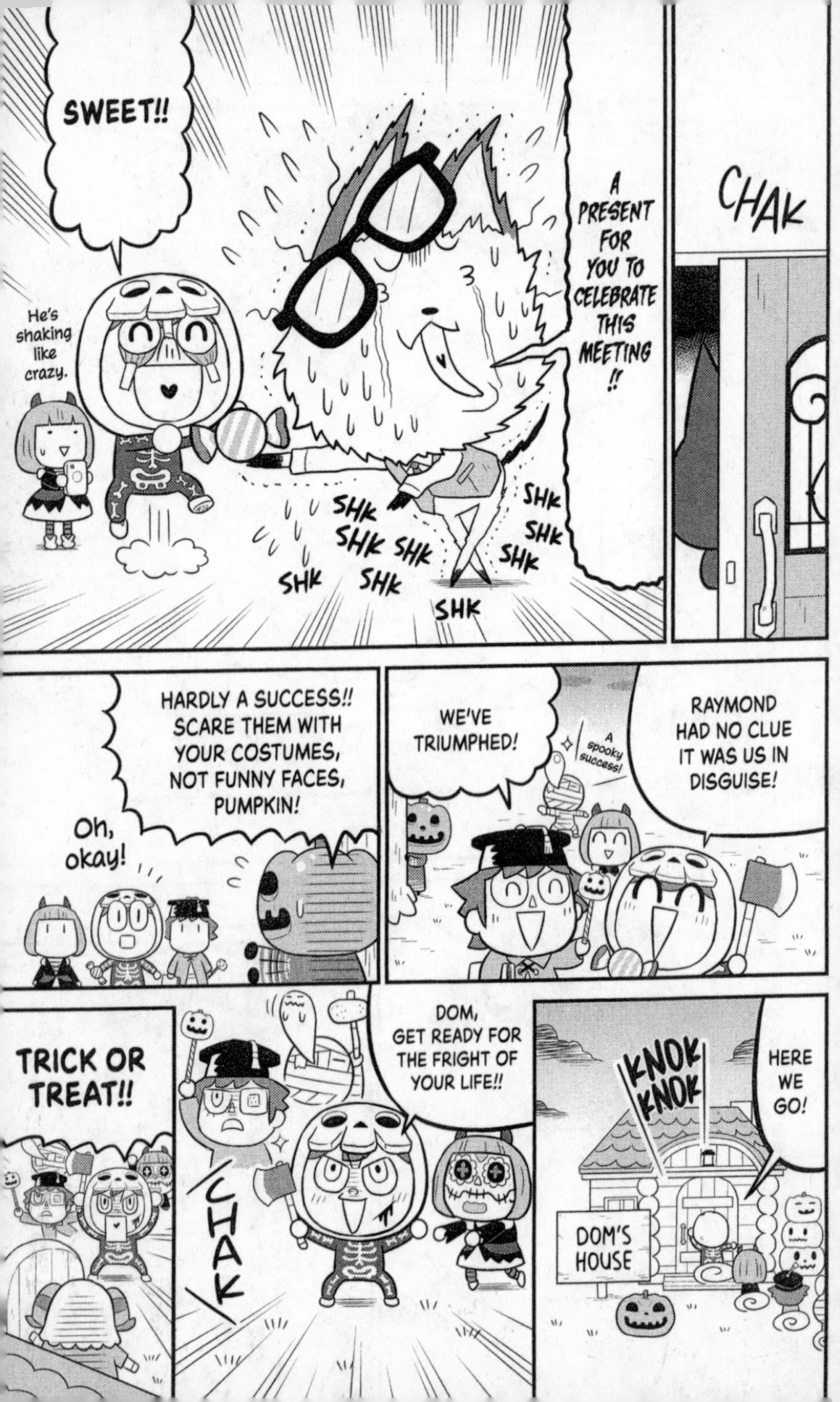
CHAK
A PRESENT FOR YOU TO CELEBRATE THIS MEETING!!
SHK SHK SHK SHK SHK SHK SHK SHK
SWEET!!
He's shaking like crazy.
RAYMOND HAD NO CLUE IT WAS US IN DISGUISE!
A spooky success!
WE'VE TRIUMPHED!
HARDLY A SUCCESS!! SCARE THEM WITH YOUR COSTUMES, NOT FUNNY FACES, PUMPKIN!
Oh, okay!
HERE WE GO!
KNOK KNOK
DOM'S HOUSE
DOM, GET READY FOR THE FRIGHT OF YOUR LIFE!!
CHAK
TRICK OR TREAT!!

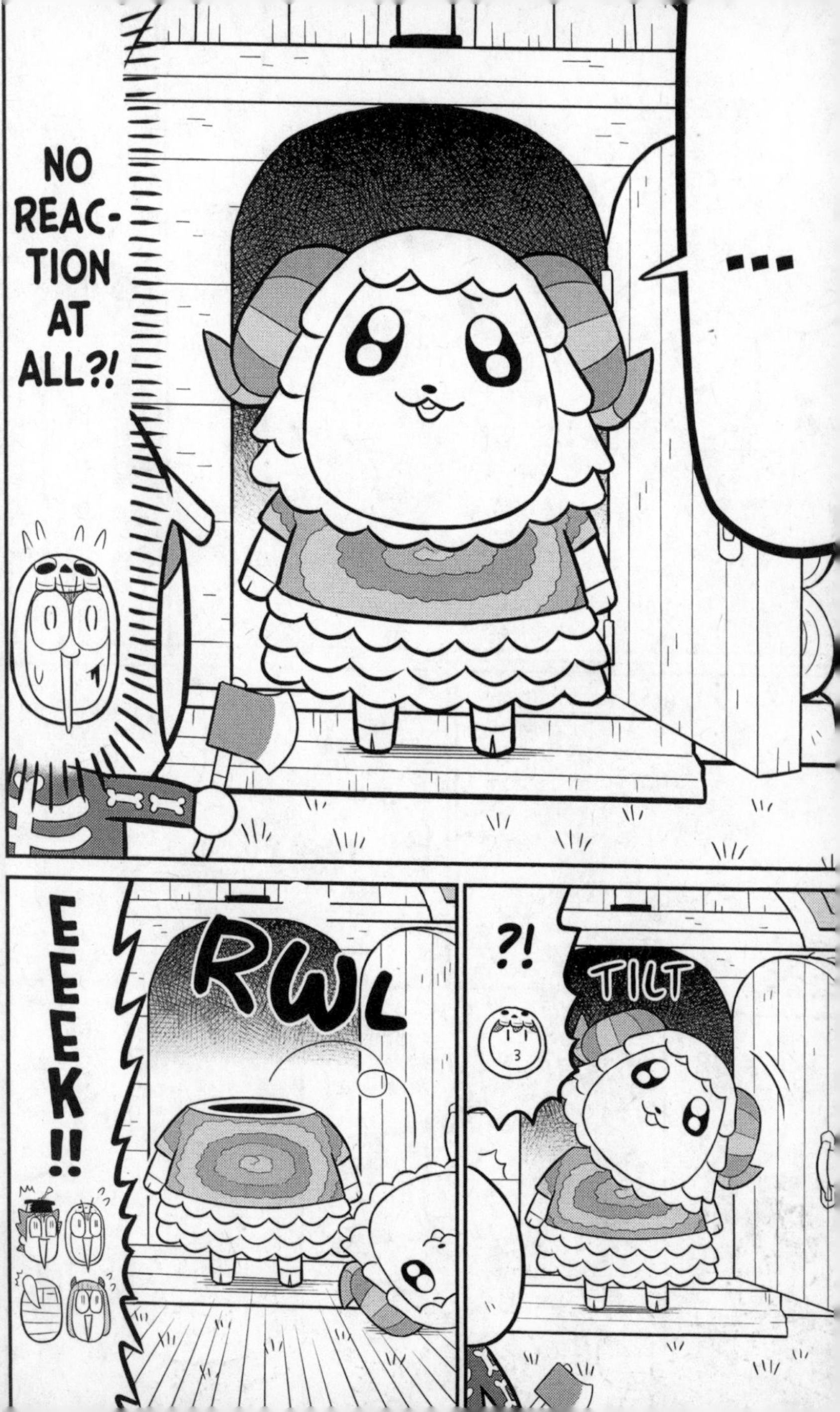
...
NO REAC-TION AT ALL?!
?!
TILT
RWL
EEEEK!!

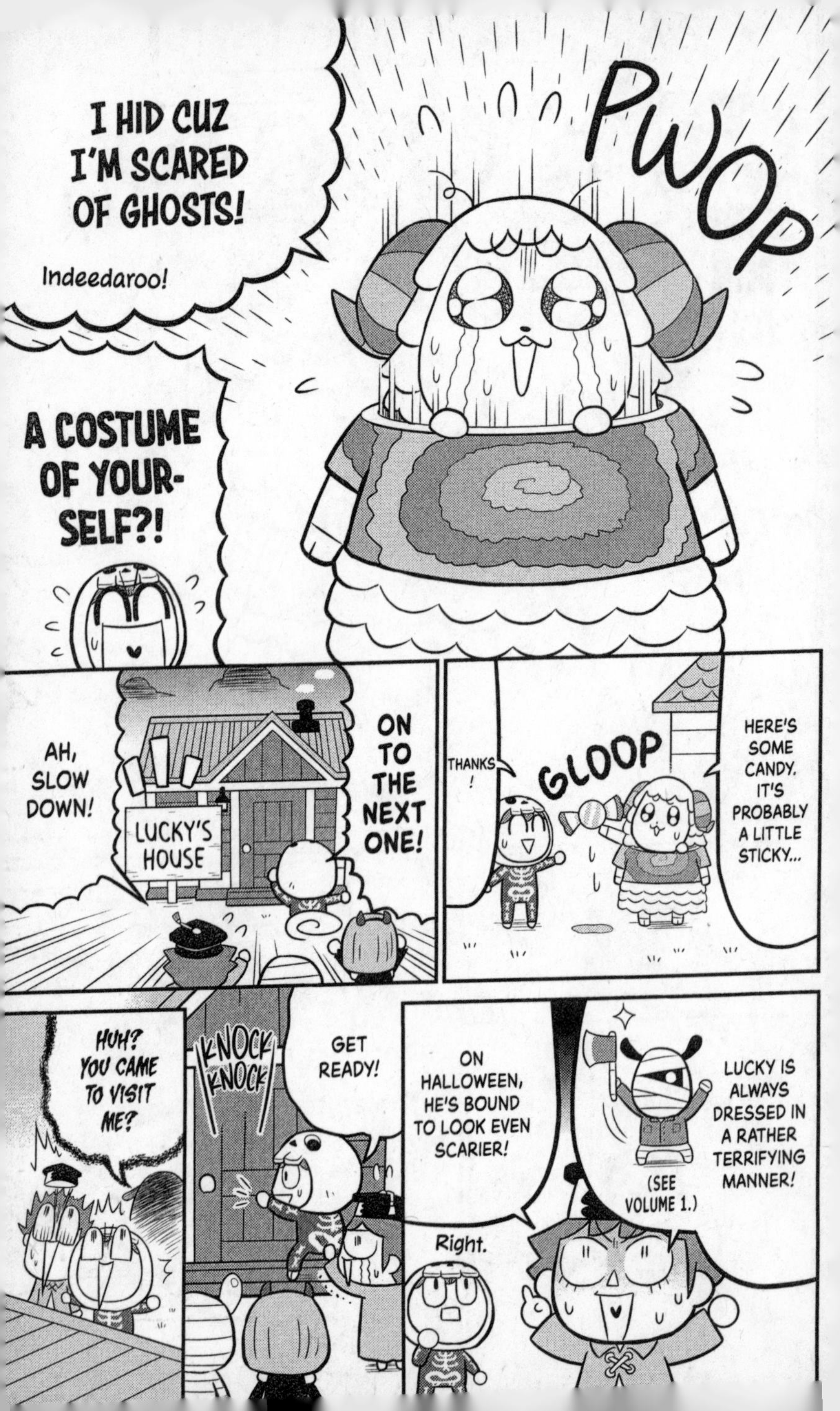

PWOOP
I HID CUZ I'M SCARED OF GHOSTS!
Indeedaroo!
A COSTUME OF YOURSELF?!
HERE'S SOME CANDY. IT'S PROBABLY A LITTLE STICKY...
GLOOP
THANKS!
ON TO THE NEXT ONE!
AH, SLOW DOWN!
LUCKY'S HOUSE
LUCKY IS ALWAYS DRESSED IN A RATHER TERRIFYING MANNER!
(SEE VOLUME 1.)
ON HALLOWEEN, HE'S BOUND TO LOOK EVEN SCARIER!
Right.
GET READY!
KNOCK KNOCK
HUH? YOU CAME TO VISIT ME?

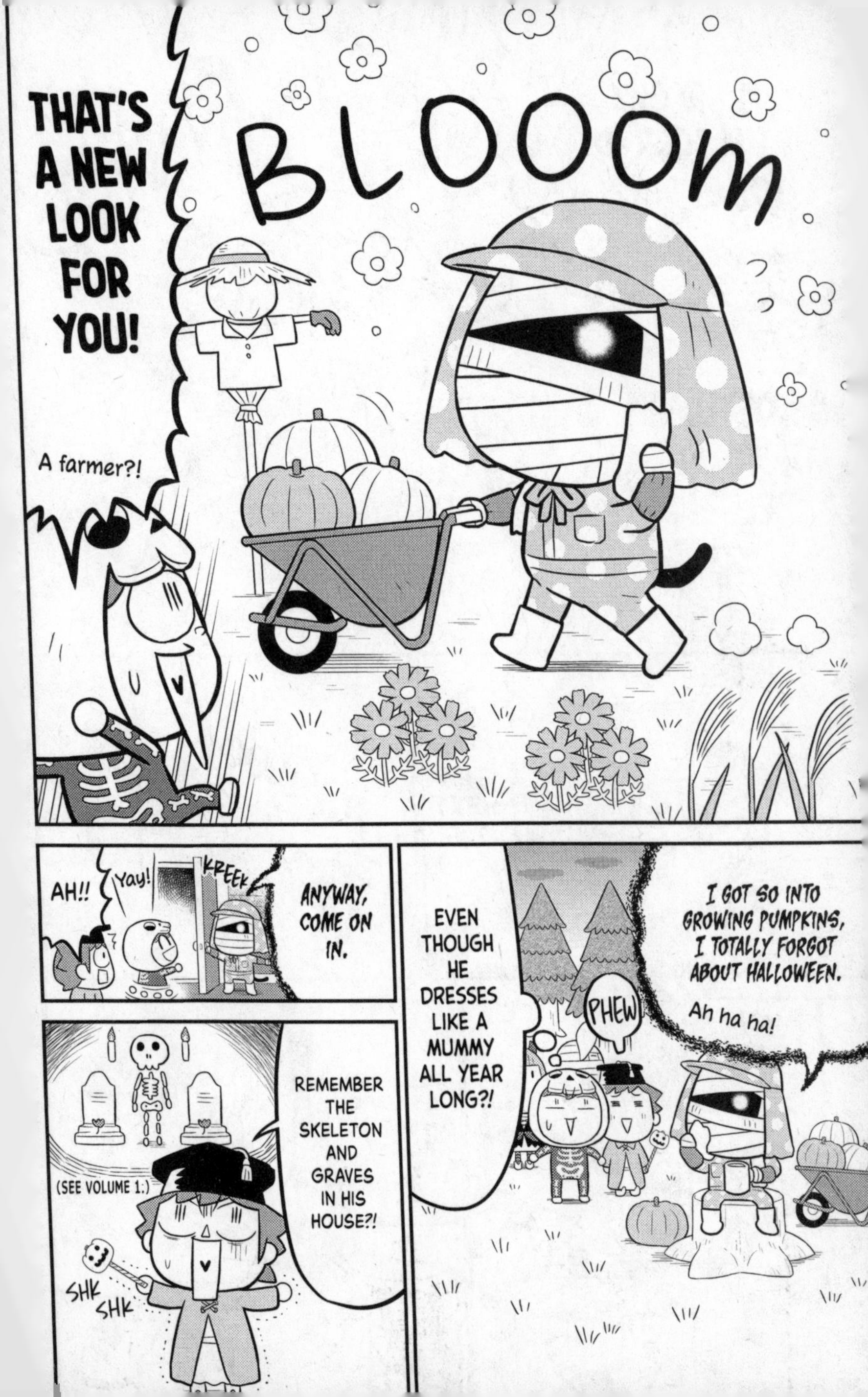
BLOOOM
THAT'S A NEW LOOK FOR YOU!
A farmer?!
I GOT SO INTO GROWING PUMPKINS, I TOTALLY FORGOT ABOUT HALLOWEEN.
Ah ha ha!
PHEW
EVEN THOUGH HE DRESSES LIKE A MUMMY ALL YEAR LONG?!
ANYWAY, COME ON IN.
KREEK
Yay!
AH!!
REMEMBER THE SKELETON AND GRAVES IN HIS HOUSE?!
(SEE VOLUME 1.)
SHK SHK

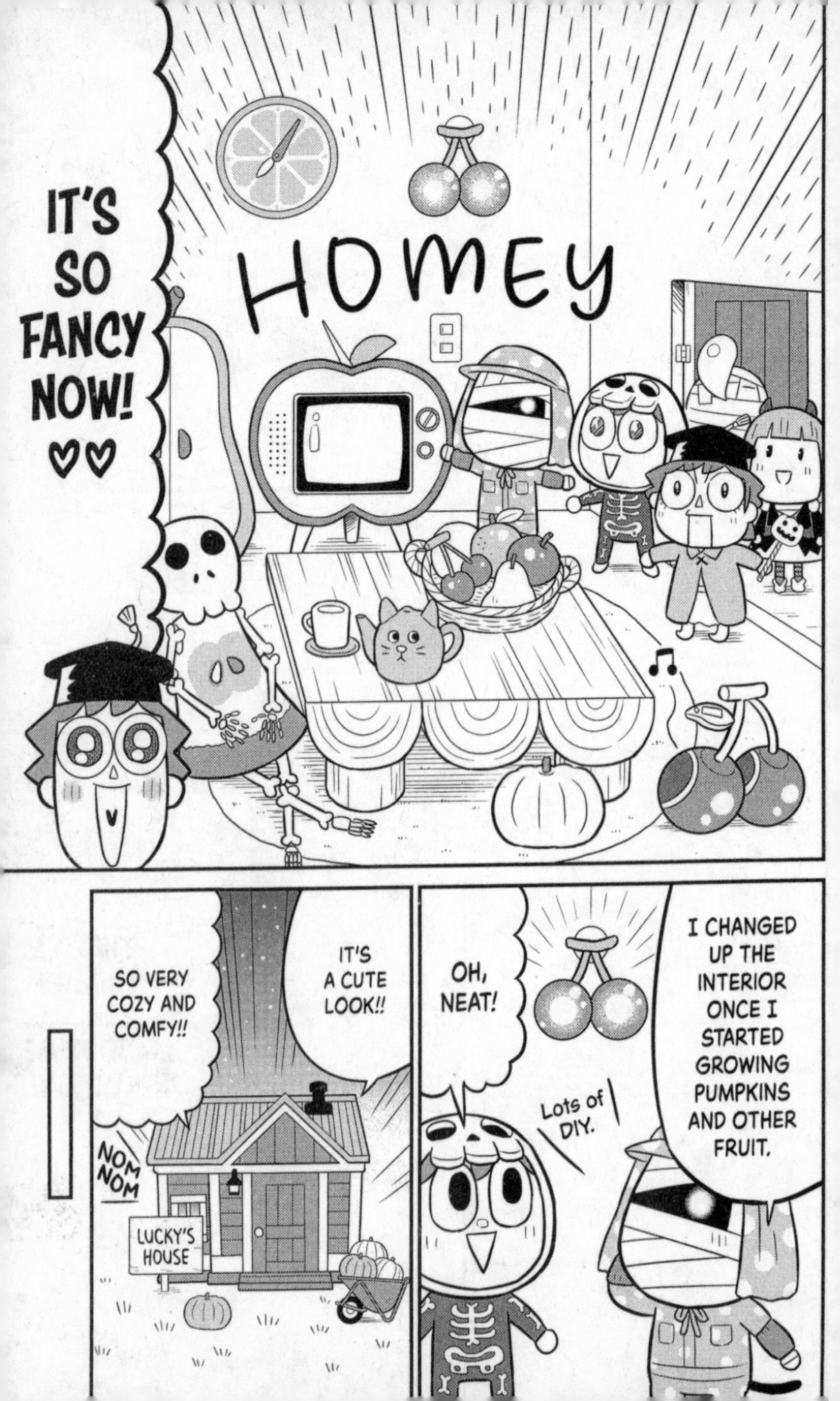
HOMEY
IT'S SO FANCY NOW! ♡♡
I CHANGED UP THE INTERIOR ONCE I STARTED GROWING PUMPKINS AND OTHER FRUIT.
Lots of DIY.
OH, NEAT!
IT'S A CUTE LOOK!!
SO VERY COZY AND COMFY!!
NOM NOM
LUCKY'S HOUSE

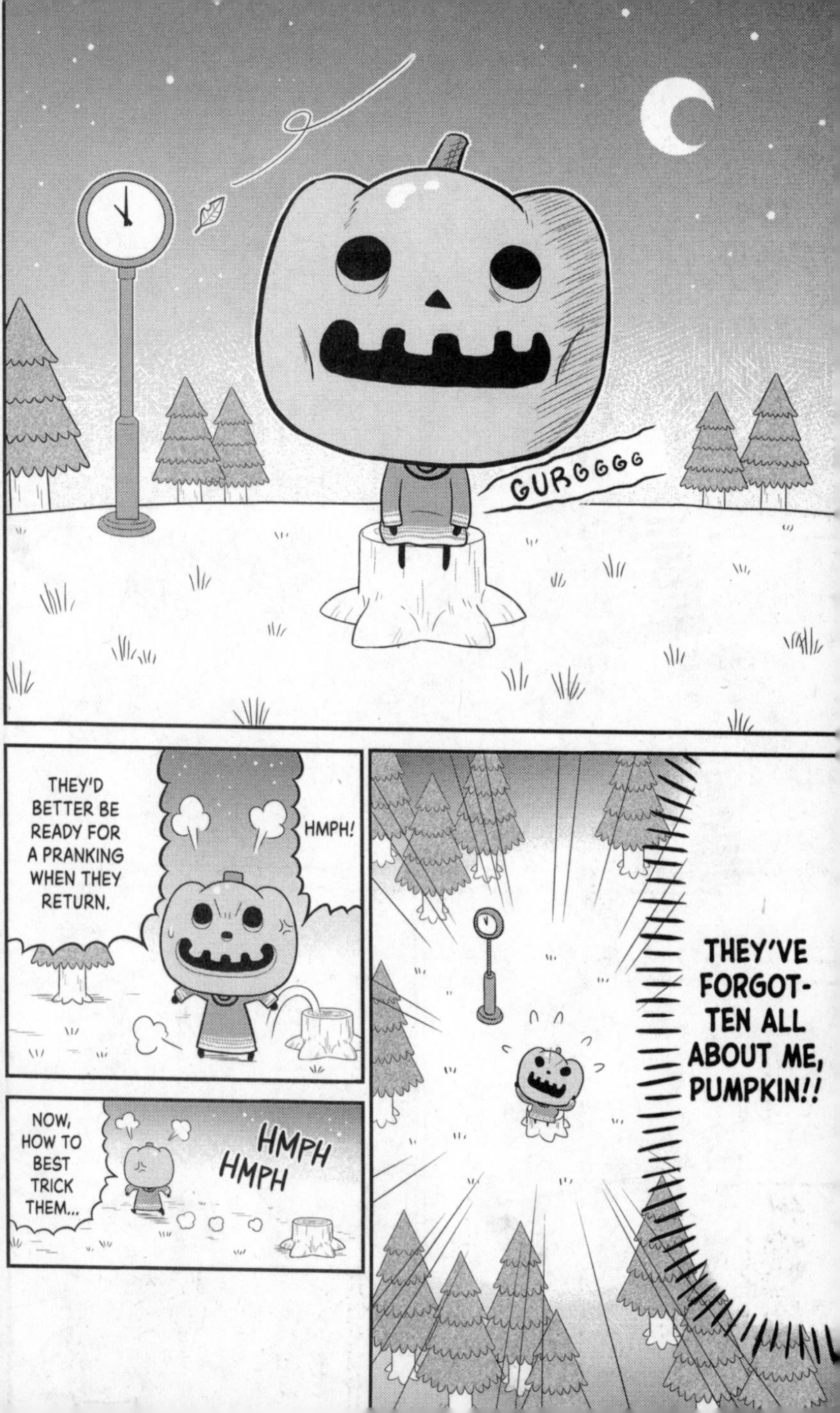
GURGGGG
THEY'VE FORGOT-TEN ALL ABOUT ME, PUMPKIN!!
THEY'D BETTER BE READY FOR A PRANKING WHEN THEY RETURN.
HMPH!
NOW, HOW TO BEST TRICK THEM...
HMPH HMPH

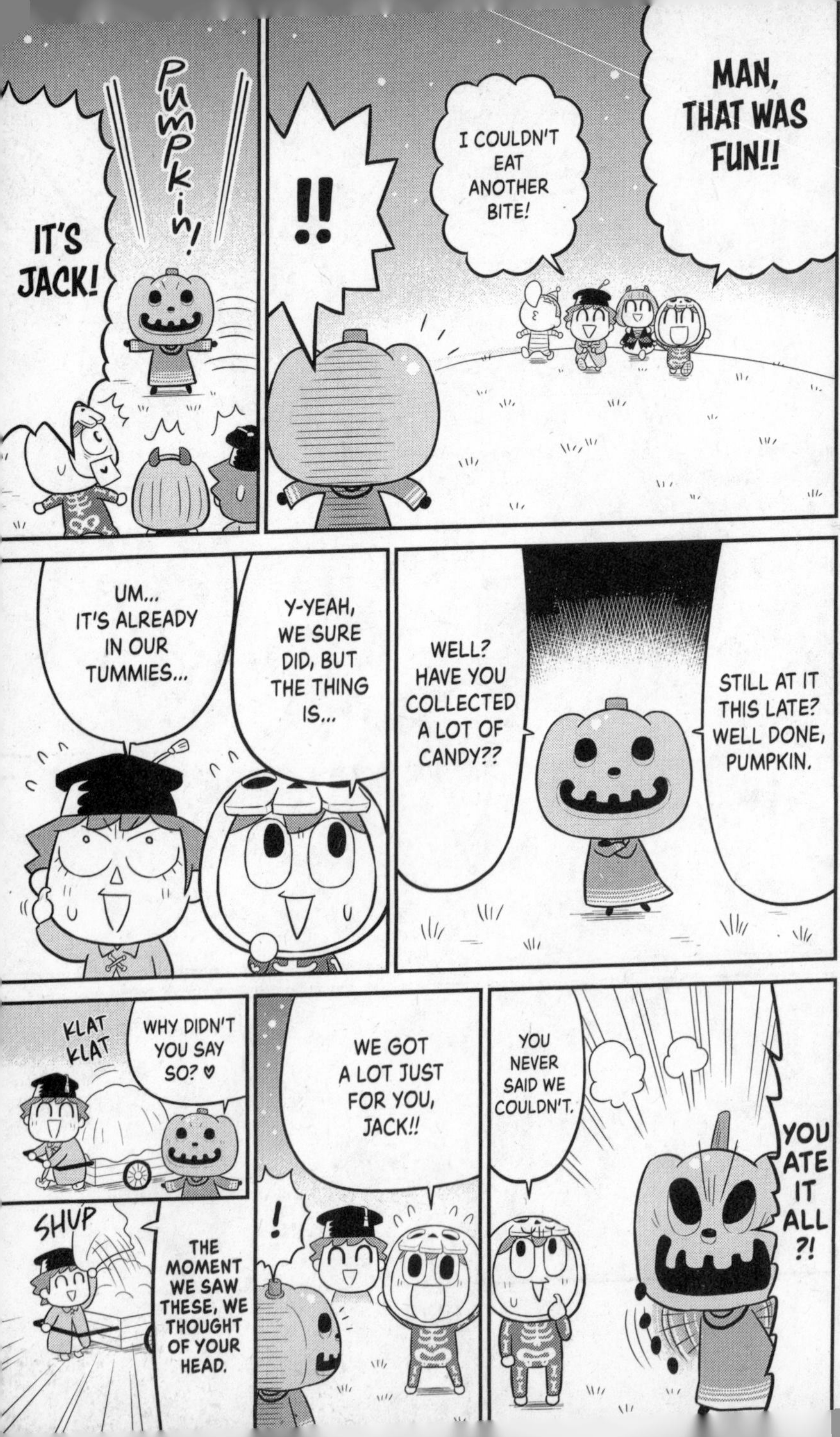
MAN, THAT WAS FUN!!
I COULDN'T EAT ANOTHER BITE!
!!
Pumpkin!
IT'S JACK!
STILL AT IT THIS LATE? WELL DONE, PUMPKIN.
WELL? HAVE YOU COLLECTED A LOT OF CANDY??
Y-YEAH, WE SURE DID, BUT THE THING IS...
UM... IT'S ALREADY IN OUR TUMMIES...
YOU ATE IT ALL?!
YOU NEVER SAID WE COULDN'T.
WE GOT A LOT JUST FOR YOU, JACK!!
!
WHY DIDN'T YOU SAY SO? ♥
KLAT KLAT
SHUP
THE MOMENT WE SAW THESE, WE THOUGHT OF YOUR HEAD.

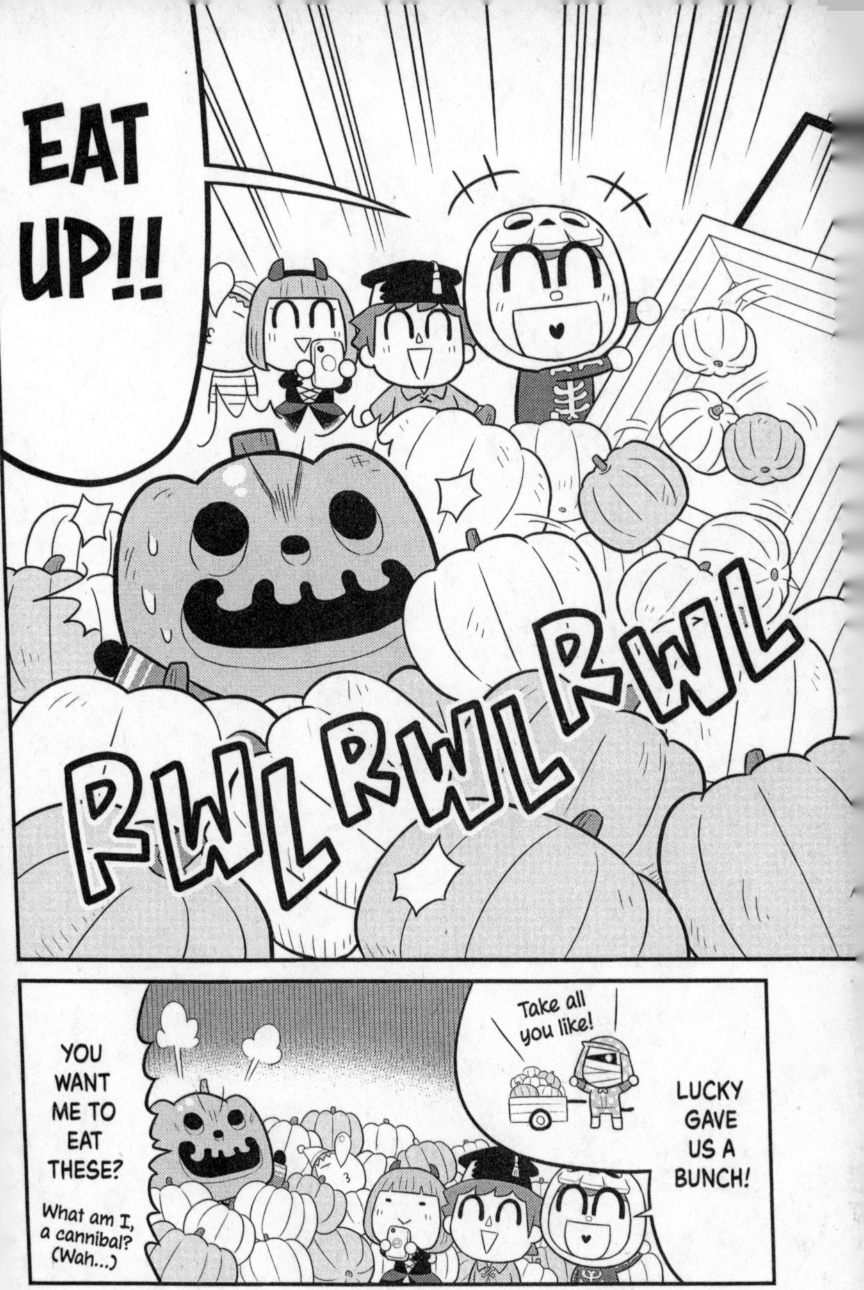
EAT UP!!
RWL RWL RWL
LUCKY GAVE US A BUNCH!
Take all you like!
YOU WANT ME TO EAT THESE?
What am I, a cannibal? (Wah...)

Bonus Diary

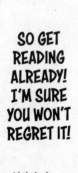

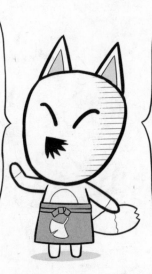

WE'VE PREPARED SOME EXTRA CONTENT JUST FOR YOU!
SO GET READING ALREADY! I'M SURE YOU WON'T REGRET IT!
Heh heh heh.

- RUMBA-STYLE ANIMAL BREAKDOWN
- RUMBA'S ACNH GAME DIARY

C.J.

PHONE

IT'S SCRATCHED AND SCUFFED BECAUSE HE'S ALWAYS DROPPING IT IN THE WATER AND LETTING IT GET NIBBLED ON BY FISH?!

JOB

HE LOOKS LIKE AN ANGLER, BUT HE'S ACTUALLY A FISH COLLECTOR.

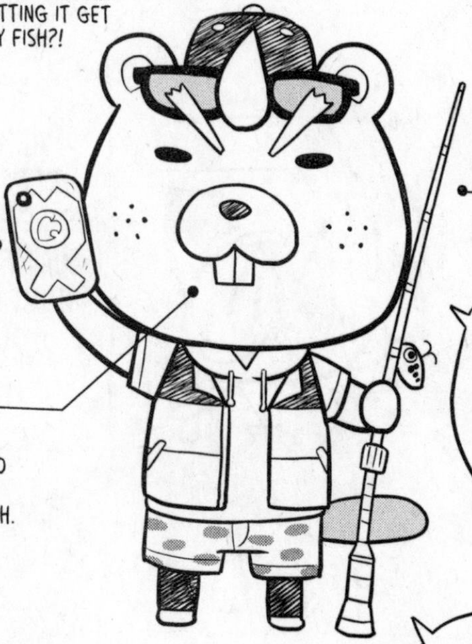

BUCK TEETH

THEY TEND TO REFLECT THE CAMERA FLASH.

I DON'T DO A LICK OF FISHING MYSELF! NYUK☆

COLLECTION

HE PROBABLY HAS MORE SELFIES IN HIS COLLECTION THAN ACTUAL FISH?!

THE FISHING POLE MAKES IT LOOK LIKE I'M GOING FISHING, AND IT DOUBLES AS A SELFIE STICK! NYUK☆

RUMBA-STYLE ANIMAL BREAKDOWN

PASCAL

SOME BOOKS ARE BEST READ BACK TO FRONT, MAAAN.

ROUND EYES

HE ALWAYS LOOKS STRAIGHT AHEAD TO PERCEIVE THE TRUTHS OF THIS WORLD?!

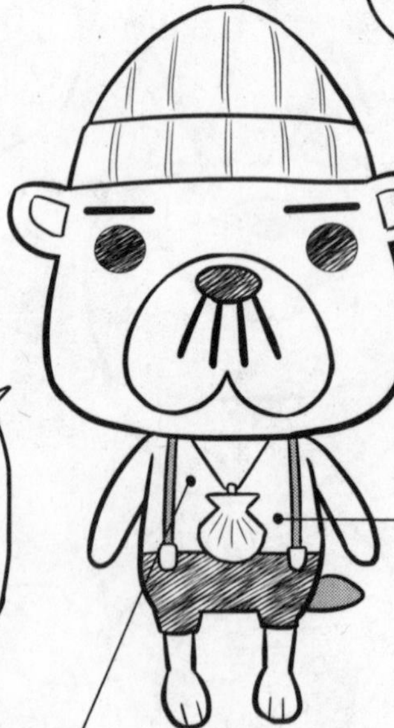

WISE SAYINGS

HE HAS AS MANY AS THERE ARE SCALLOPS IN THE SEA.

HAIR IS ONE OF THOSE THINGS WHERE YOU'RE BETTER OFF HAVING SOME THAN NONE AT ALL.

SCALLOPS

HE THINKS SCALLOPS CAUGHT BY OTHER PEOPLE ARE YUMMIER THAN THOSE HE CATCHES HIMSELF.

DEEP DOWN

HE'S GOT THE URGE TO EAT LOBSTER SOMETIMES.

AFTER IMPARTING WISDOM

HE'S OFF IN SEARCH OF HIS NEXT SCALLOP.

*THESE ARE ALL JUST RUMBA'S PERSONAL OPINIONS.

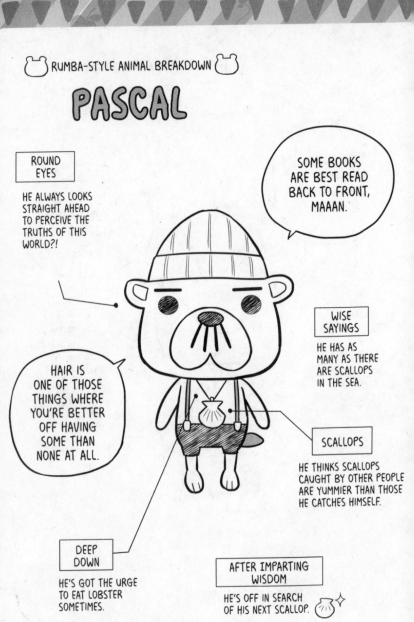

RUMBA-STYLE ANIMAL BREAKDOWN

REDD

HELLO, THERE! DO YOU HAPPEN TO LIVE ON THIS ISLAND?

I'M LOOKING FORWARD TO DOING MORE BUSINESS!

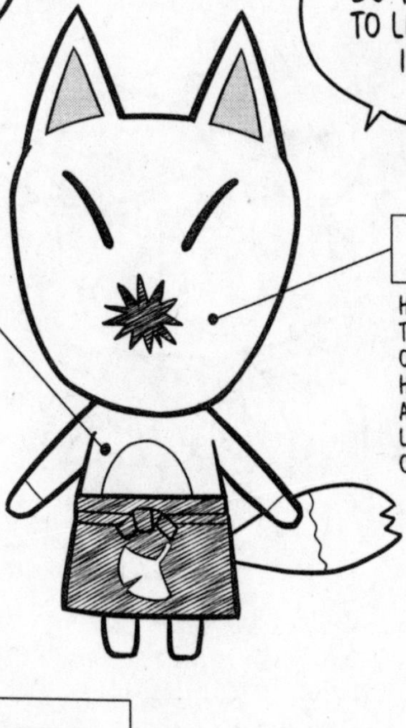

FLATTERY

HE USES HIS SILVER TONGUE TO GET OTHERS TO DO WHAT HE WANTS. HE HAS AS MANY SMOOTH LINES AS THERE ARE CUSTOMERS.

MERCHANT SOUL

AS SOMEONE DEEP IN THE WORLD OF ART SALES, REDD SEES EVERY OLD PIECE OF JUNK AS A POTENTIAL MASTERPIECE?!

TOM NOOK'S SCREAM

RUMOR IS HE MANAGED TO SELL OFF *TOM NOOK'S SCREAM* (COROYUKI'S AMAZING(?) PAINTING) ON SOME FAR-OFF ISLAND...

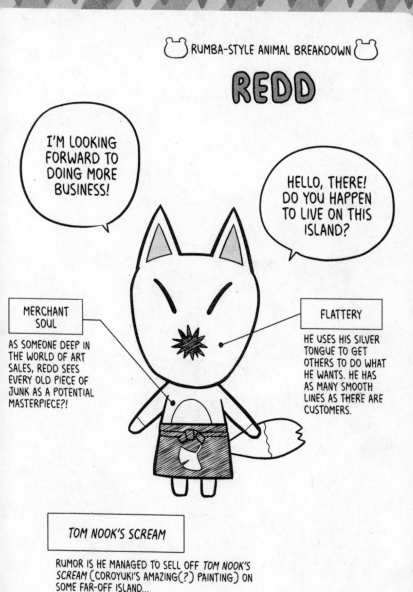

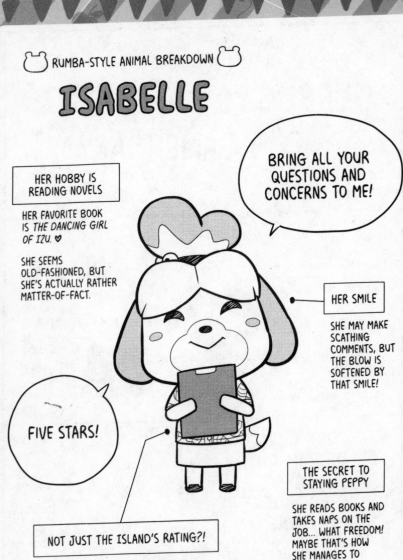

RUMBA-STYLE ANIMAL BREAKDOWN

ISABELLE

BRING ALL YOUR QUESTIONS AND CONCERNS TO ME!

HER HOBBY IS READING NOVELS

HER FAVORITE BOOK IS *THE DANCING GIRL OF IZU*. ♡

SHE SEEMS OLD-FASHIONED, BUT SHE'S ACTUALLY RATHER MATTER-OF-FACT.

HER SMILE

SHE MAY MAKE SCATHING COMMENTS, BUT THE BLOW IS SOFTENED BY THAT SMILE!

FIVE STARS!

THE SECRET TO STAYING PEPPY

SHE READS BOOKS AND TAKES NAPS ON THE JOB... WHAT FREEDOM! MAYBE THAT'S HOW SHE MANAGES TO WORK 24/7?!

NOT JUST THE ISLAND'S RATING?!

SHE MAY BE ALSO SECRETLY RANKING THE ISLAND RESIDENTS BY THEIR LOOKS. OR NOT...

*THESE ARE ALL JUST RUMBA'S PERSONAL OPINIONS.

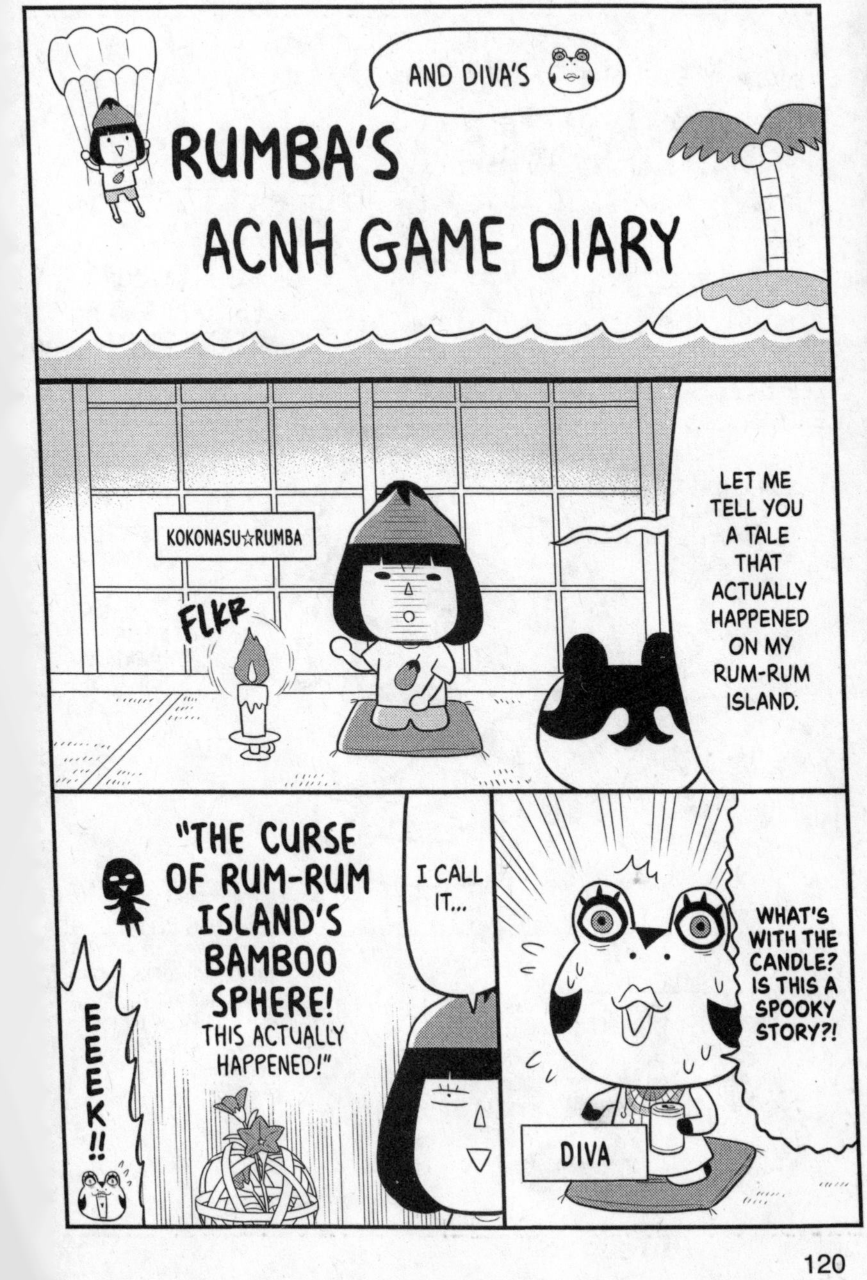
AND DIVA'S
RUMBA'S ACNH GAME DIARY
LET ME TELL YOU A TALE THAT ACTUALLY HAPPENED ON MY RUM-RUM ISLAND.
KOKONASU☆RUMBA
FLKR
WHAT'S WITH THE CANDLE? IS THIS A SPOOKY STORY?!
DIVA
I CALL IT...
"THE CURSE OF RUM-RUM ISLAND'S BAMBOO SPHERE! THIS ACTUALLY HAPPENED!"
EEEEK!!

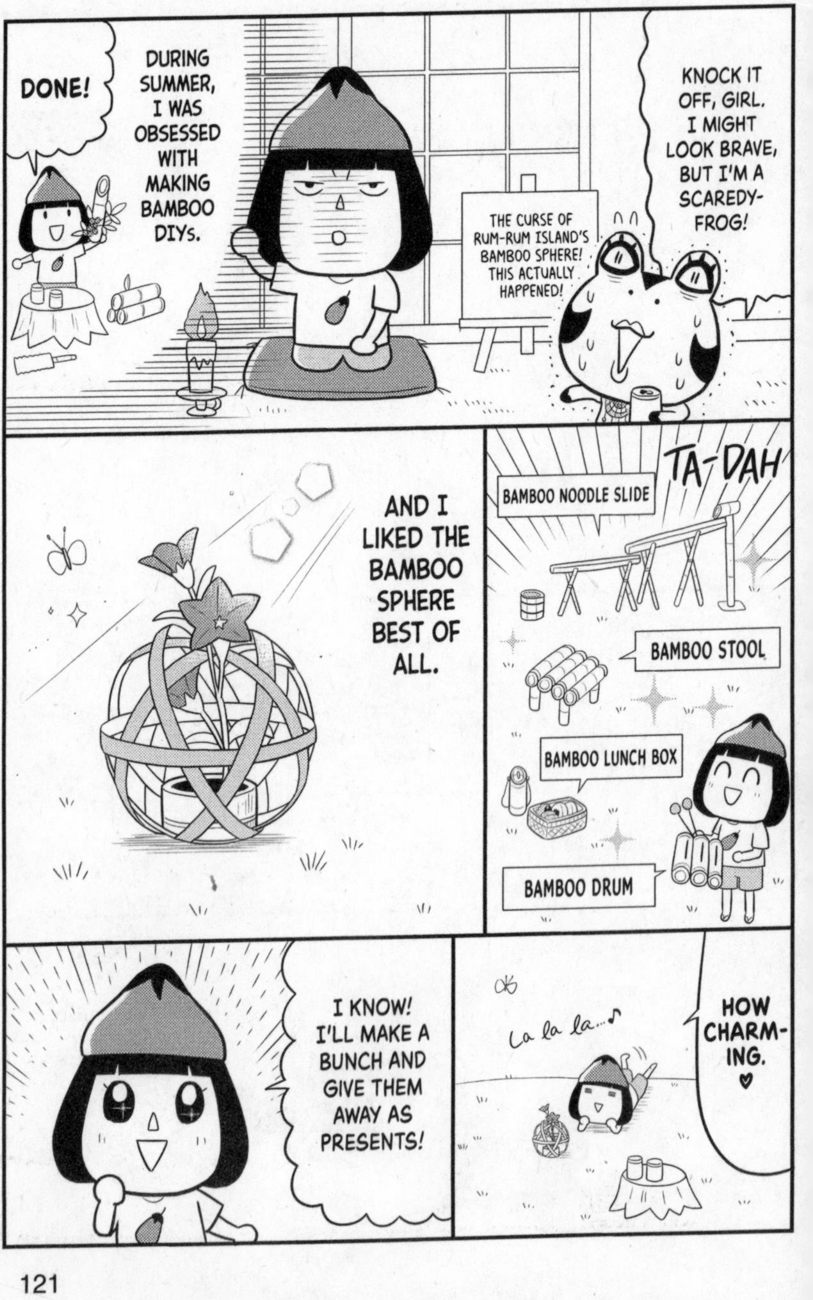
KNOCK IT OFF, GIRL. I MIGHT LOOK BRAVE, BUT I'M A SCAREDY-FROG!
DURING SUMMER, I WAS OBSESSED WITH MAKING BAMBOO DIYs.
DONE!
THE CURSE OF RUM-RUM ISLAND'S BAMBOO SPHERE! THIS ACTUALLY HAPPENED!
TA-DAH
BAMBOO NOODLE SLIDE
BAMBOO STOOL
BAMBOO LUNCH BOX
BAMBOO DRUM
AND I LIKED THE BAMBOO SPHERE BEST OF ALL.
HOW CHARM-ING. ♥
La la la...♪
I KNOW! I'LL MAKE A BUNCH AND GIVE THEM AWAY AS PRESENTS!

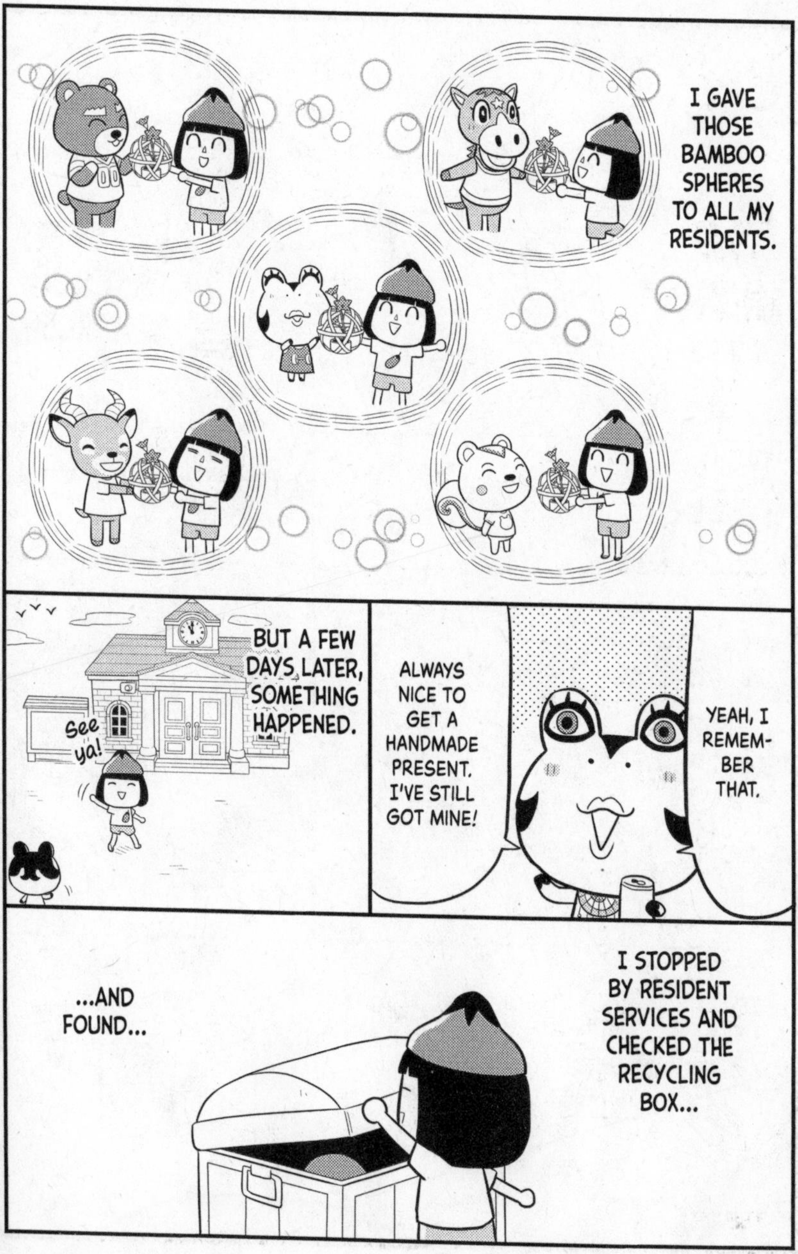
I GAVE THOSE BAMBOO SPHERES TO ALL MY RESIDENTS.
YEAH, I REMEMBER THAT.
ALWAYS NICE TO GET A HANDMADE PRESENT. I'VE STILL GOT MINE!
BUT A FEW DAYS LATER, SOMETHING HAPPENED.
See ya!
I STOPPED BY RESIDENT SERVICES AND CHECKED THE RECYCLING BOX...
...AND FOUND...

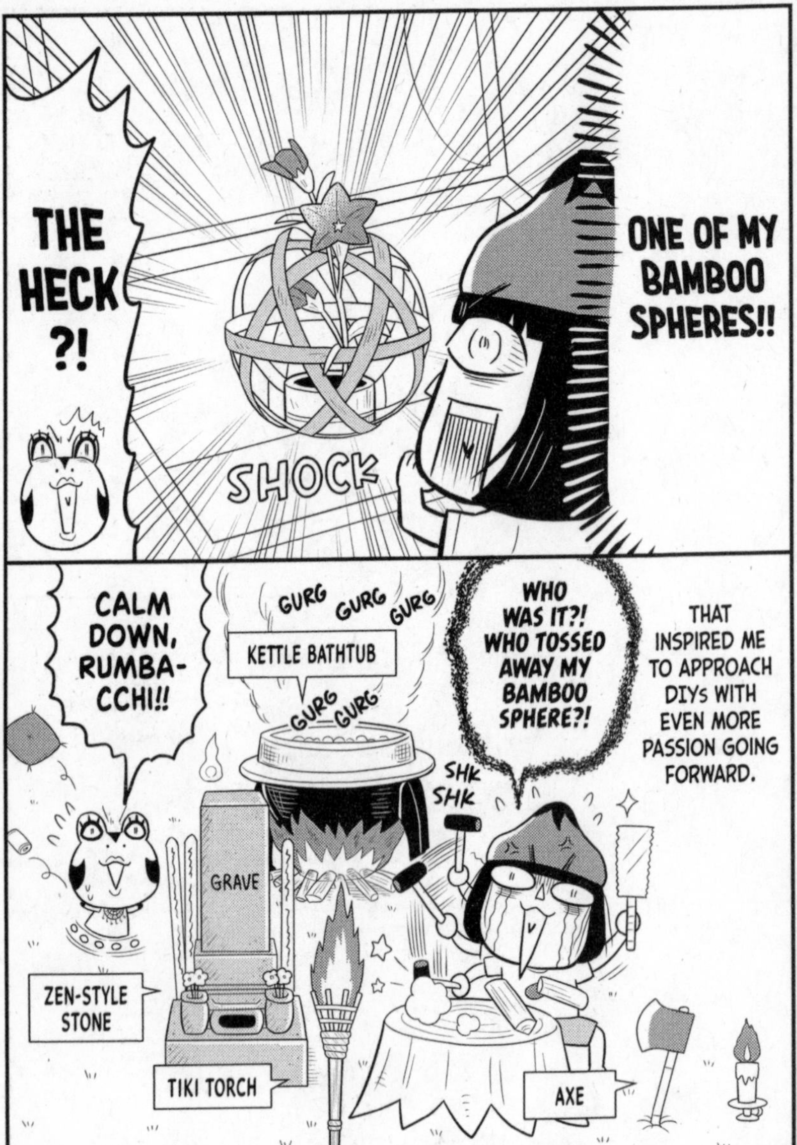
ONE OF MY BAMBOO SPHERES!!
THE HECK ?!
SHOCK
THAT INSPIRED ME TO APPROACH DIYs WITH EVEN MORE PASSION GOING FORWARD.
WHO WAS IT?! WHO TOSSED AWAY MY BAMBOO SPHERE?!
GURG GURG GURG
KETTLE BATHTUB
GURG GURG
CALM DOWN, RUMBA-CCHI!!
SHK SHK
GRAVE
ZEN-STYLE STONE
AXE
TIKI TORCH
THE END

VOL. 2/END

Celebrating volume 2 with a **party at home!!** ♪

KOKONASU☆RUMBA

A Tokyo native, she made her official *CoroCoro*
magazine debut with *Ai♡Burger Bakumaru*.
In 2013, her work *Pokupoku Pokuchin* won
an honorable mention for the 72nd Shogakukan
Newcomer Comics Prize, Children's Division.
She's best known for *Four-Panel
YO-KAI WATCH: Geragera Manga Theater*.

Welcome to Animal Crossing: New Horizons — Deserted Island Diary

VIZ Media Edition • Volume 2

Story and Art by
KOKONASU☆RUMBA

Translation & Adaptation—Caleb Cook
Touch-Up Art & Lettering—Sara Linsley
Design—Shawn Carrico
Editor—Nancy Thistlethwaite

TM & © 2022 Nintendo.
All rights reserved.

ATSUMARE DOBUTSU NO MORI -MUJINTO DIARY- Vol. 2
by KOKONASU☆RUMBA
© 2020 KOKONASU☆RUMBA
All rights reserved.
Original Japanese edition published by SHOGAKUKAN.
English translation rights in the United States of America,
Canada, the United Kingdom, Ireland, Australia and
New Zealand arranged with SHOGAKUKAN

Original Cover Design—Takuya KUROSAWA

Printed in the U.S.A.

Published by VIZ Media, LLC
P.O. Box 77010
San Francisco, CA 94107

10 9 8 7 6 5 4 3 2 1
First printing, March 2022

PARENTAL ADVISORY
ANIMAL CROSSING: NEW HORIZONS–
DESERTED ISLAND DIARY is rated A
and is suitable for all ages.

viz.com

CELEBRATE more than **25 YEARS** of **KIRBY**, the popular pink hero
of the best-selling series of video games from **NINTENDO**

KIRBY
ART & STYLE
COLLECTION

A stylish new collection of art and
designs from the best-selling
Kirby video games. Featuring
twenty-five years worth of sketches,
artwork, Japanese video game box art,
and more. With exclusive notes from
creators and artists who have brought
Kirby to life throughout the years.

VIZ

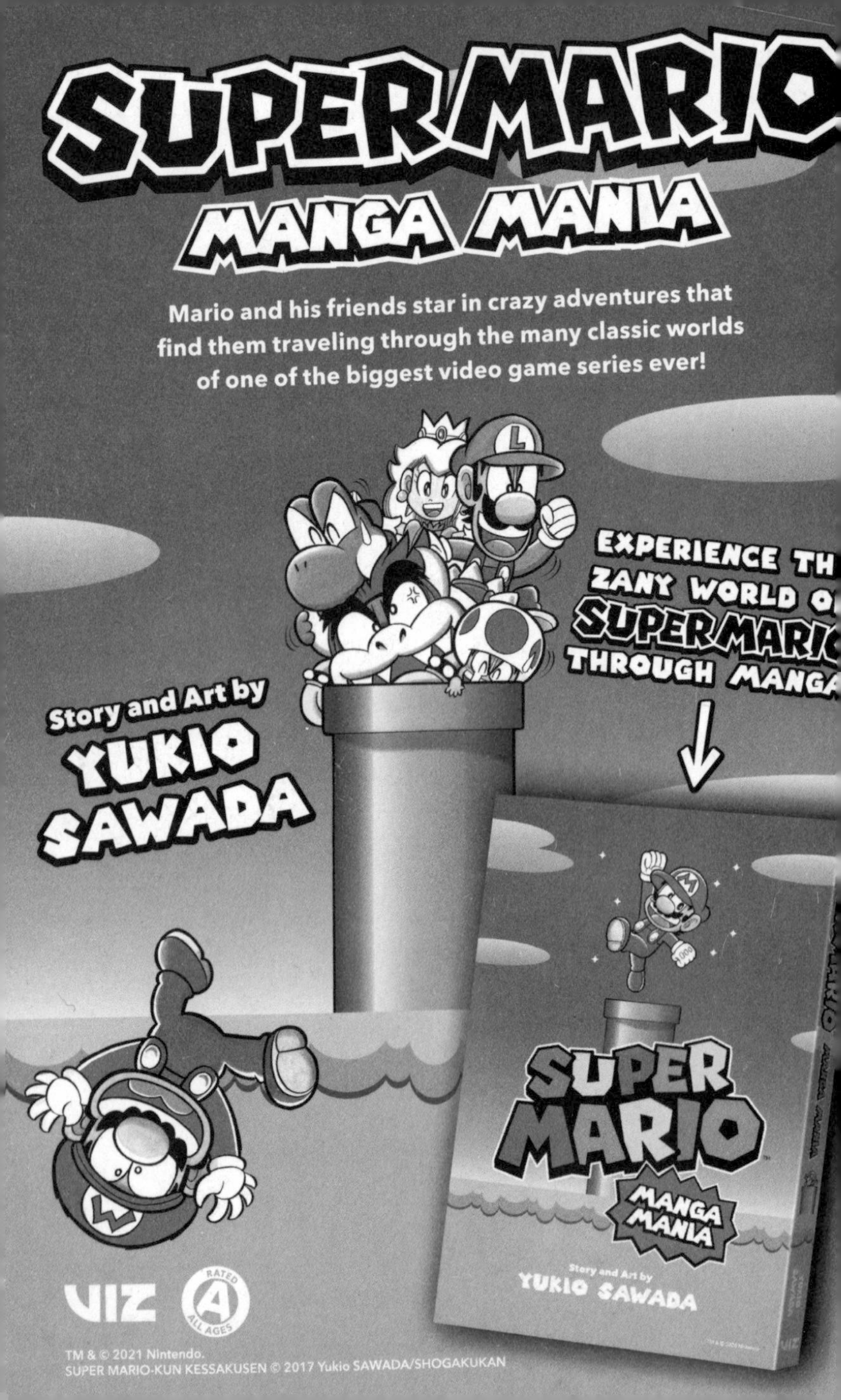
SUPER MARIO
MANGA MANIA
Mario and his friends star in crazy adventures that find them traveling through the many classic worlds of one of the biggest video game series ever!
EXPERIENCE TH
ZANY WORLD O
SUPER MARI
THROUGH MANGA
Story and Art by
YUKIO SAWADA
SUPER MARIO
MANGA MANIA
Story and Art by
YUKIO SAWADA
VIZ
RATED A ALL AGES
TM & © 2021 Nintendo.
SUPER MARIO-KUN KESSAKUSEN © 2017 Yukio SAWADA/SHOGAKUKAN

THIS IS
THE LAST PAGE!

Animal Crossing: New Horizons—Deserted Island Diary reads from right to left, starting in the upper-right corner. Japanese is read from right to left, meaning that action, sound effects, and word-balloon order are completely reversed from English order.